ALSO BY CATHRYN GRANT

THE WOMAN IN THE VINEYARD

A PSYCHOLOGICAL SUSPENSE NOVEL

ALEXANDRA MALLORY
BOOK SIXTEEN

CATHRYN GRANT

ISBN: 978-1-943142-84-5

This book is a work of fiction. References to real people, events, establishments, organizations, or locales are intended only to provide a sense of authenticity, and are used fictitiously. All other characters, and incidents and dialogue, are drawn from the author's imagination and are not to be construed as real.

Visit Cathryn online at CathrynGrant.com

Cover design by Lydia Mullins Copyright © 2024

CHAPTER 1

*N*apa Valley, California

Tess was acting as if Santa Claus was coming to town.

She'd placed a bottle of Black Mask's flagship wine on the coffee table. Beside it was the largest flower vase I'd ever seen outside a hotel lobby, filled with eighteen white roses.

"Why eighteen?" I asked.

"Because it's extravagant," she said.

"So are twelve."

"Everyone does twelve."

"He won't count them."

"But he'll know on a subconscious level there are more than twelve."

"If you say so."

"I want him to know he's special," she said.

"How do you know he's special? You've never met him. You hardly know anything about him."

"He's yours." She adjusted two of the roses. "Ow." She stuck the tip of her left index finger into her mouth and sucked on it. "That hurt."

"He's not my possession."

She laughed. "He's your man."

I wasn't sure about that either.

She went into the kitchen and returned with three enormous wine goblets. I suppose when you own a 130-acre vineyard and a five thousand square foot Mediterranean home, everything—flower vases and bouquets of roses and wine glasses—is done on a grand scale.

"I'm so excited to meet him," she said. "Finally."

"I've noticed."

"You don't seem very excited to see him … how many weeks has it been?"

"I'm excited."

She laughed. "You don't show it."

"You're giddy enough for both of us."

"Men like to know you're thrilled by their presence, that you missed them, that you need them."

"Thanks for the tip."

"You're impossible," she said.

My phone buzzed with a text from Hunter.

> Leaving the airport. Apple maps says eighty-seven minutes.

Thanks to the deadly accuracy of Apple, the doorbell rang eighty-seven minutes later. Tess rushed toward the door so fast, I thought she might skid all the way across the tiled entry, past Damien's enormous enclosure, rattling his cage, so to speak, causing an outburst of commentary from him.

I wondered if he would remember Hunter.

She flung open the door. "Welcome to Black Mask, Hunter." She stepped onto the patio. I thought she might hug him. Instead, she shoved her hand at him as if she'd changed her mind at the last minute, but couldn't quite stop her forward momentum.

He shook it with more enthusiasm than I would have expected. He wouldn't have enjoyed the hug. It was a vibe that drew me to him the moment I saw him. There was something a bit the same about the two of us. Not that he was like me in any serious way whatsoever, but he didn't thrust himself at the world, or assume that every member of the human race was someone he wanted to absorb into his life without reservation.

"I'm Tess."

"I would have known you anywhere," Hunter said.

She laughed as if it were the wittiest thing she'd ever heard, a pickup line worthy of the best bar in San Francisco.

He'd left his luggage in the rental car, but Tess wasn't going to entrust someone on her staff with that precious responsibility. "Let me get your bags." She started toward the car.

When Hunter didn't immediately follow, she waved her hand at him.

"I don't need anything right this minute," he said.

"Let's get you settled. We don't want to interrupt our evening with housekeeping tasks." Maybe she was worried he would slip out of her grip if she allowed him to keep his belongings in the car.

Hunter put his arm around my waist, pulled me close, and gave me a very nice kiss while Tess watched like an approving mother bird. Then we went to the car to get his bags.

The duffel bag, large suitcase, and garment bag suggested he planned to stay for a while.

Tess looked as if Christmas truly had come early.

I wondered if I'd made a mistake, inviting him to stay in the same house with Tess. And me. It was a lot of togetherness.

CHAPTER 2

*O*ur dinner that evening was scrumptious. Hunter gushed
to such a degree that Tess, a frequently gushy person
herself, blushed. Although she hadn't been the one to prepare it.

He praised the pork chops Marcus had barbecued, the mush-
room risotto, the salad that tasted as if every ingredient had been
plucked out of the ground that afternoon. And he didn't forget to
rave about the wine. He marveled at the magnificence of owning a
winery, and the wonder of the process itself—turning a tiny,
innocuous fruit into something that has a hundred, a thousand
different flavors, and leaves behind a pleasant feeling in the
human body.

He presented a box of truffles he'd brought as a gift. Marcus, as
gracious as Hunter, insisted all he'd planned for dessert was ice
cream because it had been a gruelingly hot afternoon.

The flattery and gushing, the attempt to outdo each other in
establishing friendly connections, offering a warm welcome, and
being a charming guest began to grow thick and heavy after a
while. It all settled around my shoulders until I felt a craving to go
for a late evening run.

I didn't, of course. Not after all that wine and all that chocolate and the incredible pork chops, of which I'd eaten two.

A few minutes after eleven, Tess stood from her place on the living room couch. "We should say goodnight. You have training for your new position tomorrow." She gave me a worried smile. Very worried. She'd worried about the training for days, asking me repeatedly if it would be better for her to sit in while Silas taught me everything I needed to know about running the Black Mask tasting room.

"It will be fine," I'd said. More than once.

"I don't want any conflict."

"He's the King of the Hill now. He'll be thrilled to treat me as his underling. There won't be any conflict."

"He's not the only one I'm concerned about," Tess had said.

"I'm here to learn."

"You won't get offended if he—"

"I think he understands the ground rules now." He did not understand the ground rules at all. The world Silas inhabited didn't have any rules.

"It might be better if I'm there," Tess said.

"He won't like that. You're trying to make him feel important with this promotion. It's not a good idea to step in and micro-manage his very first objective."

She hadn't said anything after that. She knew I was right. But I wasn't sure that was enough to allow her to let go. She was terrified I would poke at the man's easily inflamed desire for power over Tess. That any wrong move on my part would cause him to go running, skipping, gleefully singing his story to Marcus—that in a wine tasting turned to bacchanalian tragedy, Tess had had sex with him.

CHAPTER 3

*W*hen I walked into the tasting room at eight the following morning, I was relaxed from a blissful night with Hunter, during which we'd done very little talking and he hadn't once sulked about how I'd *abandoned* him in New York, how I'd waited weeks to invite him to visit Tess's winery, how I'd barely had time for him.

In fact, he acted as if none of that had happened. It was slightly surreal. I wasn't sure if it was all that flattery and good food and wine, if he'd decided to let it go, or if I should expect the other shoe to drop. Possibly, he wanted to be the polite guest. Although it wasn't like him to put on a show for anyone, definitely not for me.

So maybe we were all good.

I smiled at the thought.

Silas leered at me in return. "I hope you came prepared with an attitude of curiosity and open-mindedness."

"Absolutely."

He ran his hand through his hair, then shoved both hands into his pockets. It almost looked as if he'd raked something out from among the strands. I shivered at the imagined thought of what that might be, even though it was definitely imagined.

"Let's start back here." He gestured for me to join him in the prep room.

As I walked behind the bar, the door opened. I didn't have to hear Tess speak to know it was her. I supposed she'd placed Silas's ego and my tongue on the scales and decided she could more easily repair the damage to his ego than that caused by my tongue.

"I realized I don't know as much as I should about the operation of the tasting room," Tess said. "This seems like a great opportunity to learn."

Was she aware that no one in the room believed her simplistic story? I wondered why she'd bothered. Did *she* wonder why she'd bothered?

"Welcome, then," Silas called across the room. "Join us back here, will you? And as I told Alexandra, I hope you came with an attitude of curiosity and open-mindedness. Critical to appreciating wine, isn't that right, boss?"

"No need to call me that."

I wanted to tell her not to be combative. Instead, I smiled at her.

She got the hint. "I'm always open-minded," she said.

"You are," he simpered. "As you know, people sometimes come to a wine tasting with fixed ideas about what they do and don't like. Being open to new flavors, to experiencing each variety and vintage on its own terms is so, so important."

With that, he proceeded to go through all the wines currently on offer in the Black Mask tasting room. I was certain Tess knew them better than he did. In fact, there was no doubt she knew the profit margin on each bottle, how many were in the current inventory, and what next year's supply looked like. But she smiled politely and let him strut and crow like a rooster.

From there, he led us back out to the tasting room itself.

He went over the process for conducting a tasting in agonizing detail, from greeting the customers and how they should be welcomed, how they should be introduced to the wines, the optimal time for taking payment, and how to arrange the glasses on the bar.

The instructions even included how much personal chit chat was desirable and at what points during the tasting it should be engaged in. He told us the optimal time during the tasting to pitch membership in the wine club, after telling us how to assess what style of pitch was best for which personality type.

He told us how and when to sell discounted six-packs of wine, outlining the attractiveness of the offer because the cost of the tasting was deducted from the price of the wine, with a ten percent discount on top of that—other facts I was certain Tess was fully aware of.

I admired her ability to look curious and open-minded, pretending to learn techniques and offers she'd developed herself. I would have expected him to acknowledge this. He was looking as foolish as she had when she'd pretended she was there to learn.

The charade was making me tired.

Now that he'd moved on to telling me how to read human beings and manage them based on pop psychology, I was ready to be finished. I was confident of my abilities in that area. I could outshine Silas in any situation when it came to managing a belligerent drunk, an entitled member of the upper class, or any other type of difficult or disruptive person who might wander into a wine tasting venue.

I'd learned next to nothing about wine itself, and maybe that was to be expected. How much had I ever truly learned about wine at a wine tasting? The person behind the counter recited the marketing spiel that listed the fruits and other elements the sensitive palate would find in a glass of wine. The drinker took a few sips and by the third glass, the taste buds were so overwhelmed, the sounds and sights in the room dominating their attention until the experience began to deteriorate. Or, the entire event was simply a fabulous afternoon of day drinking. Day drinking with a classy veneer.

Finally, he was finished.

Tess thanked him. "Alex will be absolutely terrific at this. Thank you so much for giving her some instruction. I think one more training session should do it, don't you?"

"I don't—"

She cut him off. "One more is adequate. You have a lot to manage in your new role. I can't take any more of your time with this." She gave him a winning smile.

As Tess opened the door and I prepared to make my escape from behind the bar, Silas leaned close. In a low voice, he said, "Don't think I don't know what you're doing."

CHAPTER 4

$\mathcal{T}$ess and Marcus's estate was more spectacular than Alex had let on. During one of their video chats, she'd walked him around, showing him some of the gardens and parts of the house. He'd seen the suite of rooms where she was staying, but the tiny image displayed on the screen of her phone or tablet didn't begin to tell the whole story.

He'd never seen so much open space. He could get used to this.

The house was palatial. At least by his criteria—living in an 1100-hundred square foot apartment accessed by a narrow staircase, using a fire escape as a balcony on warm summer evenings, working in a kitchen where he could reach from the fridge to the stove, and rinse his hands without taking more than two steps.

And the owners were equally nice. He'd expected that. No one who owned a large, exotic bird with a charming and entertaining vocabulary could be all bad. Being reintroduced to the bird had been a riot. The creature seemed almost human at times, doling out remarks that were eerily appropriate to the situation at hand.

He would definitely enjoy his weeks off work, despite the agenda that was driving his visit. Yes, he planned to relax and have fun with Alex, but he'd decided he would find a way to figure out, once and for all, what Alexandra Mallory wanted from him. He needed to know whether or not she was the person she presented herself as.

They hadn't had much time to talk yet, but maybe now that Alex had finished her training in the tasting room, getting up to speed for her new gig as a wine server, they would get some time alone. It was a job that was absolutely on brand for her—everything from the wine to the schmoozing to living rent-free in the lap of luxury.

Instead, she'd complained of being wound up from dealing with *that guy*. She'd come back to their room, changed into running clothes, and given him a long, promising kiss.

"I'll be gone for a few hours."

"A few hours? Where are you running to, the Golden Gate Bridge?"

She laughed. "That's more than a few hours. I'm only going five or six miles. I really need to clear my mind after all that. And get my blood moving." She smiled. "Maybe I never told you I like to run."

"You mentioned it. But—"

"Manhattan cramped my style in that regard." Then she was gone.

He spent the time catching up on work email, responding to a few urgent messages, filing what he needed to address when he returned, archiving the rest. Although he was officially on vacation, he didn't have the kind of job where he could just walk away and evaporate into the ether for three weeks. Things happened, his input was required. Some issues were better dealt with now when they were minor rather than letting them fester.

It wasn't burdensome. He planned to spend thirty minutes a day, sometimes less, sometimes more, keeping up. It would make him feel grounded. As a result, he would feel freer to appreciate the time that surrounded him without obligations or schedules.

He went downstairs, checked out the gym, rode the sophisticated stationary bike for a few minutes, then wandered out to the back patio.

The problem with vacationing at someone's home, especially a home that was part of a massive operation like the Black Mask Winery, was that everyone else was working. And now he realized that included Alex. She hadn't been entirely clear about that.

He would have to figure out how he was going to occupy all this free time, enjoy all this space. It really was breathtaking. He'd grown up in a fairly small town in upstate New York, and he'd certainly traveled enough to be fully aware that being corralled by skyscrapers and walking on a grid of streets everywhere you went was not the only way to live, but this felt wildly different.

He sat on one of the lounge chairs, closed his eyes, and breathed in the warm air. It was early October, but it felt like summer in the middle of the afternoon.

"Taking a nap?"

He turned at the sound of Tess's voice. She stood near the bifold doors leading to the living room.

"Just enjoying the quiet."

"It's peaceful, isn't it?"

"Yes."

"Do you want tea? Or something cold to drink?"

He sat up, adjusting the back of the chair. "Soda would be good. Thanks."

She returned a moment later with a glass of ice and a can of cola for him and a sparkling water for herself. "Mind if I join you?"

He raised his glass to her. "I'd love it."

"Alex didn't tell me how charming you are."

"Didn't she?"

Tess laughed. "You sound certain of that fact."

"Does that bother you?"

"Not at all. I like confident people."

He waited, taking a long swallow of his soda.

"Alex has had a lot of guys, but I haven't met many of them."

He shrugged. Was she here to get him to tell Alex's secrets? He was pretty sure she knew a lot more about Alex than he did. Or maybe no one knew much about Alex. It was hard to say. It was possible that cockatoo knew more about Alex than either of them.

"I can't comment on that," Hunter said.

"That's very noble of you."

"I'm a noble guy."

"Are you?"

"I like to think so."

"How did you become so confident? Or is it simply the male ego, but shaped into something slightly more … charming and less aggressive?"

"I have no idea." He squinted. Even though he was wearing sunglasses, the angle of the sun cut through the top edge. He wished he'd worn a hat.

"Should I move the umbrella?"

"No. It's fine. I'm just not used to sitting in the sun. I like it."

She smiled as if she were pleased with herself for personally providing the sunlight for him.

"My point was, you must be really something if Alex wanted me to meet you."

"Did she want us to meet? Or she just caved?"

Tess laughed. She sipped her water. "You seem as cynical as she is, but more polite."

He wasn't sure how to answer that. He was feeling as if this conversation might be a trap of some kind. Had Alex put Tess up to it? Or was she simply probing for her own information? Looking out for her friend, trying to figure out who she was dealing with?

"Marcus thinks you're a good guy."

"I'm relieved to know I passed the test."

"There's no test." She laughed. "I just wanted you to know."

He didn't give a shit what Marcus thought of him. He wasn't here looking for an invitation to Alex's inner circle. Was that what this was? Maybe there was a test. Maybe Alex *had* put her up to this, trying to find out who he was and what he was about. Maybe while he was trying to figure out what Alex was after, she was doing the same.

It seemed wrong somehow. Shouldn't relationships be more open, unfolding naturally? Had Alex and Tess discussed this during the time Alex had been here alone, insisting she needed time to think?

"Don't be offended," Tess said.

"I'm not."

"I think you are."

"I wouldn't lie about something that absurd. I'm not offended," he said.

"Good.".

"Is it a red flag or something, if I take offense easily?"

"Maybe."

"Is that what this is? You're checking for red flags?"

She laughed. "No. Don't be so edgy, Hunter. Alex and I are friends and I'm excited to get to know the guy she's seeing. I've never met one of her guys before. Apologies if I seem a little over the top. I'm just excited you're here."

She made him sound like one in an endless string of men. Maybe she was looking for red flags. Women were always going on about that. Maybe he should let her have one, if he hadn't inadvertently done that already.

"Not edgy at all," he said. "It just sets off my radar when I'm interrogated." He took a long swallow of soda. That should get her thinking. He smiled at the garden stretched out around them. It really was incredibly tranquil. He hoped Tess would leave soon so he could enjoy the quiet. It was almost rapturous in its intensity.

"I didn't mean to sound as if I was interrogating you. I honestly wasn't."

"Good to know," he said.

He wondered if the conversation would make its way back to Alex.

CHAPTER 5

*T*alking to Hunter had been disconcerting. Tess had assumed she would have a simple conversation and get to know him a bit better. She'd thought she might find out what it was about him that made Alex so cagey. When Hunter first appeared, Alex had seemed thrilled, almost electrified by his presence. It was the same energy that shone in her eyes when she'd talked about him.

At the same time, she had a cavalier attitude about their relationship. It seemed as if she honestly didn't care one way or the other whether or not their relationship continued. Tess could not get her head around the situation.

After the four of them had eaten dinner together, she'd felt as if Alex and Hunter formed a perfect couple. Two people who belonged together. What was going on?

It wasn't any of her business, and she wasn't sure why she felt she needed answers to these questions. But she *wanted* answers. Something didn't add up and when things didn't make sense, they twisted around inside her head endlessly until she felt as if she had an unruly vine growing inside her skull. She wanted to crawl inside with a pair of pruning sheers, clipping relentlessly, until all the thick, half-dead tendrils were removed and the bright, delicate flowers could see the light of day.

Something was off.

Either Alex had concerns about this guy, or she was lying about him, or there was something else going on. But what?

Tess had left Hunter sitting on the back patio after offering him a second can of soda. He hadn't seemed disappointed to see her go. After such a pleasant evening, all four of them talking and laughing over a fabulous meal, she didn't understand why he now seemed slightly caustic. It was almost as if he *wanted* her to be suspicious of him. Why? On his second day? Did he regret the visit? Maybe he and Alex had had a fight.

She worked with her office door open, knowing that Damien would say something when Alex came back from her run and Tess could hurry down the stairs to meet her in the kitchen.

Thirty minutes later, as she'd expected, Damien shouted about wanting some mango. Tess pushed her chair away from her desk, grabbed her phone, and went downstairs. Alex was standing in front of Damien's cage, an enclosure that consumed half their large entryway, the top taller than Marcus, giving the cockatoo plenty of room for climbing from perch to perch.

Alex was telling the bird about her run, describing the wildlife she'd seen. Damien's head was cocked to one side, his crown lowered. He gazed at Alex. He was seated on a perch so they were at eye level. He seemed to drink in every word she spoke. Occasionally, he bobbed his head as if in agreement.

Tess laughed.

Alex turned.

"How was your run?"

"Good. I need water." Alex went into the kitchen. She filled a glass of water and took a sip.

Tess stood in the doorway. "How does Hunter like the Napa Valley so far?"

Alex shrugged.

"You haven't asked him?"

"No."

Tess laughed. "Why not?"

"I'm not a tour guide."

Tess laughed.

Alex drank more water, grabbed her ponytail, and twisted it into a coil.

"I hope you two won't feel like you need to be here for dinner every night. You should go out and enjoy the restaurants. Do some wine tasting. And don't think you need to sleep here either. There are some great B&Bs in Calistoga."

"I know."

"You're on vacation."

"Not anymore. I have a new job, remember?" Alex gave her a tiny smile.

"True. But the tasting room is closed Tuesdays and Wednesdays. And Hunter isn't working."

"Are you worried we'll be in your way?"

"Not at all. I just want to make sure he has a good time. That he doesn't get bored or regret coming."

"He won't."

"You seem very sure about that. He looks a little lost."

"Does he?"

"Is everything okay with you two?"

"Why are you so interested?"

"I'm concerned about my guests. I want to be sure you have a good time."

"Am I still a guest now that I'm an employee?"

"You know what I mean," Tess laughed. "I just ..." Tess walked to the opposite side of the kitchen island so she was standing a few feet from Alex. She spoke softly. "I get a weird vibe. You seem really into him, like he's the *one*. But at the same time, you seem a little ... like you're holding him at arm's length. Is something bothering you about him? Do you not trust him?"

"Everything is fine."

"I'm not prying into your—"

"Good."

"I want you to be happy."

"I am."

"Do you trust him?"

"Do you trust Marcus?"

"One hundred percent."

"Do you?" Alex raised her eyebrows slightly, a tiny smirk at the corner of her lips. "But not enough to tell him your secrets."

"That's not fair."

"It's not about being fair. You asked about trust. If you trust someone, can't you tell them everything?"

"I ..." Tess glanced at the rack of knives above the counter, clinging to a steel bar, blades pointed down, sharp as anything she'd ever seen. It was dangerous to even touch your finger to the blades of those knives. If your finger slipped even a centimeter, the blade drew blood. Even a tap at the wrong angle cause a cut. She felt as if the largest one had been driven into the softest part of her, the pain so intense she could hardly breathe.

She loved Marcus with all her heart. And she *did* trust him. Absolutely, He would forgive her. She was almost certain. Ninety-nine percent certain. Even more. Ninety-nine-point-nine. Wasn't she?

"You don't trust him," Alex said.

This conversation was supposed to be about Hunter. Were there red flags about the guy or not? Now she was utterly confused. Alex made her think there was something wrong with Marcus. That it might be a red flag, not knowing how he would react if he found out she'd cheated on him. Tess wasn't sure if she wanted to smack Alex, or cry.

CHAPTER 6

I was enduring my second mandated *training* session with Silas. He was talking, and I was studiously not listening. This was because I'd had a text from Eileen. In a decidedly irritated tone, she'd asked when I planned to remove my furniture and clothing from her apartment. She used that word—clothing, not clothes—which was the key to exposing her tone.

I'd thought I could rely on Hunter to do it for me, but that was before he'd announced he'd be arriving in California from some secret, alternate point of origin. I'd forgotten to ask him about that, in all the busyness of his first day, our dinner, and the start of my training.

But at this point, it didn't matter where he'd been before he came to California. He couldn't help. And I needed to either abandon my things, telling Eileen she could sell them, assuring her she could keep a generous fee for her trouble, or take the time to return to New York, pack up my belongings, and ship them to California. But then what? There was no doubt Tess had room to store them, but it felt like I was suddenly traveling with an enormous weight strapped to my back.

This was why I'd never wanted to acquire furniture. Until I owned my own place, the more things I owned, the heavier the burden.

I felt it pulling at the tendons in my neck; I felt it weighing at the back of my brain, sitting there like a lead ball, constantly reminding me I needed to think about it, be concerned about it, look out for it, as if I'd taken on responsibility for another living being. It wasn't unlike the weight I'd felt when I was dragging Damien around New York City, feeling responsible for his well-being. I didn't like it.

Maybe the best choice was to let it all go. Let Eileen sell it. I could see the seeping away of all that value. The lovely boots, leather jackets and wool coats, sold for a fraction of what I'd paid for them. I could see the furniture, hardly used, earning me enough for a weekend away—at best. But what was the alternative? The expense of a round-trip flight. I could also add in the cost of transporting a bed, dresser, armchair, and boxes of clothing across the country in a small moving van.

Selling everything was the only choice. I'd made it by default with my impulsive decision to accept Tess's invitation without taking care of my possessions first. It was as if I'd planned my destiny by default. Not planning was planning. Maybe that was a quote on a sweatshirt I could order off Instagram.

"Are you paying attention?" Silas asked.

"Yes."

"What did I just say?"

"I don't need a quiz."

"I can tell you're not listening."

"How can you *tell*? You don't know what's in my head."

"Your eyes are unfocused."

I laughed.

"Repeat what I said."

"You said I should always start with the lightest white."

21

He sneered. "That's what I said five minutes ago. You weren't listening."

"I got distracted."

"By what? There are no distractions here."

"I have a lot on my mind."

"Is this job going to be too much for you?"

"No."

"Then why do you have a lot on your mind?"

"My deepest apologies for not paying attention."

"What's bothering you?"

"Nothing. Let's keep going."

"I'm a good listener," he said.

"I'm sure you are. But I'm here to learn about wine."

"Are you worried about your boyfriend?"

"No."

"Maybe you should be."

I was not going to talk to this creep about Hunter. I wasn't going to talk about anything with him. And I didn't understand why Tess thought I needed any of this. I could have learned it all in a book or by reading blogs. "Are you going to catch me up after my lapse, or are we finished?"

"I'm just saying, your man seems a little controlling and you are a girl who does not like being controlled."

"Very astute of you to notice."

"I have a lot of insight into human nature."

I smiled. "I guess that's why you've been so successful selling club memberships." I very much wanted to know why he thought Hunter was controlling. Had Hunter said something to him? Worse, had Tess, with her search for some sort of *issue*, some red flag fluttering in the wind, whipped him up like an enraged bull, ready to charge at me? Or was he simply tormenting me? Knowing what I did about him, that seemed the more plausible explanation. Still, his comment was very specific. And he'd been eager to work it into the conversation. Almost as if he'd planned it, as if he'd been looking for an opening.

"Let's talk more about selling club memberships," he said. "It's critical. It's what makes the tasting room a profit center."

Clearly, he was not going to backfill what I'd missed. Which meant it probably wasn't important. Of course, it wasn't important. Nothing he'd said was anything I didn't already know.

CHAPTER 7

*H*unter and I went for a walk in the vineyard before dinner. We were each carrying a glass of Black Mask Pinot Noir. They were large glasses, not prone to spilling easily, but we still walked slowly over the rough ground between the rows of grapevines.

I told him about my wine tasting training. In more detail than he probably wanted to hear, but he acted as if he were hanging on every word. He told me about his day, which included an impromptu tour of the bottling facility with Chuck, who oversaw everything once the grapes were harvested, all the way to bottling, labeling, and shipping. I was impressed that he'd made this a priority. I'd been there for weeks and still hadn't done so, despite two offers from Chuck for a private tour.

I stopped and took a sip of wine. He moved closer as if he were about to kiss me, but I took a few steps away from him. "So where were you before you came out here? What was the big secret?"

"No big secret. I was visiting my mom, then I went to see some friends in Boston." He tipped his glass back. The rays of the setting sun touched the wine, making it sparkle like a gemstone.

Why had he been so cagey about it when we'd talked before?

He'd acted as if his location required a complicated explanation. Was his mother complicated? Was that the entire truth? Or any of the truth?

Something felt off, but I couldn't put my finger on it.

"That's a lot of time away from the agency," I said. "Are you on leave?"

"Not really. I told Pauline I needed some breathing room. She's cool with that kind of thing. She believes in her employees having work-life balance. And I'm not completely checked out. I'm still touching base every day, keeping my finger on the pulse."

"Delegating everything?"

"Some. More than some." He laughed.

"And getting paid nicely for it."

He smiled and tapped his glass against mine.

That was the kind of job I wanted. Although I wanted it on a full-time basis—freedom. It was nice he could take a month or so to do as he pleased, but I wanted something where I could live my life as I chose all the time.

It was a lot to ask. Most people wouldn't dare to ask something like that. Especially at my age. It's considered a fairy tale. Entitlement. Among other things. Lazy might be one. But that's what I wanted, and I thought about it a lot. Work that I loved, work that swallowed me whole, consumed my thoughts, filled me with energy. And absolute freedom. Why not daydream? Daydreams don't affect anyone. I had to fill my head with something. Why not that?

The sun was moving lower toward the horizon. We finished our wine, then he put his arm around me, pulled me close, and we kissed for a long while, until the sun dropped behind the foothills and the air grew cooler around us.

We started walking back, holding our wineglasses down at our sides, an unwanted burden now.

I told him about asking Eileen to sell my things.

"That's nuts."

"Why?"

"You'll have nothing but what's in your suitcase. Your whole life will be gone."

"It costs a lot to ship everything."

"But isn't there … aren't there personal things you want?"

"No."

"Photographs."

"Oh, my phone."

"Things from your childhood?"

"Nope."

He stopped walking. "Are you serious?"

"I don't like to drag boxes full of the past everywhere I go. Clutter is a lot of work. It weighs me down. And most of those things just stay in their boxes. They get older and older and look worse and worse."

"But it's your life."

"It's not my *life*." My life isn't in a box. My life is inside my head.

"Don't you want to remember things from your childhood or—"

"I remember the things I want to."

"What about childhood treasures or gifts you loved? What about family heirlooms?"

"The family *heirlooms* are in my father's house. Most of our gifts were age-appropriate—clothes or books. I don't even have them now."

"Haven't you bought things you liked when you traveled?"

I shrugged. "I'm not going to keep boxing and unboxing and paying to drag things all over the place. It doesn't make sense."

He stared at me as if I'd told him it was too much trouble to keep eyebrows on my face and I'd shaved them off.

"That's not normal," he said.

"Maybe it should be. It's a waste of money and energy and

time. Things get lost and damaged. And they sit inside boxes decaying. Once I settle, I'll buy stuff."

He continued staring at me. Maybe it was starting to sink into his head that my view made sense. Or maybe he was realizing he was more weighed down than he'd thought. Maybe he was wondering what was going to happen to us, if I was going to keep hopping around the world and he would not be able to follow me because he was chained to a very well-paying job, and an apartment full of things that apparently meant quite a lot to him.

"You could put them in storage."

"Also a waste of money."

"But worth it, if things mean something to you."

"Is it? Wouldn't it be better to buy things that mean something at a later date?"

"But ..."

He'd run out of arguments. He didn't like it. I could see that he wanted to keep going. My ability to fit my life into a few suitcases was disturbing. I wondered why. Maybe it was threatening. People want other people to be like them, to have the same ideas about how life works, to be tied down in the same ways. They want everyone working Monday through Friday, with boxes in their closets that they haven't opened for six years. Or sixteen.

"You can store them at my place."

"Your place isn't very big."

"Sell the furniture, but store your clothes and the other important things."

He didn't seem to understand that the clothes were the *only* important things. "For how long? I would still have to move them, eventually."

"What if you decide to move back to New York?"

"That's too much planning."

"I just think it's really irresponsible to toss an investment like that—a lifetime of possessions. I'm happy to help you out. Have Eileen ship them to my place. My neighbor has a key and he can stack the boxes in my living room. It's a simple solution. You can even hire someone to pack, so you're not burdening Eileen."

"I don't want to."

"I insist."

I didn't like how he was pushing me. Why did he care?

"I smell something amazing. I wonder what Marcus is cooking?"

He took my hand. "Seriously, I can arrange everything if it's too much."

It felt as if he was trying to take over part of my life. Was Silas right? *Was* he controlling? I didn't like it, but I decided to put it out of my head. Maybe it wasn't what it seemed. Or was I lying to myself?

CHAPTER 8

*O*ur evening meal was another gourmet dinner. It was
pleasant and seemed as convivial as the first night,
although now I had a different view of things, and it made me
wonder what else might be happening below the surface.

Hunter was busy mentally moving what was left of my life in
New York City into his apartment. Did he hope that doing so
would build a fence around me, keeping me close? I wanted to be
close to him, but I didn't want to be fenced in. I didn't want to be
obligated or corralled or attached to his apartment.

What was going through his mind? He'd made it sound as if
the only thing he was concerned about was a sentimentality that
he seemed to assume was lurking deep inside me. That, and my
financial status. If all my money was tied up in leather boots, wool
coats, and half-used cosmetics, it would be a sad state of affairs.

Had he cast a net around me? Was he slowly pulling the strings
through the edges, tightening it into a trap meant for a school of
fish that sometimes wrapped itself around the sleek, powerful
body of an unsuspecting dolphin?

Why was he so fixated on my possessions? Why did he think it
was worthwhile to pile boxes of old things into a metal shed,

forgotten for years? In what world did it make sense to pay a monthly bill because someone didn't want to face their out-of-control sentimentality and refusal to make a decision? It was incomprehensible to me.

As we relished our food, Tess watched the two of us as if we were microbes on a glass slide.

When she sipped her wine, she studied whichever one of us wasn't talking, staring hard into our eyes, as if she could drill right through our skulls and figure out why our relationship wasn't mapping to the pattern she and Marcus had laid out for their lives.

Marcus was the only one who seemed oblivious to the subterranean activity. Or was he? Maybe Tess had filled him in and his sharp, probing questions to Hunter were following a prescribed outline she'd given him, seeking as much information as they could gather, trying to determine whether he was worthy of me, whether he might be a danger to their business, or a threat to me in some way, or whatever it was Tess was so concerned about.

Maybe she was simply in a rush to start family life. She wanted friends who were couples. She wanted someone else she felt comfortable with buying an expensive white dress, plan a big party, take a fabulous trip, then settle down to reproduce. That way, she could have a colleague to share child-rearing strategies and goals.

After dinner, we played a board game.

Lying in bed just past midnight, my mind finally stop circling around what was happening with Hunter and Tess. But still unable to relax, my thoughts wandered back over the past few weeks to the events at the castle.

I thought about Amelia and the rebuilding going on there. Because of the fire I'd helped engineer, I still hadn't been inside either of the towers. One had been completely destroyed, and I was certain it would be different when it was complete. I wanted to see the changes, and I was also curious to see the other tower, although I'd heard plenty of stories about it by now.

I'd seen Amelia from a distance around downtown Napa, but we'd never spoken. It was only a matter of time before we ran into each other, or were introduced. I'd gone back over possible loose ends quite a few times since the fire, but recently I'd started to wonder what might happen when Amelia saw my luscious red hair that I'd adopted just before coming to California.

Would she wonder if I might be the sister of her deceased father? For a girl who had lost her entire family, so desperate for a connection she'd easily believed I was her fairy godmother, it was possible she might perceive me as that missing baby sister who was a toddler when her father was on the cusp of becoming a young man.

Amelia had been nurtured on fairy tales and the wild stories that arose in her mother's imagination. It was impossible to predict what fanciful thoughts might be dancing inside her head.

As much as I loved it, my red hair had become a potential liability.

The first item on my agenda for the following day would be a trip to a hair salon. Hopefully, I could find a place that would accept a walk-in client for a trim and a new hair color. I closed my eyes and pictured myself looking in the mirror.

Who did I want to be now? Did I want to become an exotic woman with jet black hair, or a playful blonde? Or had I reached a place, for now, where it might be best to blend in with a more neutral color? I could add a little fun with a few whispers of copper and blonde among the nut brown.

I felt Hunter's hand on my thigh. "You seem tense. Why are you awake?"

"Why are *you*?"

"I can feel your tension."

"I'm not tense," I said.

"You're thinking."

"Just making plans."

"For what?"

"A haircut."

He laughed. He was quiet for a moment, then he laughed again, harder this time. He rolled toward me and pulled me into his arms. He put his face into my neck and whispered, "Don't cut it all off."

"I won't."

"Promise."

"I don't make promises."

I thought he would ask why, but he didn't. He just held me more tightly.

CHAPTER 9

*D*ying my hair had been a very good decision.

Five days later, I was pouring Chardonnay for a retired couple who had already agreed to sign up for the Black Mask wine club, through which they would receive two bottles of signature wine every two months.

I looked up to see Amelia standing in the doorway.

Seeing her face sent a chill through my core. I felt as if I knew her as well as I'd known Eileen. Possibly because I'd rescued her in the same way I'd once rescued Eileen, possibly because she'd consumed my thoughts to the point that hers was the face that had driven me to the hair salon. Or possibly because, until that moment, I hadn't seen her up close in a way that meant we would have a personal interaction.

Why on earth had she come to this winery? Why was she standing there looking at me as if she had something very specific she wanted to say to me?

I was absolutely certain she'd never seen me at the castle. I was one hundred percent confident she knew nothing about me. She'd never heard my voice. She didn't know the part I'd played in her escape and the murder of her mother and uncle. She would never imagine me as her fairy godmother.

And yet she stared at me as if she thought she knew me.

Was it only the illusion of a mirror image due to our previously similar hair color?

It was possible I was misreading her look, so consumed by my enormous part in her life as her knight in shining armor, that I felt something in her gaze. It could be she'd heard great things about the winery. Although I knew as I tried to hold on to that wishful thinking, it was not the case.

Anything I guessed she might be thinking about me was the product of my imagination.

She stepped inside and brushed her hair off her shoulders. The way she did it appeared awkward. I wondered if I'd unconsciously done the same within the last few minutes and she was mimicking me.

She wore jeans and very high-heeled sandals, a dark brown tunic that matched her sandals, and a long pendant that looked like a wine stopper. I couldn't tell what the shape on top of the cork was. I wondered what the sentimental or fashion value of a wine stopper around your neck might be. Was she considering turning the castle back into a winery as it had been years ago? It looked uncomfortable and out of place. Maybe it was a conversation starter.

I became impatient with the couple slowly sipping their wine, discussing it as if they could remember the bouquet of every single glass of Chardonnay they'd tasted over the past ten years.

Like the wine-tasting couple, Amelia looked as if she had all the time in the world. She lingered by the door with an utter lack of self-consciousness. She seemed unconcerned whether she looked out of place or appeared to be intruding on a private tasting. She wasn't, but most people would have wandered to the gift shop area, trying to look busy. She stood there, silently watching, perfectly happy to wait, perfectly happy to continue standing, and perfectly happy to be where she was slightly out of place..

As I began pouring the next wine—a delightful Pinot Noir—I realized Amelia probably didn't read social cues very well, if at all. She'd spent her entire life alone in a castle tower. The only time she'd interacted with other people had been meal times and schoolwork done in the company of her mother.

She might not understand that standing in a room when others were having a quiet conversation was considered rude. She might not even understand the concept of rudeness.

The idea fascinated me. There was a part of me that suddenly wanted to get to know her, to experience the world through a person who had very few preconceived ideas except what she'd learned through books and movies. Was that sort of cerebral experience enough to build your instincts and give you the social awareness you need to operate in the real world?

I thought about asking what she wanted so I could fulfill her request quickly and send her on her way. At the same time, I wanted to invite her out to dinner and offer her a martini, digging into her thoughts and perceptions of the world since she'd escaped from the tower.

Finally, the couple was finished. They'd filled out their wine club application, purchased four bottles to take with them, chatted about what a terrific time they'd had talking to me, smiling and handing me their business cards as if we'd become friends, inviting me to visit their home the next time I was in Vancouver, Canada.

When they were gone, I asked Amelia if she was there for a tasting.

"No." She moved toward the center of the room, staring at me with a calculating gaze.

"Did you want something from the gift shop? You're welcome to browse. You didn't need to wait for me."

She shook her head. "No thanks."

"Then what—"

"I've seen you before."

I smiled. "It's possible."

"Running."

I picked up four of the glasses. "I go running every day, so I'm not surprised."

"You had red hair."

I carried the glasses into the back room and returned to the bar.

"Why did you dye it brown?" she asked. "And streaky?"

"I was ready for a change."

"It was almost the same color as mine."

"Was it? Well, your hair is a great color, but—"

"Why did you suddenly dye it brown?"

"There was nothing sudden. Red wasn't my natural color."

"Oh. But I—"

The door opened and Silas stepped into the tasting room, grinning as if he might have overheard us and was very curious to know about my hair color change himself. But he couldn't possibly have heard.

"How are things going, Alexandra?"

"Great."

"Are you here for a tasting?" He walked toward Amelia, thrusting out his hand. "Silas Birch. Head of Operations for Black Mask."

She shook his hand. "Hi, I'm Amelia."

"Do you have a last name, Amelia?"

She released his hand. "Just Amelia."

"How mysterious," he said.

I took a breath and held it for half a second. I began inserting the corks in the bottles that I'd used for the tasting.

"Well, I just thought it was really strange," Amelia said.

"It was just a coincidence," I said.

"What's strange?" Silas asked.

Amelia walked out the door.

Silas glared at me. "What did she want?"

"She wanted to tell me she'd seen me running."

"Why is that strange?"

I shrugged.

He hurried out the door. I hoped her eagerness to leave suggested she wouldn't tell him any more than she already had. I didn't like the idea of those two talking about me. Not that either of them knew anything worth discussing. I just didn't like it. But he was determined.

CHAPTER 10

*A*melia stood on the patio outside the tasting room. She felt like crying, even though she'd known it was a childish fantasy. She couldn't spend the rest of her life trying to find an aunt that only existed in a few old photographs. She knew nothing about this woman beyond the fact that her hair was the same shade of red as her own.

In the photograph she'd seen, the little girl appeared to be about twelve years younger than her father. That meant she might be in her thirties now, the same age as the woman in the tasting room. But it was kind of silly to think she should strike up a conversation with every thirty-something woman whose hair color was similar to her own.

Except this woman lived in the Napa Valley. That made it more likely, didn't it?

But it was really the opposite. Her aunt was probably long gone. If she was around, she and Amelia's father would surely have been in touch, and then none of those awful things would have happened. The horror show that took place inside the smooth stone walls of the castle would never have taken place, would it? Her father would still be alive. Her mother wouldn't have murdered him, so he couldn't stop her from raising Amelia under lock and key.

She sat on the stone bench at the side of the patio and grabbed the trunk of the sapling beside her, as if the tree's roots would ground her as well.

Just because the woman in the tasting room had dyed her hair a different color, didn't mean she was trying to hide who she was. She was right there in plain sight. If you wanted to hide, you had to put more effort into it than changing your hair color, didn't you? It had been a stupid, naïve question. That was the problem with growing up in a stone tower. You might know a lot about math and science and literature. You might know history, but you knew absolutely nothing about human beings and how they behaved outside of books.

And as her mother had constantly reminded her—books weren't real. Books made everyone seem better than they were. The endings of movies and books and fairytales work so it all turns out right and everything makes sense.

In the real world, as Amelia was learning very, very fast, it wasn't at all like that.

The tasting room door opened and the man who had come in after her stepped outside. He shielded his eyes, then pulled a pair of sunglasses from his pocket and put them on. The lenses were like mirrors, and she watched her tiny dual reflections as he walked toward her.

"I don't mean to invade your privacy," he said. "But you seemed upset a few minutes ago. Is everything okay?"

"You're not intruding."

"Do you mind if I sit?"

He was kind of good looking, although quite a lot older than her. Almost as old as the woman who used to have red hair.

"I don't mind."

His hair was dark. He was slim and had a nice smile. His clothes looked like they came out of a magazine. Although, what did she know? She'd seen lots of clothing in magazines, but she hadn't seen so many men that she had a clear idea about how they dressed. Most of them seemed to wear jeans and T-shirts from what she'd seen around downtown Napa, walking the streets, buying ice cream so she could sit at a small outdoor table and watch people passing by.

He seemed nice. That was the most important thing.

"Did you come for a tasting?" he asked.

"No. I just wanted to talk to ... I don't know her name."

"Alexandra. So you don't know her?"

"I've seen her running."

He nodded. "She does run a lot. Are you a runner?"

She laughed.

"Why is that funny?"

He didn't seem to know who she was. It was nice. It was very nice that he didn't know. She was tired of everyone giving her strange looks, treating her like some kind of freak. She *was* a freak, a monstrosity who had been held captive in a tower. Hers was a life out of a gothic fairytale. People almost couldn't believe it. Right after the fire, everyone had wanted to talk to her. They'd stared at her as if they were looking for evidence of damage to her psyche that would be visible on her face, as if her mother's strange ideas had left scars deep in her flesh.

She liked that he didn't know who she was, that she could be anyone she wanted. She liked that she could be normal.

"Are you going to tell me?" He touched her shoulder gently.

She felt something ripple through her body, a wave like a warm breeze blowing across a field of wild grass. He took his hand away, and she wished he would put it back.

"It's funny that you would think I'm a runner. I've never run anywhere except maybe up the stairs." She shouldn't have said that. She wanted to smack her face with her own hand. Why had she said that? He might ask why and then he would find out what a freak she was. Here he was treating her like a normal girl and she'd messed it up and told him she was a weirdo by admitting she never ran anywhere.

But he was laughing. Not just a short laugh, as if she were an idiot. He was laughing a lot. And then he touched her shoulder again. "You and I are kindred spirits, Amelia. I hate running. And the only place I've ever run was from the front door to my car when it was raining."

She laughed with him. She felt as if this might be the most perfect afternoon she'd ever had in her life. She was sitting on a bench under a flowering tree, and he was laughing because she was funny and she'd *made* him laugh. She was like a princess who had been let out of her castle, and he was almost like a prince.

He was quite a lot older than her. And she was barely nineteen, but that didn't matter. Lots of princes were older than princesses. She stopped laughing. One of her vows was that she was going to stop looking at the world through the pages of fairytales as her mother had done. She was going to be logical and serious and learn about the real world. Maybe Silas would teach her. She turned her head slightly and smiled at him.

CHAPTER 11

I cleaned up from the tasting as fast as I could, washing the glasses and leaving them to dry themselves. On a Monday afternoon in October, we weren't likely to get a rush of activity and there were no appointments on the calendar. I hurried outside, but Amelia and Silas were gone.

It eased my mind slightly that this meant they must not have spent a lot of time talking. Although it was possible he'd offered to show her around the winemaking facility. I decided not to hunt them down. If they were still together, I'd find out soon enough. For now, I'd hope for the best. It wasn't as if Amelia knew anything that could expose me. And Silas knew absolutely nothing about me except that I was an old friend of Tess's

They weren't a danger to me. Unless they became one. But for now, I couldn't imagine how that might happen. I just preferred they not talk to each other.

I went into the house, scooped some of the fancy mocha ice cream Marcus had bought into a dish and sat at the bar eating it, enjoying the brain freeze as a way to stop my thoughts from creating a problem where there didn't appear to be one. Just because Amelia thought it was remarkable that I'd dyed my hair, that didn't mean she had some sort of insight into my life.

Or was my spidey sense warning me that her interest could spiral out of control? I wasn't sure. I didn't like the tightly coiled feeling at the base of my skull. The ice cream wasn't softening it at all.

When I was finished, I washed my bowl and spoon and put them away. I wandered around the first floor, checking the back patio and the workout room, looking for Hunter. I went to our rooms and changed into jeans and a fun, low-cut top I thought he'd like. I sent him a text asking where he was.

I heard a buzz. His phone was in the drawer of the nightstand on his side of the bed.

I went out to our balcony and looked across the vineyard. I couldn't see the winemaking buildings from our balcony, but even if I could, it wouldn't have told me if he was out there. Returning to our room, I brushed my hair, slid my phone into my pocket and went out. From the second floor lounge area, I looked out to the covered parking. His rental car was there.

What was he up to?

The house felt utterly silent. I assumed Marcus and Tess were both in their offices.

I walked slowly down the long, curving staircase, enjoying the grandeur of it, imagining myself in a magnificent ballgown. I wanted to close my eyes to get the feel of it, but that seemed like the wrong choice on a staircase with nicely buffed hardwood steps.

After searching the entire first floor, I grabbed a bottle of sparkling water, went to the back patio, and settled on a lounge chair. I was now positioned front and center for Hunter to find me when he was ready. Clearly, he had something on his mind if he'd felt the need to escape his phone.

In the meantime, I would busy myself with mine. I opened it to find eight emails from Silas, all with attachments giving me background on the wine industry, information about the Black Mask grape varieties, as well as tips for working in a career that is customer-facing and requires selling a brand.

His final email informed me he would be discussing the contents with me at random times and he expected me to be prepared. I closed my phone, put it beside me, and lifted my face to the sun. Never had my phone been such an annoyance as it was at that moment. Without opening my eyes, I picked up my water bottle, unscrewed the cap, and took a long swallow.

"There you are."

At the sound of Hunter's voice, I opened my eyes, squinting into the bright light.

He moved slightly, casting a shadow over my face. "Is that better?"

I smiled.

"I was looking all over for you," he said.

"Same," I said.

He tilted his head and looked at me as if that wasn't believable. He waited as if he expected me to confess my lie. When I said nothing, he settled into the chair beside me. "I have a surprise."

"Oh?"

"I bought tickets to Alcatraz."

A prison? It hadn't been used as such for decades, but did I want to spend hours on a tiny island inside the walls of an abandoned prison, imagining life there in the forties and fifties on The Rock?

"I haven't seen San Francisco at all," he said. "The weather's been perfect, so a boat ride would be really good. We could do the tour, then spend the afternoon in the city, and have a nice dinner. Alone."

"You're already tired of Tess and Marcus?"

"Not at all. That's not the point."

"You said you wanted to eat dinner alone. Like that was the main feature of the day."

He groaned. "Sometimes it feels like you go out of your way to make things more difficult than necessary."

"I don't think so."

"I'm not tired of them. I haven't seen you in over a month. I thought it would be nice to have dinner alone and reconnect."

I reached across the space between the chairs and took his hand. "At a prison?"

"Yes, Alex. At a prison. It's a famous landmark. I thought you'd think it was unique and fun."

"It's unique."

"But not fun?"

"It suppose could be."

"If you don't want to go, I'll try to—"

I squeezed his hand. He was getting more upset than necessary. It was unlikely any of the cells locked. It wasn't a real prison. It hadn't been used as one since the 1960s. It was fine. I would be fine. It might be exciting. He had no reason to think I had any concerns about prison. And I didn't. Why was I even thinking about it?

CHAPTER 12

*I*t was a perfect October day. The sky cloudless and deep blue. There was a light breeze that would probably turn into a sturdy wind once we were out on the water. Hunter was as excited as a kid going to an amusement park. I wondered if I should be concerned about that.

What was so thrilling about a decommissioned prison? Was it the legends of the famous inmates—Al Capone and the Birdman? Or was he intrigued by the stories of the escape attempts against all odds? Maybe he wondered about the drive for freedom that caused men to risk the icy waters of San Francisco Bay, dangerous rocks, swimming in the dead of night in total darkness, knowing their chances were less than slim, because they would rather die than be locked up.

Whatever it was, once we boarded, he stood at the front of the boat, wind blowing through his hair, staring at the island as if the rocky piece of land were pulling him toward its shores like a magnet.

I stood as close to him as I could. The boat was large and the water relatively calm. There was no reason to think I would end up in the bay, but watching the waves slap gently against the sides, and thinking about the depth wasn't something I enjoyed, despite the basic swimming skills I'd finally acquired as an adult. They weren't enough to make me eager for the thrill of a boat ride.

"I'm glad you think it's romantic." He put his arm around me and pulled me even closer.

There was absolutely nothing romantic about any of it, but the rest of the day, following our prison tour, held promise. I only had to endure a few hours thinking about the description of the supposed watery deaths of escapees and a life of solitary confinement that the Birdman had endured for forty-two of his fifty-four years on the tiny rock.

When we arrived on the island, it became clear we did not see eye-to-eye on what kind of experience we were anticipating. Hunter wanted to go inside the prison. He wanted to listen to the self-guided tour and look into the cells. He wanted to see every inch of the buildings that were available to the public. I wanted to stay outside and hike around the perimeter of the old buildings, breathe in the clean, salty air, enjoy the old architecture, and look at the breathtaking views of the city.

Eventually, I yielded.

We walked the cell blocks and looked up at banks of tiny cells opening onto walkways, not unlike a hotel. The difference was each room was open to the walkway, giving the occupant a view of all his neighbors through floor-to-ceiling iron bars. There were four main cell blocks: the warden's office, the visitation room, the library, and the barbershop. The cells were primitive with zero privacy. They were furnished with a bed, desk, washbasin, a toilet on the back wall, and a few items other than a blanket. The corridors were named after major U.S. streets, such as Broadway and Michigan Avenue, which were clearly designed for mental torture.

The lecture told us about the history of the place, starting as a military prison and transitioning to a federal prison in 1933. We learned about daily life and its infamous inhabitants. Because the island is located in the icy cold waters, surrounded by the strong currents of San Francisco Bay, prison operators believed Alcatraz would be escape-proof.

That didn't stop those who treasured their freedom. We heard about the most well-known escape attempts. According to the officers who worked there, the first thoughts of every convict who arrived were centered around how to escape. I wasn't surprised. That would have been my thought as well. Although as a person who could barely tolerate putting her face in the water, much less propelling her body forward, I would have been doomed.

Not that I would ever, not in a million years, allow myself to end up in prison. Not ever. I would die first. And I would do everything I could to ensure I didn't make mistakes. Of course, all criminals and killers believe the same. I knew I had made some mistakes. I took more risks than I should have. It was probably time to give a little attention to making sure I returned to my previous level of caution. Maybe coming to Alcatraz had been a good idea after all. Peering into those cold, barren cells, and looking at all those iron bars, no matter how old and rusted, was sobering.

The prison claimed there were no successful escape attempts, but five men are listed as missing. They're presumed drowned, but who knows? People can presume whatever they like. They don't *know*.

When we stepped back onto the boat, I smiled and kissed Hunter. He lifted me off the ground for a few seconds. When he put me down, he said, "I'm glad you liked it after all."

Mostly, I was glad to be stepping onto the boat. Even more, I was an extremely happy girl when I stepped off the boat and onto the firm wood of the pier, finished with the water and the prison, ready to enjoy the rest of the day.

We spent the afternoon at Fisherman's Wharf, wandering through stores filled with souvenirs, of which Hunter bought quite a few. We had a drink at a little bar overlooking the bay, so I guess I wasn't entirely done with the water after all.

As the sun started to dip into the water, we headed to dinner. We weren't exactly dressed for fine dining, but I'd stuck a pair of high heels into my messenger bag. Putting them on made my jeans look instantly classier, and guys can get away with a more casual look if the woman beside them is wearing heels, because all eyes turn to her. We were ushered into the Italian restaurant Hunter had chosen and seated at a quiet table for two.

Hunter ordered wine. They brought a silver plate with warm bread that smelled like it had just been baked, a ceramic dish of soft butter, and left us alone.

Hunter reached across the table, placing his hands in front of my bread plate, his palms facing up. "Give me your hands."

I placed my hands in his.

"This has been the best day in a long time," he said.

I smiled.

"What was your favorite part?" He squeezed my hands, then released them as the server appeared, also momentarily releasing me from answering the question.

After the wine was opened and poured into our glasses, our meals ordered, Hunter looked at me, his eyes full of the question he'd asked.

I picked up my wineglass.

"No toast until you answer my question."

"Right now."

"Yes, right now," he said.

"No, I meant right now is my favorite part."

"That's cheating."

"Why? It's the truth."

"How can this be your favorite part?"

"Because I'm looking at you."

His cheeks turned pinkish. He liked my answer. At the same time, he wanted me to love the prison and its history. He wanted me to thrill at the devious minds and their plans to escape. He wanted me chilled at the horror of living in a tiny concrete cell, trapped by iron bars, tormented by the voices of other inmates, who in all likelihood kept up a constant stream of irritating and probably violent and threatening chatter all through the day and half the night.

"You didn't like Alcatraz?"

"It was interesting."

"How can you not wonder what it was really like to be there?"

"Who says I didn't wonder?"

"You seemed like you couldn't wait to escape." He laughed.

I really wanted a sip of wine.

"Get it?" he asked.

"I get it."

"What was your favorite part of Alcatraz?" he asked.

"I liked knowing that there were five men who might have made it to freedom."

"They didn't."

"You don't know that."

"There's no way. They said—"

"I know what they said, but they can't prove it. And you asked my favorite part. That's my favorite part." I lifted my glass. "To freedom."

"Fair enough."

As his glass touched mine, he was staring at me with an unreadable expression. I wondered if he thought I was too sympathetic toward criminals.

The rest of our dinner was pleasant and fun, with quite a few laughs, and a lot of discussion of criminals and the stories of Alcatraz Island.

CHAPTER 13

*A*s they approached the entrance to the Golden Gate Bridge, Alex plugged her phone into the car's sound system. Her message was clear as she tapped it to increase the volume—no conversation while they drove north to Napa Valley. She wanted to settle into the comforting bliss left by a delicious pasta dinner, a bottle of wine, and a chocolate dessert. She was tired of discussing Alcatraz.

Hunter couldn't figure out if she'd loved it or hated it. Her seeming anxiety about the experience was giving him a mild sense of anxiety himself. At first, he'd thought she was uncomfortable being on the tiny island, feeling trapped in the quarter mile space that was mostly rock.

Then, he'd wondered if it was the fact they were dependent on a boat ride to deliver them and take them back to the city. She'd mentioned she wasn't into water sports and wasn't much of a swimmer. She hadn't offered anymore information, but he'd taken it to mean she had some level of fear around water, that there had been a traumatic childhood experience.

Like so many things about her, she didn't want to go into the details and he was left wondering it if was a minor incident or some major tragedy that had left her deeply scarred. Should he be concerned? Was he missing something important by letting it slide and not digging deeper, no matter how much she resisted his questions?

Finally, he'd decided it must be the prison itself.

And that got him thinking about prisons in general.

Alex seemed to have an active imagination. Maybe she had too much empathy, maybe she was feeling some sort of compassion for the Birdman who, despite his crimes, had become a sympathetic figure in pop culture. Thanks to films made about the place, some of the men who had attempted to escape had also become antiheroes in the public imagination.

Was that her issue? Did she feel sorry for long dead people whose desire to make a better life transcended, and possibly blotted out, their crimes in her mind? Maybe she was more sympathetic to people who committed crimes because they found themselves in impossible situations. Maybe she was more nuanced than he'd realized.

At the same time, trying to unravel what she might be thinking, since she certainly didn't seem inclined to actually tell him what that was half the time, started him thinking about his own fear of prison, his own visceral horror when looking inside those dehumanizing living spaces.

As they'd stood outside the cell refurbished to look as it had in the 1940s, considering what it would be like to live in a space that wasn't much larger than the bathroom in his apartment, he'd felt a chill run through him that was deeper than anything caused by the rock below their feet and the concrete walls towering around them, unheated for decades.

If he closed his eyes, listening to the dramatic recorded voice of the virtual tour guide talking about life on the rock, he could feel the claustrophobia creeping up through his bones. His muscles grew stiff, then twitched with anxiety and the desire to move, just as he imagined a desire for movement must have tormented the prisoners who were only allowed outdoors one or two hours a day.

He imagined staring at the dull ceiling, the walls that appeared damp even though they were not. The constant chill from fog and the surrounding water must have been unbearable. He couldn't imagine the absolute horror of having no choices.

Prisons now were more humane. But were they? The cells were still small; the bars locked automatically, and with precision, so that all inmates were secured at once. The lack of privacy and dignity were identical. Nothing had changed.

The reality that some crimes were worse than others, the knowledge that some people had very good reasons for committing crimes, justifiable reasons, didn't matter once you were locked in that tiny cell. It wasn't as if a brutal serial killer received a smaller cell and someone who killed in self-defense had warmer blankets and a better meal plan or an extra pillow. The only differentiator was the length of time. Every day was torture for the length of time you were there, no matter what you'd done.

He looked at Alex. Her head was turned, staring out the window at the lights flickering past as they raced north, growing more sparse now that they'd left Marin County.

Was she still thinking about Alcatraz or something else? She'd seemed eager to move off the subject, so he doubted it was the tour of a now irrelevant prison, a place that seemed as if it had been invented for the backdrop of a mafia or noir film rather than a place that was an actual part of California state history.

It was such a unique and curious place. What was it about the human race that they looked at a tiny island in the middle of a sparkling, sunlit bay and said—*That's an ideal location for a penitentiary!*

"What are you thinking about?" he asked.

"The prison," she said.

It wasn't what he'd expected and her answer made him want to laugh, although he managed to keep it to himself. He gripped the wheel more tightly. He changed lanes, for no reason. "What about it?" he said, finally.

"Wondering if those guys made it to shore. If someone was waiting for them."

"I seriously doubt it."

"Yeah, probably not. But I wish they had."

"Why?"

"They were smart enough to get out."

He didn't ask any more. All he could think was that he really didn't know her at all. For the time he'd spent following her when she'd been so vague about what she was doing in California, he still didn't know any more. He didn't know what she wanted from him. He still had very little insight into how her mind worked, and he still didn't know if she posed a threat to his own freedom.

CHAPTER 14

*A*fter the dank concrete and peeling paint of Alcatraz, walking into Tess's spacious foyer felt like stepping into a spa. Even the ambiance of a fabulous Italian restaurant hadn't scraped that stuff out of my blood vessels. It lingered there like a plaque, building up in a way that made me think I was headed for a cardiac episode.

Inside Tess's clean, fresh-smelling, Mediterranean villa, I felt at peace. I relished the sensation of being able to move wherever I chose, to come and go as I pleased. I felt free. I felt calm. I felt safe.

Was I?

Hunter was looking at me as if he had a lot of questions. Or maybe he didn't have any questions. Maybe he just wanted to peel off my clothes, and I was spinning around in the foyer, chattering at Damien like a maniac. Damien clearly wasn't thrilled we'd woken him and was not in a chatty mood. His crown stood up like a stubborn weed, and his eyes looked almost beady. He refused to speak any of his usual phrases. Finally, he turned his back on us and walked to the corner of his enclosure, bowing his head slightly in a clear signal that I was disturbing his sleep.

Hunter and I climbed the stairs quickly and turned off the light that shone from the second floor down into the foyer.

In our room, Hunter kissed me and slow-walked me to the bed, pushing me gently until I fell onto my back. He collapsed on top of me, kissing my neck, pulling my hair out of the way. All I could think about was prison cells and solitary confinement and streets mockingly named after the streets of New York City and Chicago, just to further humiliate them. As if they didn't already know they'd lost their freedom to live large and bold.

But eventually, he made me forget about prison.

As we lay in each other's arms, gazing out the picture window at the stars that glittered like fairy lights, Hunter put his mouth close to my ear. "So what's the plan?"

"What plan?"

"The escape plan."

"Escape?"

He poked the soft spot just below my ribs. "Do you plan to live with Tess and Marcus indefinitely? Until they're married? Until you find a better job? Until … what? I don't really understand what's going on here."

"I don't know."

"Seriously?"

"I only just started my job."

"And how long will you be working here?"

"I don't know?"

"I had the impression you were more of a planner."

"I'm not a planner at all." That wasn't entirely true. I planned murder. But I did not plan my life. I knew I should, and I planned to start planning, but so far, I had not. There were too many choices, too many things to think about. Too many things I didn't want to give up. Hunter was now one of those things. I wondered if he knew that.

"Hmm. I thought you invited me here on a vacation. I'm not sure I want to hang around their house while you work."

"So you're leaving?"

"I didn't say that. But this is a little awkward. Everyone's working but me."

I curled into him. I pressed my face against his chest and tried to think about what to say. I did like having him there. I could also see his point. But I needed a job. And Tess had dropped one into my lap. I didn't necessarily want to live in her house, but I definitely wanted to save more money. She was paying me very well. Very, very well. And I ate up every chance I had to accumulate more money. Besides, her house was spectacular. I liked living there, for now.

I wanted more money, more freedom. A more interesting job. A fascinating job. Serving wine to bachelorette parties and book club groups, company team building events, and forty-something birthday gangs would be fun for a while. I had no doubt I would find all kinds of entertaining people walking up to the bar, sipping wine, telling me crazy stories.

"I didn't really think it through," I said. "When I invited you."

"I like being here. The time off is good, and I definitely needed some," he said. "And I didn't ask because I'm bored. I can find ways to entertain myself. I'm more curious about you. Is this how you want to live? In someone else's house? Awesome as it is?"

Should I tell him what I wanted? I'd never really done that before. With anyone. I didn't tell people I wanted to own a home. A palatial home. A castle. A compound. A place that was all mine, a world of its own.

Unless they could help me achieve that goal, it seemed like something better kept to myself. I wasn't sure why. Maybe because I thought other people could sabotage my goals. I don't know. Maybe because the fewer things people know, the less they can get in the way.

A therapist would probably have all kinds of theories about that. Tess would have *insights* about what it meant. Hunter would have comments about how it wasn't healthy, but I didn't need to know the reason. No analysis was required. It was what I thought was best, and that was all that mattered. There was no reason to discuss it.

Right now, I didn't have what I wanted, and I didn't see a path to get there. I didn't even see a sign marking the starting point for the path. So what was there to discuss? And I couldn't plan how to get to that path, so I hadn't done any planning at all.

"What about us?" Hunter asked.

Knowing I was being annoying, I echoed what he'd said. "What *about* us?"

"Are we ..." He rolled onto his back and sighed.

I remained on my side. I knew what he meant. What about us —were we a couple, were we still together, how would we stay together if I was living with Tess and he would return to New York in a few weeks? What *about* us? I had no idea. Clearly, I hadn't planned that either.

I wanted him in my life. I liked New York a lot, but I needed to be in California for now. I needed to figure things out. Why was there always something more important in the way?

Right now, that something, or rather that someone, was Silas Birch.

I wanted Silas out of Tess's life. I wanted him out of her winery and honestly, out of the world, period. But it was a very delicate situation.

And these situations continued to present themselves to me, keeping me from focusing on any kind of planning for myself. So yes, I was a meticulous planner, but all of that planning seemed to benefit other people, never myself.

CHAPTER 15

THEN: HUNTER

*H*unter wasn't sure why he thought it was a momentous occasion to be meeting his brother for dinner in midtown. At the same time, he knew exactly why it was momentous.

The occasion confirmed they were adults.

After years of childhood fights, quite a few of which had turned violent, some ending with Hunter sitting on Zack's thighs, pinning his brother's arms to the ground. Many times, he'd lowered his face over his brother's, closing the space between them to seven or eight inches. He opened his mouth, as if he were threatening to drop a loogie into Zack's eye. "Stay out of my shit. How many times do I have to tell you?"

"Language. I'm telling mom."

"Your torture will be worse if you do that. You're the one breaking the rules. Why are you always whining and crying to mommy? For the last time, stay out of my room, out of my shit." He shifted his position, tightening his grip on Zack's thin, child-like arms. Zack was only eleven. Hunter was fourteen, and he knew the fight wasn't fair. But neither was it fair that Zack was constantly going through his drawers and reading his notebooks, taking stuff and somehow, Hunter didn't even understand how, managing to get their mother on his side every single time.

"You have a responsibility to your younger brother," she said. She never spelled out what that was. He was older. He should know better, he should behave better.

Their father stayed out of it. "Stop fighting. Don't act like a couple of thugs." That was his contribution to the conversation.

"What you really need to do," Hunter said, "Is stay out of my life." He climbed off his brother, stood, and opened his mouth again as if he intended to let the saliva fall onto Zack's face after all.

Zack squealed.

Hunter laughed, then walked out of his brother's room, slamming the door behind him.

"Don't slam the door!" His mother was standing at the end of the hall. "How many times do I have to tell you that, Hunter?"

Why was she always there when he did the slightest thing wrong, but never when Zack went crawling through his room? The little creep had found the condom Hunter's best friend had given him. *You gotta practice. So you know what you're doing when the time comes*, Brian had said.

The only good thing that time was Zack hadn't gone running to their parents after finding that little gem. Maybe he hadn't known what it was.

Now, here they were—two adult men.

After ten years of hardly speaking to each other, beyond what was forced by their mother's tearful, *you're-breaking-my-heart* pleas. She'd been relentless after Hunter went away to college. Every week came the text messages to call his brother, the reminders of how Zack missed his big brother. The revision of history to suggest that Zack's irritating, invasive behavior had all been signs of his unrequited love for his older brother. If only Hunter had paid him more attention, Zack wouldn't have been such a pest, wouldn't have invaded his privacy trying to get close to him.

Occasionally she'd mixed it up with longer pleas through email, telling Hunter how upset Zack was that they weren't close.

When Hunter reminded her that Zack also had his number, she responded with silence, or a reminder that he had a responsibility to his younger brother. That old story.

Maybe it was true. Maybe the eldest had an authority they couldn't see, coming first. The younger one viewed them as some sort of surrogate parent. The first-born held the aura of a large, talking, walking human being that was a mystery to a newborn. Older children were on near-equal footing with the parents to newborns.

It was possible that position in the family was a power that an eldest child couldn't begin to comprehend.

And so, with Zack just now out of college, they were meeting for dinner like adults. It was surreal. There was no other word for it.

When Hunter walked into the restaurant that boasted of serving the most authentic Cajun food in Manhattan, Zack was already seated at the table Hunter had reserved. It was on the second floor, next to the railing, looking down into the main section of the restaurant. It was one of the better tables in the place, and Hunter wondered if Zack was aware of that.

He wanted his brother to recognize that New York City was Hunter's home turf, that he had the city in the palm of his hand. He wanted his brother to recognize who was the real adult here— the one who knew the restaurants, who was used to ordering wine, who made dinner reservations, who paid the bill. And yes, the one who took the initiative, even if it was what his mother had demanded he do his entire life.

It was irritating, but he'd given up fighting about it.

He climbed the curved iron staircase, so steep he always marveled at the servers who walked up and down countless times every night, carrying large trays of food and drinks. He pulled out the chair across from Zack. "Hey. Glad you found it okay."

"There's an app," Zack said.

Wasn't he smart. Hunter gave him a tight smile and picked up his menu.

They made small talk about the menu. They didn't order wine, which removed the opportunity to show off his knowledge in that arena.

As they ordered mixed drinks instead, Hunter decided maybe he should chill and stop trying to be the big brother. Maybe, he realized in a flash of self-awareness, if he did that, the specter of their mother might fade and they could actually talk like the adults they were supposed to be now.

They were nearing the end of the main course when Zack leaned back in his chair and placed his cutlery on the plate.

"Had enough?" Hunter asked.

"No. Just want to savor the meal. It's outstanding, by the way. And I wanted to tell you something."

"Oh? Should we order another round?"

Zack shrugged. "Might be worthwhile."

That was a strange comment. Hunter signaled the server, ordered two more drinks, cut another prawn in two, ate both halves, and waited for his brother to speak.

Zack said nothing.

Hunter put down his fork and gave his full attention to his brother. "What's up?"

"Best to wait for the drinks now. I don't want to be interrupted."

"Sounds serious."

Zack shrugged again.

What was with all the shrugging? This was getting awkward. He felt he couldn't continue eating and his glass was empty. He looked longingly at the food cooling on his plate. Was this another one of Zack's games? Not an adult after all, but wanting to turn a nice meal into a childish battle?

Finally, the drinks arrived. Quite fast, given the crowd, but it had seemed like forever in the face of Zack's silence and his ominous announcement of needing to tell him *something*. Hunter was not going to ask again. It was Zack's turn to be the actual adult.

"I wanted to tell you I'm gay," Zack said.

"Okay. All that buildup for this?"

"I wanted to give you time to react."

"Did you think I was a homophobe or something?"

"I don't know what you are. I hardly know you. If you recall, you've been a bit MIA in my life."

"For good reason."

Zack sighed. He pushed his plate farther away and took a long sip of his drink. "Probably. I was a needy kid. I wanted my brother's attention and didn't know how to get it. What I did never worked, but I didn't figure that out until it was too late. Or maybe I got the attention I wanted and the negative attention was better than nothing."

"That's a lot of self-analysis." Hunter resumed eating.

"Yeah. I had some therapy." Zack grinned. "You should try it."

"I don't feel the need."

Zack shrugged. "It helped."

"Good."

"So anyway, I wanted you to know."

"Thanks for telling me. I appreciate that you trust me."

"It's not about trust. It's not a secret."

Hunter nodded. "Okay. I get that. I probably shouldn't have said it that way."

Zack pulled his plate back and began eating again.

"Do mom and dad know?"

"Yes. Since my birthday."

"And they were …?"

"They were great. Really great. I was a little surprised, but I shouldn't have been."

"Yeah. And sorry I missed your birthday."

"It's fine. We're adults now."

Hunter laughed. Zack joined him, and soon they were laughing, not like brothers who spent ten years barely speaking, and not like the pest and the intolerant older brother who wanted to pin him to the floor, but like adults. And maybe, like friends.

CHAPTER 16

NOW: ALEX

*N*apa Valley, California

It was another spectacular fall day and the tasting room was booked almost back-to-back with group tastings. The air was cool and smelled as if the sky had been washed with mountain water. The leaves of the deciduous trees were transforming themselves to yellow and red, as if they wanted to acknowledge the importance of a change in hair color.

I'd wanted to go for a run, but after our late dinner and outstanding sex, and staying awake late for our discussion about my lack of planning, Hunter and I slept late.

Now, I was opening the blinds in the gift shop, regretting that I hadn't worn my hair up because despite the crisp air outside, it was going to get warm in the tasting room once I got busy and it was filled with groups of talking, laughing wine drinkers.

The first group consisted of three couples celebrating the fact they'd all been married twenty-five years. Their specific anniversaries had been scattered across late summer and early fall.

"And now, here we are!" Caitlin, the woman who had made the reservation, was tall and thin, with blonde hair to her shoulders. She wore a white top and pants and white tennies with silver embellishments, as did her friends. Apparently, they'd gone shopping together, wanting to recapture the bridal vibe by dressing in white, but mostly looking like they were spectators at a fancy tennis match.

One of her friends, Cassidy, was also blonde, although it looked more forced on her. The other woman, Jill, had brown hair with fine gray streaks. Jill's smile was mildly secretive, making her look like the most interesting of the three. That smile suggested she knew something they didn't. I wondered if she really did, and I wondered if it was something about them, or their husbands, or just something about life.

I wanted to talk to her, but with Caitlin's exuberance, and the fact there were six of them drinking wine, it seemed unlikely.

It wasn't the reason I was there, not according to Silas, for sure, and not even according to Tess. My sole reason for *engaging with the clients*, as Silas pompously phrased it, was to sell club memberships. My function was to get alcohol flowing through their veins as quickly as possible, reducing their resistance to spending money. Creating a desire to belong to an exclusive group of like-minded people who loved our wine.

Even Tess didn't think I should be getting into personal conversations, talking about anything deep or controversial. *Don't be combative*, she'd reminded me. More than once, which was unnecessary. It was something she reminded me of too frequently in general.

"It's not the same as being assertive," she said.

"When a person is assertive, it can turn combative," I said.

"See, there you go—combative."

"Do you think every difference of opinion is combat?" I asked.

"No. But sometimes you dig in your heels, and no matter what someone says, you have to take the opposite point of view. It's as if you pride yourself on being argumentative."

"I'm not arguing. I'm stating what I think."

"But why does it always have to be the polar opposite of what everyone else thinks?"

"Because I'm unique."

"Don't be so full of yourself."

"Isn't that combative? I don't think it's being full of myself to think I'm unique. Obviously I am if I usually have a different point of view from other people."

"It seems like you deliberately look for a different position."

"Do I? How do you know that?"

"It's a feeling."

I smiled.

"Why are you smiling like that?" she asked.

The conversation had deteriorated from there and finally ended. Neither one of us had walked away the victor from our combat, if that's what she'd thought it was.

I enjoyed disagreeing. Where was the fun in always agreeing? It was interesting to see who won. Combative was a strong word. It was a difference of opinion. An alternative viewpoint. Combative implied battle. I wasn't going to fight to the death for all my opinions. Some, yes, but not most.

I understood her wishes perfectly. She didn't want me discussing inflammatory topics over tiny sips of wine. No politics. No religion. The problem was, she also believed that a strong opinion on *any* topic was combative, heading toward the brink of verbal war over electric versus gas-powered cars, city versus rural living, red versus white wine.

It was entirely possible she'd hired me because I looked good behind her equally attractive marble countertop. I was there to glitter alongside her sparkling glassware, holding up sleek bottles with the distinctive Black Mask label beside my charming smile.

So I asked pleasant, innocuous questions about where people

had come from and what brought them out wine tasting for the day. Meanwhile, I wondered if I would get many opportunities to turn this into a more interesting job or if I would quickly be bored out of my mind.

When the group was ready to sip the Cabernet, the last tasting, I knew none of them would be signing up for the wine club. That moment had passed long ago. It had been clear from their chatter and their blank stares when I'd made a comment to test the water that any mention of the wine club would sink like a block of concrete.

They did buy six bottles, so that was considered a win, and would be credited to my list of so-called successful tastings.

Neither Tess nor Silas put a lot of stock in word of mouth. It wasn't of much interest to them that a simple tasting might be successful if the group walked out loving the wine enough that they might tell others about the winery, that they might order a Black Mask wine in a restaurant, or ask about it in a restaurant that didn't have it on the menu, or tell their friends. Only the measurable counted toward my score.

I escorted the group to the door, thanked them for visiting, and invited them to return at any time. I handed them brochures along with their wine-carrying boxes.

I followed them onto the patio. Immediately, my good mood from the tasting evaporated as if it had been punctured by a thorn from one of the rosebushes growing in the garden beside the tasting patio.

Silas and Amelia were sitting on the bench under the trellis on the path that wound through the garden.

The first time I'd seen them together had been a fluke. They'd run into each other and he'd introduced himself. But this? What was she doing here? It looked as if she'd returned to the winery for the sole purpose of meeting with Silas. The fact that they were sitting together in the garden when he should have been working in his new office suggested that she'd contacted him ahead of time. They'd made enough of a connection that they'd exchanged phone numbers.

She was nearly fifteen years younger than Silas. Barely an adult. Were they attracted to each other? Was it something else?

Whatever it was, I didn't like it. I didn't want to think about Amelia telling him the details of her story, mentioning her imagined fairy godmother who had facilitated the death of her parents.

It wasn't as if he would connect me to that act. But what if she also mentioned her father's missing sister with her red hair? Silas had made such a point of my hair color, pretending to believe it was natural for no discernible reason.

There were so many details that he might become too interested in. And for someone that hated me with the passion he possessed, knowing too many details about things I'd been involved with, was not a good thing.

CHAPTER 17

The next tasting was in half an hour. I had plenty of time to watch Silas and Amelia until that time.

From where they sat, they couldn't see me. Unfortunately, I couldn't hear what they were saying, but I could see they were having a very intense conversation. The ebb and flow was like that of two people who had known each other for a long time.

Was this only the first encounter I'd witnessed? Was it possible they'd been seeing each other for a while? Anything was. It had been weeks since the fire at the castle, the death of her parents, Amelia's embrace of her freedom.

She was a girl who was naïve beyond anyone her age. She knew absolutely nothing about the world as it existed outside of books and movies, and those had been carefully curated by her mother. She hadn't even been allowed access to the internet.

Until a few weeks earlier, she'd never encountered social media. She'd never even met someone her own age. It was possible she still hadn't. In fact, she was so out of touch with the real world, she might not even realize the age difference between herself and Silas unless they'd discussed it. And he was not a person to be forthright in his introduction of himself.

For a moment, I felt as if she needed rescuing from her tower for the second time.

Anything he told her, she was likely to believe. He could form her into whatever he chose, as if he'd stumbled upon his very own Pygmalion.

I stood in the shadows formed by the potted plants around the entrance to the tasting room. It didn't matter all that much. Neither one had turned to look at their surroundings. They were sitting close. Not entwined like lovers, but closer than two friends, definitely closer than a man she'd only recently met. Absolutely closer than she would to a man with whom she believed she should show some caution because he was a stranger.

I couldn't imagine what her interest was in him.

Maybe it was the story as old as time—he paid attention to her. He smiled at her and asked her a few questions. He told her she was beautiful.

It was now fifteen minutes until the next tasting group was due to arrive. If Silas didn't release his hold on Amelia in the next few minutes, I would have no choice but to leave them unobserved while I did my job. By the time I was finished with our guests, she might be long gone.

I could make a trek up the hillside to the castle and pay her a visit. It would be easy enough to tell her I was curious about seeing the towers, but that would draw attention to myself. And I'd already made myself stand out more than I should have with my impulsive decision, made too late, to change my hair color.

Showing up at the castle with a lecture about avoiding Silas would set off alarms in her mind, no matter how naïve she was. She would ask herself why I was so interested. And based on what I was witnessing from their budding relationship right now, she might immediately tell him everything I said.

I checked my phone—ten minutes. I could hope the tasting guests would be late. Even in my short time at the winery, I'd learned that people often were. They were on vacation. Keeping to schedules was not high on their priority lists.

As I slipped my phone back into my pocket, Silas stood. He held out his hand to help Amelia to her feet, as if she were an invalid who couldn't bring herself to a standing position from a bench without his courtly assistance.

When I saw her dip her head, her hair falling over the side of her face, I knew she'd fallen for him in a way that would not be good for me. She was infatuated. She had no idea who he was.

My stomach turned as Silas lifted the hand he was still holding to his lips, kissed her fingers, gave a slight, stiff bow, then walked along the path headed toward the wine making buildings and offices. Amelia immediately settled herself on the bench again.

I had seven minutes.

I crossed the patio, stepped onto the path, and wound my way to where Amelia was sitting. There was no time for casual theatrics and excessive politeness. "Mind if I sit here for a minute?"

She shrugged.

"Are you meeting friends for a wine tasting?" She wasn't old enough to legally taste wine, but despite my eagerness to get to the point in the few minutes I had left, I had to start somewhere.

"No."

"I don't think I actually introduced myself the last time we spoke. I'm Alexandra. I manage the tasting room."

"I know."

"How do you know Silas?"

She stared at me as if I'd asked how old she was when she first had sex.

"I met him here."

"You seem to know him really well."

"What do you want?"

"He's … a little old for you. You don't know me, so I don't have a right to say anything, but I think you should be aware … I hope you won't mention this to him, but you should be careful around him."

She scooted away from me. "Wow."

"I realize it's none of my business. But one woman to another, I thought—"

"That's really ... wow. I do not need more people telling me what to do." She bolted off the bench and turned to face me, taking a step back. "If you knew anything about me, you would know that people told me all my life what to do. I've had enough of that."

"You're right. I don't know anything about you. But he's a lot older and—"

"You probably don't know him very well either." She gave me a grin that could only be described as wicked. "He told me to watch out for you. He said you would probably warn me about him. So thanks for proving him right. He's a smart guy." She turned and walked away.

I didn't think I could have made it worse if I'd tried. I stood and glanced toward the tasting room. The group was at the door, holding it open, no doubt letting flies into the room. They were scanning the area, hands over their brows as if they were searching the desert for signs of a promised oasis.

I walked quickly toward the patio, wondering how I was going to persuade Amelia to listen to me. Or find a way to drive a wedge between her and Silas.

CHAPTER 18

THEN: ALEX

 *ortland, Oregon*

It probably goes without saying, I was not allowed to go to parties in high school. Party-going for the Mallory children ended when supervised birthday parties hosted by parents with whom my parents were well-acquainted ended.

Our social lives were rooted in the activities of Pure Truth Tabernacle.

That hadn't stopped my older brothers from trying, and occasionally succeeding. My oldest brother Eric simply told my parents he was spending the night at a friend's house. He was a friend from church—automatically pre-approved. What my parents didn't know was that his church friend was in charge of his younger sister and the house for the weekend when the parents left town to move his grandma to an assisted living facility.

There was a party. To hear Eric describe the event, it was wild, but just enough under the radar to avoid catching the attention of the police. The music thumped inside a house in which all the windows were kept closed. There were no beer kegs delivered to attract attention, only a steady stream of friends bringing six packs.

When we asked for details about what had gone on, Eric grinned and told us the rest was a secret that could only be revealed to the initiated. Those who attended parties themselves, who crossed the threshold into fighting for their *own* independence, even if it required carefully constructed lies and a significant risk of being found out.

By the time each of us reached the later years of high school, lying carried a punishment of one month's house arrest. And this was not the typical grounding that other kids experienced. This meant our bedroom doors were left open around the clock. We were not allowed to use the telephone or have friends come to the house. There were long prayer sessions supervised by my mother during the day, and by my father in the evenings and on weekends. In some cases, my mother called the school to report us sick with the flu for one week of our confinement. We did our work at the kitchen table under her supervision all day long. When we finished our schoolwork, we wrote essays about why lying was wrong, outlining why it was upsetting to god, to our father, and our mother. The details of the upset we caused were different for each of those we'd offended. If we failed to clarify the differences, we had to rewrite the essay.

Lying was risky business in the Mallory house.

By the time I turned sixteen, when I was itching to find out what high school parties were like, Tom was my only brother still living at home. I heard about parties through the stories my school friends told. Some of their stories honestly sounded more like they'd been lifted out of scenes from movies, altered slightly to fit our city and the kids at our school. They were too perfect and too filled with every possible zany event to be real.

Weren't they? It was hard to know, since I'd never witnessed one with my own eyes and ears.

Was sex truly taking place in every upstairs bedroom? Were people really walking into rooms to find their boyfriend or girlfriend naked with someone else? Was the dancing really that fabulous? Were the drinking games that wild ... the passing out, the throwing up, and the humiliating behavior that awful? Were kids waking in the morning under the parents' bed, forced to sneak out of the house before being discovered by a father who had no idea a massive party had been held at his house while he was out for the evening?

Was it fun or was it degrading and disgusting? It was hard to tell.

Were the darker stories true? Stories of girls assaulted, girls walking into clinics a few weeks later with unwanted pregnancies, or disappearing altogether amid whispers of a baby that would be absorbed into an extended family. Had a few kids, once every year or two, come close to death from alcohol, the paramedics not called until it was almost too late because everyone feared *getting in trouble*?

The dark stories were whispered about, then forgotten. Mostly, they made it sound fun. They made it sound dramatic and exciting. As if every part of you was pushed to the limits.

Drinking made you feel alive and free. It made you do things you didn't know you could, or would. It made you popular and fun. Alcohol made everyone your friend. It connected everyone in a tight bond that couldn't be experienced without alcohol. A bond that lasted a lifetime.

That's how it all sounded, that's how it all looked in my imagination.

I didn't feel the need to be connected to a group, but I did like the idea of being at the center of the action. I did like the idea of everyone going crazy and doing and saying things they didn't do and say at school. I absolutely liked the idea of experiencing the altered perception brought on by alcohol that everyone raved about, and the thrill of hanging out with people my age without a single person over thirty anywhere in sight—no parents, teachers, and if we were all lucky and didn't go too wild, no police officers.

So when I found out Tom was going to a party, even though the crowd would be mostly high school seniors, while I was just coming to the end of my sophomore year, and there would be some kids who had already graduated, which of course was necessary in order to get our hands on alcohol, I began lobbying for a seat in his friend's car.

"No," Tom said. "I have a system. I know how to avoid getting caught."

"So do I."

He laughed. "You might as well have *Risk* as your middle name."

"Why?"

"Because Dad watches you like a hawk."

"He watches—"

"It's different with you and you know it. You're a liability. You're not coming. And you better not rat me out or you'll pay for it."

"How?"

"I'll figure out a way."

He probably would. My brothers and I were better than anyone at figuring out devious means of payback and punishment. After all, we'd been enduring cunning forms of discipline since we were old enough to understand the meaning of consequences.

"I'll never get to go to a party if you don't let me go with you."

"You'll get your chance when you're a senior."

"I won't. Dad watches me, like you said. It will be easier if you—"

"No, it won't. Because they won't realize I'm gone. So it won't be easier. If they notice you're not here, they'll come looking for me."

My parents did do bed checks after we were asleep. I knew this because occasionally I wasn't asleep. They sometimes checked my brothers' rooms, but not as often. As far as I could tell, based on it happening every single time I was awake, one of them, but most often my father, opened my bedroom door every night and looked into my room.

My brothers had gotten around this with the silly and easily discovered trick of stuffing pillows and stuffed clothing into their beds. But for whatever reason, my father never advanced into their rooms for a closer look.

He didn't come into my room either, but he did sometimes stand in the doorway much longer than necessary, and I could never be sure what he was doing. Knowing him, I guessed he was praying over my defiant, wayward soul. But I never knew if he studied the rhythm of my breathing, or watched for subtle movements of my body shifting in sleep.

I had two significant hurdles to clear—Tom's absolute refusal to invite me along for the ride, and concealing my absence from the man who wanted me to exist in his ever-present shadow.

CHAPTER 19

❦

NOW: ALEX

*N*apa Valley, California

Information is power. That's what they say. I had no idea what I would do if I got information, if it would give me any power with Amelia, but I could at least look further into *getting* some information. It was information that I would have thought Tess might have sought before she bought the winery, but she hadn't.

She'd been focused on the property and business transactions of buying one hundred-thirty acres and a grape-growing and wine-making company.

The so-called soft background of what she was purchasing hadn't been uppermost in her mind. She knew nothing about Silas's relationship with the previous owners. She knew nothing about his role beyond the job description itself.

I'd begun to think it was a blind-spot. Because Tess certainly knew from her career managing large groups of people that a job description, and the individual who performs that job and how they fit into the role, adapting it to their personality and their quirks and flaws, can't possibly be captured in a resumé, or even in a rigorous interview process and background check.

It was possible she knew absolutely nothing that truly mattered about the man. For all she knew, she was not his first blackmail victim. For all she knew, blackmail was his primary source of income.

There were a hundred things that might help her escape from his grip if she knew more about him and his relationship with the previous owners. He'd come highly recommended, but why? Was he really that amazing, or had he blackmailed them into recommending him? It was absolutely possible.

I started with Google, which is always the starting place. Or it was until it was infected by AI, but it still worked, most of the time. I suppose a normal person would have considered the starting place to be Tess Turner, but I didn't want to discuss this with her. She would tell me not to go poking around. She would tell me not to do anything that might get back to Silas, anything that might upset him, anything *combative*. If he was rattled or annoyed in any way, it would blow back on Tess.

Not that I didn't recognize this fact, but it was still something that had to be done. I would be careful. Discreet and careful. An internet search would not blow back on Tess. A social media search wouldn't make any waves.

After that, I would see where things stood.

I learned that the previous owners—Gordon and Jillian Harper—were in their mid-fifties. They had a twenty-five year-old daughter named Rosé—a name that made me laugh out loud. It sounded as if the wine business had taken over every cell in their brains. Now that the family had left the wine business and moved to Italy, I wondered how that name was working out for her. Maybe the Italians loved it. Maybe they found it charming and romantic and right in keeping with the delightful mood of that country.

The information available online told me all about their public life, which was to be expected. I learned about the history of the winery, the date of their marriage, and the sale of the winery. I learned about the galas thrown at Black Mask and their philanthropic activities in the Napa Valley.

Rosé Harper had graduated from San Francisco State College, which struck a slightly off-key note for a family that had a lavish lifestyle and seemed to want to present themselves as hugely successful. I would have thought they would want to send their daughter out of state, or at least out of the local area, to a school with more prestige.

Maybe she didn't have the grades. Maybe she wasn't all that interested in an education she could brag about. Maybe she planned to enter the family business and college was just a bow on her home-grown education. At the age of twenty-five, when they'd sold the winery, she appeared to be living at home. She'd moved to Italy with her parents.

The most intriguing part of the Harper family online portrait was Rosé. Her age suggested someone who would have caught the attention of Silas. There probably wasn't a woman within ten years of his age, in either direction, who wouldn't catch his attention.

But this was all wild imaginings on my part. And more than a little bit of a combative attitude toward the man, but I was fully aware I was out to get him. I was completely conscious of the fact that he couldn't do anything right in my eyes.

In fact, I didn't even have to scratch the surface of my thoughts to recognize that I was digging in the hopes of finding something troubling. I wanted something that I could place in front of Amelia, waving it in her face so I could show her she needed to stay away from him.

Without too much stretch, it might appear that the family almost fled the country after a quick sale of their winery. The circumstances whispered this might be a family wanting to escape from a slimy man. At the same time, I wondered if I was giving him too much credit. To think that a family with that much money and local influence couldn't manage an employee, but instead, sold their business and left the country.

I was spinning a story in my head because I needed something to sever the bond growing between Silas and Amelia. Or, I could remove him from the picture immediately and solve two problems at once. But I hadn't figured out a way to do that.

With web pages bookmarked, I turned to social media.

There, I encountered a black hole. The social media for the winery itself was stunning—years of elegant photographs from wine tastings and weddings, anniversary parties and twenty-first birthday bashes. There were shots of luscious food flanked by glamorous glasses filled with silky liquid. The accounts had all been handed over to Tess when she purchased the winery, and the enticing displays continued without a hitch.

No personal accounts existed for Jillian or Gordon Harper. More surprisingly, there was nothing for Rosé Harper. Given her age, and a name like that, there was no doubt I would have found an account somewhere if one existed.

Had she deleted her accounts, or had she never started any for some inexplicable reason? I had no way of knowing.

I combed through local high schools, looking for the names of people who might have graduated around the time Rosé Harper should have, trying to find a mention of her, a stray photograph that resembled the handful of professionally posed family shots buried in the history of the Black Mask Instagram feed. There was nothing.

The same was true for San Francisco State University.

There seemed to be no further corners of the internet for me to poke into on my own.

I sent a text message to Scott Ruiz, the reporter I'd met in a bar when I was seeking information about the history of the castle and its occupants. The manner in which we'd parted suggested he might be expecting a message about meeting for a drink to hook up, so I phrased my message carefully, to be sure my intentions were clear.

Alex:

We met a few weeks ago and chatted about the history of the Windy Hills Castle. History buff that I am, I have a new curiosity worm in my ear. Are you open for me to pick your brain? Drinks on me, obviously.

I read it three times before hitting send. The intention seemed clear to me, but it was hard to know sometimes.

CHAPTER 20

$\mathcal{B}$y dinner time, there was no text back from Scott. He was probably working on a story, conducting interviews, rushing toward a deadline. I decided to wait a day before calling him.

Tess and Marcus had invited Hunter and me out to dinner at their favorite restaurant. It specialized in seasonal menus and locally grown food, and, of course, served wine from Black Mask, as well as a few other Napa Valley wineries. I wondered if they would order their own wine or try something different. I wondered if they would make that decision themselves, or leave it to Hunter and me.

We were escorted to a table on a patio surrounded by a private garden. We were offered complimentary sparkling wine and given our menus, as well as a charcuterie board that Tess had arranged in advance.

After ordering, which turned out to be a special offering that included wine pairings to go with each course, the wines coming from a variety of wineries, we settled back in chairs so comfortable I expected we might end up sitting there until after midnight.

We talked about the winery. We talked about my new job and

my old job. Hunter told them what it was like working in PR for a top New York modeling agency. We talked about Australia and cyber security. Marcus had a way of making it sound like a series of true crime stories rather than a lecture in technology, carrying us all the way through the main course.

Then, as if someone had tapped her on the shoulder, alerting her that now was the moment she was tasked with disrupting the flow of conversation, Tess turned to Hunter. It might have been partially caused by a lull at the completion of the main course. More likely, it was caused by weeks of pent-up questions and ruminations, blended with her own fixation on marriage and living happily ever after.

"We know almost nothing about you, Mr. Hunter Pierce. I think it's time to reveal all."

Hunter laughed.

"You won't be charming your way out of this," Tess said.

"I doubt we have time to hear his entire life story," I said.

"We have plenty of time. A dessert so rich we'll want to savor it. Another drink. A cup of coffee ..." She waved her hand in the air as if all kinds of other drinks and food would follow.

I placed my hand on my stomach, letting my gaze drift down the small menu again, trying to decide what I wanted.

We ordered our desserts and after-dinner drinks. Tess placed her elbow on the table and rested her chin on her upturned palm, and fixed her gaze on Hunter's face. "Parents still together? Siblings? Childhood traumas? Who did mom love the most? First drink? First time you got laid? Worst thing you ever did? College pranks that went bad? Let's *seeee* ..." She drummed her fingertips on her chin. "What else?"

"That's enough for a two-hour monologue," I said.

Tess straightened and turned sharply. She gave me a slow, wicked grin. "Is that right? I'm assuming then, that would be the case for you? I know very few of these things about you, Alexandra. Maybe that's why I'm so eager to know Hunter. He's the doorway to you." Her smile spread, convincing me the thought had come to her only a split second before she'd spoken, maybe even as the words were coming out of her mouth.

Hunter picked up his glass of whiskey. He took a sip, then set it down firmly. "Parents stayed together, but dad's gone now. Very much in love until the day he died, as far as a kid can know that about their parents, which obviously, they cannot. One brother, younger. Gay. Owns a bookstore and coffee shop. Mom loves him best. First drink, age fifteen. First time I got laid, age fifteen." He winked. "Worst thing I ever did, not saying. Didn't engage in college pranks. So, maybe Alex needs a two-hour monologue, but I do not." He picked up his glass and took a liberal sip.

"That's the dullest life story I've ever heard," Tess said. "But you strike me as a fascinating person. Mysterious and deep."

"I don't know why," Hunter said.

"How many glasses of wine have you had, Tess?" Marcus placed his arm across the back of her chair. "You sound like you're a little ..." he laughed and kissed her cheek. "But you are entertaining, so carry on, if Hunter doesn't mind."

"I think there are a *lot* more chapters in some of those stories," she said. "First, why won't you say what the worst thing is? It must be pretty bad. Am I right?"

Hunter shrugged, but looked unconcerned.

I wondered if he was playing with her. It was hard to say.

"I'm curious why you needed to mention your brother is gay," Tess said. "It doesn't seem relevant. A hint of homophobia?"

"Not at all," Hunter said. "Zack has a lot of speakers and book signings for authors writing about issues facing the gay community. He hosts activist meetings, so it always comes to mind when I think about his bookstore."

Tess nodded. "If you say so."

"I do."

"It just stood out, in such a bare bones bio."

Hunter shrugged again.

"You didn't mention your parents' sexual orientation. Or your own, for that matter."

"Tess," Marcus said.

She sat back and picked up her drink. "Just trying to break through the surface."

"Did you?" I asked. "Break through the surface?"

"No." She laughed.

Hunter laughed. I joined him, and finally, Marcus chuckled softly.

It was obvious Tess was eager to conjure up another list of questions, or to push him harder into a corner where she could make him squirm so he would say something that would give her whatever she was looking for—exposing a secret, or showing a darker side. She seemed to think there was something she needed to know that Hunter wasn't telling her.

I really didn't understand it, but if she wanted to keep searching for something elusive, I didn't care. I was fairly sure Hunter didn't mind, either. He looked amused, not offended. And he wasn't volunteering anymore information.

"I hope she didn't put you on the spot," Marcus said.

"Don't apologize for me," Tess said.

"Not at all." Hunter sipped his whiskey. "She can ask whatever she wants. I'll feel free to do the same, if any questions come to mind."

Tess looked suddenly uncomfortable.

I glanced sideways at Hunter. It sounded as if he was making the same teasing conversation we'd been carrying on while she tried to put him under the spotlight. But maybe he had been offended. Maybe he had a good poker face. And maybe, Silas had said something to him that made him think Tess had darker secrets than he did.

Was it possible he thought her question about the worst thing he'd ever done had come from worried thoughts swimming to the surface on a river of alcohol? Was it possible he thought her sudden deflection to his brother's sexuality was her attempt to cover a question she'd immediately regretted asking? A question she didn't want him to answer because she definitely did not want him returning it to her in front of her fiancé—asking about the worst thing *she'd* ever done?

Maybe she didn't trust the strength of her own poker face if she were asked that question with Marcus's gaze focused on her.

CHAPTER 21

*A*s we lay in bed, our bellies full, our heads in the hazy disconnected state that comes from too much alcohol, I wasn't sure whether I should ask Hunter what he'd thought of Tess's interrogation. He'd seemed to go with the flow, seemed to not care much how she wanted to pry. He'd tossed out simple answers and deflected her interpretation of his response.

Was he finished with it all?

What *was* the worst thing he'd ever done?

I couldn't ask, because it would prompt the identical question to me. I could say anything I wanted, but I wasn't in a state to create a well-thought-out lie that I'd be willing to carry on with indefinitely.

Why hadn't he answered? I supposed most people wouldn't. No one would, unless the worst thing was fairly innocuous. *I stole a candy bar when I was five.* Or, *I lied to my teacher about a fight on the playground.* That sort of thing. Childish things. Things that are only bad if you don't even fully comprehend the meaning of that word.

Hunter wasn't going to shrug and admit to armed robbery or embezzlement. He wasn't going to tell us all he'd left the scene of a car accident or, like me, committed multiple, calculated murders.

Tess wasn't even thinking along those lines when she asked the question. She couldn't be.

No one thought about murder when they had those kinds of conversations, when they played truth or dare, or two truths and a lie. Because most people you meet have not committed murder.

It was entirely possible Hunter had forgotten all about her questions.

Listening to his breathing, I wasn't sure whether or not he'd fallen asleep. We didn't normally go to sleep without a kiss and cuddling, even if we didn't have sex, which, most of the time, we did. Even if we had a lot to drink. Almost always when we had a lot to drink.

We hadn't moved into the world of a couple where we analyzed and discussed an evening spent with others after it was over. Mostly because we hadn't spent more than one or two evenings with other people. Did he want me to ask about it? Did he expect me to ask about it? Did he have complaints about the questioning? It wasn't as if I could do anything about it after the fact, and it wasn't as if I were inclined to soothe him if he was deeply upset that my friend had accused him of being homophobic.

I didn't think he was. And I honestly didn't think Tess thought he was. What I thought was that she wanted to get a reaction out of him. She wanted to find out why I wasn't longing to move to the next phase, whatever that was—sharing an apartment or hoping he would slide a ring onto my finger.

She was absolutely certain this meant there was something wrong with him and she needed to figure out what I was hiding from her, what he was hiding from me, or from her.

When Marcus stopped her before she achieved her goal, she'd looked defeated, then worried.

I felt as if I were in the middle of a game of four-player chess.

Tess wanted to expose every facet of Hunter's life. At the same time, she was hiding her own secret. She was literally sitting on a ticking bomb, letting a man walk around her winery, holding keys and an enormous amount of control over her business who could detonate that bomb at any moment he chose.

She didn't seem all that motivated to do anything about it. I'd invested more time than she had in trying to gather information about the man who was threatening her. I didn't understand what was going through her mind. It must be some form of denial. It seemed as if her plan was simply to wait and see what happened, to do nothing but clean up the mess when it was over.

In the meantime, she would spend her time interfering in my life.

I wondered, too, at the glibness of Hunter's responses to the questions. They'd almost sounded rehearsed. It was doubtful he'd experienced that series of rapid-fire questions before. He'd probably expected her to ask. She'd been aggressively interested in him since the moment he stepped out of his rental car and shaken her hand.

But they still sounded too smooth.

And why *had* he made a point of his brother being gay? It seemed irrelevant. The story about his bookstore and coffee shop sounded inflated somehow. There was something that made him highlight that single, small, personal piece of his life. It wasn't as if I didn't know other pieces of his life, but he hadn't mentioned that, and now he had, in a very pointed way, and I wondered if he'd intended to do that.

The sound of his breath moving in and out of his lungs told me nothing about his state of consciousness. Experience and my logical mind suggested he was awake. And if that was true, that meant his thoughts might be as busy as mine, reliving the evening, analyzing the conversation, wondering how I'd interpreted things, and considering what he wanted to do next.

There seemed to be something between us I couldn't identify. I wasn't sure if it was his desire to have a more conventional relationship, his irritation that I'd left New York suddenly and permanently, or something else. Was he hiding something, and he was concerned he'd stepped too close to the edge, allowing Tess to get under his skin, even though he hadn't stumbled?

I turned onto my side. I placed my hand on his stomach, feeling his warmth and the soft, light growth of hair. I moved my fingers through it, waiting for him to respond. His breathing remained steady. His body remained motionless.

I wriggled closer, curving my arm around his waist, resting my head on his chest.

He lifted his arm and placed it around my shoulders. His breathing hardly changed at all. He placed his other hand on the back of my head, closing his fingers around my skull, holding it tightly. The pressure was pleasant. I sighed softly.

His breathing remained steady.

"You survived the interrogation," I whispered.

"Is that what it was?"

"That's not how it felt?" I asked.

"Not really. Did you think it was?"

"She's very curious about you."

"It's flattering."

Was that the truth? It didn't sound like him. I decided to let the lie settle between us. Waiting could be a good thing. Sometimes, things reveal themselves without probing. I had enough other things to probe right now.

CHAPTER 22

THEN: HUNTER

*A*fter five years of teaching high school English, Hunter's brother decided he wanted to open a bookstore and coffee shop. Zack had spent the best days of his college life hanging out in a gay-friendly coffee shop, reading books that opened a whole new world to him. He'd participated in discussion groups and heard authors speak who made him feel as if they saw inside his thoughts and had lived lives like his.

The moment Zack announced his plans, their mother began recounting her worries to Hunter on a weekly basis, as if she were ticking off rosary beads, working her way through the things his brother had said.

"He wants to give back. He wants his life to have meaning. He needs a job with purpose. He wants to be part of a community." She repeated each item every time they spoke on the phone. She sent the phrases in text messages as if they were mantras.

"Sounds great," Hunter said.

"I don't like it," his mother said. "He has all that as a school-teacher."

"Tell him that, not me."

"I have, sweetie. I have. He won't listen."

Hunter wasn't fond of his mother calling him sweetie. Couldn't she come up with a nickname that was more fitting for a man in his thirties? It made him feel like a fluffy baby duck.

"It's his life," Hunter said.

"It makes him a target."

"I don't think that's how you should look at it. He's just living his life."

"But there are a lot of hateful people out there. You know that. He's advertising who he is and his opinions and how he—"

"He's not advertising anything. He wants to own a bookstore and coffee shop."

"But if he promotes speakers and groups and draws attention to—"

"Are you uncomfortable with who he is? I thought you and dad accepted him? That you love him?"

"We do. You don't understand. People are awful. I don't want to see him hurt."

"He's been hurt already."

"But he doesn't need to invite it."

Each time, Hunter reassured her that his brother knew what he wanted, knew what he was doing, was free to make his own choices. He reminded her it was a bookstore, not a nightclub. He told her to stop worrying. It was a small town. It was upstate New York. It was fine.

But she worried, and she wanted Hunter to listen to her worries. She wanted to persuade Hunter that her worries were the truth, that they were accurate predictions of the future.

"He needs to listen to me. There are so many jobs he could have that he'd do really well in. He was an incredible teacher. After only two years, he won teacher of the year."

"I know that, Mom. But he wants to do this now." It was another part of the lament that Zack had been teacher of the year. And after such a short time. Such an accomplishment. Teaching was a secure job. A job for a lifetime.

His mother worshipped security. It was her whole reason for living. Maybe it came from raising two boys, spending the best years of her life trying to keep them safe, trying to give them security, and so it became the central theme of her life. If she could ensure security, she'd done her job.

Now that they were out of her sight, out of her care, she couldn't do it physically, but it didn't stop her from trying to steer them toward it in every way she could think of. His father's lack of concern, his absolute certainty that security could be ignored and everything would just work out, seemed to inflame her desire to lock things down.

"You need to talk to him," she said. "Please."

"No."

"What if there's a boycott, and he goes bankrupt?"

"Don't be so negative. He knows what he's doing. He has a solid line of credit. He has investors."

"That could all be gone. Sometimes people want to—"

"Let him do what he wants. It's a great idea. He has a solid plan and he has a focused market. It's a better idea than most. He's not competing with ten other people trying to do the same thing."

No matter what he'd said, his mother continued with the anxious, repetitious calls and texts. It was as if every fear she'd had for either of her sons was wrapped up in that store. After a while, Hunter wasn't sure if it was because she worried Zack would be targeted because he was gay, or because she didn't like the idea of him starting his own business. She seemed to be afraid that the lack of a weekly paycheck was equally dangerous, that she viewed an employer as a surrogate mother, someone to watch over her boys and provide the illusion of security in her absence.

It was exhausting.

But later, it made him wonder if his mother had some sort of special maternal insight that had allowed her to see what was going to happen. As if she felt it in her bones, like she claimed to feel it in her bones when a thunderstorm was coming.

CHAPTER 23

NOW:ALEX

Napa Valley, California

It was possible I had an ulterior motive when I invited Tess out to lunch. My purpose wasn't solely to shift her fixation away from Hunter, although that was part of it. There wasn't anything particularly wrong with her probing into his life. He didn't seem bothered by it, but I was bothered. I wasn't sure why. Maybe because anything she learned about him might give her the upper hand in some way I couldn't define. Maybe because I thought she was making him a more significant part of my life before I'd decided where he fit in.

She questioned him as if she were doing a background check, as if she wanted to be sure he wasn't hiding something that would reveal him as a dangerous choice for marriage.

I wanted things to be easy and fun. Marriage was not on my mind. She should focus on probing the depths of her own relationship, not mine. She was the one walking on the edge of the precipice. She had everything backwards.

So it wasn't truly an ulterior motive, but she would see it that way.

For that reason, I didn't waste any time. Once two large wine glasses, with tiny splashes of Chardonnay at the bottom, and two beet salads sprinkled with pine nuts and goat cheese and raspberry dressing had been placed in front of us, I looked directly at her, waiting for her to meet my gaze.

She lifted her glass for a toast, but I left mine on the table.

"What do you think Silas actually wants from you?"

"What?"

"The blackmail."

She jerked her head to one side, then the opposite, her dark hair swinging wildly, as if someone had slapped her cheek. She leaned across the table, glaring at me. "Shh."

"It's fine."

"It's not fine," she hissed. "People can hear you."

"They aren't listening. And if they are, they have no idea what I'm talking about."

"You shouldn't be talking about it. So please don't."

"You had no problem grilling Hunter about his private life in a restaurant."

"It wasn't …" She looked around, then back at me, "And we were at a secluded table. This place is crowded. That was entirely different. I asked friendly questions. And that word …" Her stare hardened.

"You're making it look strange by jerking your head around like that. Calm down."

"Are we going to toast?" She clicked her glass against mine without waiting for a response. "To discretion."

I wondered if she recognized the irony in her toast, given that her blackmail was all about her lack of discretion. First, the quantity of wine she'd consumed, then allowing it to gain the upper hand. Even when alcohol has been swimming too freely in my head, there's still a tiny voice in the background warning me when to be cautious. I'd never been to a place where I was beyond hearing that voice. Whether you listen to that voice is another matter entirely. What had happened to that voice when Tess was with Silas?

We sipped our wine, staring at each other over the tops of our glasses, eyeing each other to see who would make the next move.

"Avoiding the word that upsets you, I think we can still talk about it. And what I wanted to ask is—what do you think he actually wants?"

"I already told you."

"Did you?"

She nodded. She put down her glass, picked up her fork, and stabbed a beet with a bit of butter lettuce. She shoved the food into her mouth and bit down much harder than was required, as if she were tearing into a piece of steak.

I waited for her to finish, leaving my own food untouched for the moment. "And what did you tell me?"

"I said, I don't want to talk about it. Not now, not here."

"You won't be able to get free from him without knowing what he wants."

"I won't be able to get free. So let's not talk about it, as I already said."

"Refusing to talk about it isn't going to change anything. Is that how you want to live the rest of your life? Is that how you want to start your marriage?" If she did, it was her choice. But it wasn't my choice to allow a man like Silas to continue doing as he pleased, even if Tess thought it was acceptable. Or if she assumed he had all the power, or whatever it was she thought.

Clearly, she'd made a stupid mistake. But that didn't mean she had to keep giving him power over her business and her marriage for the rest of her life. I couldn't understand what was happening inside her head. It seemed as if she was perfectly fine with having more money than she could ever hope to accumulate, a gorgeous, intriguing man, a business that thrilled her, and yet she didn't mind having this worm crawling around beneath the foundation of everything, eating away at the core, until the whole thing rotted, ultimately collapsing on her head.

What was she thinking? I didn't know because she wouldn't tell me.

I suppose she thought the same about me.

"What does he want?"

"I don't know."

"So you're going to sit in your office, terrified of what he might do, just waiting for everything to come crashing down?"

She stabbed another beet, then placed her fork on the side of her plate, the beet still impaled, and picked up her wineglass. She took a long swallow.

I knew what I was planning for Silas. I also knew that I had to find a way to make it look like he'd removed his own self from the world, or had an accident. Tess was aware that I wanted to be rid of him, although she obviously did not know what this really meant. Still, his departure had to look natural and unrelated to me.

I didn't have the slightest idea how I was going to make this happen. I wondered if I would ever figure it out, but until then, I would keep searching for every little thing I could possibly find out. "It seems to me, he can only want two or three things."

She ate her beet, glaring at her plate while she chewed.

"He either wants a relationship with you, a cash payout, or some kind of control over the winery. Those are the most likely. The final one is that he's simply a sick individual and the only thing he wants is to watch you suffer. He wants to destroy your relationship with Marcus for the fun of it."

She shrugged. She stabbed another beet.

"Can you think of anything else?"

"What difference does it make?"

"It's important to know."

"Why?"

"You're giving him all your power. Can't you see that?"

"He has all my power. I gave it to him that night. There's nothing else I can do."

"I don't think that's true."

She picked up her glass and finished the wine in a single swallow.

"Which of the four do you think it is?"

"I have no idea. I can't read his mind."

"He didn't give you any hint?"

"No."

"He hasn't said a word?"

"He uses it when he wants something. No matter how small."

I took a sip of wine.

If he wanted to destroy her relationship with Marcus, I would have thought he'd have done that by now. It seemed as though it would be the same if he wanted a cash payment, or ongoing payments.

Tess was no help. I'd almost eliminated two without any input from her.

"Has he mentioned it recently?"

"No. The job promotion seems to have distracted him."

Or maybe it had moved him closer to what he wanted. So maybe it was the winery he was after. This thought made me even more determined to find out what had happened with the previous owners.

CHAPTER 24

*D*uring every free moment, when there were no tastings on the schedule and no cars pulling into the long drive leading to the Black Mask estate filled with day trippers ready to try something new, I slipped out of the tasting room to pursue Silas like a stalker.

His office was on the second floor of a small building near the winemaking buildings. It featured a reception area and a spacious room with a large conference table. The office had belonged to Gordon Harper, who had preferred being close to the operations of the winery rather than working from inside the house like Tess did. She viewed her presence that close to the operations as micro managing. The previous owner had viewed it as keeping his finger on the pulse.

This was told to me through Silas's filter. I wasn't sure if it was meant to be a criticism of Tess or a pat on his own back that he was now the one with his finger on the pulse. It further confirmed my suspicion that the objective of his blackmail might have something to do with seeking control of the entire operation.

I couldn't imagine how he thought he would accomplish that. The winery had cost Tess millions, and although he seemed to be doing well for himself, there was no way he had the resources to purchase 130 acres of land, the well-tended grapevines, the operations and all the equipment, not to mention the brand reputation of Black Mask.

Did he think he could blackmail his way into all of that? Did he think if he kept Tess under psychological pressure long enough, she would eventually break and he could move in to mop up the mess? He was also assuming Marcus didn't love her enough to forgive one indiscretion.

In fact, this entire mess was based on the assumption that Marcus was a certain type of man. Maybe he wasn't that kind of man at all. And maybe the simplest thing was for Tess to find out. But she didn't seem inclined to do that. At least not yet.

It was difficult to get much insight into what Silas was doing because he was holed up in his office and I couldn't very well stand outside with a pair of binoculars. There was no reason for me to be inside the building that also housed Chuck's office, as well as the business center, and a few other small offices used by people who did the PR and marketing work that Silas supervised.

Lurking anywhere in the vicinity would draw unnecessary attention to myself, so most of the time, I went to the third story of Tess's house and used binoculars to see if I could catch him coming or going. When I saw his car leaving, I noted the time of day, even though I was aware it was a useless detail. If I didn't know where he was going, it only told me he had meetings in downtown Napa.

Leaving the tasting room unattended was risking my new job, and I felt torn in two as I tried to be everywhere at once, learning nothing new about the man who was out to destroy Tess, and slacking off in my responsibilities at the same time. Still, I couldn't stop myself. I was obsessed with knowing where he was every minute of the day.

As I stood at one of the bedroom windows on the third floor, offering a panoramic view of the winemaking and bottling facilities, I saw an unfamiliar car coming up the road that led from the side entrance. It stopped near the office building. The door opened. Amelia emerged and went into the office building.

There was nothing more to be seen through the binoculars. I placed them on the table and stared out the window. I crossed the room and looked out toward the front of the property in time to see two cars moving slowly up the drive. I hurried downstairs and out to the tasting room in time to greet the visitors.

I gave the fastest overview I'd ever offered, hardly saying anything about the wines beyond the vintage. I mentioned the wine club, but didn't give my usual enticing sales pitch. To hurry them out the door, I offered a free bottle of wine. This prompted them to buy three more bottles, which would look good on my sales record. Later, I would come up with an explanation for the free bottle.

I smiled and shook hands. I smiled more. I touched shoulders and forearms as I moved toward the door. I gushed about other wineries and how amazing their tasting rooms were—the gardens and the glamor of it all.

Finally, they were gone.

Without bothering to rinse the glasses, I shoved the corks into the open bottles, locked the door, and scurried along the pathways leading back to the warehouse and office building. Amelia's compact car was still there. The Mini Cooper that Silas normally drove to work was also parked outside, but there was still no way to linger without looking like I was out of place. I wandered over to the open doors of the warehouse. Inside, people were working and paid no attention to me.

I leaned against the frame of the large opening and watched people perform the complex tasks that were everyday habits for them, wondering if they found it fascinating to be creating something that most people found so mysterious they took tours to learn how it was done. It was probably like any other job. Once you knew all the steps and processes, unless you were alert and awake in every moment, it felt as mundane as making a bed or washing a dinner plate.

They might think the things I did were equally mysterious. But how many times had I dropped Rohypnol into a glass of alcohol and ushered someone into unconsciousness and then ended their life without thinking about the shocking, mind-shattering thing I was doing, focusing only on the mechanics of each step?

I slipped out of the building and returned to the house. I went in through the door that led to the pantry. I filled a glass of water from the fridge and carried it upstairs. I stopped in our room and grabbed Hunter's keys to the rental car, certain he wouldn't need them because he was spending the afternoon working on a massive jigsaw puzzle Tess had put out on a table in their library. I went up to the third floor and took my spot at the window, keeping my eyes on the office building, hoping I hadn't missed them while I was making my way back.

What had they been talking about all this time? Trying to guess what their relationship might be turning into gnawed at my stomach. I had a good idea, but I wanted to *know*. And I wanted to figure out a way to stop it, if that was possible. I felt as if I'd turned into a surrogate parent, worrying over a wayward teenager who had fallen in with a man who was poised to manipulate her and take advantage of her in ways she couldn't begin to comprehend, leaving her a broken and empty shell.

Not only would she destroy her own life, just as it was beginning, she had the potential to destroy mine, or at least inflict quite a lot of damage.

CHAPTER 25

THEN: ALEX

 ortland, Oregon

Clearing the easier hurdle of convincing Tom to take me to the party with him came first. I needed more time to figure out how I would clear the more difficult hurdle of escaping from my father's always open eyes. It was possible Tom might help me with that, if he was already fully on my side.

It was obvious to me I was old enough. Tom should recognize that. He agreed it wasn't fair that my father had one set of rules for the boys and another for me. He'd even argued with my father about it, always on the losing side, of course, but he'd kept at it. I appreciated that about him.

Since he was sure I would mess up his own plans, I needed to convince him I'd be an asset.

I talked to girls at school, asking them what they liked about parties and how the guys behaved. I asked about beer and how it tasted. I asked them to tell me what it felt like to get drunk.

It was clear from the way they looked at me, sad smiles on

their faces, that they felt sorry for my stupidity, my silly questions, and my complete lack of experience. I didn't care about any of that. All I wanted to know were a few important details about the party experience that I could use to convince Tom he would be better off with me by his side, or at least somewhere in the vicinity.

As they talked about good parties, lame parties, okay parties, and legendary parties, it sounded as if the best ones were those where everyone got wildly drunk but didn't go so far over the edge that they ended up sliding around in vomit or passed out, forgetting forever what had happened to them that night. Good or bad. Sometimes very good. But sometimes, very, *very* bad.

None of this got me any closer to finding a way to prove why I would be valuable to Tom. Knowing my brother, it was doubtful he got more than a little tipsy. I didn't know much about drinking alcohol since I'd never tasted a drop. A bottle of alcohol had never entered our house and my parents didn't associate with people who drank even wine or beer. When beer or wine was served at neighborhood parties, my parents didn't attend.

I imagined Tom drinking a few beers, then sitting back and making snide comments about kids who got out of control. He preferred to sit back and make snide comments about life in general. It was his favorite sport.

He didn't need me to keep him from taking too many shots. He might appreciate my presence if it kept girls from puking on him, but could I really do that? Besides, I didn't want to go to the party and hang out with my brother the entire time.

Maybe my approach was wrong.

I could blackmail him into it, but that would turn against me after one time. My brothers and I had always stuck together. Threatening to tell my parents he'd tried alcohol would spoil a good thing.

I just needed to go to that party and I needed him to change his mind about thinking my presence made it more likely he would get caught.

Trying to figure out a solution was keeping me awake at night. It was distracting me from my homework. It was coming dangerously close to giving myself away, because at dinner, my father asked me a question about school.

I stared at him as if he'd seen what was inside my head and asked why I wanted to drink the devil's potion—a beverage that caused people to turn away from god, caused them to do the worst things, and sent them sliding down the slippery slope into the pit of hell.

But he hadn't asked that. I had no idea what he'd said.

He narrowed his eyes at me. "Are you losing your hearing?"

"No."

"Then you must be daydreaming. Have you forgotten that letting your sinful nature control your mind leads to death? Romans eight—"

"I wasn't daydreaming."

"You certainly weren't paying attention to my question."

"I was thinking about my English assignment."

"What is it?"

"I have to write an essay about The Scarlet Letter."

His face turned its own shade of scarlet, as I'd known it would. He would forget all about whatever he'd asked, all about my daydreaming.

He turned his attention to my mother. "Why do they read that kind of trash?"

"I don't know."

"I thought you contacted the school when the boys were assigned that book?"

"I did, but it's a classic."

"There are many classics to choose from."

My parents continued discussing it as if I wasn't there. Tom looked at me across the table, curious about why I'd thrown such an inflammatory comment into the middle of our meal. I returned to daydreaming about how I could twist his arm into inviting me to the party.

In the end, I decided the best approach was to put Tom in my debt. He was prepping for the SATs. It was all he did on the weekends. My father thought it was a waste of money to take the tutoring classes that were offered to give kids a leg up, getting them ready to perform well and increase their chances of acceptance into a top college.

That weekend, I dragged our push mower out of the garage and spent the morning cutting the grass in the front and back yards to my father's specifications. I trimmed the hedges along the back of our property.

When my father asked why I was doing it, I told him Tom was studying and I wanted to help. He looked suspicious, but he couldn't seem to find a hole in my story, no matter how long he stared into my wide, guileless eyes.

Just before lunch, Tom came outside to cut the grass. "Don't think I don't see what you're doing."

I smiled.

That afternoon, I washed and waxed the fifteen-year-old sedan that had been passed from Eric to Jake to Tom. A car that each of my brothers in turn had worked part-time jobs in order to pay for insurance and gas and maintenance.

"It's not going to work," Tom whispered after my father commented on how it was nice to see the car had finally been properly waxed.

When I mowed the lawn the following weekend, Tom caved.

"If you get caught, it's on you. I'm not covering for you. And you better not tell them you went with me. Got it?"

I nodded.

I wondered if a few beers or some Jell-O shots were worth all this trouble.

CHAPTER 26

NOW: ALEX

Napa Valley, California

I stood at the window sipping water for thirty-five minutes. During that time, no one drove onto the winery grounds looking for a tasting. I wondered how long I had. I wondered what would happen if someone showed up and found the tasting room locked.

I already knew what was going to happen to me. The moment Amelia emerged from that building, I was going to run down the stairs, slip into Hunter's car, and follow her wherever she went. She and Silas were making me extremely uncomfortable, and I wasn't sure who was the bigger threat. I also wasn't sure how I would be rid of either of them.

On the surface, Amelia was harmless. She knew absolutely nothing about me, but her curiosity about the change in my hair color was still nagging at me. Living a sheltered life might have made her more observant than most. Or perhaps she was longing for connections in a world where she was alone inside a massive castle. All she had to cling to was the slightly unique color of her hair, hoping she might find missing relatives by pursuing that single feature.

My water glass was empty, and still the main door to the office building remained closed. I placed the glass on the table beside me and leaned against the window frame. I was getting bored. Bored and impatient. I wanted to look at my phone. I wanted something to distract me, but a distraction that was effective might pull me away just long enough that I would miss what I needed to see.

It was another twenty minutes of twitching muscles and random itchiness before the door opened.

Amelia walked out, followed by Silas. His hand was on her waist in a way that suggested he was guiding her with a great deal of loving concern along the pathway that led to the parking strip between the two buildings. He went to the passenger side of his car, opened the door, and she climbed inside. A moment later, he was getting in the driver's side.

I hurried from the room, down the sweeping staircase, and past Damien's cage.

He squawked after me before the door closed—*Dangerous woman!*

I started slowly down the main drive. The access road that circled the entire vineyard joined the road into downtown Napa at two points. Silas would have to pass by the main gate and I would be able to follow him from there.

Driving wasn't something I did often, and following someone in a car was completely outside my experience. I hoped I would be able to do it without making myself obvious to them. The nondescript style of Hunter's white rental car was the only thing in my favor.

A few seconds later, the Mini Cooper zipped by. I waited until it was well past the gates, then pulled out and followed. There were a few other cars on the road, but thanks to the somewhat unique style of his car, he was easy to keep sight of.

I followed them into and through downtown Napa, staying a

constant two cars behind them. Finally, he turned onto a quiet street, slowing in front of a luxury condo complex. He pulled to the curb and stopped. He got out of the car and literally ran to the other side to open the door for Amelia, as if he were afraid that moving too slowly would allow her to get out of the car herself before he could demonstrate his chivalry.

It looked as if he'd already zeroed in on her affinity for fairy-tales and decided that phony princely behavior was the way to worm his way into her affection. It appeared to be working. When she emerged, she looked up at him, tipping her face up. Her hair fell down her back in a cascade of red waves that shimmered in the sunlight. She smiled as if she were gazing at her savior. I remembered the moment I'd heard Tess call him the savior of her winery and felt a sense of foreboding wash over me.

Silas placed his hand on her jaw, tipping her head back even farther, until the angle of her neck looked painful. He bent down and kissed her. A long, forceful, sloppy kiss that seemed to make her want to squirm.

Her hands, fingers extended and rigid, seemed to want to push him away. She looked as if she was aching to readjust her position, but because of the angle of her head, it was almost impossible for her to move. Even though he wasn't restraining her arms, it appeared as if she was trapped between the car and his oppressive force against her.

After several long minutes, the kiss ended. He stepped back and released her jaw. He took hold of her upper arm and helped her onto the curb as if he were leading a horse out of its stable and into the corral to perform its training exercises.

They went up the main walk, opened the gate into the front garden, and disappeared from view.

There appeared to be about twenty condos in the complex. Each one was two stories, with a large deck on the first floor and a spacious balcony on the second. The second floor looked large enough to accommodate a loft area and vaulted ceilings.

I longed to follow them, but of course, that was impossible. The thought of more waiting, which could just as easily be thirty minutes or thirty hours, was not appealing. Would she spend the night? Or was this a quick meeting to finish whatever had started at the office? Or a quickie, period?

After several minutes of staring at the buildings, wondering if I would be lucky enough to see any movement through one of the windows, telling me which unit belonged to Silas, I decided the kiss told me what I needed to know. I had his address, and I had an understanding of their relationship.

I definitely had an additional insight into the threat the two of them posed—double what I'd believed.

CHAPTER 27

$\mathcal{T}$he sun was coming through the blinds, hitting her computer screen, turning everything into a blur that made her feel she was underwater, not unlike the sensation inside her head. Tess stood and went to the window. She pulled the cord, closing the blinds tightly. The room was now dark and gloomy, but the screen glowed with everything in sharp contrast. She returned to her chair and cupped her hand over the wireless mouse.

A knock at the door caused her hand to twitch, and she let go of the mouse. The door opened, telling her it was Marcus. They both had the same habit—agreed upon without ever discussing it —a quick knock and then opening the door. Because they had access to each other's calendars, they knew when the other was in a meeting and couldn't be interrupted.

She turned and smiled, wondering why her hand had twitched as if giving away an underlying anxiety, even though she'd known it was him.

"Hey, you." He closed the door and crossed the room. He kissed her lips, then turned and settled on the small sofa adjacent to her desk. "I won't stay long. I know this is your territory, but I just wanted to get your reaction to what happened with the tasting room."

She sighed. Of course, that was why her hand had twitched. She'd known this was coming, yet she wasn't entirely sure what her reaction was, much less how she was going to explain her feelings to Marcus. She closed her eyes and pressed her thumb and forefinger to the bridge of her nose, a gesture she immediately regretted because it told Marcus something she wasn't ready to talk about.

When she let her hand fall to her lap and opened her eyes, she saw a look of relief on his face, an assumption that she agreed with his concern. But she didn't. At least not in the same way. She was absolutely concerned — upset that Alex had closed the tasting room for no reason, abandoning her responsibilities, disappearing for several hours. But Tess was quite sure that overall, she would ultimately choose a different course of action than what Marcus would recommend.

"I'm not sure it was a good idea to hire a friend," he said. "Especially such a close friend."

"Anyone might do the same thing. Friend or not."

"But it's easier to deal with when there's no personal relationship. What are you going to do?"

"I haven't decided."

"It's unacceptable." He straightened. "I know you know that. And I know it's none of my business. I'm just ... concerned. The boundaries here are starting to blur."

She laughed. She wasn't sure there had ever been any boundaries. Alex decided where the boundaries were. Tess had always known that about her, and she was okay with it. She was okay with a lot of things about Alex, because, for whatever reason, for reasons she could never fully understand, she liked Alex. She might even say she loved her. Alex felt like a sister, and like a sister, Tess put up with a lot from her.

There were times when Alex took gross advantage of her,

treated her in a way that some might consider manipulative, but she really didn't care. She felt as if she could be herself around Alex. That alone was worth the world. And she always, *always* ... almost always, knew where she stood. That was also worth more than she could say. Their relationship was something she didn't fully understand, so she didn't bother trying.

"It's complicated," Tess said.

"That's lazy," Marcus said.

She shrugged.

"That's not how you run a business."

"Don't tell me—"

"I'm not. But I think if there's anything we've agreed upon in our relationship, it's that we can be straight with each other. That we can say what we think. And I think you have some blind spots with this woman. She's living in our house—blurred boundaries. She's in our wedding—blurred boundaries. Now her boyfriend is here for an indefinite period of time. And she's working for you in a key position. All of this means the boundaries are—"

"I'm aware, Marcus."

"Why won't you talk to me? I thought we talked about everything?"

"We do."

"But Alex is off-limits?"

"No."

"Then what is it?"

She shrugged.

"You're acting a little ..." He cleared his throat. "How do you plan to address it?"

"I haven't decided."

"Why not?"

"Because she already knows she screwed up."

He laughed. "Are you serious?"

"I'll probably dock her pay."

"Is that enough? She lives here rent-free. Docking her pay isn't going to hurt much."

"She's not living here rent-free. She's our guest. She's my maid of honor."

"Exactly. Blurred boundaries, as I said."

"The winery is mine. I know what I'm doing. She's worked for me before."

"She wasn't your maid of honor and she wasn't living in your house."

"Actually, in Australia, we did live together."

"But you weren't her manager then."

"I don't know why we're discussing this."

"Because I'm concerned that you have a major blind spot. I'm concerned she's not taking her responsibility seriously. I understand that hiring her makes sense in terms of her customer finesse, but she doesn't have any background in the wine industry."

"That's easily learned."

He crossed his legs. He ran his hand through his hair and turned his head slightly, looking toward the side window, where the blinds were also closed. "Why is it so dark in here?"

"There was a glare on my computer."

He stood and walked toward her. He stood behind her and began massaging her shoulders. "Are you okay? You seem tense."

"I'm fine."

"Why would she close the tasting room? Doesn't she realize how that could hurt the Black Mask brand? It's not just the lost business for that afternoon. It—"

"I *know*." She put her hand on his wrist, squeezing it until he stopped rubbing her muscle. The massage felt good, but she couldn't deal with the mixed messages of his challenge to her decisions and his soothing, supportive massage. "I'm taking care of it, and I'll come up with a solution. I just need time to think."

He moved away and walked to the door. "I'm just wondering if this isn't a good time to have a conversation about what her goals are. It might be worth revisiting your offer, whatever it was, and trying to reshape it into something temporary."

"I can't do that."

"You can, if that's what's best for the winery. I'm here to help, but I'll back off now." He raised his hands, palms toward her. "I won't mention it again. Let me know if you want to bounce ideas off me." He lowered his hands, made an air kiss in her direction, opened the door, and went out.

Tess put her elbows on her desk. She rested her forehead on her hands. Hiring Alex had been the right decision. It had been a way to pacify Silas. It was a brilliant decision. And she was absolutely sure Alex was not taking advantage of her.

It would all work out. She was not going to dock her pay. She would talk to her. Alex would make her usual excuses, but it was unlikely to happen again. That was the thing about Alex. She was impulsive and unpredictable, but she rarely did the same thing twice.

CHAPTER 28

I was standing behind the tasting room counter, wishing it was one o'clock. At that time, a corporate group was due to arrive for a tasting and catered lunch. The caterers were busy on the patio, fretting about the weather that was windier than expected.

They were spoiled in California, assuming they could plan an outdoor lunch in October, knowing it was unlikely there would be rain or temperatures so cold even outdoor heaters wouldn't help. Wind was nothing. If they were in New York, they would be laying out their charcuterie boards in the tasting room because the temperatures would be turning everyone's fingers stiff and white with cold.

The door opened, and Tess slipped into the room. She looked like a snake, gliding through the narrow opening as if she hoped no one would see her. She smiled and came to the counter, resting one hand with navy blue polished fingernails on the counter, slipping the other into her pocket, trying to look relaxed, appearing anything but.

"All ready?" she asked.

"Can I expect you to check up on me every day now?"

She looked relieved that I'd brought it up, eager to have a conversation about my dereliction of duty the day before.

"You have to understand how unsettling that was. I know you realize it was incredibly unprofessional."

"I do."

"Then why?"

"I had an appointment."

"You should have told me. I would have covered."

"You already said that."

"I know, but it makes no sense that you didn't, and I can't stop thinking about how simple it is to let someone know you need coverage."

I shrugged. "It was urgent, and I wasn't thinking. Can we let it go now?"

"What was so urgent?"

"It's personal."

"I don't think that's an adequate explanation in this case."

"Why not?"

"Don't you realize what this could do to our reputation?"

"You already said that. Twice. And I already told you, I do. Twice."

"Then why?"

"It won't happen again. Why do you want to keep talking about it? We can't go back and have a do-over."

She heaved a dramatic sigh, as if I were acting like a five-year-old. "If you would at least tell me what the big emergency was, I could understand and maybe I could —."

"How would that change anything?"

"I would *understand!*"

"Why do you have to understand?" I wasn't about to mention Silas. I needed to stop telling her anything about him. Whatever ended up happening to him couldn't appear to have any connec-

119

tion to me stalking him, looking into him, being involved with him in any way. Even though she thought I might find a way to get him out of her life, my way was not at all what she was thinking.

If she thought closing a wine tasting room for an afternoon was an outrage, I couldn't imagine what she would have to say about ending a man's life. I had to bite hard on the inside of my lip to avoid laughing as I imagined the way her eyes would grow so wide it would appear as if her eyelids had disappeared completely. Her mouth would open until it seemed as if her jaw had been locked in place.

"We can make some adjustments if you need time away," she said. "I just have to know what's going on."

"It was a one-time thing. It won't happen again."

"How can I be sure of that?"

"Because I said so."

"I'm not at my peak level of trust in you right now."

That wasn't a surprise, but I couldn't do anything to make her believe me. You never can. It's always a choice to believe someone or not. "The group will be here in a few minutes," I said.

"This isn't resolved."

"I don't know what you want from me." I straightened the wineglasses on the counter. She probably thought I was doing it to avoid meeting her gaze, but I wasn't. They weren't lined up, and I liked them to be perfect.

"I want to be able to trust you. I want the tasting room open during its stated hours."

"It will be."

"It wasn't."

"One time."

"We're going in circles." Her voice was louder, losing patience.

"*You're* going in circles. I had to leave. And I *said* it won't happen again. I won't close the tasting room without telling you I need to leave. My bad."

"Don't trivialize this."

"I'm not. But it's over and I don't know why you want to keep talking about it."

"Because you were careless with our reputation. Don't you understand that?"

"I see that now, but it didn't occur to me at the time. I said, my bad."

"You're making it sound like you borrowed my shirt and spilled wine on it."

I laughed.

"It's not funny."

"The analogy is funny."

"It feels like you're not taking this seriously. Do I need to dock your pay or something to make you understand how important this is?"

"I get it. If you want to dock my pay, that's fine. Do what you have to. I'm just tired of talking about it."

"You haven't even apologized."

"Are you listening to me? It won't happen again."

"You're so frustrating. I'm surprised you haven't been fired if this is how you behaved in other positions."

"Are you going to fire me?"

She yanked her hand off the bar as if she'd been burned. She glared at me and shoved it into her other pocket. "This winery is really important to me. And the tasting room is our face to the public. I need you to be passionate about it. I need you to care about promoting our brand. I need you to be responsible and professional."

"I'm every one of those things."

"Are you?"

"Absolutely."

When she was gone, I wondered why she'd come back for this second round. She'd already told me she was upset, and she'd already tried to find out why I'd abandoned the tasting room midday. What had made her start up the conversation all over again when she'd known I wasn't going to tell her where I'd gone? Was the curiosity eating her up, or was it something else?

CHAPTER 29

*T*he corporate group that had come for a tasting and lunch dragged their drinking out until five-twenty. Because the tasting room closed at five, I'd made a date to meet the reporter at five-thirty. After Tess's freak-out over my unapproved closing to follow Silas and Amelia, there was no way I would be able to sneak out while the business gals and guys spent a Thursday afternoon getting drunk together, slowly forgetting the sexual harassment training they'd surely taken some time during the past year.

I stood behind the bar, looking across the tasting room toward the French doors in the gift shop that opened onto the patio. The lunch food had been packed away long ago. All that remained were tiered plates of fancy cookies and tiny pastries. Most of what was left of those had been reduced to crumbs or partial pieces that people had sampled, leaving the rest behind for others to share. But others hadn't wanted to share. They'd wanted samples of their own.

Mostly, they wanted wine.

In a steady stream, they wandered through the gift shop, never wasting time looking at what was displayed, walking directly to where I stood. Each one held out an empty glass, sometimes a second, for a friend. They stated their preferred variety and waited. Some of the women pouted if the pour was skimpy. Some of the women and men both assertively demanded, "More, please."

Their company had chauffeured them to Black Mask in an air-conditioned bus with reclining seats, bathrooms, and Wi-Fi, meaning no one was worried about how much alcohol they were consuming. They were having fun, and they were doing it at company expense, in more ways than one.

I wanted them to leave. I wanted the bus to honk its horn. I wanted them to stumble over, trip up the steps, and collapse into their seats. I didn't want Scott Ruiz leaving the bar, assuming I was a no show. Surely, he would text first.

I hadn't yet texted him that I was running late because I didn't want to provide an opportunity for him to change his mind. If he had thought our exchange of business cards suggested a hookup, a text might make him decide more brain picking wasn't how he wanted to spend the evening after all.

It was growing dark. The fairy lights across the patio were on. The heat lamps were on. These people needed to leave. Who was in charge?

Several men and one woman strutted around as if they owned the estate. The woman had grabbed a bottle of Pinot Noir off the counter when I wasn't looking, carrying it with her and offering pours to whomever she was talking to, topping off her own glass each time. Definite boss behavior. Or a dropout from AA.

I took a deep breath. I picked up my phone from under the counter and sent a text to Scott.

Alex:

Running late. Does six work?

Scott:

No worries. See you then.

I smiled and filled the glass of the man holding his out to me. He pouted at the tiny puddle of red in the bottom of his glass. I emptied the bottle into it.

"That's more like it," he said.

"You're very welcome."

He grunted, took a sip, and turned away. I put the empty bottle on the recycling shelf and glanced at the time. Five-thirty-one. I hoped my text hadn't been too optimistic.

Finally, the woman carrying her own bottle hugged it close to her chest. She raised her voice and told everyone what an amazing team they were, what a privilege it was working with them, how in awe she was of their brains and talent. She announced in a voice tinged with hysteria that she was *raising her glass to them*. Then, she instructed everyone to head to the bus.

She began walking in that direction herself, carrying the bottle and her glass.

I sent a message to Tess that I would clean up later because I was meeting a friend for a drink. Predictably, she wanted to know what friend, whether Hunter was going, where we were meeting. Then, her messages circled back to ask how I'd made a friend when she hadn't been aware that I'd gone anywhere or done anything without her since arriving in California. I reminded her I used to live in California, and that was enough to stop the questions. For now.

Hunter already knew I was meeting a friend and had agreed to let me use his car, with only a brief amount of arm twisting, since technically the rental agreement didn't allow for anyone to drive it but him.

"I'm only driving a few miles," I'd said.

"Something could happen."

"It won't. When was the last time you had a car accident? Probably never."

His silence answered the question. Finally, he'd said, "That's why they're called accidents. You never know when they might happen."

"If anything happens, I'll pay for it."

"That could cost you a lot of money."

"It's fine."

He studied me as if I were the riskiest gambler he'd ever encountered. But he gave me the keys.

Scott was seated at the bar with a beer in front of him. I slid onto the stool next to him and ordered a vodka martini.

"Are you ready for another beer?" I asked.

"This is good."

"It was supposed to be my treat."

"No worries."

When my drink came, Scott clicked the neck of his beer bottle against the rim of my glass. "So what's up? You're warming to the thrill of researching local history? Writing a book?"

"No. Nothing as interesting as that." I took a sip of my drink. "I'm the hostess in the tasting room at Black Mask Winery now."

"I thought you were here on vacation?"

"Things changed."

"Sounds like it."

"I want to find out as much as I can. So I can be really interesting for our customers."

"Don't they give you training for that?"

"Absolutely." I took another sip of my drink. As the alcohol seeped into me, I realized how tense the corporate wine drinkers, taking their sweet time with *my* time, had made my muscles. I was becoming a prisoner inside the tasting room. I wasn't sure how long this cushy job was going to last.

Between Tess's oversight of every move and the fact that I was tied to that room, that bar, those bottles of wine, it was looking less cushy every day. Free rent and the serene environment were nice, but I didn't want to live in a beautiful cage.

An unattractive free range existence would be more endurable.

"They taught me all about wine, their process, and the sanitized history of the winery. But I want the interesting things. The gossip. The dark stories. The secrets." I gave him a wicked smile.

"What makes you think I have any of that? I report the news."

"But when you're digging into the news, you learn all the real stuff at the same time, don't you? Isn't news the things people do and say, the lies they tell and the secrets they keep, the crimes they commit?"

He laughed. "I've never heard anyone describe the news quite like that."

"How would you describe it?"

He took a long swallow of beer. "Can't think of a better way."

"I just want to have some interesting stories that are more than a list of dates and facts."

"Unless I've written a story about something, I'm unlikely to know any more than you do. So what made you think—"

"But you could look into it."

He laughed. "I'm not a private investigator. Did something happen there you think is newsworthy? Another rumor of a body buried?"

"Not that I'm aware of, but you never know."

"I'm a journalist. I don't go around looking for rumors or trying to dig up crime stories for scandal-clad docudramas."

"That's not what I'm asking."

"Then what is it?"

"Do you know the man who managed the tasting room before me? Silas Pierce?"

He laughed, harder and longer this time. "Why would I know him?"

"He seems like a notorious kind of character." The words slipped out too fast. This was not good. I shouldn't have mentioned his name. I shouldn't have referred to Silas at all. I was tying myself to him in so many ways. My obsession with finding out something that would give me control over him was dulling my brain and loosening my tongue.

If Silas disappeared or turned up dead—*when* that happened—would my negative opinion of him be the first thing that entered everyone's mind?

"Is it possible for me to go through back copies of the paper?"

"What are you looking for? You need to narrow this down. It sounds like you have some kind of objective in mind, but it's so vague it's nothing."

"My boss has owned it for less than a year. Do you know anything? Did you hear anything about why it was sold?"

"I don't travel in those circles. I'm not involved with expensive real estate. Or the wine industry."

"You report on the Napa Valley community."

He laughed. "But I don't know the ins and outs of who buys what."

"Can you ask around? I'd treat you to dinner. Or I'll get you a gift certificate if you want to take someone out. Or ..."

He held up his hand. "I did hear one thing. It was a fast sale. No one even knew it was on the market, then suddenly, it had changed hands."

"That sounds newsworthy."

He laughed, as if I was being ridiculous. "It's not newsworthy. Not at all."

"Do you know why it happened?"

"I don't think it's the tasting room chit-chat you're looking for."

The fact that it wasn't ideal for tasting room storytelling made me believe it was exactly what I was looking for.

CHAPTER 30

I ate one of my olives and placed my hands flat on the bar. I studied my fingernails and thought about what color I wanted for my next manicure. My nails were currently burgundy. Tess had said it was important to have my nails done on a regular basis as part of presenting a nice façade to the wine drinking public. Even Silas had gotten regular manicures when he oversaw the wine tasting room. Of course, he hadn't had his nails painted, but they'd been trimmed and shaped regularly. Maybe a champagne color would be nice.

"Why was it a fast sale?" I asked.

"Can't you get this information from your employer?" Scott asked.

"It's nice to have an outside perspective."

"Do you think there are issues? I'm not sure why you're asking me at all—"

"No issues." I said no, but the question gave me pause. She hadn't said anything, but anyone who is in a hurry to get rid of something, especially a multi-million dollar property and wine-making business, should cause the buyer to raise their eyebrows. It should cause the buyer to move forward slowly.

"I hope she did her due diligence."

"I'm sure she did. She's an experienced businesswoman."

"Glad to hear it."

I didn't like his tone. It sounded as if he thought Tess was a spoiled little rich girl who wanted to play winemaker. Maybe I was reading into it. Or maybe he didn't like that an outsider had purchased some of their Napa Valley property. It was a very cozy community. Tess had given me the impression there were some who wanted to draw a line between families who had grown wine for generations and were *true* winemakers, versus those who were hobbyists, coming in looking to park the millions they'd made elsewhere, always having dreamed of doing something exotic, but about which they knew absolutely nothing. Winemaking was half farming. It wasn't slick and glitzy and high society. It was nurturing vines and caring for soil, paying attention to the weather and working together as a community.

"Do you know why they were in a hurry to sell?" I asked.

"The winery was started by Jillian Harper's great-grandfather. I think they hoped, rather, they assumed their daughter would—"

"Is that Rosé?"

"So, you did some homework already?"

"It's not homework. It was on the Black Mask social media feed. Tess took over their social media so she could maintain continuity."

He put his beer bottle to his lips but didn't take a drink.

"Rosé wasn't interested in wine?"

He shrugged. "All I know is that no one knew it was for sale. People thought something strange was going on—that maybe they were having financial problems, although that wasn't clear. The tasting room was closed for a while. There was some gossip because people were speculating about why that was."

"For how long?"

"I'm not sure. Two months, maybe a little less. Then they were gone. And then Tess Turner popped up and announced she'd bought it."

"They must have had a lot of friends. Someone must—"

"They kind of just vanished. I heard they moved to Italy."

"Maybe they bought one of those villas you can buy for a dollar if you promise to renovate it."

"What?"

"You haven't heard about that?"

"Sure. But I don't think that was it. They wanted to get far away. That was my impression."

I sipped my drink. "Who gave you that impression?"

He turned to face me. "Why are you *so* interested? None of this has anything to do with pouring wine for people. What's going on?"

"I like to know the history of things."

"This isn't history. It's gossip."

I ate another olive. "It's a fine line, like I said. Gossip. News. History. How many times does yesterday's gossip turn into tomorrow's news? And today's news is tomorrow's history."

"You're quite the philosopher."

"Am I?"

"So why all the interest in this family and the sale of the winery? And again, why don't you ask your employer? Are you concerned about something not being above-board?"

"Not on her part. Absolutely not. But aren't you curious? Don't you think it's interesting when someone abandons something that belonged to their family for decades, then suddenly leaves the country for no obvious reason? With their adult daughter? You don't think that's strange?"

"They didn't abandon it. They sold it."

"Cheap."

"Was it cheap? Or a fair deal? Below market, sure ... maybe, but fair."

"I have no idea. You're the one who said it was cheap."

"I didn't use that phrase."

"I had that impression."

"I choose my words carefully, so don't go drawing conclusions from impressions you're grabbing out of thin air."

I laughed.

He didn't. Nor did he smile. "I'm not sure I can tell you any more."

"You seem put out."

"Not at all. It has nothing to do with me. Why would I be put out?"

"Your tone changed."

He laughed. "My tone changed? I think you like to stir up things out of nothing. Is that what you do? Provoke people to get a reaction?"

I did. I wondered if he was asking, or he'd already decided that was the truth about me. I took another sip of my drink. I was getting hungry. It was late and although I'd watched people eat a fabulous lunch, none had been offered to me. I hadn't expected it, and I'd nibbled on some apple and nuts while I poured wine, but now, I was famished.

If he knew more, I could find out by inviting him to dinner, but it didn't seem as if he did. And he didn't seem inclined to look into it.

I thought it was strange the family had moved out of the country without a backward glance. I thought it was curious they'd sold a lucrative family business with a great reputation for a good deal, or cheap or whatever you wanted to call it.

The more Scott danced around how normal it all was and how it was none of my business and I was just looking for gossip, the more I thought there was a very good reason they'd taken off. Was it possible that reason was Silas? But what on earth could he do to them that would cause such a dramatic reaction?

132

If I pushed on that angle once again, I would expose myself. A woman running around asking questions and flaunting her animosity toward a guy who later turns up dead, even if it absolutely looks like an accident, is not the way I liked to handle things.

CHAPTER 31

THEN: HUNTER

Zack's bookstore and coffeehouse had been in business for nearly a year before Hunter's mother mustered up the courage to visit. By then, his father, who had always kept himself at arm's length from family life, had departed altogether. Resting comfortably in a beautiful coffin beneath a well-kept lawn, he would have been proud of.

It wasn't clear to Hunter why it took her so long. She'd insisted she loved his brother as much when she learned he was gay as she had the moment she gave birth to him.

It was the bookstore that seemed to bother her.

Maybe she loved Zack because he was her flesh and blood. Because he was her son, her baby, her little boy. He was hers and she loved every cell in his body, every thought in his mind, every feeling in his heart. But maybe she wasn't so sure about other gay men and women.

That was the only thing Hunter could think of.

Or maybe she truly did think the bookstore and the speakers he hosted were a magnet for trouble. Their parents had lived quiet lives. They didn't *make waves*, as she called it. They didn't paint their house a color that *attracted attention*. They didn't even plant trees that might irritate the neighbors by dropping sticky pods on the sidewalk. They parked their cars in the garage instead of taking curb space.

His parents kept their opinions to themselves, often failing to speak up even when they should have. Like the time his mother's best friend told everyone his mother had spoiled her birthday party by not making a reservation in time when she'd promised to book an event room for a fortieth birthday gala.

Everyone blamed his mother that the party had to be postponed. As a result, many of the guests weren't able to attend because the party date slipped into summertime when vacation trips had already been arranged. In truth, booking the room had been another friend's responsibility. But his mother thought it would be *mean* and *petty* to call attention to that fact.

So maybe having a son who wanted to stand up in his community, making his sexuality public, fighting to become normalized in a culture that had abused and excluded men and women like him for centuries, went against her grain. Inside her, a battle raged—love for her son against her devotion to keeping the surface of the water calm at all costs.

She wanted him to teach school, to lead a quiet life. She wanted him to have a solid, long-term relationship. She did *not* want him to put himself in the spotlight where people who believed he should stay in the closet, or worse, sometimes far worse, might come after him.

And even in New York state, even in the twenty-first century, there were people who objected to his brother making even the smallest ripples on the surface of the lake. They objected to his light-filled bookstore with its white walls and bookcases, its rolling ladders and leather armchairs, its coffee shop and pastries from the bakery next door. Most of all, they objected to its Thursday night readings from newly published autobiographies and novels, poetry and political books written by people whose sexuality differed from what some of them considered god-ordained.

His mother trembled in fear that some of those people also thought it was their god-ordained purpose to silence those voices. She was wiser than her quiet life might have suggested.

So, one summer evening, Hunter and his mother finally visited Zack's bookstore. It wasn't a Thursday. They weren't there to hear anyone read from their book or participate in a discussion. There wasn't a crowd. In fact, business on that beautiful, warm evening was light, and maybe that's what made Zack vulnerable.

They walked inside and despite her misgivings, a smile crept across his mother's face, sweeping away the lines of concern and fear.

Zack stepped out from behind the counter and approached them. He wrapped his arms around their mother, holding her tightly.

"It's absolutely charming," she said as he released her. "You've done a beautiful job."

"I had help."

"I'm sure you did, but it's your idea. Your vision."

"Thank you."

"It's so welcoming. I feel like I could spend the entire evening here."

"That's the idea."

He led them through to the coffee shop and introduced them to the barista on duty. Kimberly made iced lattes for both of them. His mother had never had one.

They sipped the drinks slowly and talked to Zack for a while. His enthusiasm was more invigorating than the caffeine flooding their bodies from the cold coffee. The longer they sat there, the faster Zack talked, excited to finally have his mother's full attention. He was obviously thrilled that her anxiety seemed to be fading now that she was sitting in the peaceful setting, realizing there was nothing to be concerned about.

The ambiance of the place was palpable, and even though there were only a trickle of customers, people lingered among the shelves of books and no one left without making a purchase. Those who stayed for coffee carried on quiet conversations. The atmosphere was a blend of someone's living room and a college café.

Hunter had to give it to Zack, he'd done a brilliant job.

It was five minutes to closing time when they finally stacked their plates and got ready to leave.

The bell at the front of the shop tinkled gently. Hunter could have sworn, although maybe this was the distorted memory of the aftermath, it seemed as if the atmosphere changed immediately.

The place was quiet. Hunter had been aware of his brother at the front of the store, getting ready to put up the closed sign and lock the doors, but he was still near the checkout counter. His mother was carrying their dishes to the counter. The barista had cleaned up because the coffee shop closed half an hour before the bookstore, so she'd gone home for the night. Zack had told them to leave the dishes. He would wash them later.

Hunter heard a low voice, then Zack, speaking distinctly. "Please leave. We're closing."

"But what happens here after hours? That's when the real party begins, doesn't it, you fucking fairy?"

"I asked you to leave."

"We're not going anywhere. Isn't this a place that welcomes everyone?"

Hunter glanced at his mother. She looked scared and angry at the same time. "Stay here." He walked quickly to the front of the store.

Two men stood near the counter. One, a tall, muscle-bound guy with dark hair and a full beard, had his hand splayed on the counter. He was leaning forward slightly, emphasizing how large he was compared to Zack. The other stood beside him, a few inches shorter, wiry, with wavy dark hair mostly covered by a white ball cap. His arms were folded across his chest, but as Hunter approached, he grabbed a book off a display in front of the cash register and flipped through it. Then, he took half in each of his hands and tore it in two.

"Hey!" Hunter spoke at the same time his brother raised his voice and asked them again to please leave.

"If you don't, I'm calling the police," Zack said.

The one with the beard laughed. "You think the cops *like* queers holding parties and talking about their perverted *feelings*, trying to convert confused teenagers?"

"We're not converting anyone and we don't have parties," Zack said.

He sounded polite, respectful, his voice carrying the authority he'd acquired teaching school. But authority only works when people respect it. They didn't care about his opinions or his rationale.

The wiry guy moved away from the counter to a table in front of the doors with displays of new and featured books. He knocked several to the floor.

Zack picked up the handset. The guy with the beard, well over six feet tall, leaned easily across the counter and grabbed it out of his hand.

Zack's authority and polite requests were useless. At that point, Hunter wasn't sure reaching for his cell phone was going to be any more effective, but across the street and two doors down was a Mexican restaurant with an outdoor patio. According to Zack, cops loved taking breaks there, chowing down on a quick a plate of nachos and large glasses of soda on warm summer evenings—a snack that was served hot and fast and could be abandoned just as fast when a call came.

He hurried to the door and shoved it open, cursing those ridiculous bells, terrified that the odds of finding a cop eating chips and cheese were slim, as he left Zack and his mother in a situation that was poised to turn violent. But he needed help fast. He couldn't fight these two brutes. He would double his efforts by calling 911 as he was running across the street to drag any cops he could find away from their break time. If it wasn't already too late.

CHAPTER 32

NOW: ALEX

*N*apa Valley, California

When I came home from talking to Scott, I was famished. I'd found a power bar in the bottom of my bag that looked a little defeated, but the package was still sealed, so I ate it while I drove, speculating about the Harper family.

I wondered if Scott was curious enough to look into them on his own. If he did, would he let me know if he found anything? It was a question that might remain unanswered. I certainly wasn't going to ask him. I'd let my curiosity show far too much already.

Hunter had taken Tess and Marcus out to dinner. They'd just returned and Hunter and Marcus were playing pool in the game room on the third floor.

Tess informed me of this as she sat at the kitchen bar sipping tea.

I opened the fridge and began pulling out eggs, cheese, and sausage to make a spicy scramble.

"Didn't you eat?" she asked.

"No."

"Why not?"

"It didn't work out."

"I thought you were meeting a friend."

"We just had a drink."

"You were gone a long time for one drink and no food."

"We talked a lot." I turned on the gas, broke two eggs into a bowl, and started whisking them into a froth.

"Was it a good catch-up?"

"Yes." I started grating cheese, slicing off a piece to nibble on while I waited, feeling the hollow sensation in my stomach. "I ran into that reporter."

"What reporter?"

"Maybe I never mentioned him. I met him when I was trying to find out about the castle."

"Oh?"

"We ended up talking about Black Mask." I washed the tomato and chopped half of it, then diced half an avocado.

"How did you end up talking about that?"

"I mentioned I worked here. He said the previous owners moved to Italy."

"I know."

"Why?" I sliced two scallions and dropped them into the pan, inhaling the aroma as they immediately began sizzling in the olive oil that had been heating for a few minutes.

"I have no idea," she said.

"Did you know they have a daughter?"

"Yes. What does that have to do with anything?"

"Do you think it's strange an adult daughter would move out of the country with them? And don't you think it's strange they would sell a winery that's been in their family four generations?"

"It happens."

"Do you know why they sold?"

"Where are you going with all this? I hope you weren't gossiping about it to some reporter, and whatever friend you were meeting with. It sounds like ... I don't know what it sounds like, but what are you trying to say?"

"People come into the tasting room and ask about the winery and it got me thinking about the history."

"No it didn't."

I poured the egg and cheese mixture into the pan. I added the pre-cooked sausages I'd sliced into thin disks.

"What's going on?"

"I just think it sounds strange. I'm curious about what happened."

"It's not really any of your business." She sipped her tea. She slid off the bar stool, still holding her mug, and moved toward the window. "It feels like you're trying to dig up dirt. This has nothing to do with the history of the winery. I gave you the historical information that's of interest to our customers."

"People like human interest ... not just grapes and the year buildings were constructed and who the architect was."

"Architects are people."

I laughed. I turned off the gas, scraped the scramble onto a plate, and took a forkful. It was as amazing as I'd imagined. Spicy and filling and so cheesy.

"Aren't you going to sit down?"

I took another forkful, stabbing a piece of sausage on the end.

"Please don't ask strangers anymore questions. If you have questions, you can ask me."

"But you don't know. You're not even curious."

"It's their private business. And who cares? Maybe they were tired of running a winery. It's a 365-day a year job."

"You'll never get a vacation?"

"I will, but I'm always thinking about it. I always have to be available. Maybe it was too much. Maybe they wanted to enjoy the fruits of their labor."

"To be honest, I just wondered if it had anything to do with Silas. Maybe he—"

"Are you serious? Please tell me you didn't ask this random reporter about Silas."

I ate some egg and sausage. All I'd asked was whether he'd ever met him. That was innocuous enough.

"Did you?!" Her voice rose slightly.

"No."

"Is that the truth?"

"Yes." I ate more egg and took a few sips of water.

"Why don't I believe you?"

"I have no idea."

"You cannot be asking people about him. Especially reporters. Do you get that?"

"Of course."

"You could destroy my life." Her voice trembled slightly.

"*He's* about to destroy your life, not me."

"Don't talk about him! I thought I could trust you. I thought you—"

"You can trust me."

"I'm not sure. You don't tell me anything, and then you show a total lack of discretion about the most horrible secret I've ever—" She glanced toward the door, a look on her face that made me think of a wild animal, caught in the blinding beam of a high-powered flashlight, fearing for its life. She tried to put her mug to her lips, but her hand shook so badly, she had to support the mug with her other hand, and even then, some of the tea splashed onto her fingers.

"Don't be so upset. I didn't tell him anything."

"Oh my god, you're absolutely clueless about this. Why would you even say that?"

"Say what?"

"Tell me you didn't say anything about him! To a total stranger. To a—"

"I was trying to reassure you." I couldn't understand why she was having such a meltdown. All I'd done was ask if Scott had met the former head of the tasting room. Tess was acting as if Silas had given me photos of Tess and I'd been passing them around the bar.

Had he crept so far inside her head that she was imagining things? Or had he said something else to her that had made her more afraid than ever? "What's wrong?"

"I don't want you talking about him to *anyone*. Ever. And I don't want you asking about the former owners. I don't want you talking to anyone about anything."

I laughed. "Are you serious?"

"Yes."

"Maybe you need to talk to your fiancé about this. Or Silas is going to destroy this winery, and you."

"I'll take care of Marcus and my business. You just need to show you have an ounce of discretion."

"I'm trying to help. I'm trying to find out what he's after. You don't even know why he's doing this. He hasn't asked for money. He hasn't done anything except scare you so badly you can't even think straight."

"I'm thinking just fine. You need to stop talking about him. Got it?" She came around the bar and poured her tea down the drain. She put her mug in the dishwasher and walked out of the room.

I finished eating my eggs and sausage and thought about Tess. I knew nothing about marriage. I didn't even really know much about relationships, since most of mine had been very brief, and very different from the norm, as far as I could tell. But I didn't think it was going to work with her and Marcus if she didn't either trust him enough to tell him what had happened, or find out what Silas was up to and get rid of him.

It seemed like a logical guess that the sudden evacuation of the Harpers might have had something to do with Silas. He was working at the winery that had been in the family for generations when they suddenly decided on a below-market sale and an apparently final departure from this country of the entire family. He was the common thread between that unusual situation and the open-ended blackmail of the new owner.

CHAPTER 33

*T*ess grabbed her running shoes out of the closet in the workout room. Despite having eaten a heavy dinner of Chinese food with more potstickers than she should have, she needed to do something to drive the fear out of her bloodstream that was threatening to overwhelm the cells of her brain with a hundred thoughts of disaster and ruin.

She kicked off her sandals, pulled on a pair of thick socks, and shoved her feet into her shoes. She shimmied out of the silky top she'd worn to dinner and grabbed a tank top out of the narrow closet.

After twisting her hair into a messy bun, she climbed onto the treadmill, set a medium incline, and started walking fast. She hit the control repeatedly, increasing the speed faster than normal until she was running almost as fast as she could, her heart pounding. She was breathing hard, but it felt good. She didn't want to think. All she wanted to hear inside her head was the sound of her breath rushing in and out of her lungs and the thud of her heart pushing blood to her legs.

It had been obvious from Alex's simultaneously shocked and amused expression that Tess had overreacted to the news that

Alex had been talking to a reporter about the previous owners of the winery. Tess had been curious about the sudden sale. She'd also been pleased at what seemed like a golden opportunity and hadn't seen a need to pry into their reasoning. If they wanted to sell below the market, she was eager to buy.

It had been an incredible deal, and after assuring herself, with the help of experts in the field, that there were no hidden issues with the health of the business, the property itself, the quality of the vines, or anything else forcing the sale or driving the low price, she'd made an offer. Marcus had heard about their desire to sell from a friend who had recently purchased a winery as a place to park some of his windfall earnings. Because of his friend, Tess had been first to the table before anyone else knew Black Mask was up for sale.

She felt lucky that Marcus had an inside track. Yes, she'd wished she'd done it all on her own, without what looked like special favors, the privilege of moving in the right circles. But she'd worked hard all her life, and she had the resources to buy a winery and the skills to run a business of this size and complexity. She wasn't going to feel bad if some things came more easily to her than they did to others. That was how life worked sometimes.

At the time, Silas was just a key employee who knew a lot about wine and a lot about Black Mask in particular. He'd seemed like an asset. It had never even tickled at the back of her mind that the sale, or the previous owners' sudden departure, was remotely connected to him.

Why was Alex talking about him so freely without recognizing how dangerous it was? Silas was out to destroy her. She didn't know why or how he planned to. And she didn't know when, but clearly, he wanted to hurt her very badly. He was dangerous. And Alex was acting as if it were a silly high school game of who was in and who was out of a clique. She sounded as if she'd been talking to anyone who would listen, asking questions about the Harpers.

People remembered stuff like that. And they talked. What if someone had overheard?

She jabbed her finger at the controls, increasing the incline. She was gasping for air, but she wanted it that way. She wanted her body depleted so that all these thoughts would drain out of her skull, unable to torment her for another moment. She wanted her brain squeezed like a sponge until nothing was left but the pure awareness of the life inside—the blood and bones and viscera.

The workroom door opened and Alex stepped inside. She closed the door and leaned against it. "What does he want from you?"

Tess stabbed the button to increase the speed.

"Talk to me. You can't live like this. Why are you even trying?"

"Because that's how I am." Tess could barely get the words out. She gulped in air, running faster to keep up before the machine tossed her to the floor.

"Running won't help."

"Yes, it will."

"Not for the long term."

Tess ran faster. She wanted to close her eyes. She didn't want to see the accusing expression on Alex's face. But closing her eyes risked falling off the treadmill. It was easy to lose her balance on the moving conveyer, especially with the incline.

"Have you asked him what he wants?"

"Why would I do that? It's giving him control." Tess's voice was strained and thin from the effort of running at full speed.

"He already has that," Alex said.

Tess felt tears pushing against the backs of her eyes. They burned in her sinuses. They filled every space inside her skull, as if the liquid had been manufactured on the spot and was ready to pour out like a torrential rainstorm, making her look like a helpless child.

And that's what she was. A helpless child. There was no escape from him. She'd thought about it endlessly. She'd believed telling Alex about it would provide relief, that somehow, it might show her a path toward escape, but it hadn't. Talking about it had made her feel better for a brief few minutes, slightly less alone for several days. But now, she felt worse. She was more terrified because she was certain Alex was not going to be able to keep her mouth shut. She was going to poke and prod and push at this like she did with everything.

It was like a giant blister, and soon pus would explode all over Tess. She would be left with a raw wound that would never heal.

She slammed the heel of her hand on the control panel. The machine beeped wildly, but it kept functioning. The conveyor continued moving.

"You can't just do nothing," Alex said.

"What do you suggest?" Tess pressed the button to lower the incline. "What the hell do you suggest I do?"

"Find out what he wants. Find out why the former owners ran for their lives."

Tess laughed. "They didn't run for their lives."

"They were definitely eager to get out of here. And the only thing they left behind was Silas. It's interesting, don't you think?"

Tess slowed the treadmill until she was walking calmly. She didn't feel calm, but she did feel ... different.

She couldn't just keep doing nothing. It was killing her. The problem was, she still had no idea what to do, aside from telling Marcus. And she wasn't ready to do that. Not yet. The torment of not knowing his response was more bearable than the terror that he might walk away.

CHAPTER 34

*H*unter was getting bored fast. Alex was either working or running off to meet friends, or running, period. She liked to run alone, and if he was honest with himself, that was fine. He didn't mind going for jogs in Central Park but running along seemingly endless miles of highway, breathing in dry California air, constantly alert for loose gravel, wondering if the relentless sun had lured rattlesnakes out of hiding, wasn't something he relished.

He'd done some hiking. He'd made good use of the heated swimming pool, which he was still enjoying in the middle of the day when the temperatures were balmy. Even though there was a crisp chill in the morning air and the evenings were cool and breezy, the early afternoons felt like summer. California was a surreal place. He understood why people who lived here, at least in the central and southern parts of the state, behaved as if life were a constant party.

Maybe New Yorkers did that too, but in an edgier way.

Californians acted as if they were always splashing about in the sunshine, always glowing with the good health of being outdoors, constantly wearing sunglasses. He'd seen a fair number of people wearing sunglasses indoors, as if the frames were glued to their faces, their eyes fully adapted to the dark lenses, making them forget they were wearing them.

He didn't mind the rest and relaxation at all. He couldn't remember when he'd last had a vacation like this. Most of his vacations involved travel, with itineraries and lots of sightseeing, must-try restaurants and a change of hotels every few days, boarding trains or planes every five. This was nice. Keeping in touch with everything at the agency was working well. He felt as if he was doing his job, but utterly relaxed and disconnected at the same time.

Still, it had its uncomfortable aspects. It seemed as if there was no end. There was no plan. If he allowed himself to think about it too much, he felt he was in the way.

Neither Marcus nor Tess made him feel that way. Just the opposite. He hardly saw them during the day, and they seemed almost honored when they could cook for him, in Marcus's case, or take him out to dinner and introduce him to their favorite wines and foods, in Tess's.

Neither had Alex made him feel unwelcome, but she was distracted. Extraordinarily distracted. So ... was she the one making him feel he wasn't welcome? Or was that his imagination?

Now he stood outside the tasting room. The afternoon sun hit the glass on the French doors that led to the gift shop. He couldn't see into the room beyond, but Alex was in there, pouring wine and talking.

The job seemed like a step backwards, a major step backwards, but he hadn't mentioned that to her. He saw the appeal—standing around talking to strangers. He imagined she liked that. She liked asking questions; she liked getting into conversations that left people wondering what had just happened to them.

But other than that, where was the challenge? It was no different from a somewhat mindless clerical job. She had no creative control over her work. It wasn't really work at all. It was pouring drinks in a predefined way. It was telling the same story about the wine every single day, multiple times a day.

He imagined she would quickly be far more bored than he was.

Had she agreed because she wanted to hang out in Tess's spectacular house? Did she simply want a place to stay and was going to take advantage until Tess and Marcus were married next spring?

The two of them hadn't talked about it. They hadn't talked about anything. That was his fault as much as hers. He was still on the fence, and he wasn't getting any closer to deciding where he was headed with her. He wasn't any closer to deciding whether this had the potential to be a normal, satisfying relationship, or if she had targeted him and was on her way to setting him up in some way he couldn't quite work out.

It was the reason he'd followed her out here without her knowing, watching her from a distance, before she'd invited him to join her. That had been a scramble—trying to explain why he wasn't flying to San Francisco directly from New York. Her invitation to visit had caught him by surprise because he'd been only a few miles away, staying in a nondescript motel, watching her from a distance, following when he could.

When she'd followed up her invite with a request to pack up her things at Eileen's apartment, he'd had to feed her a vague story about traveling that he hadn't explained with a lie until he'd arrived. She'd accepted it, which startled him, because usually, she accepted nothing. It was a relief in more ways than one. He didn't want to pack her things. And he didn't want to explain her vanishing act to Eileen, whom he'd never even met.

The whole situation was disturbing. It added more to the mildly paranoid side of the scale that was constantly weighing whether she was interested in a relationship with him, whether she'd been attracted to him the moment they met. Or whether she'd been stalking him with some greater purpose in mind, and nothing had been an accident at all. Every single date and gesture and word out of her mouth designed to lead him to his death. Which was it? He changed his mind every day.

"So you're her man, but you were following her?"

Hunter felt as if he'd been punched in the back of the head. The voice was too loud, too close, and too unexpected. He jerked around. The guy who had run the tasting room before Alex maneuvered herself into the job stood behind him. Even as Hunter turned abruptly, almost bumping into him, the guy didn't take a step back. He stood so close, Hunter could see each dark hair of the stubble along his jaw, and the fine line of dry skin on the bottom edge of his lower lip.

Repulsed, he moved away.

The guy laughed.

What was his name? Simon? Silas.

"Didn't mean to scare you, buddy."

Hunter grimaced.

Silas slapped his hand on Hunter's shoulder. "Relax."

"I'm relaxed."

"Then why are you standing out here staring at her? Or trying to. You can't see much."

"I'm not staring at anyone. Just enjoying the quiet."

"Doesn't look that way to me."

Hunter shrugged.

"Troubles in paradise? She's a wild one, isn't she?"

"No troubles."

Silas laughed, throwing his head back, howling up at the vine-covered lattice overhead. "You're the very picture of a man in trouble. Creeping around asking questions about your girlfriend, if that's what she is. Then showing up here to stay with her. What's going on, buddy?"

Hunter's jaw tightened. He wanted the *buddy* thing to stop, but antagonizing this guy didn't seem like a good idea. Hunter suddenly realized he needed a significant favor from this moron.

Although Silas did not seem like someone he could trust to follow through on a favor, no matter what he might say when he asked.

"You know, every relationship has its quirks, right?" Hunter said.

"If you say so." Silas clapped him on the shoulder again.

"So I'd appreciate it if you didn't mention it to Alexandra that I was asking about her."

"Following her. I think you meant to say. You'd appreciate it if I keep your secret that you were *following* her."

"I wasn't—"

"Come on, buddy. Don't play games."

"It's complicated."

"Aren't they all … aren't they all?" Silas laughed.

"So you'll keep it between us?"

"I don't even know you." Silas smiled. "I don't think she'd like that, would she?"

"I'd just rather not—"

"What will you do for me?"

"What will I—"

"Yeah. It's only fair." Silas grinned.

Hunter squinted as a beam of sunlight cut through a space between the vines, stabbing him in the eye. He laughed. The guy was joking, wasn't he?

"Think about it," Silas said.

Hunter continued laughing.

"Seriously, give it a little thought." He slapped Hunter's shoulder, turned, and walked away.

Hunter found himself still laughing, even though he stood there alone, looking like a madman, if anyone was watching. Standing on a patio laughing at nothing. Was it a joke? He was fairly sure it wasn't.

CHAPTER 35

THEN: ALEX

 *ortland, Oregon*

My ability to fool my father turned out to be the result of a miracle, not my own doing.

Unfortunately, if he'd known about it, his rage would have blinded him to the miraculous nature of the event that took place right inside his own home.

His sister, unrepentant and therefore unsaved, was dying. He was certain god had called him to her deathbed to convince her that her entire life had been a waste—ugly, horrible, and displeasing to god. If she didn't open her eyes and see this, if she didn't allow my father's reading of page after page of the Bible, interspersed with his own interpretations and addendums to highlight her flaws and failures, bringing her to her knees in tears, she was destined to spend eternity with flames licking at her skin. She would suffer eternal separation from god. She would know pain in her soul unlike anything she'd ever experienced. Despair would consume her endlessly and the regret would be so deep, so pervasive, she would beg for the flames to devour her.

These details were vivid in my mind because my father discussed them every night at dinner while he and my mother made plans for their trip to Canada where my aunt lived in sin with her partner of twenty-seven years—a man who did not want my father to visit. Because this man was so antagonistic, my father insisted my mother needed to go with him. My mother's *sweet, godly nature* would soften the path and allow them entry through the dark doors of his sister's home.

Of course, it was out of the question that Tom and I would be left alone—at the ages of eighteen and sixteen—to watch over our easily misled selves. A friend of my parents was coming to stay with us. But this was not a hurdle anywhere near the height of what I would have had to clear in trying to escape the house under the sharp eye of my father.

Even though he gave our caretaker a list of instructions that filled two sheets of paper, spit out of the computer and handed to her the day she came over for a meeting to review everything she needed to know to care for his precious children, I knew I would find a way to disarm her.

This woman did not know what she was up against. My father might give her warnings about me. He might issue a stern directive about bed checks, but I knew from talking to other kids that most parents, nearly all parents, were quite different from mine. Even the other parents at Pure Truth Tabernacle.

No one I knew experienced nightly bed checks. No other kids lived through the elaborate punishments my brothers and I had experienced since we were small.

Mrs. Baxter would be easy. She would be charmed by me and then she would be cowed by me. I would attend the party, carried on the wings of angels, as the Bible proclaimed. My prayers had been answered, even though my father would call them desires that came from dancing with the devil.

I had a smile on my face that was almost impossible to conceal, but I managed, most of the time.

"Why do you look so happy?" My father watched me clearing the plates from the table. I stacked them, carefully lining up the flatware on the top plate to ensure the utensils didn't clatter as I carried the stack to the kitchen.

"I got an A on my trig test."

"Don't use slang. It's sloppy."

"On my trigonometry test."

"Well done."

"Thank you." I grinned.

"It's good when you do well. But don't let the pride make you too full of yourself."

"I won't. But I studied hard, and it feels good."

He gave me a warm smile that was somewhat unlike him. Maybe he was feeling sentimental about leaving us. It had never been done before. He'd hated it when my older brothers left home for college. Despite his harsh ways, and his decidedly dystopian ideas about raising children, I never doubted that we were the center of my father's life.

It wasn't necessarily a good thing, because he saw us as projects—clay to be shaped into figures that he envisioned inside his mind, that he believed with all his being, had been placed in his hands by some infinite, all-powerful, unseen creature.

I don't know if he was afraid of what might happen to us without his vigilant oversight, or if he didn't know what to do with himself without constant attention to his projects, or if he'd had a sudden vision of his future. His number of projects was dwindling. Soon, no matter how hard he tried, we would all be gone.

Every so often, I wondered why he hadn't gone the extra mile. He might have been one of those religious cult leaders who purchased land far from civilization and kept us around him forever, securing our life partners for us, and building an isolated community of his own.

From that perspective, maybe he wasn't at the extreme end of the scale.

So, my parents left and Mrs. Baxter moved into Eric's old bedroom.

I began my seduction of her the very first afternoon. I baked a batch of brownies. I asked her what her preferred beverage was.

"Anything you have, sweetheart."

"Tea?"

She looked disappointed.

"Coffee? Juice?"

She looked almost ill, and a bit anxious.

Finally, we settled on water. She ate four brownies and sipped the water. Her gaze darted anxiously around the room. I sat across from her and asked what I could do to make her feel comfortable in our home. We talked about her own children, who were still in elementary school, currently under the watchful eye of her husband and mother, while she stayed with us for the next six days.

When she reached for the fifth brownie, her hand shook.

"Are you okay?" I asked.

She gave me a grim smile and nodded.

"Your hand is shaking."

"I just need my medicine."

"Can I get it for you?"

"Not now, honey. I'll take it later." She gobbled the brownie and reached for another.

I loved brownies. Everyone in my family loved brownies, but I'd never seen anyone eat as many as she did. And with nothing but a few sips of water to moisten her lips, I wondered if she would start choking on all that chocolate and sugar. Brownies truly are meant to be consumed with a beverage.

"Are you sick?"

"No."

"Then why do you take medication?"

"Sometimes people have chronic conditions and they need medication. It's personal." She smiled, her teeth outlined in gruesome ridges of thick, wet chocolate, glued along her gums and in the spaces like clotted blood.

"What's your condition?"

"I'm not going to discuss that with a child."

"I'm not a child."

"You are. And you shouldn't ask such personal questions."

"Why is it personal?"

She stared at me. She opened her mouth, but no sound came out.

Our church believed in miraculous healings. Maybe she realized she should have walked down to the altar on a Sunday morning and knelt before the elders so they could place their hands on her head and pray for the healing of her condition. If she kept it a secret, she wouldn't be healed. Maybe she realized I could see she was lying.

I wasn't sure how I knew, but she was keeping something important from me.

She picked up her glass and took a long swallow of water. Her hand shook so badly, I thought the water would spill out onto the table. If it did that and left a mark, I might be blamed.

I moved the coaster toward the edge to be sure it was within easy reach when she was finished.

"Thank you for the brownies," she said.

While she made dinner, I went upstairs and slipped into the bathroom she was using, quietly closing the door behind me. I found the small zippered bag with her toothpaste, hairbrush, and other toiletries. There was a bottle of acetaminophen, but no other medications. I went into Eric's room and opened her suitcase. Wrapped inside her bathrobe were four small, clear bottles with yellowish gold labels and black letters—Seagram's Extra Dry Gin.

There was really nothing else I had to do. As the bible so clearly said —*This was the day of my salvation.* Or something like that.

Her *medication* would put her to sleep the moment Tom and I were in our rooms with our lights turned off. All I had to do was keep her well-supplied with sweets, so she was comfortably lulled into a sense of security. Leaving the house would be easy. And there was no chance she would notice the slightest hint of alcohol on our breath the morning after the party.

It was a miracle.

CHAPTER 36

NOW: ALEX

Napa Valley, California

I poured more than the standard amount for the second to last red. The two women and one man standing in front of me were busy talking to each other. They had no interest in Black Mask or in joining the wine club. The guy was working overtime, flirting with both women. The result was, they had zero interest in me or in anything I had to say.

I'd spent much of the time trying to work out what the relationship was between the three. I hadn't come to a conclusion.

Just as I was lifting the bottle for the final pour, my attention was captured by movement on the patio. Hunter was out there. He stood facing the French doors, looking as if he was trying to see inside. It was clear from his expression, he couldn't. Every few seconds, he moved his head slightly, as if he thought he might be able to look around the wood frames dividing the glass and get a better view. After a few minutes, he seemed to recognize it was impossible, but he didn't leave. He remained with his attention focused on the doors, staring at nothing.

I poured the wine and watched him, wondering what he was thinking about. It didn't seem as if he was necessarily waiting for me. He seemed to be drifting, unsure about what his purpose was.

Then, as I began easing the cork into the bottle of Pinot Noir that was still on the counter, Silas walked up behind him. He put his head close to Hunter's. He must have said something, because Hunter jumped as if he'd been smacked on the side of his face.

I watched them for nearly ten minutes as they carried on an intense conversation, punctuated by Silas laughing like a hyena every few minutes. Hunter looked like his prey. Not that he was cowering before him, but he didn't look happy. He looked like he wanted to escape. And yet, he didn't. He stood listening to whatever nonsense was oozing out of Silas's lips, taking a step back each time Silas moved closer.

I was so caught up watching every gesture; I ended up serving and extra pour of the signature Cabernet. No one pointed out my mistake, and I didn't notice until I started the man's glass. By then, I couldn't correct it without wasting the wine in the women's glasses.

Part of my job was to account for every tasting, tracking how many bottles were consumed each day. I wasn't sure how I would explain this overage to Tess, but I would figure that out later. Right now, I was far more interested in explaining to myself what Silas might have to say to Hunter.

As far as I knew, they'd never met.

At least they didn't appear friendly and chummy. For now.

I thanked our guests, gave them business cards, was surprised when they purchased six bottles of wine, and ushered them out the door.

Before cleaning up, I went outside to meet Hunter, hoping no one else dropped by for a late afternoon sip of wine on yet another crystal clear fall day.

"You met Silas?"

Hunter kissed me, long and slow.

I was impatient to hear what they'd talked about, but he pulled me closer, kissing me as if he'd only just arrived, as if he wanted to pull me into bed. What had Silas and he been talking about that he wanted his tongue so far down my throat that no more questions could slip out?

I let the kiss go on. Then, after another half a minute, I felt a laugh bubbling inside me. If Tess saw me, would she consider this another dereliction of duty? Kissing on the patio when I was supposed to be washing wineglasses, calculating the ounces poured and entering them into the spreadsheet? Wiping counters and preparing for the next drop-in day drinkers?

In my mind, it seemed like a good way to entice people wandering the Napa Valley, looking for a pleasant, out-of-the-ordinary experience. What more exciting finale to six small tastes of spectacular wine than a delicious kiss with a good-looking guy on a vine covered patio on a fall afternoon?

Hunter pulled away from me. "I like a reaction when I kiss you, but laughing isn't what I dream of."

"I wasn't laughing at the kiss." I brushed my lips across his. "I was thinking that Tess might not appreciate me kissing you when I'm supposed to be working."

He ran his fingers through my hair. "Can I help you clean up or anything?"

"What were you and Silas talking about?"

"Just small talk."

He was lying.

The aggressive way Silas kept slapping Hunter on the shoulder, the way Hunter was backing away from him, the very air around them as I'd stared out the window, over-pouring wine, had told me they were not having a conversation about the sunny afternoon or the beautiful grounds of Black Mask, or a quick exchange of who's who. In fact, it hadn't looked like an introduction at all. They hadn't shaken hands.

"Was that the first time you met him?"

"I've seen him around."

What did that mean? Why was he giving me non-answers? "What kind of small talk?"

"Why so curious?"

"You should probably keep your distance."

He laughed. "Should I?"

"Yes."

"Why is that?"

"He's creepy."

"How is he creepy?"

I shouldn't have used that word. I shouldn't be using any words about Silas. I just didn't want the two of them talking. I wanted to be rid of Silas. I wanted to slice him out of Tess's life, but he was like the vines creeping across the lattice, sending new shoots in every direction, twisting his way around everyone and everything.

I couldn't explain any of that to Hunter. I couldn't say anything about the man. Every time I mentioned his name, I drew a neat, black arrow, pointing directly at me that would raise questions when he turned up dead.

Unless I found a way to be rid of him in a way that his body was never found. Unless I could make it look as if someone else had killed him. But who would that even be?

Looking at Hunter's expectant expression, I felt as if Silas stood behind me, his icy fingers around my neck, pressing into my throat, choking the breath out of me.

The things I imagined doing to him were starting to look impossible. All the usual stealthy ways of enticing a man to his death, all my usual methods of achieving anonymity, were out of the question. And because I was obsessed with removing his entitled, probing fingers and death-like grip from Tess's throat, I'd slowly and wantonly painted myself as the singular person who was unreasonably fixated on him.

I couldn't tell Hunter that Silas had forced himself on me. I absolutely couldn't mention what he'd done and was doing to Tess.

"Are you okay?" Hunter asked.

"I'm fine."

"You look like you're having trouble breathing."

I laughed. "Not at all."

"How is he creepy?"

"Didn't you pick up on that? A lot of people do."

"What people?"

I pulled him toward me and kissed him again. When I let him go, I laughed softly. "It's probably just one of those chemistry things. He was condescending when he was training me. He's a player, and we didn't hit it off."

"That's it?"

I smiled. "Why are we even talking about him?"

"Good question," he said.

It was clear we were both relieved to change the subject. But I wanted to know why Hunter was so relieved to stop answering my questions.

CHAPTER 37

THEN: HUNTER

*A*s Hunter raced across the street, hoping to find the cops snacking, he pulled out his phone, fumbling, trying to tap the three critical numbers onto the screen to call the police while simultaneously scanning the outdoor patio of the Mexican restaurant.

He stumbled onto the opposite curb, having accomplished nothing because he wasn't focused on either task, thinking about those two assholes and his brother trying to defuse their intense antagonism ... worse than antagonism ... *How* much worse? And his mother. Alone and vulnerable. Scared out of her mind.

Fear grabbed at his throat as he thought about what could happen in the moments he was gone. Why had he left Zack and his mother alone? But what choice did he have? Finding police officers just a few yards away rather than waiting for some to respond to a call seemed so much better at the moment when he'd realized what might happen. He'd acted without thinking. Even now, he still hadn't managed to tap out 911, still fumbling to focus on the screen while scanning the outdoor tables.

He saw three cops sitting near the railing, large glasses of soda in front of them, a plate piled with chips and beans and guacamole and cheese that looked as if it had just been served.

"Help!" They looked at him with curiosity, but none of them stood. "Help me!" He waved his arms at them. "Some guys are threatening my brother." He gulped for air, more from panic than the effort of running. He gestured toward the opposite side of the street.

"Threatening your brother?" The female cop echoed.

"Can you come, please? He owns the bookstore. Two guys came in and they're making homophobic slurs and vandalizing the place."

"Vandalizing it how?" The female cop pushed back her chair, but without any sense of urgency.

"Hurry. I don't know what they'll—"

"What do you mean by homophobic slurs?" The larger male cop with a shaved head plucked a nacho from the plate and shoved it into his mouth.

"Just come. I'll explain … It's probably escalating right now … while we're talking. They were destroying books, throwing them on the floor."

The female cop stood.

The smaller male cop, a slender guy with short dark hair, also stood. "Some people around here are a little upset about the bookstore. Sooo … He's your brother?"

"Yes. Hurry!"

"It was suggested to your brother that he should just sell books, which is what a bookstore is supposed to do. He's been inviting people who don't even live in the area to give speeches, drawing large groups. It attracts attention and—"

"So that makes it okay for two thugs to vandalize his store?"

"I'm not saying that."

"Will you hurry? We can talk later." His chest felt tight. His breath was getting shallow. He wanted to reach across the railing and grab the guy's arm, yanking him over the side instead of waiting for him to walk around to the opening. What was wrong with them? They were acting as if he was telling them a raccoon was trapped in the store and he needed help cornering and capturing it.

He should have called 911 first. From the store. But would it have gone the same way? They were acting as if Zack had invited this because he offered community events.

"Hurry!"

"A few books on the floor aren't an emergency," the shaved head cop said. He picked up his soda and took a drink. He'd obviously decided not to join the other two because he hadn't made a move to leave the table.

"I don't know what's happening now. They seemed really angry." Hunter's voice shook, the pitch was higher, making him sound hysterical. He needed to calm down, but their lack of concern was making it worse.

After what seemed like another ten minutes, but was probably less than two, the smaller male cop and the woman ambled out of the eating area and followed him across the street. The guy lectured him as they walked, telling him it was a quiet town, that people didn't like political issues shoved down their throats, that a bookstore was intended to sell books, that people read books to escape the daily grind. He told him he'd met Zack himself and he was a stubborn guy. He told Hunter that *he* didn't seem gay.

As they stepped onto the opposite curb, Hunter realized the black sedan that had been parked in front of the ice cream shop next door, a woman at the wheel, the car running, was no longer there. He knew before the female cop opened the door that the guys had been in that car and they were long gone.

He felt a cold wash of silence as they stepped inside, hating himself that he hadn't stopped to take a picture of the license plate, knowing what he would see before he saw, because the silence told him everything.

The first thing to greet him was the powerful odor of urine.

Zack was sprawled on the floor in front of the cash register, his face and neck covered with blood. It was a face Hunter hardly recognized as belonging to his brother. The shape of it beneath the blood looked as if it belonged to a stranger, or a creature not fully human. Zack was surrounded by torn books that were wet with what was obviously the piss of the fuckers who had beaten him so badly, Hunter feared his brother wasn't breathing.

Before the cops could do anything, Hunter had tapped 911 into his phone—far too late, almost useless now—and was speaking in a voice that sounded absurdly calm and matter-of-fact, the voice of a bored clerk, the voice of a robot, demanding paramedics.

As Hunter spoke to the paramedics, he knelt beside Zack, placing his hand on his chest.

"Stay away from him," the female cop said. "You can't be touching him. There's evidence."

Hunter thought about the evidence that had driven away while she and the others acted as if he were inquiring about the quality of nachos at the restaurant.

He took Zack's wrist and felt for his pulse. As he touched him, Zack groaned, making Hunter feel he'd been punched in the chest, but also filling him with relief that brought tears to his eyes.

Zack seemed unable to move. His eyes were swollen shut.

"Are you ... can you sit?"

Zack groaned again.

"Where's Mom?" Hunter stood as quickly as he'd fallen to his knees and bolted to the back of the store. His mother lay slumped against one of the half-height book cases just outside the entrance to the coffee area.

She had a large bruise forming on her left cheek, dark, painful-looking red marks on her forearms, and huge purple bruises that ran along her shins. Her face was streaked with tears and makeup.

He was overcome with a sense of shame that he'd never experienced. He'd abandoned her. He'd left her alone, handing her over to the lowest form of humanity imaginable, while he walked away with some self-important mission regarding justice and following the law, without a thought for her life.

A choked sob filled his throat. He sat beside her and pulled her onto his lap. "Paramedics are coming. I'm so sorry. I'm so, so sorry."

"It's not your fault, sweetie."

And then, he hated himself more for shunning that endearing, childish name she'd refused to let go of. He hated himself like he'd never hated anything in his life.

CHAPTER 38

NOW: ALEX

N apa Valley, California

I cleaned up the tasting room.

Hunter went for a swim. He was still in the pool when I was finished. He was swimming laps as if he were crossing the bay from Alcatraz to Fisherman's Wharf, chased by twenty armed prison guards. I could see him from a distance, but I avoided walking through the garden to the gate surrounding the pool.

Watching someone submerged in water, using their limbs at full capacity to propel themselves toward the opposite end, or shore, whichever it might be, was not something I wanted to do. Even a man as good-looking as Hunter. If he chose to lie on the chair on Tess's back patio, without his shirt, I could sit beside him and admire his shoulders and back for hours, noticing every ripple of muscle when he shifted his position. I would follow him around a gym and lose myself in the fluid movements of his body as he lifted weights. But all that water was too much for me.

I turned my head toward the seemingly endless acres of grapevines as I passed by the swimming pool on my way to the winemaking facility.

It felt like walking a tightrope, not that I'd ever done anything even close to that circus trick, but I imagined that's what it would feel like, easing one foot in front of the other, curling my toes around the wavering rope, the ground far below, driven beyond reason to find out what Silas wanted from Tess, knowing I had to get him out of her life, because she certainly wasn't going to do it, but knowing that every step forward was risking my own life as people watched from the ground far below.

One shift of my body in the wrong direction would send me plummeting to the earth. I would be nothing but a bloody pulp on the ground, indistinguishable from the crushed red grapes and torn skins that went into the wine vats.

Silas wasn't the sole person who had stayed on when the Harpers fled to Italy. Chuck had also stayed on, and although he'd already labeled me unnaturally and obsessively interested in things that had nothing to do with me, he did like to smoke. And people who smoked, as I knew better than most, were sitting ducks for people who wanted to ask questions.

With the pool behind me, the sound of Hunter's splashes fading in the distance, I walked quickly toward the buildings, wondering how often Chuck went out for cigarette breaks.

When I arrived at the spot where I'd seen Chuck before, the ground was free of his extinguished butts, but speckled with a faint covering of ash. I turned and went toward the building that housed Silas's office. I settled on a bench under a small leafy tree.

The risk I was taking in talking to Chuck brought a chill to my bones that felt like they were packed in ice, but there was nothing else I could think of. I had to find out more about the people who had left this spectacular setting and all the money it generated, not to mention their family history. It wasn't normal that a woman in her twenties would willingly move with her parents to another country rather than setting out on her own. Was it? I couldn't imagine doing that when I was twenty-five.

And even though I'd had more reason than most to want to escape from the people who had raised me, nearly everyone I'd met throughout my life had been the same. They wanted to live their own lives. They wanted to be free, to follow their own rules, set up their own way of doing things. Not continue living like a child.

And there was Silas himself.

He'd kept Tess sweating and sleepless and worried. Cowering in terror that with a single phrase, he could destroy her life. Was that all he wanted? The thrill of her palpable fear, sucking it out of her like a vampire sucks blood? It was possible. There are so many perverse desires in the human race. There are certainly people who get enjoyment from the sheer thrill of watching others suffer.

But was Silas one of them?

I had the sense Silas preferred to be *The Man*. He wanted to impress. He wanted to be feared and admired. He wanted power. Not just the power that came from watching Tess be miserable, but real power. So why hadn't he asked her for money? He could bleed her dry with the photographs he had.

The longer I sat there brooding over Tess's inaction and Silas's unspoken desires, my thoughts shifted to what he and Hunter had been talking about.

How long it would be until Chuck took a break for a smoke?

I found myself longing for a smoke of my own. My thoughts drifted back to the days when I'd sat on benches and stood outside buildings with a cigarette between my fingers, inhaling smoke and blowing it out through my lips. My thoughts had seemed more orderly. The smoke calmed me. The actions associated with smoking gave me something to focus on.

Now, my mind sometimes spiraled out of control unless I was running or lifting weights. I needed to be doing something. I couldn't just sit here feeling the breeze on my skin, watching grapes grow.

It had been nearly thirty minutes, and I hadn't seen a single sign of human life. There wasn't a flicker of animal life, for that matter. I hadn't seen a bee or a fly or an insect creeping along the ground.

I stood, my legs jittery with the need to move, my fingers itchy with the desire to touch something besides the fabric of my skirt, or the bones of my wrists. I walked toward the warehouse.

The doors were open.

Inside, voices echoed around the large space, but their words were indistinguishable. I stepped closer to the entrance, ready to enter the building, needing to do something to divert my mind from gnawing and chewing on my own thoughts like an animal gnawing its own leg to escape from the metal teeth of a trap.

"You can't be here." A woman dressed in white coveralls seemed to appear out of nowhere. The aroma of fermented grapes surrounded her like some strange, off-putting perfume. It wasn't the lovely aroma of an open bottle of wine, but more like alcohol spilled on concrete.

"I'm the new tasting room—"

"I know who you are, Alexandra. But this area is for employees." She smiled in a way that said this was her territory and although I might consider myself an employee, I was not one of *them*.

As I considered her unwelcoming smile, I saw Chuck walking toward us, a cigarette already in place between his lips, a lighter in his hand. The moment he was a few feet outside the building, he flicked the lighter and touched the flame to the tip of the cigarette.

"Chuck," the woman said, her tone a reprimand.

He strode away from the building. I turned and followed.

"I hear you're an employee now," he said.

"Yes."

"Are you here for your tour of the facility?"

"I wanted to schedule one."

"Friday at three?"

"Sounds good. Does it include a history of the winery?"

He laughed. "No. It's about winemaking. We're about wine here, not history. There isn't a lot of history to tell. Four generations." He shrugged.

"But there's history in four generations of one family."

He took a drag on his cigarette. "So?"

"Why did they sell?"

"How would I know? I'm in charge of winemaking."

"Were you worried about losing your job when you knew they were selling?"

"I'm not a worrier."

I looked toward the rows of grapevines that stretched out and up the gently sloping hillside. "Did you just assume you'd be re-hired by the new owner?"

"I didn't give it a lot of thought."

His answer felt evasive. I couldn't imagine someone who had the responsibility he did never thinking about the future of his career when the winery he worked for was being sold. "Were you guaranteed you would still have a job?"

"Why all the questions?"

"I'm curious about the sale. I heard it was really sudden."

"You seem to have a lot of time on your hands for asking questions about things that have nothing to do with you."

I inhaled the smoke coming from his cigarette. I longed to take his cigarette between my own fingers, recalling the taste as if it had been inside my own mouth just moments before. The moment I was finished talking to him, I would go for a run, inhaling the cool fall air, reminding myself why I'd quit, letting the oxygen soak into every cell of my lungs. I took a step away from him, offering a friendly smile at the same time, so it didn't appear as if I was offended by his smoke or his comment.

"You'd be amazed by the questions people ask when they're tasting wine."

"I doubt that. I give tours to the same people. I've heard all the questions. And there's never been a single one about the owners."

I laughed. "Women get asked different questions than men, trust me."

He put the cigarette to his lips and took a long, slow drag. "Trust you?"

"Yes. You can't know until you've experienced it."

He laughed. He tapped his cigarette, letting the column of ash fall to the ground. It formed a neat pyramid, almost as if he'd practiced the trick. "How can you possibly know that? You've never experienced the questions a man is asked—if you're going to make wine tasting all about the war between the sexes."

"Is it a war?" I asked.

"You're the one who made the distinction," he said.

"I didn't call it a war." His description had sounded like something out of the 1970s. Given his age, it made sense, but I wondered why he'd turned it into that. I suppose he didn't like it that I suggested I might have had a different experience than he had. Of course, everything I'd said was a story, and maybe he'd guessed that.

"So you never wondered if you would lose your job when the winery sold? You weren't at all curious why a family who had a connection to this piece of land, and the buildings, who had created the Black Mask label, would so easily walk away from it?"

"Italy is a nice place," he said.

"So is this."

"Their daughter needed a change of scenery."

"She didn't need her parents. She's an adult," I said.

He shrugged. "None of my business. I'm here to make great wine. It's none of your business either. And not the business of tourists who drop by to taste the wine. If that's what anyone actually asks about, which I seriously doubt." He dropped his cigarette on the ground and squashed it with the toe of his boot, as firmly as he had the conversation.

But I had my answer. Even though she was an adult, they whisked their daughter away as if she needed saving. I was sure of it. Because that was how I felt about Tess and now Amelia. They needed saving from that snake—Silas Birch.

CHAPTER 39

*A*s I walked back toward the house after being dismissed by Chuck, I saw Hunter standing outside the gate to the swimming pool. His skin was wet, his hair dripping onto his shoulders. A towel was wrapped around his waist, but it didn't look as if he'd used it to dry off at all.

He took my hand, his wet fingers weaving through my dry ones, his damp palm pressing against mine. The sensation wasn't unpleasant, but I wondered why he hadn't bothered to dry himself. He surely couldn't walk inside the house, leaving wet footprints and drops of water on the hardwood floors.

"What have you been up to?" he asked.

"Getting more familiar with the winemaking side of things."

"Is this a permanent gig for you?"

I shrugged.

"It feels like we're living in alternate realities," he said.

"Why?"

"My life is in New York."

"I know."

"Are we ever going to talk about what's going on with us?"

"Yes."

"When?"

"Why are you all wet?"

"I was *swimming*." He stopped walking and kissed my cheek, trying to move closer toward my lips.

I stepped away. "But you're sopping wet. You didn't dry off."

"I will. You're changing the subject."

"I needed to get away from New York and I haven't figured things out yet."

"When are you going to figure things out?"

"I don't know."

He sighed. "You can be really frustrating. I don't know if you're playing games or there's something …"

"Something like what?"

"Never mind," he said.

"What were you going to say?"

"This isn't a vacation, which I thought it would be. And I can't just hang around forever. It seems like it doesn't matter one way or the other whether I'm here."

"I like having you here."

"I thought you were staying with Tess to help with the wedding or something. And you invited me to explore California with you. But you're … I don't know. Distracted. Not really here, even when you are."

"I have a new job."

"But that's the question. Why?"

"Isn't it obvious? I need to support myself." I laughed. If he hadn't been sopping wet, I would have wrapped my arm around his waist and pulled him close, steering his body and the conversation off this topic. But I didn't feel like getting wet, as divine as he looked with his glistening, lightly tanned skin.

"But why did you quit? I thought you loved being a photographer?"

"Working with Diana was intolerable."

"All jobs have—"

"She made it impossible. It's over. There's no reason to talk about it."

His sigh was so loud, it was more of a groan. "But why *this* job? It's so ... it seems like you took the easiest and the first thing that came up. I don't get it. You're basically a bartender."

"What's wrong with that?"

"You're more talented. You have more skills. It's not at all related to your experience."

"Why does that matter?"

He stopped walking. He unwrapped the towel from around his waist and dried his hair roughly. He dragged the towel down his body, removing most of the water. "I just don't understand your thinking, your career plan."

"I don't have a plan."

He laughed. "That's obvious. But I thought you did. I thought—"

"Why are you so worried about it?"

He didn't answer. We were almost at the house. He walked toward one of the lounge chairs on the patio but didn't sit down. "I don't understand anything about this relationship. You seem like you're really into me. But you don't tell me what you're thinking about your life. I guess you aren't returning to New York?"

He didn't wait for me to answer, but rushed on, talking so fast it sounded like he was firing bullets at me. "Obviously you're not. You want to get rid of everything you own, which is the weirdest thing I've ever heard. You walked out of a great job that I thought you loved, without even trying to negotiate for a better situation. You're living here, but you're not enjoying what they have to offer. You keep disappearing. You have a job that you already seem a little bored with after only two weeks. You already have some antagonism towards one of the guys you're working with, who seems like he should be your manager. Although the structure is so unclear, I can't even tell if that's the case. I just don't get it. You invited me here like it was a vacation, but you're working and I'm sitting around with nothing to do."

"You seemed really put-out that I hadn't invited you when I first came, so I told you to come."

"That's the only reason? What the—"

"I thought you wanted to be together?"

"I do, but not like this. If you're planning to stay in California, I don't see how we can have a relationship. If that's what we even have."

I didn't like talking about relationships. Why was he making it so complicated? I knew he was right—I hadn't thought that through. Things just happened. I had to get away from Fly Higher. He was also right that I really liked being a photographer, but I wasn't going to live in a prison to do something I liked. Plus, Ned. And killing Carolina. And the others. I needed some space.

I could find other things I enjoyed doing. It wasn't taking photographs I liked most about my job; it was talking to people, making them feel unsettled, capturing a side of them they weren't aware they were revealing. Maybe I should start my own Fly Higher, but with a less ridiculous name.

I knew I wouldn't, but I could, if I wanted to.

Things happened. Silas happened. I had to take care of that. I had to get away from Diana. And Eileen.

It felt like a problem from High School Algebra. Hunter in his New York apartment. Hunter with a job that he considered a career, that made him a lot of money, that he'd never once mentioned changing. Me, unable to stay in New York, with a need to be free, to be able to breathe.

I knew I wouldn't stay in the wine tasting job for very long, but I would stay until I figured out what to do about Silas. And I might stay until I was finished with Tess's wedding. It was a good way to save more money. Her house was amazing. The food Marcus prepared was like eating in a restaurant every night.

There was a lot to be said for staying here for a while. Hanging out with Tess was fun.

I was at point A and Hunter was at point B. Point C didn't exist. The problem was unsolvable. For now.

Hunter seemed to realize there were things I wasn't telling him. Maybe he had too much time on his hands to pay attention to everything I was doing. Maybe he was too much like me in that he spent a lot of time watching what people were doing, noticing little things. Little things like Silas. I'd made my antagonism far too obvious, or Hunter was perceptive. So what had they talked about? And why didn't he want to tell me?

"Should I take your silence as a *no?*" he asked.

I wrapped my hands around the back of his neck and pulled his face toward mine. I kissed him softly. "I have things on my mind."

"Obviously. But if you aren't going to talk to me about them, what are we doing? If this is just sex …" He took a few steps away from me and moved his hand back and forth in the space between us. "… I'm okay with that for a while. But I'd appreciate knowing."

"I don't think so."

He laughed. "Then what is it?"

"I don't know." I honestly didn't. I'd never had a relationship like other people had them and I wasn't sure that was possible for me. I wasn't going to tell him all about my life, if that's what he was expecting.

"That might be the first honest thing I've heard from you," he said.

Maybe it was. But it was also probably the last, for a while.

CHAPTER 40

Silas had said it would be easy, but Amelia wasn't sure about that. Amelia felt as if Alexandra was reading her mind, staring at her with a smirk on her face.

He'd insisted everyone loved to talk about themselves, especially narcissists like Alexandra. All Amelia had to do was start asking questions and Alexandra would talk.

Silas had said he needed to know more about her. He'd explained that in the business world, it was considered inappropriate and almost unethical to hire people who were relatives or friends. Tess had made a terrible mistake hiring Alex, forcing Silas to go outside the normal process to learn more about her because Tess hadn't done her due diligence.

Because the two women were friends, no background check had been done on Alex.

"Normally," Silas said, "checks are done to make sure someone hasn't committed a crime or been fired from other jobs for doing anything to damage the company. Tess isn't thinking clearly."

Amelia had felt a thrill pulse through her heart as he looked at her, holding her gaze, touching the back of her hand. It felt almost magical, knowing he trusted her with his concerns, and with such a serious part of his job. Even though she knew absolutely nothing about the business world, nothing about getting or holding a job of any kind, he was treating her like she was equal to him in her experience of the world. He acted as if she had wisdom and a special kind of intelligence.

"If Alex does something that hurts the winery or its reputation, I'll be the one who has to correct the problem. It could be really serious. And if Tess doesn't think Alex has done anything wrong, I could be the one who ends up losing my job," he'd said.

Still, Amelia was nervous about starting a friendly conversation with Alex. All she had to do was ask how she knew Tess, ask about her experience in the wine industry. From there, Amelia should get Alex talking about her career so she could get company names. With those details, Silas would be able to make his own inquiries.

"What if she asks why I want to know? What if she asks a question I can't answer?"

"You'll figure it out," Silas said. "You're smart."

She felt like her heart would explode with pride when he'd said that. Besides, she was curious. She didn't tell him that, but she still wanted to know why Alexandra had dyed her hair. It had been such a beautiful red, almost exactly the same color as Amelia's.

She knew the chances that Alex was her missing aunt, that she was the little red-headed girl Amelia had seen in the photograph of her father taken years before Amelia was born, were almost impossible. But she couldn't stop thinking about it. Every time she looked in the mirror, every time she brushed her hair, she thought about it. And every time she went into the tower and looked at the urn containing her father's bones and ashes, every time she opened that photo album her mother had kept, wondering about all the things she didn't know, the things she would never know, staring at the photograph, she wondered.

Then, Alexandra had suddenly dyed her hair another color. Why would she do that? Did people change their hair color for no reason? Amelia wasn't sure. But she'd never seen anyone else do it. Not that she had any experience with such things. Because, thanks to her mother and her uncle, she had no experience with much of anything. Every moment of her life was a guessing game, trying to figure things out, trying to understand people and how the world worked. But something told her, from what she'd observed so far, that except for girls who liked to experiment with blues and greens, most women rarely changed the color of their hair.

This made her think Alexandra had a reason for hiding the color that was almost identical to Amelia's, as well as her father's and her aunt's.

So it wasn't just because Silas told her to find out more about Alexandra's background. She wanted to know herself.

When she'd opened the door to the tasting room and stepped inside, Alexandra was standing at the bar. She was holding a wineglass up to the light, turning it slowly, peering through the glass as if she were looking for flaws. She'd placed the glass on the counter and looked at Amelia. She didn't look pleased.

"Hi." Amelia smiled and walked toward the bar.

Alexandra said nothing.

"I wanted to try some of the wine," Amelia said.

"I didn't think you were twenty-one."

"I'm not."

"I can't serve you."

"I've had wine before."

"It doesn't matter. I have to follow the law."

"Do you like working here?" Amelia leaned against the bar. She smiled and picked up one of the cardboard coasters with the Black Mask logo on it.

"Yes." That was when the smirk appeared on Alexandra's face.

This would not be as easy as Silas had said. How did you start a conversation with someone you didn't know? Books and movies made it look easy. People smiled and asked questions and the other person started talking. But what if they didn't? What if they didn't want to talk to you?

"Did you work at another winery before this?"

"No."

Amelia's cheeks hurt. She was used to smiling when she was happy, not because she was trying so hard to look friendly. She was sure if there was a mirror behind the bar, she would look like a lunatic, smiling at nothing, smiling too hard. "Where did you work?"

"Why do you want to know?"

"I'm just curious, since you didn't work at a winery."

"Why are you curious?"

"I'm just being friendly?"

"Did you take my advice about Silas?"

Amelia felt the smile on her face crack and break into something that she wouldn't be able to describe if she had seen it in a mirror. She wondered what Alexandra was thinking as she stared back at her. The expression on Alexandra's face was smooth and calm. She didn't seem at all uncomfortable. There was no sign her mind was racing to think about what she should say next or that she was worried about what Amelia thought of her.

"Why don't you like him?" Amelia's voice trembled. She was glad she hadn't answered with a meek-sounding *no*. It felt good—refusing to give in and making it seem as if she should have taken unasked for advice from someone she didn't know. It was none of Alexandra's business who she was friends with. Or more than friends.

"It has nothing to do with liking him," Alexandra said. "He's manipulative. I'm not sure you recognize that."

"You know nothing about me."

"I know enough."

"You don't."

"I know you were raised in captivity."

"I'm not a zoo animal."

Alexandra laughed.

Was that a good thing or a bad thing? Amelia wasn't sure. But she was very sure she wasn't going to get the information about Alexandra that Silas had asked for. She would not get an answer to even the simplest question. Alexandra wasn't going to answer any questions she didn't want to. Amelia felt as if she'd walked into a trap.

She felt as if Alexandra was the one who had started the conversation. Alexandra was in control, and Amelia didn't have a chance of finding out what Silas wanted.

He wanted too much information. How did you ask all those questions without sounding like you were prying, asking things that were none of your business? It wasn't as if they were at a party, talking about life, getting to know each other.

"Why are you here?" Alexandra asked.

"You probably know I live at the Windy Hills Castle."

"I've heard that."

"It was a popular wedding place and—"

"Was?"

"I don't want to do weddings. It's not really—"

"Why not? I heard it was booked all the time. Your mother must have made a fortune. And you must have weddings that were already scheduled for the next year, or more."

She wasn't here to talk about weddings or the castle. Or her mother. She was forced to do the weddings. Her mother had contracts. And she hated it. Every part of her hated thinking about those awful, horrible, macabre weddings. But the lawyers had told her she had no choice.

"Weddings don't interest me. So I wondered what's involved in starting a winery."

Alexandra laughed. "You're asking me what's involved in

starting a winery? I'm the last person who can answer that. Isn't your boyfriend the expert? In fact, you should ask Tess. She's the real expert. So why are you really here?"

Amelia wondered if the heat filling her body was visible on her face. Alexandra was still staring at her as if she could read her mind, but she'd been doing that since the moment Amelia opened her mouth. Maybe it didn't show. All she needed to do was stay cool. That's what Silas had said. And she knew that. She might not be experienced in talking to people, but she knew about people. She wasn't a complete idiot.

She'd figured out her mother and the lie they'd tried to create around her—pretending her uncle was her father. She wasn't a child. She wasn't stupid. Silas had told her she was smart. She needed to trust that. Alexandra wasn't some brilliant mastermind.

"I thought you might know something about it because you're close friends with the owner. I didn't want to talk to Silas about it because it's something I'm only thinking about. You seemed like a nice person and someone that I might be able to trust. Maybe I was wrong." She took a few steps away from the bar.

Her clever words did the trick. Although the expression on Alexandra's face didn't change, her attitude seemed to.

"I've never worked in a winery, so I really don't know anything about it, but you can trust me. To answer your question, I've had a lot of different jobs. Before this, I was a photographer." Alexandra shrugged. "The only help I can offer is to tell you that Silas is not someone you can trust. I know that from experience. You can believe me or not."

"How does a photographer—"

"I can't talk any more. There's a tasting scheduled at two." Alexandra turned away and took a bottle of wine off the shelf behind her.

Amelia said goodbye. As the door closed behind her, she wasn't sure if her attempt at getting information was a complete failure. She'd learned a few details. She felt Alexandra would talk to her again and trust her enough to say more. But Silas probably wouldn't think it was all that great.

Being warned about him twice was making her stomach feel squirmy. Should she be worried? She hated someone telling her what to do. But why would Alexandra keep saying that, since it didn't matter one way or the other to her?

CHAPTER 41

*H*unter climbed out of the pool after yet another afternoon swim. It was the thing keeping him grounded, if it was possible for water to do such a thing. He grabbed his towel off the lounge chair and dried his face. As he pulled the towel away, he saw Silas. The man was only six or seven feet away from him, staring as if he'd been watching the entire time he'd been swimming laps.

"What's up?" He knew. The aggressive slap on the shoulder and the suggestion he should do something for Silas in return for not telling Alex he'd been following her had not been a joke. He'd known at the time. And he knew that's why Silas was standing there now, like a wannabe mafia dude ready to collect his weekly blood money, or whatever they called it.

He'd never been into mafia films and lore. He didn't drink the stuff up like some people did, feeling the vicarious thrill of a large family and the assurance of protection, as well as revenge for wrongs that were done to you. Although, considering how his life had played out, maybe those would have been nice connections to have.

"I realized I misspoke the last time I saw you," Silas said. "Why would I ask what you want to do for me? I'm gonna *tell* you what you need to do. It's not like you offered me a choice, right?"

Hunter wrapped the towel around his waist. Water ran down his spine, but it felt somehow submissive to dry himself while this guy was standing so close, watching him with such interest. He didn't like it. And he really didn't like the fact that he felt as if he was essentially on the cusp of a blackmail threat.

Maybe he should just tell Alex what he'd done. She'd be upset, but the whole situation between them was becoming so convoluted, a good clearing of the air might be in order. He should lay all his cards on the table and see where things stood.

It couldn't continue like this. They were at a crossroads, no matter how he looked at it. In a week or two, he would return to New York and she would remain in California. If she wasn't even willing to make a trip to the East Coast to pack her belongings, it was unlikely she would be visiting often, if ever. He'd pushed his time off to the limit, and it would be a long while before he could return for more than a three-day weekend here or there. With a five-hour flight between them, was a three-day weekend worthwhile?

Yes, he was consumed by her. Even now, when she was gone for a few hours, he couldn't think about much else but her. At the same time, if she didn't start talking, if he didn't decide once and for all whether he believed her interest was genuine or a set-up—

"Hey!" Silas snapped his fingers in front of Hunter's face. "Where'd you go? I asked you a question. Twice."

Hunter shifted his gaze to make eye contact, although that wasn't technically possible since the man was wearing mirrored sunglasses.

"How soon can you do that?"

"Do what?"

"I'm serious? Are you having blackouts or something?"

"I have a lot on my mind. What did you say?"

Silas let out a barking laugh. "We all have a lot on our minds.

Don't act like you're stupid. I said I need you to go through Tess's office and find any contracts that pre-date her ownership of the winery."

"No."

"Not a choice. Equal exchange of favors."

"There's nothing equal about that. All I asked you to do was show some discretion."

"What you asked me to do, is to lie to your girlfriend. This tells me you're terrified of her. If she finds out you were following her, she'll dump you so fast you'll crack your skull. She's out of your league and you know it, and you don't want to get kicked to the curb. Sooo ..." He grinned, his lips wide, exposing his gums.

Hunter looked away from the gruesome sight.

"Now that I think about it, you're right," Silas said. "It's not at all equal. I'm doing a helluva lot more for you. You have easy access to her office. A quick pass through in the middle of the night. I'm not even asking you to take anything. Just snag a few photos of any contracts that were in place. Easy."

Hunter clenched his jaw. He wanted to point out that ease wasn't the issue. It was the ethics. But discussing the finer points was suggesting he was considering it and he was not going to do this. At the same time, he was irritated with himself that this loser was going to be the one to push him into a serious, confrontational discussion with Alex. He should have done it before she left New York. He should have done it a hundred times. All those times when she'd dodged his questions, changed the subject, directed his attention away from her life and onto her body.

This was his mess. But he was not going through Tess's office and he was not doing any favor whatsoever for this guy. "Not gonna happen." He started walking toward the gate.

Silas grabbed his arm just above the elbow. His grip was unbelievably strong. The pressure on his tendons hurt like something he'd never experienced. Pain shot up his arm and into his shoulder. Despite his desire not to give Silas the advantage, he grunted.

"You have no choice, you little fucker. I want a photo of every contract she has. By Friday. Or that hot chick in your bed is gonna find out you're a stalker."

"I'm not a stalker." Hunter hated the squeal of pain seeping through his words. He sounded like a thirteen-year-old boy.

"What kind of insecure guy follows his girlfriend, trying to find out what she's up to? And then has to run around asking everyone not to rat him out?" Silas cackled, then released his grip. "Friday."

The needles of pain traveling through Hunter's arm remained for several minutes after the clang of the metal gate faded.

CHAPTER 42

*M*arcus was in San Francisco for the evening, taking clients to dinner.

Tess had ordered enough Indian food to feed six people. We'd stored the leftovers in the fridge and were sitting in the living room watching the flames of the gas fire dance behind the glass. She and I were sipping martinis. Hunter was drinking a beer. Or not drinking it. Mostly, he was carefully peeling the label off the bottle in strips, pausing to stare at the flames as if he needed to keep a watchful eye on the fire because he thought the flames might burst through the glass at any minute.

During dinner, he'd picked up each tender strip of chicken as if he were a surgeon, extracting some invasive substance from the open cavity of a person lying on the table in front of him, studying it with intense distrust before placing it in his mouth.

Now, he placed the bottle on the coaster, still half full. He leaned back on the couch and pulled up his leg, resting his ankle on the opposite knee. "What made you buy this winery, Tess?"

"I thought it would be something I'd love doing, and I knew I'd be good at it."

"I mean this particular one—Black Mask."

"It had a good reputation." She gave him a wry smile. "It wasn't as if there were twenty on the market."

"So you didn't consider others?"

"Not really."

"How did you decide it was a good investment?"

"I had our accountant look at the books."

He nodded.

"Is it complicated? Were there a lot of entanglements?"

"What does that mean?" She sipped her drink. She looked thrilled that he was asking about her beloved winery.

I wasn't so sure. The questions weren't casual cocktail conversation. I wasn't aware he was so interested in the wine business, and now he seemed to want to know details that were only important if you were thinking of buying a winery yourself. It reminded me of my conversation with Amelia. Poking around for information, but why?

"Because it's such a complex operation. Did you have to take over a lot of existing contracts with shippers and distributors? Things like that?"

"Of course, but that's a good thing. It freed me up to focus on building the brand and working with the vintner to make sure the wine quality was top-notch instead of having to worry about the logistical stuff."

"Sure. I can see how that would be valuable."

I sipped my martini and nibbled my way through my first and second olives while Hunter asked increasingly detailed questions about the winery and what Tess had known about it when she purchased it, what she'd learned after buying it, and what had surprised her the most about running such a complex operation.

Her glass was empty, and she was smiling, leaning forward as she talked on and on, gazing at him as if no one had ever paid such flattering attention to her in her life.

Just as I was scooting to the edge of the couch, ready to offer Tess a second drink, Hunter grabbed his bottle, took a long swallow, and stood. "I'm going to call it a night. I'm really tired. I'm not used to all this fresh air and swimming." He laughed.

Tess grinned as if she was thrilled that he was enjoying all that her home had to offer, but to me, he sounded as if he was making excuses. He didn't look or sound tired. What he looked like was a man who couldn't wait to end the conversation and escape from the room.

A moment later, he was gone. I took our glasses to the kitchen and while I ate my final olive, I mixed two more martinis and thought about Hunter. I wondered what he was doing upstairs. I wondered if I would find him sleeping when I went up. I wondered what all his questions had been about. Was he just being the polite guest? Was he giving back a bit of the grilling she'd given him when we'd gone to dinner?

I didn't think so because none of his questions had been of the personal, potentially uncomfortable variety that she'd asked him. He didn't seem interested in making her squirm, or in finding out about her past. He seemed to want to know something very specific about the Black Mask Winery, but I had no idea what that was. Or why.

In order to give my mind space to consider Hunter, I handed Tess her martini, tapped my glass ever-so-carefully against hers, and changed the subject.

"Have you chosen the caterer yet for the wedding?" I settled back to listen with one ear while she ran through her thoughts about food. In the background, I let my mind spin around Hunter and his questions.

When our glasses were only half empty but Tess's thoughts about appetizers and main courses, and buffets versus plated dinners had exhausted themselves, I told her I was also going to bed. She was shocked that I wasn't finishing my drink. I ate my last olive and said I had a headache.

I slipped off my flip-flops and held them in my hand. I walked quietly up the stairs, keeping to the right side, hoping Damien wouldn't see me pass by and make a comment that could be heard on the second floor. I paused on the landing.

Something didn't feel right. Something about Hunter's questions that were so uninteresting and so unlike him. Something about his slightly anxious and distracted behavior and his sudden departure. I thought about checking our guest suite, but I already had a feeling he wasn't there.

I turned in the direction of Tess's office, my feet sinking into the carpet as if I was walking on clouds, my approach silent except for my breath, soft in my ears.

Tess's office door was closed. I pressed gently on the handle and opened it.

Hunter stood in front of her credenza. He held his phone over an open file folder that lay on top. He didn't look up. He was too busy taking photos of whatever was in the file.

CHAPTER 43

THEN: HUNTER

*A*lthough Zack was in terrible shape, covered with blood, lying on the floor of his bookstore, surrounded by piss-soaked books, the female cop went through the farce of interviewing him.

"Have you ever seen either of these men before?"

"No." Zack's voice was a torn whisper.

I hated she was talking to him before he received medical help. At the same time, I wanted them to get a description. I wanted every cop in town out on the roads with a description, looking for them.

"Can't I answer these questions? I saw them. I saw the car. I can—"

"We need to speak to the victims," she said. "In fact, it would be better if you would wait at the back of the store. Or outside."

I was standing beside my mother, who was slumped in a chair we'd brought from the coffee shop. "I'm not leaving them."

"Then please don't interfere."

She returned her attention to my brother. "Can you describe them?"

"One was tall." His words were thick and inarticulate, as if his tongue was glued to the roof of his mouth. "Really big guy ... a beard," he mumbled. "Other one was smaller." He grunted. "Wearing jeans. Dark T-shirts. Not sure—"

"Black shirt for the big guy," my mother said.

"We'll get your statement in a minute," the cop said.

"Don't speak to her like that," I said.

The cop glared at me. "I need you to stop talking."

"She's hurt. She's traumatized. You need to—"

"What did they say when they came in?" the cop asked Zack.

It continued this way. I could see that the descriptions, even with the combined efforts of Zack and my mother, were vague. They could fit hundreds of men. There were no scars, no tattoos, nothing to distinguish them.

Finally, I was allowed to describe the black sedan and the woman in the driver's seat, although I had even fewer details to offer. They were clearly disgusted with me for failing to get the license plate number.

Amid their questions, the paramedics arrived.

Zack moaned as they cleaned up his face and bandaged his wounds to stop the bleeding. After lots of prodding that caused him to cry out several times, once with a scream of pain, they announced they would be taking him to the hospital. My mother would also be taken for X-rays and an examination for internal injuries.

When they were gone, before going to the hospital to be with Zack and my mother, I talked to the cops. "Have there been other hate crimes in the area?"

"We don't know this was a hate crime," the female cop said.

"It's obvious."

"It's not obvious. Your brother could have been a target for another reason. Until we can talk to him further, we won't know. And we'll need to talk to patrons of the store."

"Why?"

"To get a clear picture of what his gatherings are like."

"What does that have to do with anything?"

"If we're going to throw labels around, we need the complete picture."

"Are you sending a sketch artist to the hospital? Or do you have one of those computer programs that comes up with composite drawings from descriptions?"

"We don't have those resources here. We have the description and the make of the car."

"It would be helpful to know if there have been other hate crimes. You must track—"

"I said, once we decide if that's what this is, we'll look into it."

"How are you going to find them?"

"We'll do our best."

"I want them caught. And prosecuted."

"Of course you do. Everyone wants the same when they're the victim of a crime. But you have to recognize the realities of the situation."

"What does that mean?"

"Your brother doesn't recall seeing them before. We don't have good descriptions. There's no security camera, and you didn't get a license plate. In summary—there isn't a lot to work with."

"Are you telling me you aren't going to do anything?"

"That's not what I said. You have to understand the realities of what we have to work with." She gave me a condescending smile. "Unless you have some suggestions."

"I do. Talk to people. Check your hate crime database! Find out about anyone who has a history of aggression toward gay people. People who make slurs and—"

"It's not against the law to express your opinion about perv ..." She paused and looked down at her notes.

I glared at her. I glanced at the other guy who had become offensively silent. "Is that how you're looking at this? No big deal because you wish Zack's bookstore didn't exist?"

"You're distorting my words. I didn't say anything close to

that. But people have a right to their opinions and we're not going to question everyone who's been known to express an opinion that your brother might find objectionable."

I pounded my fist on the counter. "Are you going to actively pursue these guys and that woman in the car, or not?"

"Calm down. And if you make a threatening move like that again, this conversation is over."

"Threatening?" I laughed. "That's ironic. It sounds like this *conversation* is already over. Because it sounds like you don't plan to do anything."

"We'll do everything we can. I'm simply trying to set your expectations so you're not frustrated and ultimately disappointed. You need to control your emotions. We're deeply sorry your brother and your mother were so badly injured. Please don't misinterpret our reaction. But there's only so much we can do with very little to go on."

"You collected DNA."

"If they haven't committed a violent crime in the past, their DNA won't be in the database." She pressed her lips together. "We'll see. My gut tells me this was an isolated incident."

"How do you know that?"

"When you're in this business, you develop instincts. And as I said, I'm trying to set your expectations. I could be wrong."

"It seems like you don't really care."

"It's not my job to be emotional about crime. That would interfere with my work." She gave me a tiny, incredibly calm smile, as if to prove her lack of emotion.

We talked for a few more minutes, but the conversation deteriorated further. It became increasingly clear she thought it was highly unlikely they would catch the fuckers. She implied even more strongly that the lack of a security camera, which my brother thought was oppressive to his patrons, as well as my failure to get a license plate, meant that their inability to bring these assholes to justice was our own fault.

It was hinted repeatedly that the existence of Zack's *provocative* bookstore caused the crime, and our failure to be vigilant meant the perpetrators would remain free.

When they left, I went into the bathroom in the back of the store and vomited. Then, I made an inventory of the books that had been destroyed, took them out to the dumpster, and cleaned up as best I could. I turned out the lights, locked the doors, and drove to the hospital.

CHAPTER 44

NOW: ALEX

*N*apa Valley, California

As I watched silently from the doorway, Hunter continued taking pictures of the files spread across the credenza in the corner of Tess's office. I waited for him to become aware of my presence. He closed a file folder and opened another, positioning his phone over the document.

"Why are you taking pictures of her files?"

He fumbled with his phone, almost dropping it as he jerked around to face me. "I …" He turned back and began straightening the papers from the open file. He closed the folder and returned it to its place, closing the drawer quietly. He slipped his phone into his pocket.

"You need to delete those. Whatever they're for."

"Can we get out of here?"

"Why? Are you worried she'll hear us?"

He didn't answer.

"She might not think you're so amazing after all."

He took a few steps toward me.

"You need to delete them."

"Okay. But let's go to our room. We should talk."

"We probably should."

He glared at me, then crossed the room. I didn't move out of his way. He stopped, looking down at me, his face unreadable. I moved out of the doorway and we walked down the hall and around the corner to our room.

Inside, I dropped my flip-flops on the floor. I sat on one of the armchairs in the corner and dragged the footstool closer. I folded my hands on my lap and waited.

He sat in the chair beside me but didn't look at me. "Silas asked me to take pictures of her contracts. Anything that pre-dated her purchase of the winery."

"Why?"

"I don't know."

"Why would you do that?" I was aware, as each word slid off my tongue, that if Hunter knew the things I'd done, things that were slightly more disagreeable to most than sneaking into a friend's office and handing over her business information to someone who might want to destroy her, he would be horrified by my hypocrisy. But he didn't know.

And horror at my situational choices never affected me. The thoughts of others rarely entered my mind, except as points of curiosity and obsession, but not to dictate or direct my behavior.

He looked uncomfortable. He looked as if he might be sick to his stomach. I crossed my ankles and waited for him, wondering how long he was going to take to explain. It wasn't something I would have imagined him doing. I couldn't begin to guess why he would give Silas more than a second's thought or why he would even listen to a request like that, much less consider it.

"It was a return favor."

"Favor?"

"Not the right word, but yes. I asked him to do something for me and he turned it into—"

"What did you ask him to do?"

He sighed. A sigh that sounded like a groan. A groan that sounded like he'd lost a contest of some kind, as if he'd given up, as if he'd reached the end of the road. "It's a long story."

"We have all night."

"Do we?"

"Yes."

"You need to get up for work."

"I need to know what's going on. I've survived on a few hours of sleep before." I could not survive not knowing what was going on around me, especially knowing what he'd said so far. Knowing mattered more than sleeping. I could feel the adrenaline pumping through my veins, as if I'd consumed two espresso martinis.

"I was in California before you invited me here."

"What?"

"I came out a week or so earlier. I wanted to know what you were up to."

"What I was up to? I was helping Tess make plans for her wedding. I told you that."

"It didn't feel right."

I laughed. "What didn't feel right?"

"I don't know. Something seemed off. Maybe it was in my head. But it was so dramatic and sudden. Leaving work for such an extended time to help with a wedding that's almost a year away. What was there really to help with? And then quitting your job like that? A job that I thought you loved." He was quiet.

I said nothing, waiting for him to explain more. I thought I was seeing what had happened. I recalled the expression on his face when I'd told him I was resigning from Fly Higher.

He'd followed me? Was that strange expression his moment of decision? Something about quitting my job triggered him. But why? Why would he do that? What did he imagine he would find?

And what was he worried about? Had he guessed something about me?

My mind moved with relative calm over the things I'd done while I'd known him—the murders of James and Carolina. It wasn't possible he could know even the slightest detail about any of that. I'd kept my activities well away from him. What was bothering him so much that he came to California to follow me? It was almost funny. What did he think he would learn, watching me run or go out to eat, or take my trips to the castle?

I felt my rapidly pumping blood turn chilly. I'd noticed someone following me because he was so clunky and obvious. I'd been aware of a man speaking to Silas about me, but what if he'd done more? What if he wasn't as inept as he'd seemed? What if those were slip-ups and his other moves had been stealthier?

"I followed you." His voice was so quiet, I almost didn't hear. And by now, his confession was superfluous. "I asked Silas about you. And after I arrived to stay, I asked him not to mention it. He jumped on it and demanded a return favor."

"You followed me?" I didn't ask why. I left lots of wide open space for him to tell me everything.

"You're not like any woman I've ever known and I can't figure out what's going on with us or what you really want—from me, or even from your own life."

"Okay."

"Not just different because I'm really into you, but crazy different. Impossible to figure out, and not like women are difficult for guys to understand, but sometimes I wonder ..."

I waited for him to finish the sentence. The silence continued. It went on for so long, I wondered if he'd forgotten he'd stopped mid-thought. I wondered if he'd forgotten what he'd planned to say.

"It was really aggressive and not normal how you were waiting for me in front of my office building that day."

"What day?"

"When you asked me out to breakfast. When we first met."

I laughed, but my throat felt cold. "What does that have to do with anything?"

"I've sometimes had thoughts that this might be a set-up."

"That what's a set-up? What are you talking about?"

"You and me. That you have an agenda."

"An agenda? For what?"

"Did someone ask you to come on to me?"

I relaxed slightly and started laughing with more relief. What was he thinking? That I was a spy? What did that mean about him? Was his job at the modeling agency a cover for something else? I felt like I was acting in a film. Or having a dream. I couldn't stop laughing. Maybe he'd had too much to drink. Or maybe he'd had too much time on his hands ... he'd met someone and experimented with psilocybin. What was going on with him?

"Does that mean no?" he asked.

The question made me laugh harder. "That might be the most bizarre question anyone has ever asked me."

"I'd appreciate an answer."

"We're not talking about me. We're talking about why you would betray Tess."

"I told you."

"Because you followed me and you asked Silas about me and you were so worried about me knowing that, you agreed to do whatever that guy asked? Giving information about her business to someone who might want to hurt her?"

"He works for her."

"Asking for photos of contracts behind her back doesn't sound like he's trying to help her."

He stood and walked across the room. He took off his shoes and flopped onto the bed. He stared up at the ceiling, putting his hands over his eyes as if the dim light was too much for him. Or maybe, because he didn't want to see my face, even from that angle.

"I should have said no." His voice was rough. "I should have had this conversation first. But it's not something I wanted to talk about."

"Why?"

"I don't know. Maybe because you tell me almost nothing about yourself. So I also keep more to myself than I probably should." He sat up. "Not a great way to establish a good relationship."

I had no idea how to establish a good relationship, so I said nothing.

"Why don't you?" he asked.

"Tell you about myself?"

"Yes." His voice was sharp, as if I'd missed the obvious.

"I don't know why I quit my job and I don't know how long I'll be staying here. I don't always know what I'm planning. That's all I can say."

He heaved an enormous sigh, as if he couldn't be bothered to say another word.

"Will you delete the photos?" I asked.

"Absolutely." His tone was sarcastic.

He was annoyed that all I cared about was the photos, but I'd told him the truth. I couldn't answer any of those questions right now.

"If you want to know more about me, I do know I don't want to be a wine tasting hostess or whatever it is. But it works until I can figure out something else."

"You act like you're nineteen years old."

"I didn't know figuring out a career had an age limit."

"Fair enough." He was quiet for a moment. "Let's go to bed."

"Sure. After you—"

"I'm doing it now."

Even though he was clearly irritated with me, he managed to get over it when I came out of the bathroom and slid into bed beside him, wearing nothing but a short, silky top.

I fell asleep with a smile on my face, but I wasn't sure the smile on his face carried him into his dreams like mine did.

CHAPTER 45

The moment I woke, I wondered why I'd insisted Hunter delete those photographs. Because, of course, my curiosity outweighed my irritation at Hunter. I absolutely didn't want Silas getting his hands on them. And I didn't like it at all that Hunter would so easily rip open the curtain of Tess's privacy to that slimy man, but I wanted to know why Silas was so interested.

What did he think was hidden in her filing cabinets? He already had a grip on Tess that would force her to bend to any wish he expressed. Why did he think he needed to bring Hunter into the mix? Why did he need to see contracts for the winery without her knowing? He had leverage over her to demand anything he wanted. Was he fishing for information, or looking for something specific?

I hadn't stood over Hunter while he was deleting the photos. They might still exist in his recent deletions file. But I had no way of easily getting into his phone. And I didn't want him to know I was interested.

We were together enough. He was on his phone often enough … was there a chance he might put it down and turn his back or leave the room before the screen locked, giving me a chance to dive into it without him knowing?

If he caught me with the phone in my hand, whatever paranoia he had about my agenda would double. But it sounded as if that paranoia was already quite strong, eating at him from the moment I'd asked him out, since the first time we'd had dinner together. If that was the case, why had he said yes? There were so many questions. If he thought I had an agenda, maybe he had one of his own, and he'd said yes because he wanted to know what I was after.

I truly felt as if I was in some weird, low-budget spy movie. A cat-and-mouse game that I didn't have the script for. What was going on that he would think I'd asked him out with an agenda?

It was something that required more discussion, but not now.

First, I needed to know what Silas was after. Something so important, he enlisted Hunter as his spy. Something buried in Tess's files that must be part of what he needed in order to dismantle her life. His photographs of her having sex with him weren't enough? Drunk and disconnected from her real self, lost in a moment of whatever happens when alcohol soaks through every brain cell and turns it into an unrecognizable, unthinking creature that some compare to animals.

Although that's a deeply offensive comparison to the clever creatures who share the planet with the human race. They never do the risky and foolish things that human beings do. They never lose their instinct for self-preservation, even for a moment. While human beings deliberately and regularly numb those instincts, drowning them as if they think they're unnecessary, hardly worth possessing.

What else did Silas need from her?

After telling Hunter he had betrayed Tess by prowling through her office and photographing critical pieces of her business in the dark, I needed to find the time to do the same thing myself. Without being discovered. It would be risky, but probably not all that difficult. A late night with lots of wine, a quiet departure from our bed at the darkest hour, and a silent walk down the hallway to Tess's office.

The following evening, Marcus presented me with my opportunity by making spaghetti with freshly baked garlic bread and a salad with vegetables from the farmer's market. I took charge of liberally refilling Hunter's wineglass with their signature Cab. He seemed eager to comply. Maybe, despite thinking I had an agenda, he was feeling bad about betraying our hosts and wanted to appreciate their generosity by savoring their wine and good food.

After dinner, I suggested we try some of the single malt scotch from the collection Marcus was obviously proud of to complement the tiramisu.

When we went to bed, Hunter was clearly feeling it. I was clear-headed from keeping myself to only two glasses of wine and a few sips of the scotch. It was a constant fascination to me how easy it was to conceal how much I was drinking once others got going, watching how they assumed my laughter and enthusiastic, rambling conversation suggested the same amount of alcohol flowed through my veins as was soaking into their bodies.

Hunter was snoring within moments.

I set my phone to vibrate at two-thirty in the morning and placed it under my pillow.

I didn't really need the alarm. Knowing I wanted to wake did something to my body clock and at twenty minutes after two, I was awake, my hand sliding under my pillow to find my phone and confirm the time.

In Tess's office, I kept the lights off and used my phone light to find my way around. I opened the drawers in her credenza and read the labels on the hanging folders, removing the ones that looked interesting. I figured when, and if, I stumbled across whatever it was Silas might be looking for, I would know.

It took me until four in the morning. By that time, I only had another half hour or so left before I risked Tess or Marcus getting up early. I risked Hunter waking and noticing I was gone.

But at ten minutes past four, I found it.

The document wasn't a contract. It was a letter of intent, an agreement for the future.

It referred to Rosé Harper and her fiancé—Silas Birch—outlining their ultimate ownership of the Black Mask Winery upon the retirement of Gordon and Jillian Harper.

CHAPTER 46

THEN: ALEX

*P*ortland, Oregon

When Tom and I arrived at the party house, it looked proper and quiet. The drapes were closed. The lights inside offered a warm glow. The thumping music wasn't audible until we were close to the front steps. Because it had rained all day and the night air was cold, I expected all the neighbors had their windows closed.

Knowing party protocol, Tom didn't knock. He simply opened the door. Music spilled out onto the front porch. We went inside and closed the door behind us.

The music was loud enough that Tom raised his voice and put his mouth close to my ear. "You can get lost now."

I turned toward the living room to see if I recognized anyone.

Tom grabbed my wrist and pulled me back. "Don't drink too much or you'll regret it."

"Is that a threat?"

"This is your first time. You need to be careful."

"What's too much?"

"No Jell-O shots. Two beers. Maybe three. I'll find you when it's time to go."

"What time is that?" I shouted.

"When I decide."

"How will I know?"

"Don't be a PITA." He gave me a light shove, and I turned back toward the living room. He immediately disappeared.

Seven or eight kids were dancing on the hardwood floor. The rest were sitting on the couches, more like piled on the couches—all three were overloaded with ten or twelve people, a tangle of arms and legs and hands holding plastic cups filled with beer.

I wanted to try a beer, but first, I wanted to see if there was anyone I could hang out with. I saw some kids from my year, but none of them were people I usually talked to. I kept walking, weaving through the room where people stood in groups, shouting at each other and laughing as if everything everyone said was the funniest thing they'd ever heard.

The living room had a large opening into the family room and that was more of the same—kids piled on couches and armchairs. Some people were sitting on the floor, and a few couples were half-lying down, leaning against the walls, kissing and groping each other.

Three girls I knew were crammed into one armchair. They were holding clear plastic cups with pale yellow beer that honestly looked a little like pee. I said *hi*. They wiggled around and told me to climb on.

"Wait," Jennifer said, "You don't have a beer. Everyone on the chair needs a beer." They all giggled.

"Where's the beer?" I asked.

Jennifer pried herself off the chair. "Come on." I followed her to the kitchen. A large silver keg sat on the counter. She put a cup under the spigot, filled it and handed it to me. "Now you're ready."

I put the hard plastic to my lips and tipped the cup slowly. The foamy stuff touched my tongue. The taste was cold and sour and doughy. It smelled like wet bread. I didn't see the appeal, but I took another sip because I knew the appeal wasn't the flavor, although my brothers had claimed it tasted great. Maybe it was like pickles or sauerkraut, and you liked it after you tried it a few times. Or a hundred times, in the case of sauerkraut.

As I followed Jennifer back to the family room, I took a few more tiny sips and looked around at the other kids, trying to figure out whether they were acting differently because of the beer, or because there were no adults in the house telling them they couldn't dance like that or let a guy lay on top of them and kiss them.

Jennifer squeezed herself back into the chair with the others. It was already overcrowded, so I perched on the arm and continued sipping my beer, waiting to see what would happen.

They were talking about a teacher everyone hated, which seemed boring to me. Why would you come to a party, with dancing and beer and no adults, and talk about school? It made me want to laugh, but I didn't. I just kept sipping beer.

When my cup was empty, Jennifer noticed right away. It seemed like she'd been keeping a close eye on it, watching the liquid disappear. She wriggled out of the chair. "I'm all empty too." She giggled. "I'll get us more."

I was tired of sitting on the arm of a chair. I didn't come to a party to sit on a chair and talk about school. I wanted to have fun.

"I can do it." I pushed her gently back into her crevice in the chair. She folded into it as if all her muscles were Jell-O. She giggled. "I might have to pee." She grimaced and wriggled slightly.

"I'll be back in a while," I said.

She didn't seem to notice what I'd said, maybe because she was trying once again to get off the chair and seemed to be having trouble with it. I decided the others could help her. I was tired of the chair club. I turned and went into the kitchen.

A boy I didn't know was standing by the keg.

"What do you want?"

"Isn't it obvious?" I asked.

He grinned. "Lots of things are obvious."

I smiled and put my hand on the tap.

"I didn't give you permission."

"Is it your keg?"

"Maybe it is."

"Well, is it?"

"What's the magic word?"

I wasn't sure if he was flirting but wasn't very good at it, or if he was kind of a jerk, or maybe more than *kind of*. "Please."

"Please is for little girls. Girls who drink beer need to know the real magic word."

"I'm here to party, not play fantasy games with trolls."

He threw his head back and laughed a great, bellowing, roaring laugh that turned into something almost sinister, making me think that possibly he was a troll. Except he was incredibly cute. One of the cutest guys I'd ever seen, although I'd never noticed him around school. He looked like he was probably a senior and I hung out with kids in my year.

"Do you know who I am?" he asked, when he'd finally stopped bellowing.

"No." I stuck my cup under the tap.

Before I could touch it, he closed his large hand over it.

"Seriously? No clue?"

"None."

"So you're clueless."

"Yes."

He gave me a mocking smile. I gave him one back.

"Harrison Andrews."

"Alexandra."

"You still don't know who I am?"

He was utterly disinterested in my name. He seemed agitated that his name didn't register with me. He seemed almost angry that I didn't recognize it, that I wasn't embarrassed by my ignorance.

"*Football?*"

"I don't go to football games."

"You've never looked at a yearbook? Never listened to the Monday morning announcements—"

"Nope."

"You really are clueless. Maybe that's why I've never seen you at a party."

"Maybe it is. I'd like some beer now."

"Have you ever had beer before?"

"Yes."

"When?"

"Is that the magic word? Football?"

He snorted. "So Alexandra, I'm the quarterback of the football team. I'm the one who led our team to the championship last year, and I'm heading there again this year."

"Congrats."

"That's all you have to say?"

"I don't watch football."

"What do you do?"

I shrugged. "This is a lot of talking just to get a beer."

He moved his hand away from the tap. "Don't you like talking? 'Cuz I'm having a good time."

"It's not too bad." I filled my cup, lifted it to my lips, and took a long swallow.

"Want to dance?" he asked.

I held up my beer.

"Chug it."

I did. It was not a pleasant experience. The taste and the carbonation felt like a bathtub full of chilled water and foam going down. But after spending my time so far teetering on the edge of a recliner, I wanted to dance more than I wanted to continue sipping beer, and now I was done with it. Besides, the faster I drank it, the sooner I would find out what it felt like to have alcohol inside my body.

So far, I hadn't felt much except a mild desire to smile a little more easily than usual, a slight willingness to smile at Harrison's less than funny comments, even though he thought they were hilarious.

Dancing would be the most fun I'd had since I walked in the door. He was nice to look at, and dancing meant I wouldn't have to listen to him tell me how awesome his football stardom was. Hopefully. We'd be close to the speakers, so even if he did continue telling me how important he was, I wouldn't be able to hear. I could let the beer bubbles create easy smiles on my face and lose myself in the music.

There were a few more people dancing than earlier. They were looser and more seductive than they'd been when I arrived, so it was definitely fun watching.

We danced for seven or eight songs, getting more wild as the time passed. I could feel that the beer was changing how I moved. I noticed my arms were free, my smile disconnected from my thoughts, my body developing a mind of its own.

After a while, someone handed me a tiny plastic cup filled with Jell-O. Despite what Tom had said, I wanted it. The Jell-O smelled sweet, and I was sick of the taste of beer. I didn't feel anywhere near tipsy. I was definitely not drunk and wasn't that why I was here? I wanted to know what it was like, and the thought of drinking two or three more beers made my stomach rebel.

I popped the sweet treat into my mouth.

With Tom's voice thrumming in my head, background music to what was coming out of the speakers, I declined the second cup of Jell-O.

Soon, I felt myself dancing as if no one else was there, the feeling of my brain disconnecting from the rest of me growing stronger. I was laughing at nothing. When Harrison moved closer and pulled me close, I let myself fall into him, my thoughts drifting and vague.

Slower music came on and he wrapped his arms around me. The lights that someone had already turned low, were turned off. A few strings of Christmas lights that had been wrapped around the tables and light fixtures and draped over the picture frames provided tiny pricks of light that made everyone look warm and friendly.

Harrison danced me slowly toward the doorway. From somewhere, another Jell-O shot appeared in his hand and I opened my mouth.

CHAPTER 47

NOW: ALEX

Napa Valley, California

Knowing that Silas had expected to become the owner of the Black Mask Winery explained his behavior. In his mind, Tess had managed to sneak in and take it away from him just as it was about to fall into his hands.

For whatever reason, the Harper family had suddenly changed course. The engagement must have ended and Silas was left with nothing but a mid-level management job, a lot of bitterness, and a bank account that couldn't begin to accommodate an offer of his own.

Now, what was he waiting for? Why hadn't he used his leverage over Tess to try to take it away from her?

It was also clear that Tess *knew* he'd expected to own it himself, but she'd never said a word about it to me. Even as I'd looked her in the eye and asked her what Silas wanted from her. She wouldn't be happy if I looked her right back in the eye now and told her I knew because I'd rummaged through her files.

If I continued asking her what he wanted, would she eventually tell me the truth? Why hadn't she?

Maybe none of it mattered. All that mattered was getting rid of him, and this was simply a distraction. I didn't have to know, did I?

But I *did* have to know. I always had to know. She'd sat in front of me multiple times, stared at me with her dark eyes, wide and bottomless as the ocean, outlined in dark, artfully applied shadows, looking utterly immobilized by fear. Looking as if she were being held captive by that pompous, posturing fool who strutted around her property in his aviator glasses as if he owned the entire Napa Valley.

No wonder he acted as if he owned the place. In his mind, he did.

I had to know why she hadn't bothered to give me this important piece of information. All these acres had been placed in the palm of his hand, one wedding vow away from becoming his to nurture and reap the rewards from for the rest of his life. Then, his bride was swept away to Italy, and the vineyard was sold to a woman who materialized out of nowhere, who began her venture knowing almost nothing about wine, and had no connection to a place where he'd spent most of his life sinking his roots into the earth.

He'd meticulously set her up for a blackmail scheme. And yet, he was sitting on it. He hadn't tried to destroy her marriage; he hadn't yet tried to force her hand. Were Silas and Tess involved in some delicate negotiation she hadn't told me about? Why had she told me at all, if that was the case? She'd acted as if Silas was poised to tell Marcus she'd betrayed him. She'd acted as if she wanted my help. With what? Now that I saw the things she'd kept from me, I wondered what she'd expected I was going to do?

I stood at the bar in her massive kitchen, sipping my third cup of coffee. It was too much caffeine—my thoughts were already racing over the questions I wanted to ask her.

I wasn't sure I wanted to confront her head on. It was better to creep up slowly, but I wasn't quite sure how to accomplish that. I didn't want Hunter to walk into the room unexpectedly. Or Marcus. I rarely saw Marcus in the mornings. He usually got up before dawn, drank a smoothie, worked out, and was in his office, deep in virtual meetings with colleagues in Europe by seven o'clock. But it wasn't something Tess liked talking about if he was anywhere in the house.

I poured the remainder of my coffee down the drain. I rinsed the mug and placed it in the dishwasher. I grabbed a cup of yogurt from the fridge, opened it, and started eating.

She would refuse to discuss this in a local restaurant as well. My choices were limited.

In the end, I suggested a pleasant lunch in San Francisco. A long car ride, even though she would be distracted by driving, was the safest solution. And although I wished I could tease her thoughts out slowly without her knowing where I was headed, I didn't have that luxury. I launched immediately into a discussion of Silas.

"Silas is in a relationship with Amelia—the girl from Windy Hills Castle," I said.

She accelerated onto the freeway, silent for a moment as she checked her mirrors. "I know who Amelia is."

"She's so young. And very naïve."

"How is that any of your business?"

"He's a predator. And she—"

"You don't know that."

"You don't think he is?"

"I have no idea."

"After your experience ... what do you think he is?"

She changed lanes. "I don't want to talk about him."

"I think you need to. You can't keep pretending it's not happening. Are you just going to live with him holding this thing over your marriage?"

"Until I figure out a way around it, yes."

"But you haven't."

"I will."

"You honestly have no idea what he wants?"

"I said I don't want to talk about it."

"It feels like you haven't told me the entire story."

"I just needed to get it out of my head. I didn't think you'd start talking about it all the time. You're making it worse."

"How?"

"By talking about it."

"How does that make it worse? It's not possible to make it *worse*. I thought you told me because you wanted my help."

The car was going well over the speed limit now. She was changing lanes whenever necessary to keep herself flying faster than the traffic around us. I loved the feeling of the high speed, but the freeway here was well-patrolled. Did she not care about risking a ticket? Maybe her record was pristine and she could afford one black mark. Maybe she wasn't thinking about the risk and she simply needed to speed up to get my nagging voice out of her ears.

"I don't want your help," she said. "There's nothing you can do. I wanted you to listen and be a friend."

"Don't friends help? You said —"

"There's no way to help the situation."

"What is the *situation*?"

"Why are you torturing me like this?"

"I just get the impression I've only heard half the story. You got drunk, you did stuff you shouldn't have, and he threatened to tell Marcus. But he has to want *something*. It makes no sense that he wouldn't tell you what that is. So what is it?"

"I thought we were going out for a nice lunch to talk about my wedding?"

"How can you enjoy lunch, or think about your wedding at all, with this hanging over your head?"

"It's called compartmentalization, Alex. You should try it. Otherwise, you can't accomplish anything in life because your runaway thoughts are in charge of your mental state. I focus on what I can control. And right now, I can't do anything about Silas and what he might be thinking. I have no idea what he's thinking. All I know is what he's said and what he's done so far. Speculating about another person's thoughts is a useless way to spend your time."

I didn't think it was useless at all. She was right that she couldn't know what he was thinking or planning. But speculating was a very good use of time. It allowed you to consider your own choices. "Why won't you tell me what's going on?"

"I have."

"I don't think you have. Because what you told me makes no sense. No one blackmails a person with no purpose. All he's done is threaten you. He absolutely wants something from you. What is it?"

She drove in silence for three miles, finished with her wild lane-changing, before she spoke again. "Why are you so relentless?"

"Because you said you wanted to tell me something awful in your life, but you only told me part of it. And you seemed to want help, but I can't help if I don't know what's going on."

"I never said I wanted your help. And I meant, why are you relentless about *everything*?"

"Why are *you* always changing your mind? No one can say why they're the way they are."

She laughed.

We were approaching the Golden Gate Bridge before she spoke again. "I regret telling you. Before, it almost seemed like it hadn't happened. He threatened to tell Marcus. I begged him to give me some time to work things out, and he hasn't spoken to me about it since. So it's started to feel as if it never happened. As if I imagined it. Especially after I promoted him."

"A brilliant idea of mine," I said.

"A deferment. Which is helpful. But it feels like a horrible dream. When you keep talking about it, the dream becomes real, and it gets worse every time you mention it."

"I'm your dose of reality."

"It's not something I want to make jokes about. So please stop." She sighed. I saw her knuckles grow white as her grip tightened on the steering wheel.

"What he wants is the winery." Her voice was low, heavy with defeat. "He was engaged to the daughter of the former owner. She decided she didn't want to be in the wine business. He told the family they had a *contract*, and it didn't matter if they were getting married or not. They insisted the contract was tied to his future marriage, and it was now void. He threatened to sue them, to make it public, to post pictures and videos of their daughter and him having sex—basically destroying the reputation of Black Mask. Finally, since Rosé wasn't interested in going into the family business and they knew they would probably have to sell eventually anyway, they decided to sell now and move to Italy."

"Silas told you this?"

"Not in that way. I knew part of it when I met the Harpers prior to the sale."

"Why did you keep him on?"

"His employment contract had a clause covering the sale of the winery. I had no choice."

"There's always a choice."

"You don't know what you're talking about. There's not always a choice. Contracts dictate your choices when you own a business, and when you're buying a business."

"A lawyer could have—"

"You don't know what you're talking about, Alex. So stop talking. I told you because I needed someone to know what I was going through. At least I thought I did. I thought it would make me feel better. Now, I'm not sure. But I absolutely do not need ignorant advice."

"I'm not ignorant."

"About this situation, you are."

"Then you have to tell Marcus."

"What I have to do, is think about it without you constantly talking about it and asking about it. Can you do that for me? Can you just be silently supportive?"

I didn't say anything. It seemed as if she was truly handcuffed to Silas, or at least she believed she was. This was the thing about relationships. Why did she want every part of her life connected to a man whom she wasn't sure she trusted enough to stay with her if she revealed every part of her life to him?

"Thank you," she said.

I wasn't supportive, but I could be silent. Apparently, she was happy, at least about that.

CHAPTER 48

*C*onsidering how to kill Silas was unlike any situation I'd encountered before, but I had to get him out of Tess's life. She was clearly incapable of doing it herself. Even if she did find the courage to tell her fiancé what she'd done, she claimed she was still obliged to keep Silas on the payroll. There had to be some kind of limitation to that, but she didn't want to discuss it. No employment contract is for life, unless you work for the Mafia, I suppose. Or you're a member of a royal family or have a seat on the Supreme Court.

Either way, she was facing a man who would likely find a way to harass her on the fringes of the law. A man who would be vindictive in all kinds of petty ways. He was in a position to damage the winery, even if he couldn't take it from her.

And if she didn't tell Marcus, which seemed to be her current trajectory, if for no other reason than she appeared to be immobilized by indecision, then Silas seemed poised to take the thing that made her thrive, the thing she'd poured all her passion and energy into. She would not only lose millions of dollars, she might end up losing Marcus anyway.

How on earth would she explain that to him? Had she even

thought about that? Marcus would think she'd lost her mind. He would never sit by and let her watch an investment of that size dissolve into nothing, so he was sure to find out about Silas, one way or another.

I couldn't understand her thought process.

She was terrified, and it seemed to have made her mind incapable of shaping any rational thoughts about the situation. Her brain had frozen into a block of ice and she simply went through the actions required to keep the rest of her life functioning, labeling it *compartmentalization*.

To me, it looked like self-sabotage.

The thing was, my usual method of eradicating slimy scum from the surface of the planet, leaving the water a crystal clear, sparkling sapphire, was impossible. I had zero anonymity. My relationship with Silas made it impossible to seduce him. He would never believe I was suddenly attracted to him, overcome by the desire to fall into a luxurious bed with him, or even something quick and urgent.

On the long shot that I could make him believe I'd been hiding an attraction, which, given his ego, I might be able to achieve over time, there were other obstacles. And his corpse in a hotel room, even in San Francisco, would raise too many questions. The threads tying him to me were countless and tangled, visible to everyone in Tess's house, to those working at the winery, possibly even to Scott Ruiz, with my urgent, unnatural questions.

I'd set my own trap. I'd painted myself into a corner.

Tess was right about that. I couldn't stop talking, and I'd talked myself into looking like a prominent person of interest, as the police liked to say.

I either needed to find a way to kill Silas that appeared without question to be an accident, or make it look as if he'd taken his own life, also without question.

Living in a rural area, without subways and thousands of anonymous cab and Uber drivers, without the ability to easily walk from a bar to a hotel, slipping unseen into an alley, merging into a crowd of people, none of whom were looking at me, who cared nothing about me or what I was doing, millions of people looking at their phones who wouldn't recognize my face even if I didn't bother to change my hair color, to wear glasses or a hat or eye-catching high heels, made my work close to impossible.

I had some access to Tess's car, but at some point, she would notice. She might notice the additional miles on the odometer, the dip in the gas supply. Even if I was careful to refill it, there were things I couldn't hide from her. The car was hers and she was intimately familiar with every part of it.

Each time I got behind the wheel, I risked doing something that would damage her car, even if it was a tiny scratch. If her car was seen, the license plate would expose the owner.

There were too many details to consider. Even starting to work through the possibilities made the rush of adrenaline into my blood feel like an overload of caffeine that I couldn't manage. My heart pounded and my eyes felt as if my lids were permanently opened wider than they should be.

I would explore the idea of an accident first, but I wondered if I'd been given a cleaner path to the second option. Silas had lost his fiancée. It had only been seven or eight months. Perhaps he could be presented as a corpse with a broken heart. It was possible I could create that illusion. There was no question this would also have its own challenges, so first, I would explore the opportunities for an accident.

There was one thing I was absolutely sure of. I was not going to wait any longer for Tess to work out whatever was going on between her and Marcus that prevented her from telling him she was being blackmailed. I would not wait for her to figure out how to get control of her life. I was not going to continue looking at the smirking, sinister, seducing, predatory face of Silas every single day.

That man needed to be removed from the Black Mask estate.

He needed to be permanently removed from Tess's life, along with his phone and its incriminating photographs.

He needed to be wiped off the face of the earth.

I wasn't sure I had the skills to accomplish everything that needed doing, but it wouldn't stop me from trying.

CHAPTER 49

*H*unter was thrilled that I suggested we go for a romantic drive along the coast, bringing along a picnic lunch. He was looking forward to more conversation. I was looking forward to locating a secluded and treacherous turn in the highway where I might force that cute red mini Cooper and its driver over the side of a cliff.

They were very different objectives, but I was certain we would both enjoy our picnic and the scenery.

I wanted to get a sense of the highway, to experience the shape and feel of the road and its traffic flow, with a mindset of intimidating a car until it drove too close to that spectacular cliff, with its sheer drop hundreds of feet onto the enormous boulders and into the Pacific Ocean below.

My mind was completely devoid of thoughts about how I would entice Silas to take this imagined drive, how I would time it so I might follow him, how I would instill enough fear that he would exceed the speed limit, taking the sharp turns too quickly. All of it seemed like a plan that could happen only in a fantasy, but for now, it was all I had.

In some ways, it was a matter of crossing the first thing off my list. Clearing it from my mind would make way for ideas on how I might execute the next steps.

For so many years now, I'd used a single method in nearly all situations. Unless I was stalking and killing another woman, my techniques hardly varied at all. I wasn't sure whether I liked the challenge and welcomed the change of pace, the freedom from the sameness, or if the idea of something new and unproven was a risk that would take me too far.

I made roast beef sandwiches with lettuce, tomato, and paper-thin slices of red onion. I packed small bags of chips, a container of sliced apples, and a small package of soft cheese as well as one of Tess's fancy cheese spreading knives. She had a nice wicker picnic basket with a leather strap to hold a bottle of wine and space for two wine glasses.

We took a leisurely and peaceful two-hour drive toward the coast. Highway One extends from Southern California, just south of LA, to the redwoods in Mendocino county at the uppermost part of the state. It runs along the coast for most of that distance, occasionally forced inland by the terrain, but most of the time offering incredible views of deep blue stretching to the horizon, waves crashing against boulders and cliffs that curve and jut at impossible angles where the water has made dramatic cuts into rock, leaving impressive formations that are impossible to describe.

The driver loses out, but passengers in a vehicle can enjoy hours of breathtaking beauty.

As we drove, I felt the thrill of places where only a thin metal barrier, only as high as my knees, and often, nothing at all, separated our car from a few feet of ground and the edge of the cliff. A skid of the tires, a wrong turn, Hunter's lack of attention, and we could easily flip over the inadequate barrier, or simply skid sideways and find ourselves flying in a vehicle without wings, falling for a few seconds before we were plunged into chilling water, sinking to the bottom of the sea and a watery death.

The waves would close over us before anyone even saw we were there. No one would find us, nothing would indicate where we'd gone in. Trapped and injured in a tiny enclosed space, unable to escape. If we opened a door, water would rush in, filling the car and our lungs within seconds.

The ends of our lives would be eternal mysteries.

Considering this outcome for Silas Birch occupied me as we drove. It made the deep blue water all that more majestic. It filled my mind and made the sides of the cliffs more treacherous. It kept my body focused on the speed of the car, imagining it accelerating out of control. It prevented me from speaking.

As a result, Hunter's frustration accelerated.

"It feels like you don't want to be here."

"I do."

"You're a million miles away."

I laughed. "I'm right here."

"I asked about your lunch with Tess three minutes ago and you never answered."

"I guess my mind was on something else."

"This was your idea. Where else would your mind be?"

"Just drifting."

"Drifting to what?"

"I'm not sure."

"That's a lie."

His tone was harsh. I was shocked that he was so blunt about calling me out on not telling him what I was thinking. I wondered if it was too late to ease him back to something less ominous than lying. "Not a lie … just not something I can put into words because my mind is all over the place. You know how that is, too many things at once."

"Give it a shot." He didn't sound any more friendly.

"I was wondering if you told Silas you weren't going to take pictures of Tess's files. Then I started wondering what he wanted them for, and then I was thinking about my job and how I need to figure out what I want to do, and then I was thinking about all my jobs and how I've bounced around, and then I was—"

He laughed, although he still sounded annoyed. "Okay, I get it."

We drove in silence around more sharp turns, Hunter carefully managing each one at slightly below the speed limit.

"Did you?" I asked.

"Did I ... ?"

"Did you tell Silas you aren't doing it?"

"I haven't seen him."

I felt the car slow again for a turn that pushed us outward, giving the sensation we were driving straight toward the water. The car slowed further. As a New Yorker, Hunter rarely drove. He didn't own a car, and he hadn't driven on a regular basis since he was in college.

With this thought, I saw the biggest flaw in my plan. I lacked the skill to drive in a way that would force Silas over the cliff into an invisible grave on the ocean floor without risking winding up there myself.

There might be possibilities for an accidental death, but this wasn't one of them. I was annoyed with myself that it had taken me so long to recognize the obvious.

CHAPTER 50

THEN: HUNTER

Zack was in the hospital for three days after his brutal beating. My mom was released the following afternoon, but the psychological effects lingered for a long time, and then sank deeper inside, where I knew they would live forever.

For the first week, the cops answered my daily phone calls, but their responses were so similar, I seriously wondered if they were reading off a script.

We're doing the best we can.

We don't have much to work with.

When we have something to report, we'll be in touch with you.

Eight days after the violent attack, they stopped picking up. Three days after that, they stopped returning my calls.

I knew then what I'd known the night it happened—they believed my brother invited the assault. They were going to put zero effort into identifying those monsters and bringing them to justice.

As I lay awake at night staring at the ceiling, trying not to picture the bruised, swollen face of my brother, or the terror in my mother's eyes, I wondered what would happen if I tried to find them myself. Would they be arrested? The police had the DNA evidence. But how would that work?

If I found them, how would I get disinterested law enforcement to even listen to me, much less go to the thugs' location, and make an arrest? Would they argue that their appearance didn't match closely enough to what we'd described? Would they say they needed probable cause to take DNA from anyone I located? What else was required to make an arrest? If one of them owned the black sedan, they would still be reluctant because the make and model were too common, and due to my *absolute failure*, there was no way, from a police perspective, to ensure it was *the* car.

Did that mean all of this was my fault? There was no justice because I'd cared more about getting the police there in time before they murdered my family in cold blood than I had in stopping to write down the numbers and letters on a license plate, in pausing to peer through a windshield without the help of a streetlight to get a better look at the woman with her hands on the steering wheel?

Were the police really that helpless? Why did we have them if they simply asked questions that disappeared into an unread computer file, collected evidence that sat in a locked cabinet, and refused to even tell me if they had a hate crime database?

I couldn't go on with my normal life, knowing those guys were out there, smiling as they sat around the table eating dinner while my brother felt a residual pain in his gut when he tried to swallow the smallest morsels of food?

It wasn't only his body they'd damaged.

Zack startled every time the bells at the entrance jangled, feeling his nerves do the same. He assessed every person who passed through the doorway into the bookstore, wondering what their mood was, wondering about their intentions. He no longer assumed everyone was an eager customer or a curious browser. He felt he needed to consider every face, imprinting it upon his memory in case this one, too, turned out to be a monster who hated him. He found himself maneuvering every standoffish patron so their face was captured on the new surveillance camera, which he loathed.

My mother worried constantly. She begged Zack to sell the bookstore. She pleaded with me to make him realize the danger. *Those beasts are still out there*, she cried. Despite the new thread of anxiety running just below the surface of his mind, Zack refused.

I felt the opposite. I felt a need to rid the world of these creeps. I felt compelled to do the work of not only the police, but the entire, cumbersome, often ineffective, introspective, over-burdened justice system.

If they were arrested, would a deal be made and they would be let off? If it was a first offense, at least the first for which they'd been arrested, would prosecutors go easy on them? What if a deal was made? What if they had a good reputation in the community? What if a jury pool agreed with their views?

What were the odds that a jury would decide in my brother's favor or theirs? What kind of judge would he get? All of it was a roll of the dice—a great big gamble with your life and your sense of fairness.

And it all took so damn long. It could be years.

If they found them. If they arrested them.

If they even looked for them, which they appeared not to be doing.

In my mind, the police should have gone door-to-door. They should have combed their database for reports of verbal attacks against gay people. They should have asked questions. They should have spoken to people who ran organizations that supported the gay community and asked about anyone who was known to harass their clients.

But they didn't.

So I made my decision. It was my responsibility. I'd never imag-ined myself as a vigilante. I'd never dreamed I had any traits even

THE WOMAN IN THE VINEYARD

THE WOMAN IN THE VINEYARD

close to the kind of person drawn to that behavior. But I'd never imagined myself in a situation where two of the people I loved most in the world had been horribly brutalized. I couldn't sit there and let a crime like this fade into the background of everyone's consciousness.

I couldn't accept that my desire to get the police as quickly as possible, to get them running across the street to pull those ugly hands away from my brother's face, to silence those hate-filled voices, without stopping to write down a license plate number, meant there was no justice.

That wasn't the kind of world I'd imagined I lived in and it wasn't a world I *wanted* to live in.

So I methodically set about looking for them myself. I didn't stop to consider what I would do once I found them. I knew the police wouldn't follow me and make an arrest, so maybe I already knew I was headed down an ever-darkening path, but I didn't consciously think about it. I took it one step at a time, one day at a time.

Using a spreadsheet, the geekiest approach imaginable, I looked up every support service for gay people in the county. I didn't bother with phone calls. This required a personal touch. I laid out a plan for visiting each one, and day by day, I met with directors and staff members, receptionists and group leaders, physicians' assistants and counselors.

I heard stories of vandalism and violence. I received descriptions, sometimes vehicle types, and less often, the names of known antagonists. They freely shared information when they had it, telling me where some of the perpetrators liked to hang out, occasionally where they worked. More often than I'd expected, they told me when a police report had been filed.

Apparently, the police had a robust database, after all. They just didn't utilize it. Or maybe it didn't exist as a database. Maybe all these crimes simply floated untagged within a much larger database of crime and there had been no effort to collect them into a group of actions taken against people solely because of who they were.

It was pathetic. We were well into the twenty-first century. The battle to simply live a normal life, equal to everyone else, was still raging. It wasn't something I'd paid attention to, until now, but it must have been exhausting.

It took me three months of lurking around town, hanging out in bars, following people who showed up at counseling and job support centers for the sole purpose of intimidating or harassing people, usually managing to stay within the confines of the law, but making life miserable for the people they targeted.

Every weekend, I left Manhattan and drove two hours north to spend the weekend with Zack. He thought I was wasting my time. He was mildly concerned my efforts, whatever they were, might bring additional trouble to his store.

"What will you do when you find them?"

"I'm not sure."

But when I saw them, I absolutely knew what I would do.

After that, I began to dial it back with Zack. I stopped staying at his house. I told him he'd been right all along. The police wouldn't arrest them anyway because our descriptions weren't specific enough. There was no point in locating them.

Instead, I booked a room in a motel in the next town over.

I'd found both guys working at a custom tile shop. They were co-owners. A counselor at a job placement center had told me about the guy with the beard. Because of his size and all that solid muscle, because of the larger-than-life beard, the counselor said he sounded familiar. A guy who looked exactly like that had lurked around the placement center for a week. He'd catcalled everyone who came and went, casting out slurs like he was tossing pennies into a fountain. They'd called the police, who came and asked the guy to move on, but he'd returned every day to repeat the same behavior.

The tile shop, the thugs' craftsmanship, almost made it worse, in some ways. They knew from their own experience how Zack must have poured his heart into his own business. They knew what it took, what inventory cost, and how losses devastated a business. Yet they'd gone out of their way to destroy a small business, trying hard to survive and thrive under the watchful eye of a single person who was the visionary, procurement officer, PR, greeter, closer, accountant ... everything imaginable for his small place. Just as they were. They were more like Zack than they were different, but that's not what they saw.

I found them, greeting their customers and discussing tile layout as if they were the nicest guys in the world. Smiling and talking, pretending they hadn't come close to murdering my brother. Acting as if they hadn't had the shameless gall to kick and punch my sixty-year-old mom.

Two guys who vomited whatever was wrong with them—whether it was simple hate, or some deep form of insecurity—all over Zack and some beautiful, unread books, waiting to bring pleasure and knowledge and a few evenings of escape into someone's life.

I began watching them, absolutely certain of what I wanted to do, wondering whether I was capable of doing it.

CHAPTER 51

NOW: ALEX

apa Valley, California

After a luscious picnic without any discussion of what was wrong with me or any talk of how our future was doomed because Hunter was inevitably returning to New York and I was hurtling to nowhere I could define, we drove back along the coast, using the outside lane, which was even more thrilling. Although now there was no purpose to the thrill beyond my own enjoyment.

As we entered downtown Napa, we stopped for a red light. I looked out the side window to see Silas and Amelia sitting at an outdoor table in front of an Italian bistro. They'd pulled one of the chairs around so they were side-by-side, as if they couldn't bear to have the extra space of a table between them for an hour or so. Amelia leaned into him, as if she was famished for the strength of him, clueless to the fact that there was no strength at all to be had in that man.

The server beside their table looked impatient — invisible to their private fantasy world.

Silas flapped his hand at the server. She shoved her pad into her pocket and walked away. He pulled Amelia even closer until she was halfway on his lap. Her hair swept across the table as her back was now toward us. He began kissing her almost violently, oblivious to anyone around them.

The light changed, and we began moving.

I faced forward and closed my eyes. After Amelia had approached me with her awkward questions about running a winery, I'd thought she might consider my warning about Silas. She'd seemed to hesitate, seemed less dismissive than the first time. Or maybe she'd only continued asking questions because the answers were more important to her than her objection to being told what to do.

Either way, she hadn't listened. She seemed to think I could tell her everything about running a winery despite the fact I had the lowest position at Black Mask and clearly knew nothing about the business itself. But she refused to believe I had anything worth listening to regarding the man who was seducing her.

Of course, I would have been the same if someone had warned me about a man when I was her age. But I was also able to identify predatory men myself. Most of the time, I felt it the moment they looked at me, or touched me with a proprietary hand. It was her lack of acceptance of adult input I could identify with. I understood her refusal to listen to me. Absolutely.

But since she wasn't inclined to listen, since she was captivated by that man without any questions regarding what he might want from her and without appearing to have any doubts or questions about a single word that came out of his mouth, maybe she could unwittingly help me be rid of him.

I wasn't sure how, but I was severely restricted and I needed more than my usual resources.

An unquestioning devotee could be helpful. At the same time, I could rescue her once again. This time, she didn't know she needed rescuing. This time, being held captive was her own doing, but she was trapping herself all the same. And he was surely using her for something. Even if it was only sex. But I had a feeling it was more than that. Maybe he wanted more property than just the Black Mask. Maybe he now had his eye on the Windy Hills Castle and its fallow vineyards as well.

He'd lost one wealthy heiress, perhaps he thought he'd found another. Now, it looked as if he might be maneuvering himself into a second marriage scheme and the acquisition of a valuable piece of land.

Opening my eyes, I watched the rows of grapevines slide past the window, the stately wineries at the end of long, straight drives, some marked by rows of palm trees, others by oaks. All of them promising an entrance to a magnificent experience.

It didn't matter what Silas's game was regarding the castle. All that mattered was that Amelia was smitten with him. As long as she was blinded by her lust and longing, she was available for me to use to lure him to a place where I could be rid of him. I just needed to figure out where that was, and how I would do that without Amelia being aware of what was happening.

CHAPTER 52

$\mathcal{F}$inally, I was taking the tour of the winemaking facility that Chuck had been offering since the first time I'd met him, when I'd been far more interested in digging for details about the Windy Hills Castle than learning about the craft my friend had become so passionate about.

I walked slowly along the path that wound its way through gardens and past the swimming pool, leading from Tess's secluded back patio to the winemaking facility. I was in no hurry to be indoors, breathing the overpowering odor of fermented grapes, listening to more detail than I cared to know about how it all came together. It wasn't something the visitors to the tasting room wanted to hear from me. If they were seeking an education in winemaking, they took a tour themselves.

From me, they wanted to know about the varieties, at best. Occasionally, they were interested in hearing about food pairings. Mostly, they wanted to sip wine and learn which offerings fell into their price range, or hear the advantages of joining the club, or simply relax and talk to their friends.

Tess insisted knowing more about how grapes were grown, harvested, and turned into wine would give me more depth and authority. Silas said I wouldn't be taken seriously without that background. Chuck had assumed that anyone associated with a winery at all would have a burning desire to know the secrets of turning small pieces of fruit into delicious and subtly varying alcoholic beverages.

Chuck met me at the open warehouse doors. Before we entered the building, he explained the harvesting process. He talked about rain and sunshine and soil, barrels and grape skins. It was more interesting than I would have thought, but at the same time, I felt the details sliding around in my mind in a way that suggested they wouldn't linger for more than a few days.

I followed him around the warehouse, learning about everything that went into the making of wine. I listened and asked questions. I marveled at the details and the careful execution required. I was truly fascinated by the fact that differences in weather and the timing of when the grapes were plucked off their vines changed the taste of the wine that was ultimately poured into glasses.

In the end, what captured my interest were the vats that held the juice from the grapes while it was fermenting—forty thousand gallon steel tanks. I couldn't imagine how many bottles of wine that might be, but I didn't interrupt Chuck to ask that question. I was mesmerized by those enormous tanks.

They appeared to be formed by a single sheet of steel, curved into a column, welded to the curved bottoms where huge spigots allowed the liquid to be released. High above our heads, accessed by ladders and walkways that ran between the tanks, were covers with openings held in place by huge latches.

I stared at the covers and thought about all the liquid inside those tanks. If a man slipped, or was pushed through the opening while he was inspecting the wine, and the cover re-sealed, he could remain floating in all those gallons of wine for weeks before anyone became aware. Until someone came for a sample taste to assess the fermentation status, no one would know.

Would they notice? Would they simply think the batch had gone bad?

Would the pickled body give off a terrible flavor? *Would* it be pickled? Would it be something akin to embalming, so that decay was halted and there were no ill effects?

Assuming there would absolutely be some kind of horrible, rotten, stomach-churning taste bleeding into the wine, what would they do? They would empty it and write off that batch of wine as a loss. They would rinse and clean the tank. Would they look inside? Or would they assume something had gone wrong with the grapes? How long would it *be* until the body was discovered? Was it possible another forty thousand gallons might begin the fermentation process and then be deemed undrinkable before someone looked inside?

Was wine like acid? Did the body survive intact, or would it be broken down into something unrecognizable?

The possibilities fascinated me. I lost the thread of what Chuck was telling me about bottling and labeling. I lost the thread of everything else he had to say. I nodded and smiled, bobbing my head like one of those bobble-head dolls, making myself look foolish and slightly brainless. But I couldn't do much else because it was impossible to stop thinking about pushing Silas into one of those vats.

From there, my mind wandered to what would be required to lure him up the metal steps onto the platform where access was given to the openings. The skill required to draw him close to one of the vats, to open the top and wrestle him into the opening, seemed out of reach. Someone who didn't want to go inside would be extremely difficult to force through the moderately small opening. But the fantasy wouldn't leave me alone. It was too enticing. It was too perfect. On the surface, it was absolutely clean. No one would guess in a hundred years that I'd had a hand in it.

They would be left wondering how on earth he'd gotten

inside. They would scratch their heads, staring at each other. They would never stop muttering to themselves—*Why was he up there? What was he doing? How did he fall in?*

It would be such perfect justice to think of Silas immersed in wine, his lungs filled with that liquid with which he claimed such expertise. The stuff would fill his pores, stain his skin, and discolor his fingernails. Even the whites of his eyes would turn the color of a light Pinot Noir.

By the time they found him, I might be long gone. They would have no idea when it had happened. There would be nothing to tell them how long he'd been there. Surely, the preservative effects of alcohol would impact what they knew about how long a body had been deceased.

It would be an exquisitely perfect murder.

Except I had no idea how I would lure him up to those platforms twenty feet above the concrete floor. I couldn't imagine how I would release the latches without him asking what I was up to. And the physical maneuvering required to get him into the opening was beyond my ability to manage alone.

The perfect murder would have to remain a fantasy.

The tour ended. I thanked Chuck for an enlightening experience. He looked pleased with himself.

CHAPTER 53

*B*efore I could do anything about Silas, I needed to find a way to make him believe I was no longer his enemy. I wanted him to think I was on his side. Thinking I was on his side, whatever that meant, might be going too far, but I could at least let him think he'd misjudged me as an enemy, if it wasn't too late.

I planned to see him in his office, where he would be the man in charge, and I would be his subordinate. He would be enthroned behind his desk like a member of the ruling class in his plush office, while I would be the guest, asking for time and attention.

Ultimately, his office or his home were the only places I could get him alone. And any death that didn't appear to be an accident, or by his own hand, would potentially turn the spotlight on me.

I wasn't sure Tess could imagine me as a killer. I wasn't sure Scott Ruiz or Chuck, or even Hunter, could think of me that way. It's quite a large step to put that on someone you know, especially a woman. Most people are incapable of doing it.

At the same time, I'd made no secret of how I felt about Silas. Would they wonder? Would they recall the things I'd said about him? What would they report to the police?

Once the police got involved, they might have an entirely

different view. I could work meticulously, I *would* work meticulously to remove every cell of my DNA from the vicinity of Silas's corpse, but in the past, I'd always had anonymity on my side.

I'd never had the police looking specifically at me as someone closely associated with my victims. They'd never collected my DNA. Even though I was a peripheral acquaintance, the location and manner of their deaths had always made the killer appear to be a total stranger.

This would be very different.

The challenge was enormous. But it wasn't impossible. Nothing is impossible.

I walked into the building that housed the offices. The main floor had a central open area filled with plants and comfortable couches. There were several offices where I could hear people talking on the phone, and the voices of three women holding an impromptu meeting. I walked to the staircase leading to the second floor landing. Silas's office occupied the entire second floor. It included a reception area, a spacious office, a bathroom with a shower, a small conference room, and a room set up for VIP wine tastings with a balcony that looked out on the vineyard.

I hadn't told him I was coming, but I knew he was there because his bright red car was parked out front.

No one was seated at the desk in his reception area. He hadn't hired an assistant, preferring to control his schedule himself, which wasn't surprising, given his sneaky nature. It was something I could identify with, which made it easy for me to recognize.

His office door was open. I'd chosen my time carefully—just before the end of the day. He was on the phone, talking about an upcoming wine competition and the entries from Black Mask.

I leaned against the doorframe.

He looked up, frowned slightly, and waved his hand at me to go away.

I smiled and settled myself more firmly against the doorframe, suggesting I was willing to wait as long as necessary.

He flapped his hand at me again. I smiled again.

His voice rose, and he continued talking. He swiveled his chair so his back was to me. After a few minutes, sensing I was still there, he stood and crossed the room. He tried to close the door, but I remained where I was, making it impossible without shoving me out of the way.

After a few more minutes, he said he would call back with the rest of the details. After a clipped *goodbye*, he shoved his phone into his pocket. "You're very rude."

"I didn't mean to be. I wanted to talk to you. I didn't mean to rush you off the phone."

"It was a private call."

"It sounded like business."

"You shouldn't have been listening. It has nothing to do with you."

"I didn't mean to upset you. I came here for the opposite reason, actually. Do you mind if I sit down?"

"Is there a problem?"

"No. I just wanted to talk."

"About what?"

"You and me."

"What about you and me?"

"We need to get along."

"You don't try very hard."

"Neither do you."

"And that was a perfect example of how you don't try. I made a suggestion that would improve things, and you immediately turn it on me."

"Because the first thing you did was blame me."

"You're the one who wants to get along so badly all of a sudden. I'm not that keen on being buddies with the bitch who bit my tongue."

I smiled.

"Is that you trying harder?" he asked.

"It is. And how about this for trying harder. I heard you're interested in some of the contracts related to Black Mask."

To give him credit, his face remained unreadable. He wasn't going to betray Hunter as easily as he believed I just had. "Where did you hear that?"

"Hunter told me."

"What did he say?"

"He mentioned you're interested in the contracts and you asked him to get photographs of them."

"What else did he say?"

"That's all," I said.

"Why would he tell you that? And why are you telling me?" Now he looked nervous. "Tess is your ... are you threatening me?"

"Have I said anything even remotely threatening? Don't be paranoid."

"Then what's this about?"

"You're in a powerful position now. If Tess is withholding important information from you, that's not right. She can be ..." I shrugged, letting him fill in whatever he wanted, leaving myself plenty of room to deny whatever accusation he might throw at me if he ever mentioned this to Tess. It was doubtful he would, but just in case. "I'm happy to help. And I have much better access to her office than Hunter."

He looked at me with great skepticism. "Why would you do that?"

"Because sometimes she's too secretive. And that can cause problems. I also want to see the winery succeed. And I get what an asset you are, even though you pissed me off when you overstepped."

"You were flirting with me."

"I wasn't. You need to read the signs better. But you're young. I'll give you a chance to redeem yourself."

"I don't need redemption," he said.

"You know what I mean."

"I don't know what you mean, and I don't like your tone."

I gave him a soft, meek smile. "A second chance, okay? Let's not argue about every little thing."

"I won't, if you won't."

"How do you know there are contracts? What are you concerned about?" I asked.

"It's important for me to know everything she's committed this company to," he said.

"Absolutely."

"I know because I was ..." He ran his hand through his hair, tugging gently at the strands with his knuckles, as if pulling it taut to trim it with a pair of scissors held in his other hand. "I was involved in a lot of ... there was ..." He let go of his hair, turning slightly to look toward the doors leading onto a small balcony. "How do I know I can trust you? Until ten minutes ago, you hated my guts."

"I never hated your guts. Did I say that?"

"It's been your attitude."

"I didn't like you trying to kiss me."

"You made that clear."

"You can trust me because I'm risking my friendship with Tess by working with you on this."

"That's another question," he said. "I'm still not clear on why you're doing it."

"I think I was clear."

"It's for her own good? How does that benefit you?" he asked.

"I'm trying to help you. I want this place to be successful."

"Why?"

"Because I work here."

"It's not like you get profit sharing," he said.

"How do you know?"

He stared hard at me.

"Anything can happen."

He laughed. "Fine. Cards on the table. I know there are contracts because I was engaged to the daughter of the former owners. This place was supposed to be mine when we were married. But my fiancée decided she didn't want to be a wine-maker, or a fiancée, after all, so they sold it."

"And you had a contract? Why don't you have a copy?"

"It wasn't like that. There were a lot of verbal agreements. An understanding. I want to see what was actually documented."

I couldn't understand why he didn't use his massive leverage to get this information from Tess. I couldn't figure out why he was hesitating. Did he think it wasn't enough? Did he sense she might decide to tell Marcus, and he really didn't have all that much leverage after all?

If there was a contract, or anything that put Tess's right to purchase the winery at risk, would she have kept it? I didn't think so. The winery had belonged to the Harpers, and they'd made a clean sale to Tess. I knew her well enough to be certain that was the case.

Silas was dreaming if he thought there was something in Tess's office that would allow him to assert a right to ownership. He was fantasizing about a promise that had been made and broken and he couldn't let go of his bitterness and disappointment—a piece of gold placed in his palm, then snatched away before he could close his fingers around it.

I stood. "I'll get you photographs of everything that looks relevant."

"Looking forward to it."

I gave him a winning smile, pivoted, and walked out of his office. It had been easier than expected, but it was also likely to be far more difficult than anticipated going forward.

CHAPTER 54

THEN: ALEX

 *ortland, Oregon*

After Harrison eased that second Jell-O shot into my mouth, things unfolded in a fast, but almost dreamlike, state. Or maybe I should say they *unraveled* in a dreamlike state. Because that was the best way I could describe it. I felt as if I was dreaming. I felt as if I was disconnected from myself, talking to myself, as if I were narrating my life.

And that was due to the alcohol.

When I tumbled out of the living room into the hallway with Harrison, half dancing, half simply hanging onto each other, I heard a voice in my mind, like that of an announcer, but also mine, telling me that I was now definitely drunk.

The voice laughed—*Oh, yes, Alexandra. This was what they were saying. You are out of your head. You don't really know what you're doing.*

Then another voice, clearly also mine, said—*I do know what I'm doing, because I know that I'm telling myself I don't know what I'm doing and if I know that I don't know what I'm doing, then doesn't that mean I know what I'm doing?*

And then I giggled.

"Why are you laughing?" Harrison asked. "Are you drunk?"

"I don't know," I said. "I've never been drunk before."

But I did know. I knew why I was laughing. I just didn't want to tell *him*.

The voice said—*You're being an idiot.*

Harrison started kissing me. After a few seconds, he paused. "I like you," he whispered. Then he continued kissing me.

I wasn't sure if I wanted to kiss him. But I wasn't sure how to stop him from kissing me, and I wasn't sure if I should stop him or why he'd started. I wanted to giggle because it seemed like those were a lot of thoughts about kissing when it shouldn't be that complicated. I couldn't really giggle because his mouth was covering mine and his tongue was inside my mouth, so giggling was impossible, actually. Also, why not kiss him? He was cute. It wasn't unenjoyable.

He started walking backwards down the hallway, pulling me with him. I stumbled along, trying to keep myself from sliding onto the floor.

The voice, my voice, said—*He's taking you to one of the bedrooms and that means more than kissing and since you aren't sure you even want to be kissing, you probably better stop.*

I tried pulling my mouth away from his, but he was holding the back of my head. The kiss was kind of nice and I kind of liked him. *Kind of.* I'd had fun talking to him. He was fun to wind up, but I didn't like him in the way that I wanted to be around him a lot. I liked him because it was fun knocking him off his game, saying things he didn't expect.

All these thoughts were making the kiss less fun. My mouth was hurting. His saliva felt kind of icky. It tasted like beer that was too warm. I tried to duck out of his arms, but he pulled me into a room and closed the door.

In the darkness of the room, I felt myself suddenly relax as more alcohol rushed into my bloodstream.

The voice telling me what I was doing said—*Oh, this feels very nice now. This must be the other Jell-O shot. This is nicer than the beer. Another Jell-O might be good. But Tom said no Jell-O shots. Maybe Tom was just being a little mother bird, and he didn't want you to have fun because this feels kinda nice. Fun and nice.*

Harrison's kissing wasn't as hard now, and the saliva wasn't as gooey and all over. Now, I liked it better.

"That's more like it," he said. "You just needed to relax, little girl."

I giggled. "I'm not a little girl."

"Aren't you?"

He started backing up again. A moment later, I felt myself falling.

Then, he was lying on his back on the bed, and I was on top of him.

I tried wriggling off, but he held on tightly. "Where are you going?"

I laughed. "I'm getting up."

"Why?"

I wasn't sure why. It felt good, but I didn't like where it was headed. Was it headed somewhere? I was sure it was, but I couldn't necessarily assume that, could I? From the stories I'd heard, it was definitely headed somewhere.

Making out took place in the other rooms. Bedrooms were for going all the way. And I didn't want to go all the way with this guy. And I didn't want to do it with my head spinning and whirling as it was starting to do. I didn't want to do it with my brain firing questions at me and pointing out what I was doing as if there were two different Alexandra's in there, having a conversation with each other.

Mostly, I didn't want to do it with this guy. He was too full of himself. He was very good looking, and I liked tripping him up, but he didn't make me laugh and he didn't make me curious and he didn't make me want to keep talking to him. Those things made me less than thrilled about having him all over me and inside me.

I wriggled harder.

"You can't go until you answer the question."

"I want to go back to the party."

"Why? I thought we were having fun at our private party?"

"I liked dancing."

"We can dance more. Later."

"I want to dance now."

"The way you dance made me want to do this." He bit my neck.

"Ow."

"It was just a little love bite."

"I don't love you. Let go of me."

"Hey. Calm down."

His words sounded strangely soothing. I should calm down. What was I so annoyed about? I didn't like being bitten, but I didn't have to dance. It felt nice being on top of him. My body was soft and relaxed. I liked the feel of his arms around me.

I wasn't exactly sure what I wanted. I wasn't sure I cared. I wasn't sure what I was thinking. Did it really matter? Did I care? What was wrong with my brain? It felt as if it was slipping sideways. All my thoughts were running over the edge, pooling on the floor. I felt as if I wanted to look over the side of the bed. If I did, would I see my brain in a puddle there?

CHAPTER 55

I laughed. I felt a little dizzy and a little bit like I didn't care what happened next. I wondered where Tom had gone and what he was doing. I wondered if Jennifer and those other girls were still sitting in the chair. I wanted another Jell-O shot. They were really good, and I liked how I was feeling. I liked feeling buzzy and calm and not-caring.

I liked not really thinking about anything much and not having to make a decision about what I was going to do or what I should be doing right this minute. I wondered what Mrs. Baxter was up to and if she'd finished her entire bottle of *medicine*. I laughed. I laughed harder and realized I enjoyed feeling this way, too.

"What's so funny?" Harrison asked.

"Nothing."

"Not me, I hope."

"Not you. I wish I had another Jell-O shot."

"That could be arranged. But if I go get you one, how do I know you'll stay here? You don't seem like a very cooperative girl."

"I'm not." I giggled. "My father thinks I'm very uncooperative."

"Is that right?"

I giggled. I sounded stupid. At the same time, it felt really good. I liked laughing, although I didn't like the giggle because it felt like I was happy to be with him and I still hadn't made up my mind about that. I didn't have anywhere better to be. I'd wanted to come to the party for excitement, to find out what it felt like to be drunk. I was pretty sure I'd found that out. So far, it wasn't all that exciting. Dancing drunk was fun in a different way than dancing sober. But it wasn't necessarily better.

And in some ways, the party was boring. Sitting in the chair, crushed up with Jennifer and the others, had been boring. What *was* Tom doing? Was he just drinking beer and talking to his friends? Had he found a girl? Maybe he had a girlfriend he was meeting here. I didn't even know if he had a girlfriend. He never talked about stuff like that.

"One Jell-O shot, coming up," Harrison said. "But you can't move." He rolled me off him and jumped up. He took two long strides to the door, flung it open, and called out. "Need some shots in here!"

As if there'd been a butler waiting to service the room at a private club, I heard voices. The next thing I knew, before I could think that maybe I should get off the bed, or at least sit up, I heard the door close. I heard the lock click.

Harrison was lying on top of me, holding a cup with Jell-O inside. "Here you go. Open up."

I opened my mouth a tiny bit, and he squeezed the Jell-O inside. As I tasted the strawberry, I wondered why I was doing this. I didn't really know what would happen. I liked not knowing, but I also wondered why Tom had made a big deal out of it. And I wondered whether I was already giggling too much and my brain was already really disconnected from itself and maybe this Jell-O that had just finished sliding down my throat was going to be a little too much.

He was on top of me again, pushing his tongue back into my mouth. And then, his hands were squeezing my breasts.

"Don't do that."

"Why not?"

"Because."

He laughed. "That's not a reason."

"It is."

He ignored me. He slid his hand up my shirt, poking his fingers under my bra. I tried to grab his wrist, but he beat me to it, grabbing mine and pinning it to the bed. He shifted to the side and moved his hand down over my ribs and belly, shoving it behind my waistband. He pulled it out again and started undoing my belt, then unfastening my pants. He yanked them partially down my hips.

I twisted from side to side as much as I could, but I felt like a caterpillar inside a cocoon, with only inches of inside the tight space he'd formed around me, with my head wrapped in long strands of fluffy cotton, my thoughts still speaking to each other as if they were strangers, watching what was happening—furious and upset and shocked all at the same time. Not believing it was real.

It couldn't be real. I came to the party to have fun. To flirt. To dance. To maybe make out with a cute boy. To see what drinking felt like. But not this. I was not going to let this happen to me. I refused. I would kill him before I let this happen to me, no matter how fluffy my head felt and no matter how I wanted to giggle, even when something made no sense.

"Get off me right now."

"Come on. You like me. I could feel it the minute you came looking for beer. Even if you didn't know who I am. But now you do, right?" He laughed and his hand poked deeper into my pants because he hadn't managed to pull them over my hips. "Help me out here."

I put out my tongue.

CATHRYN GRANT

"That's more like it." He brought his mouth close to mine.

I licked his lips and as he moved closer, I bit hard on his upper lip. He howled. He let go of my wrist and placed his hand over his mouth. He yanked the other out of my pants and smacked my cheek. Hard. "You little bitch." He rolled off me.

I rolled the other way, got off the bed, and pulled up my pants. "I told you not to do that." I went out of the room and asked the first person I saw if they knew who Tom Mallory was.

Now, there was only a single voice speaking inside my head. I no longer felt as if I were talking to myself, telling myself what I was doing, and laughing about it. I was ready to go home.

I wouldn't tell Tom what had happened. I would never tell anyone. And I wouldn't tell him about the Jell-O shots.

CHAPTER 56

NOW: HUNTER

*N*apa Valley, *California*

Hunter had managed to avoid Silas for days. Although he was relieved that Alex knew he'd been following her, he was quite sure Silas would not take his failure to get the photographs sitting down. He would still demand the favor, even though he no longer had anything to hold over Hunter's head. The threat was empty and dead now, but Silas would try to find a way to revive it.

He'd decided to spend the day in San Francisco. There were a hundred things he wanted to do and see in that city and he was done with hanging around the house waiting for Alex. Besides, she'd lived in San Francisco long enough, she'd probably done half of them already.

He decided to start with the MOMA. He bought his ticket online and was there when the doors opened. He wandered around the permanent exhibits for most of the morning, went out for lunch at a highly rated Thai place, and returned for the featured exhibit titled, The Intersection of Tech and Art, in the afternoon.

Just as he was about to enter the darkened gallery that promised to *expand his mind with new possibilities*, according to the printed sign at the entrance, he felt a nudge in the small of his back.

He turned and was greeted by the smirking face of Silas. "If you have time to burn looking at art, does that mean you have my pics?"

Hunter stared at the man's face. Silas looked as if they'd casually crossed paths outside the tasting room. He acted as if this were the most natural encounter in the world.

He felt slightly ill, realizing that his own outrageous behavior toward Alex was being inflicted on him. Had the guy put a tracker on Hunter's car, or managed to hack into his phone, or simply followed him all the way from the winery while Hunter had been totally unaware? His hand went instinctively to his pocket, checking that his phone was where it usually was, even though he'd just read his messages twenty minutes ago.

"How did you find me?"

Silas grinned. "Did you do what I asked?"

"How did you know I was here?"

"That's not important. You have a job to do and it's been several days. I'm getting impatient."

"I want to know how you found me here."

"I'm not gonna discuss that. I need to see the pictures."

Hunter took a few steps away from him. "I've decided I don't want to do that. I told Alex about following her, and we're good." He smiled.

"That's it? You break your word that easily?"

"I don't consider it breaking my word. You pressured me into doing it. You blackmailed me into doing it, honestly. And I don't want to."

"You said you would."

"I agreed to do something I didn't want to do because you were going to break my trust. Now, I don't have to trust you. I told her myself. Which I should have done ages ago."

"You still owe me. I kept your secret before. You owe me."

"I don't. You can tell her and she won't care."

"Won't she?"

Hunter grinned. "Not at all."

"Sounds like the relationship has done a one-eighty since you first popped up here."

Hunter shrugged.

"From stalker to knowing her so well, you knew you could tell her you were a stalker, and she'd be cool with it."

"I know her pretty well. Following her was a mistake. It was ..."

"It was what?"

"Not important."

Silas gave him a lazy, knowing smile. "Glad to hear you two are so in sync. You don't see that very often. Lots of couples *think* they know each other. They feel like they have that trust, but they've never had the hard conversations, so it's an illusion. It's sad, but it can be a little funny to watch. They're kind of smug about it. It's good to know you're not like that."

"Not at all. Absolutely not at all," Hunter said.

"So ... you're taking in the art? Scoping out the place for a date that will impress your girl?"

"I'm not scoping out anything. I like art and I'm interested in this exhibition. I'm gonna get going now."

"I should tell you ..." Silas looked past him. His expression went blank for a moment. He seemed to be staring at someone across the room, or maybe thinking of something unrelated to their conversation.

Hunter didn't want to give him the satisfaction, but the words were out before he realized it. "Tell me what?"

"About Alex. The woman you know inside and out. To whom you can confide your darkest secrets."

"I didn't …" He wasn't discussing anything more about Alex with this guy. It was none of his business. He didn't like that he was inserting himself into their relationship, acting as if he knew Alex, taking that superior attitude.

"You should know … she was hitting on me."

Hunter laughed. "No she wasn't."

Silas raised one eyebrow. "She definitely was."

"She wouldn't do that."

Silas laughed, slapping his hand against his thigh. "She absolutely, positively would do that. She's a very flirty girl. You must know that."

"You make her sound like she's thirteen."

"I'm telling you what happened. She came on to me. Very intensely, I should say. She came to my office, uninvited. She wouldn't leave, even though it was clear I was busy. And she was talking, telling me about your relationship, talking about how she felt about things. It was definitely a changed dynamic with her. And then—"

"She wouldn't hit on you. Whatever happened, you misinterpreted it."

"Nope." Silas shook his head. "I misinterpreted nothing." He grinned. He slapped Hunter on the back. "Enjoy the art. If you figure out the intersection of tech and art, I would love to have you enlighten me. But maybe you should skip it and get back to the winery. You need to keep a tighter leash on that girl." With another thump on Hunter's back, he turned and disappeared into the crowd.

Hunter stared after him. The guy was a liar all the way through. There was no way Alex had hit on him. She wouldn't. Not ever.

CHAPTER 57

I was in the yoga room, standing in a tree pose, impressed with myself that I'd held it for nineteen seconds so far, when the door opened. I lost my balance and was forced to put my other foot on the mat.

Hunter stood in the doorway, looking like he'd just seen me standing on my head at the bottom of the swimming pool, instead of in a perfectly natural position—doing a yoga pose on a yoga mat, in a room designed for yoga.

"What's going on?" he asked.

"I'm doing yoga."

"Right."

"How was the MOMA?"

"Great."

"Where did you eat lunch?"

"A Thai place. Have you been talking to Silas?" He closed the door. "I guess you smoothed things out between the two of you?"

"A little. Just trying to have a better working relationship. So things are calm when we have to interact, especially when customers are around."

"I didn't know you had that much interaction."

I wanted to do the tree pose standing on my right leg. I didn't like feeling unbalanced, doing it only on one side. It made me feel as if my body would remain unbalanced, and maybe other things in my life would start losing their balance. It made me feel off, as if something was unfinished or hadn't been done right. It was the same if I did bicep curls. I couldn't do just one arm. I felt twitchy and unfinished until I completed the other side of my body.

I started to move my foot up my leg, directing my gaze above his head, looking at a swirl in the wood on the door. It was difficult with him standing there, and I could feel myself swaying. I returned my foot to the floor.

"Do you?" he asked.

"Enough. We both work here, so we should have a solid, professional relationship. I don't want this to be like my previous situation. And it was headed that way."

"He said you hit on him."

I laughed.

"Did you?"

"Do you believe that? Even for half a second?"

"No."

"Then why are you asking?"

"Because he said it, and I wanted to let you know."

"But you didn't let me know. You asked as if you wanted to know whether I had."

He put his hands in his pockets. "Okay. Sure. He sounded very certain about it."

"He sounds certain about everything. That's meaningless. You know that. Lots of people sound certain." I wondered if he really believed certainty meant something, or there was another concern rattling around his brain.

"I didn't hit on him," I said. "He disgusts me."

"That's what I thought."

"Hold that thought."

He smiled. "Do you want to go out to dinner?"

"Marcus is already—"

"Yeah. Okay. Maybe tomorrow?"

"Maybe."

"Do you want to go to the MOMA on your next day off?"

I thought about the effort required to get Amelia to see Silas for who he was. All the things I still needed to do to be rid of him. This was taking too long. I wanted to be finished. At the same time, maybe it would be better to wait until Hunter went back to New York.

The fewer people asking questions and giving their thoughts about Silas's death, the better. Especially Hunter. As I looked at his curious face right now, I knew it would be better to answer his questions from a distance.

But I didn't want to wait. I was impatient to get Silas out of Tess's life, out of my life, out of Amelia's life, out of the life of every woman he might encounter in the future. But somehow, I needed to find a thin scrap of patience buried inside myself. I needed to dig it up and hold on to it tightly.

This required so much planning and finesse. I couldn't afford the tiniest mistake. "Sure. Let's go to the MOMA."

"I don't want to force you."

"You're not."

"You don't sound very enthusiastic."

"I think I do. Besides, does that matter? I said *yes*. Isn't saying *yes* enough?"

He looked as if it wasn't even close to enough, but he didn't say that. He gave me a grim smile. "I'll let you get back to your yoga."

"Thank you."

When the door was closed, I did a perfect tree pose for exactly nineteen seconds. I felt sublimely balanced as I lowered my left foot to the floor.

CHAPTER 58

THEN: HUNTER

Five weekends of Hunter's life were consumed with watching the creeps laugh and run their business without worrying or looking over their shoulder a single time. Resentment and rage crawled through his belly until it growled as if he hadn't eaten in days.

What right did they have to carry on with their lives, to run a thriving business when they'd been able to damage his brother's in such a sick manner, walking away without even a slap on the hand? The police didn't want to be bothered. Those fucking assholes seemed to know that.

They could do it again, and they would probably get away with it again.

Nothing about their demeanor suggested they carried a shred of guilt or remorse. Had they once asked themselves if they shouldn't have beaten his brother, punched and kicked his *mother*? What kind of men were they? They weren't men. Not by his standards.

If he'd gone into their shop looking to have his kitchen floor re-tiled, he would have thought they were great guys. Talented guys.

How could they be such a complete contradiction? So filled with vile hatred one night, then living such outwardly decent lives every other day? It made his head ache and the rage fester. It made him want to throw open the car door, charge across the street, and beat them up as badly as they had his brother, not stopping until his fists were bloody, ragged stumps.

But he knew, looking at them, he didn't stand a chance. Even taking on one of them wasn't a sure thing. Especially the big guy. There was no way.

So he watched, and pressed his fist into his gut, trying to get it to stop grinding and churning with bile. He watched, hating their customers for no rational reason whatsoever. He hated them for their blindness and ignorance, even though they couldn't possibly know. Or could they? Did those violent creeps ever make comments in casual conversations? Comments that were over-looked, or worse, silently agreed with by their customers?

Hunter carried on vicious conversations of his own inside his head, telling each customer who they were doing business with, telling them how despicable they were for supporting that tile company, for letting their money go to people who were violent thugs—people who pissed, literally, on something as beautiful and valuable as books.

When the tile store closed for the evening, he carefully pulled out of his parking space and followed them home. First, he followed the bearded guy.

He lived in a nice house. Very nice. It was a cottage that looked as if it had been built at the turn of the twentieth century, but expertly refurbished into a modern home. He'd added a two-car garage that fit with the design. A wide porch spanned the front. When he went inside, the lights came on and the curtains closed, making it appear cozy and comfortable. A blissful American home populated by a law-abiding family. Hunter assumed there was a family inside. A minivan was visible when the garage opened so the monster could drive his truck inside.

The next weekend, Hunter followed the other guy. He lived in a condo. It wasn't as warm and inviting and all-American, but it was nice. It was well-landscaped, sleek, and modern.

Neither of them seemed to live like the cretins they were.

Did they make a habit of terrorizing and beating up gay people, or had his brother been the first? The people Hunter had spoken to said they verbally harassed their clients and customers, but had they ever done anything like what they'd done to Zack? It seemed as if he might have been the first.

Maybe this escalation of their hatred had gotten into their blood. They'd enjoyed it and were planning more. Maybe they were excited they'd gotten away with it and couldn't wait for another opportunity, salivating at the thought of slamming their fists into bone and flesh, watching it split apart, licking their lips as blood spilled out.

Hunter had decided the bearded one's house was the best place for what he was planning.

And what *was* he planning? It was coiled at the back of his brain like a snake, sure of itself, ready to slither out and devour everything in its path. At the same time, it lay there with its eyes closed, not entirely sure what was coming.

There was only one solution. After weeks of brooding, he'd come to realize it was the only solution that would satisfy him and deliver justice. It wasn't one that Zack or his mother would ever approve of, or one that he'd ever dreamed he might be capable of. It wasn't something that had ever entered his thoughts until now. But it was the only outcome that would allow him to sleep at night as he'd done before he'd seen his brother lying help-lessly on the floor with his blood smeared across his face, his limbs useless, his well-curated bookstore smelling like piss. It was the only one that would settle Hunter's stomach and cut that snake out of his brain.

The third week he watched them, the wiry guy followed the bearded one to his house, and they sat on the front porch and drank beer until after midnight. They'd stopped on the way to pick up two pizzas, which they devoured with bared teeth, tearing it in big mouthfuls, yucking and talking and looking more like he remembered them that night.

He bought a gun. It took a while for the paperwork, but he spent the intervening weeks productively — continuing to watch, working out that it was the last Saturday of the month when they got together for pizza and beer on the front porch.

Even as the weather grew colder, the routine remained the same. Last Saturday. Close the shop at five. Stop for pizza. Drive to the bearded one's house. Plop down on the porch and never move except when one of them walked down the steps and over to a pine tree to piss in the front yard. Nice.

CHAPTER 59

NOW: ALEX

*N*apa Valley, California

Amelia was thrilled when I told her I wanted a tour of her castle.

"Are you and Hunter thinking of—"

"Oh, absolutely not. It's just such a gorgeous building." I smiled. "It's unique, and the towers are absolutely fascinating."

"I'm sorry to hear you and Hunter aren't—"

"We're good." I gave her a contented smile.

"But you must—"

"Everything is perfect the way it is."

She nodded. "I suppose not everyone believes in fairytales."

"They aren't real." She should have known that better than anyone. This was part of what made it confusing that she seemed look at Silas with the eyes of a girl smitten by fairytales. Maybe first love, or rather first lust, conjured up fairytales no matter what — the powerful pull of a man who claimed to desire her, eliciting an instinctive response that's rooted in the subconscious.

"I know that. But they're still fun to think about." She smiled.

"I'd love to show you the castle. Maybe it will make you realize you want a fairytale after all."

"It would be great to see the towers. Tess was considering it for her wedding, before the fire."

"Oh! I didn't know that."

"So I've already seen parts of it because I was there for her cake tasting. But I only saw the grand hall and a few other rooms on the ground floor."

"That's nothing."

"That's what I thought."

She told me she would be happy to take me there that afternoon after her meeting with Silas.

"Meeting?"

"We've talked a little about the viability of turning it back into a winery, like I was telling you."

"That's a huge learning curve."

She nodded. "But he knows everything about running a winery. He might be able to work out an arrangement where he can act as the general manager while I get up to speed."

I bit down on my tongue so I wouldn't laugh. "Interesting. Well, text me when you're finished." I went into the tasting room and tried to busy myself getting organized for a tasting scheduled in ten minutes. It was impossible to focus. All I could think about was how quickly Silas had moved, and how ludicrous it was that he knew *everything* about running a winery. He knew absolutely nothing about the growing and harvesting side of things.

Only a few days ago, he'd been acting like her lover. Less than a week ago, she'd asked *me* about running a winery. Now, she was having meetings with him about turning Windy Hills back into a winery? It wasn't simply a matter of planting a few vines and opening a tasting room.

I was quite sure it took years to get the soil in the right condition and the vines established. Not to mention developing a signature wine. That was the impression I'd had half-listening to

Chuck's enthusiastic lecture about the science and art and crafts-manship of winemaking.

The scheduled tasting was unremarkable—three couples who kept themselves entertained with a non-stop flow of loud conversation and laughter. They hardly paid attention to my descriptions of the wines. They barely noticed which variety they were sipping. They asked for a second taste of some, which I honored, because one couple had immediately signed up for the club.

In the end, they stopped talking long enough for me to sell club memberships to the other two couples. I was proud of my club sales record. Tess was thrilled with how often I was able to get people signed up, and even Silas had noted my ratio was above the norm. He didn't mention the norm or tell me how far above I was.

When they were finished, I washed the glasses as quickly as I could, expecting Amelia to walk through the door at any moment. By five-thirty, she still hadn't appeared. I'd hoped to see the castle while it was still dusk, hoped to look out the tower windows and see the valley stretched out around me, watching the hawks drifting on the breeze.

At this rate, by the time we reached the castle doors, it would be fully dark. I wondered if I should reschedule. I also wondered what she and Silas could possibly be talking about for going on three hours. Was she seriously headed toward starting a winery on her own? She was nineteen years old. She'd lived in captivity until just a few months earlier. She had no vineyard, no staff, no business experience at all.

Clearly, Silas had something in mind. Possibly, he was convincing her she was ready for all that, while he was planning to move in to rescue her when she quickly faced disaster. Was she so naïve she believed she, with only some gentle guidance from Silas, could face an undertaking like that?

The tasting room door opened, and Amelia stepped inside. The light above the doorway made her long red hair glow. She wore a light brown dress, brown leggings, and dark brown leather boots. She looked like she was headed out to ride a horse. I could picture her on the back of one, galloping across her property, her hair flying behind her. She looked as if she'd stepped out of a broken fairy tale. She did not look like the owner of a winery. She looked frail and almost helpless.

Was there any way I could get her to recognize who Silas truly was? I needed her to see him clearly without shoving it in her face. I needed her to cut him out of her life of her own volition. And I needed her to do it fairly soon.

If she caught him with another woman, would that be enough? Or would it be more powerful if she realized he wanted her castle, not her? That he desired the land she owned, and she was simply the key to acquiring everything he'd been waiting for? That he was doing what he'd tried, and failed, to do with the Black Mask Winery?

If she found out about Rosé, would she recognize the parallels?

CHAPTER 60

$\mathcal{I}$t was dusk by the time I climbed into Amelia's car and we drove out of the Black Mask property, headed toward the castle. The only view I would see from the towers would be scattered lights from the vineyards and wineries surrounding it, and from the town of Napa. But at the same time, it might be eerie fun to wander around inside the darkened, echoing castle after dark. I could have rescheduled, but part of my purpose was to get closer to Amelia. Canceling didn't seem like the right move.

When we arrived, she led me through the enormous main doors, past the gargoyle in the entryway, and into the grand hall. It was exactly as I remembered. The only difference was that the small metal trees that had been placed around the hall when we'd done the cake tasting were scattered about now, as if she wanted the interior to mimic a garden, instead of showing guests a bare, cavernous room and leaving brides to imagine the place transformed into a lavish setting for a banquet and dancing.

She gave me a tour of the first-floor rooms I'd already seen, including leading me down the torch-lit tunnels leading to the main entrances to the towers.

"Since you mentioned them, I assumed you want to see the towers first, before the second and third floor bedrooms and living areas?"

"Yes, please."

She laughed. She began climbing the curving staircase into the first of the two towers.

"Do you want to see all the rooms on the way up?"

"Absolutely."

"Just a warning—they aren't that exciting. The only thing unique about them is that they're round, and they have better-than-average views."

We'd already passed the room on the first story, which had been made into sleek, modern office space. We paused now outside the doorway to the room that occupied the second floor of the tower. "This tower used to belong to my mother … and uncle. But I'm slowly transforming it into something entirely different. They used a lot of it as office space, and I'll do the same, but I'm changing the feel of it. This is where all the wedding planning takes place. There's a staff of three that works here."

I glanced at the desks and arrangements of chairs. She was right—aside from the curved walls, it hardly felt like we were inside a tower. We continued our climb, pausing to look at a library, a sitting room, and finally, a room that had been stripped bare, waiting for its transformation.

"I changed what was on each floor. I didn't want it to be anything like when they were here. This is the tower where I found my father's ashes. They'd murdered him." Her eyes were glassy but focused, her gaze holding mine for several long seconds.

The best part of the tower, as I'd always imagined, was the stone staircase that wound from the ground floor to the peak. Climbing the stairs of the second tower, running my fingertips over the smooth stones that formed the curved wall, immersed in the shadowy light of flickering torches, was as magnificent as I'd thought it would be.

At the top of the second tower, where Amelia had her living quarters, was a luxurious sitting room. The walls were hung with photographs of horses, some showing Amelia as a child on the back of a horse. There were curved couches, several low tables, and a sleek TV mounted to brackets that had been specially designed to attach to the curved stone wall.

We went to the window, and I looked out. A breathtaking array of lights sparkled across the valley. I would have liked to sit by the low window with my feet in Hunter's lap, gazing out and dreaming about possessing a hilltop castle of my own. Or simply drinking in the lights, feeling the warmth and pressure of his body against mine, surrounded by quiet and darkness and the unbroken circling stone walls of the castle tower.

"Silas thinks it will be a fabulous draw to hold tastings for private parties up here. We could charge a premium. Because of the view."

"We?"

"He and I will be working on it together."

"It sounds like your plans are really coming along."

"I'm so excited. The weddings are fine, but it makes me feel as if I'm re-living my mother's life. And after what she did to me, locking me up, I don't want my life to be anything like hers." She looked away, then spoke softly. "Silas has helped me see that she was mentally ill,"

I nodded. I continued gazing out at the valley, wondering how I could make her see past the glittering lights and sparkle in Silas's words. She thought he was something fabulous himself, a man who had swept her off her feet and made her believe he was her prince charming.

It was astounding to me that she could be so eager to cut herself free from the past, so definite that she wanted to live a different kind of life, but at the same time, so blindly eager to lock herself into another person who clearly wanted to control her life and take possession of her.

I wasn't even sure he even wanted her. At least her mother had that in mind. In Ella's own sick way, she loved her daughter and had wanted to keep her close. She'd had the deluded vision of somehow protecting her from ever being hurt or damaged in any way.

But that wasn't the case with Silas. I would put money on it.

"What other plans does he have?" I asked.

As if she'd been waiting to tell me since the moment we'd passed by the ever-vigilant gargoyle, the words gushed out of her mouth, telling me his plans for the towers, the grand hall, the planting of the vines, the varieties, the amount of grapes they needed to procure from other wineries. They could expedite the opening by starting with the bulk of their grapes purchased elsewhere, taking time to nurture their own crops. She told me how the bottling facility would be built, but even the bottling could be done elsewhere at the start.

"Is he thinking he can use The Black Mask facility?"

"I'm not sure, but he has it all worked out. He said the Windy Hills Castle is one of the premier properties in Napa Valley and—"

"It sounds like he wants the castle more than he wants you."

She looked both hurt and angry. "That's not true, and it's really cruel. Why would you say that?"

"I just think you should be careful. You're young. You haven't had a lot of experience, and—"

"That's why he's *helping* me. He can advise me on everything. And since we're in love, we're in this together. We're building something *together*."

I nodded. "You fell in love very fast. But not all princes are charming." I gave her the warmest smile I could manage.

The look she returned was cold.

"Didn't your mother read you the story of the Wicked Prince?"

"No."

"Not all fairytales, not all stories are happy. You must know that. The wicked prince acquired all his power by conquering and pillaging the neighboring towns."

"It's a story." Her voice was hard and clipped.

"That's true." I turned back to the window. "The Wicked Prince was eventually driven mad. But I was just reminded of it—"

"Silas isn't at all like that. It's just a story."

"You don't need to tell him I said so. But it's something to think about. You know better than anyone that sometimes love has a dark side. Your mother loved you more than life."

Amelia didn't say anything else. A moment later, she was turning off the lamps and starting down the staircase. I followed, strangely dissatisfied with the time I'd spent in the tower. I'd expected more, but I wasn't sure what.

CHAPTER 61

melia didn't speak to me during our drive back to Black Mask. Although she seemed chilly, I crossed my fingers that her lack of conversation was a good thing. It could mean she was thinking about Silas, considering what he wanted from her. She might be comparing him and his control over her life to her mother's. Maybe she was thinking about my mention of The Wicked Prince fairytale.

I told her goodnight in the warmest possible tone. I thanked her for the tour and complimented the work she'd done to restore the castle after the fire. She thanked me without much enthusiasm. She said nothing more about her plans for a winery or the help she would get from Silas.

All I could do was hope for her cooperation in the elaborate plan unfolding in my mind. It was a plan in which she played a key role. I could probably make it work without her active participation, but having her play her part would be much more effective.

Still, I wouldn't coerce ... not yet.

I went inside and found Hunter talking to Damien. Hunter

looked relaxed and calm, as if he had nothing better to do than wait there for me, but Damien seemed agitated.

Chardonnay time! Chardonnay time! Watch out. Watch out. Watch out!

I wondered if Hunter had been chatting to him the way I often did. I wondered if Hunter had told him any secrets that I might be interested in knowing.

"Hi." Hunter kissed me lightly on the lips. "Where'd you go?"

"I had a VIP tasting. At someone's home."

"You weren't gone very long." He eyed my jeans and top with criss-crossed spaghetti straps on the back. "You don't seem very dressed up."

I shrugged. "It was private. Private doesn't always mean black tie."

"I guess not. You were gone for less than two hours."

"I'm hungry. Should we go out?"

"You didn't eat there?"

"No. I never eat when I'm working. And I'm famished."

"Sure. Where should we go?"

"Chinese?"

"Let me get my keys." He ran up the stairs two at a time. When he returned, we went out the front door together, but the minute it closed behind us, he moved ahead of me, turned, and stopped. "So why was this tasting so short?"

"It just was. They only tasted three varieties."

"Seems strange, to go to all that trouble for a private event and make it so short."

"They had other things going." I started toward the car and he followed. He opened the door for me and I climbed in, wishing he had a convertible so we could put the roof down and cut off this conversation with a blast of cold air.

"What else did they have going on?" he asked.

"A big dinner."

"What was the group?"

"Why so many questions?"

He started the car.

"I definitely want pot stickers, but I'm also craving wonton soup. Do you think that's too much?"

"You're definitely changing the subject. I didn't even know you had a private tasting. And it's strange that it lasted less than two hours. Where did you go? Really?"

"Why don't you believe me?"

"You never mentioned it."

"Do you tell me every little detail of your job?"

"No, but you're not sitting in my office watching me work."

"Neither are you."

"I might as well be. You're living at the winery. I walk past the tasting room every time I go out. I can see it when I'm headed toward the pool or going for a hike."

"I still don't mention every single thing I'm doing."

"I thought you would have said something about this. Since it's not typical."

I turned to look out the window. "This is getting boring. Why don't we talk about what we want to order?"

He punched the gas, accelerating onto the highway. It felt good to be going fast, and I leaned back in my seat.

"We can talk about whatever you want, Alex. I just think it's really weird that you went out in jeans and a T-shirt to a private tasting you never mentioned. It sounds … off."

I laughed. "How can it *sound off*? It's what happened."

"If you say so."

"I do."

We drove in silence to the restaurant. Hunter parked, and we went inside. We were seated, handed our menus, and he remained silent. He didn't believe me.

Had my lie been that transparent? Was this all about my *clothes*? He might not have been bothered by the brief timeline if I'd dressed up, but there was no way to sell him on the idea of a private tasting, no matter how much I talked about casual events and not everything being black tie. Jeans and a T-shirt were a very long way from black tie. He knew I wouldn't have worn these clothes to a tasting of any kind. But it was the lie I'd chosen, and I was stuck with it now. I would have to repeat it for the rest of the evening, knowing he saw through it.

We ordered our food—both pot stickers and wonton soup, as well as all the other things we loved—ending up with more than we could possibly eat. We paired it with a bottle of Zinfandel.

We sipped and talked. We ate the pot stickers dipped in soy sauce and chili oil. They were divine, as was the soup. We devoured savory and spicy and sweet and salty foods until both our bellies were completely satisfied, although I could see on Hunter's face that in his mind, he was not at all satisfied.

We finished our wine and talked about other things.

The lie sat in the middle of the table, like a puddle of chili oil, impossible to clean up easily. It gnawed at me, and I could see it eating at Hunter too.

CHAPTER 62

THEN: ALEX

 *ortland, Oregon*

After those endless minutes I'd spent trapped beneath Harrison Andrews and his probing fingers, I had a single-minded focus. I would find a way to pay him back for what he'd done.

He hadn't hurt me physically. He hadn't accomplished his objective. A lot of people might have said he didn't deserve payback because nothing *that bad* had happened. I had no bruises. My body was still my own. But was it? Maybe he hadn't put anything unwanted inside me, but he'd put his hands where I didn't want them, grabbed me and squeezed me and tried to remove my clothes as if they belonged to him.

He'd tried to steal my self-respect.

Worst of all, he believed he had the right. He assumed he had the right. He thought a few dances and a couple shakes of my hips, some laughs and some kisses, meant I was offering myself up to him. In his calcified brain, he *knew* he had the right.

He didn't bother to ask if that was what it meant. He didn't bother to ask anything at all. And when I told him to back off, he rushed forward. I wasn't a football field. Maybe that was all he knew. Rush toward the goal, pummeling every object in sight until he got there, triumphant, spiking the ball and prancing around in a victory dance.

He was going to pay.

But making a football player pay is not easy. Everyone worshiped the guy, as I discovered the following Monday. No wonder he'd been shocked that I didn't know who he was, insulted and unable to believe I could be so clueless. He was the star. To hear him talk, the school revolved around him, his skill, and his wins.

No one would be on my side in trying to deliver payback. I was on my own. And that narrowed my options. I doubted there was anything I could do to him on the football field itself, in front of hundreds of fans. Even afternoon practice was probably a non-starter. Trying to get into the locker room wouldn't work—there were too many people.

He drove a classic Mustang—black with orange stripes. I considered letting the air out of his tires, but that was a minor inconvenience and easily fixed. I could puncture a tire, but I might be caught and the punishment would fall right back on me.

For nearly two weeks, I considered my options as I walked to school each morning. Because I was so fixated on public humiliation, I couldn't find a suitable solution to my problem. I wanted to yank his pants down in the school quad at lunchtime. I wanted to stretch a wire across the hallway and watch him trip and fall on his face. I wanted to leave something disgusting on his chair and laugh as he sat on it.

But each of those punishments would expose me, leaving me open to attack by a squad of six-foot-two-inch guys and a flock of cheerleaders defending their hero. Their retaliation would be far worse. Some of those ideas risked inflicting punishment on the wrong people. He would walk free. He might even be the one to laugh and mock the unfortunate person caught in my trap.

And even if those things did happen to him, he was so golden. Would they even affect him the way they did others? An average high school kid who tripped and fell would feel embarrassed and awkward. But Harrison might turn it into a moment in which he could leap to his feet and mime a spectacular football play.

Finally, the perfect idea came to me while I was talking to Jennifer about the party. Even though it had now been weeks ago, it was the first I'd spoken to her.

"How did you like it?" she asked. "You never came back after that beer."

"I was dancing."

"By yourself?"

"No. With a bunch of people."

"What people?"

I wondered if I should tell her. If my name became linked to his, whatever I did to him would point to me. But not if I didn't tell her everything. Dancing was just dancing.

"A few football players. Harrison Andrews and ..." I didn't know the name of a single other football player. I should have thought through the details of my lie before I started spinning it out to her.

"Oh. He's kind of ..." She rolled her eyes.

"Kind of what?"

"Well, handsy."

"Oh. We mostly just danced."

"Mostly?"

"We kissed some. But mostly danced."

"I'm glad he didn't get all ..." She grabbed her breasts, laughing. "He can be that way. And he doesn't listen to *no*. So full of himself. And kind of dumb. If he doesn't get his English grade out of the toilet, he can't play next quarter. If he's out of the playoffs, that'll really screw us."

"Might not get to play football at all?"

"Nope. He's failing. Literally. F average. Who gets an F average?" She cackled as if she'd told a joke. "If he can't get it up to a D, he's off the team for the quarter."

"I didn't know that was a rule."

"You can't just show up to play football. You have to at least *pass* your classes." She cackled again.

I laughed too, thrilled with my sudden idea. All I had to do was get my hands on one of his homework assignments. If he already had a failing grade, it wouldn't take much to sink him completely. I couldn't have cared less about our school's chances in the playoff games.

For the next few days, I followed Harrison to all his classes. I learned he had English right after lunch.

From there, I began sitting where I could see them in the quad, watching him with his friends, eating their lunches and laughing, throwing wadded up wrappers from burgers they bought at the fast food place across the street. They tossed fries in the air and tried to catch them in their open mouths, missing more than half the time. They left the fries on the ground where the crows flocked in to gobble them up, cawing and calling to invite other crows so that the quad was sometimes overrun with large jet, black birds, flying at other kids trying to eat their lunches while fighting off hungry, aggressive birds with sharp, shiny black beaks.

Harrison never had his backpack with him, so I assumed his homework assignments were in his locker.

He'd had at least as much to drink as I had at that party. Was it possible he didn't really remember the details of what had happened between us? Was it possible I could become friendly with him, getting close enough to see his locker combination?

CHAPTER 63

It was worth a try. Harrison was so impressed with his own charm and popularity, he wasn't likely to notice someone quietly noticing his combination as he twirled the dial. Especially a smiling, admiring girl.

When the first bell rang, announcing the end of lunch, all the football players remained on the benches in their territory at the center of the quad. The other kids began packing up, headed toward lockers and classrooms. Finally, moments before the second bell, the players lumbered to their feet and began strolling toward the main building.

I followed and came up alongside Harrison.

"Hi. Remember me?"

He snorted.

"That's not very friendly," I said.

"Neither were you."

I laughed. "I was, but you got kind of grabby with me, for someone you'd just met." I gave him a flirty, friendly, submissive smile.

"I don't think I was."

"I don't even know you." I slapped his arm playfully.

"Oh yeah?" He grabbed my wrist.

I giggled.

He tugged me after him and I stumbled along into the building. He didn't let go until he came to his locker. He spun the dial, then turned it slowly to the first number. I watched, pretending I was gazing up at his face with a look of pure lust, while he worked through all three numbers in the combination.

After he grabbed his books and folders, he slammed the locker. "Where are you headed?"

"Trig."

"Oh, a brainy girl."

I smiled.

"You should come to the game Friday night."

"I should." I grinned.

"See you there." He reached over to pinch my cheek, but I managed to be just out of reach. He looked annoyed.

"Bye!" I gave him a little wave and turned around.

The next day, I cut my English class right before lunch. I would get detention, but it was so very worth it. Absolutely worth it. An investment was how I looked at it.

I went to Harrison's locker, opened it, and took out all his folders. Rather than standing in the empty corridor where I might be noticed and questioned by a teacher with a free period, I took the folders to the girls' bathroom and into a stall. Perched on the edge of the toilet, I went through them. The folder labeled English had two essays inside. One was marked with red pen and included a note that it needed to be rewritten according to the corrections. I took that. The other looked like a half-finished essay.

It seemed risky and over-the-top to take both. It might be obvious that someone had been messing around in there. One missing essay he would blame on himself for losing. Two looked like sabotage, although given his level of intelligence, he would have a hard time figuring out how on earth his folder had been sabotaged inside a locked metal cabinet.

I folded the essay that was due for a rewrite and shoved it inside my shirt. Then, because I just couldn't leave it at that, I took the last page of the half-finished essay, tore it into tiny pieces, dropped them into the toilet, and flushed it.

I closed the folder and left the bathroom.

The hallway and locker banks were still deserted. I'd wondered if someone would be out looking for kids cutting class. By this time, my absence would have been reported. On any given day, there were always a few cuts, although most of them hung out near the football field, or in a grove of trees where kids sometimes tried to get away with smoking weed on rainy days when teachers and other school staff didn't feel like going out there to check.

I went to Harrison's locker, opened it, placed the folders exactly as they had been, closed it quietly, and walked quickly past the row of lockers and around two sections to where my locker was located.

I opened it, pulled the essay out of my shirt, and tucked it into the back of my own English folder.

After school, I took a longer route home. I stopped in front of a taco stand where I sat on the curb and tore the essay into long strips, then tore those into smaller pieces. I put all of them into a brown paper bag that I'd found blowing across the quad after lunch. I crumpled the bag and tossed it into the dumpster behind the taco stand.

Walking home, I heard crows cawing in the pine trees at the edge of the park. Their cries sounded victorious. I smiled all the way home.

CHAPTER 64

THEN: HUNTER

*H*unter decided he was never going to get up his nerve unless he settled on a date and made it just that—a date. Otherwise, he would sit in a rental car every weekend for the rest of his life, watching them conduct business, following them home, and once a month, watching them drink beer and chow down pizza on the front porch.

Those two guys needed to be wiped off the face of the earth.

If law enforcement would not do their part to start the wheels of justice turning, then he would have to do it himself. There was no other option. It was settled. He'd had countless hours to think it through, and he was certain he was doing the right thing.

People couldn't be allowed to brutalize other human beings simply because they didn't like the way they lived. If they were, the human race hadn't evolved at all. Millenia of evolutionary social change might as well be wiped from history as cleanly as a computer hard drive was wiped clean—the story of humanity reduced to a blinking cursor on a blank screen. After centuries of progress, decades of change, this was where they were?

He did see the hypocrisy in the fact that he was choosing death as his solution. He definitely saw that. He felt it in the marrow of his bones. But he didn't call it anything except righteous death. It wasn't murder by any stretch.

Those two deserved to rot in prison—literally. They could not be allowed to do the same thing again, or something worse. And he had no doubt, despite the sunny, upstanding life they presented to the community surrounding them, that they were capable of much worse. Once someone crossed that line into violence, they only went deeper.

And that did give him concerns about himself. Who would he become after he was finished?

But he couldn't think about that. He had a job to do. He had to seek vengeance for his brother, for his right to live a life free from harassment and intimidation and violence, especially violence. To run his business and be the person he was born to be. Hunter felt he'd failed as a brother, and even more, as a son, if he didn't punish these monsters for what they'd done to his family, for the peace of mind they'd stolen that might never be recovered.

So he made a date with his destiny as a killer.

November 27. The creeps would be having their monthly beer night. He trusted it would be the same even though it was Thanksgiving weekend. Their store was only closed for the Thursday holiday itself, so there was no reason to expect they wouldn't continue their same habits.

A snowstorm was forecast for Friday, and he thought heavy snowdrifts would provide assistance in keeping them from moving too quickly. On the horrible chance Hunter missed one of his shots, their escape would be slowed.

His plan was to create a disturbance by the pine tree they used as a public urinal. He would lure them both off the porch, shoot them, and be on his way. It sounded simple enough when he rehearsed it in his mind. But it was the most difficult challenge, filled with potential missteps, he'd ever faced.

The biggest weakness in his plan was ensuring they both came off the porch to check out the issue. For this reason, he needed a disturbance that was more than something that sounded like a squirrel running through the underbrush.

He'd purchased a few fireworks that shot out a spray of colored sparks. In the darkest hours of the night, with heavy snow on the ground, he was certain this would startle them enough that both men would come barreling out into the snowdrifts to see what was going on.

He'd taken lessons and spent time at a shooting range in the city. He was well-prepared in every way he could think of. The only weak spot was getting them both off the porch, but he was confident, especially after the bloodlust they'd displayed in Zack's bookstore, that the fireworks would do the job. A rocket of crackling sparks shooting into the sky on a winter night, a few yards from that massive pine tree, would surely bring them leaping off the porch in an alcohol-fueled frenzy of either fear for the safety of the tree, or testosterone-riddled delight at the pyrotechnic display.

He'd rented a black truck to better conceal himself a few houses down the dark street in an area between streetlights. The gun was on his lap, the fireworks on the seat beside him. He held the butane lighter in his hand, his palm damp with anticipation, his breath quick in his lungs. The sound of it moving in and out of his chest filled the car, steamed the windows, made him feel more anxious and conspicuous than he was.

A calm peace had been with him all day. This was the right decision.

Just after midnight, he got out of the truck, slipped the gun into the pocket of his jacket, and grabbed the fireworks cone. He walked casually along the side of the street the bearded guy's house was on, cut across the neighbor's yard where kids had disturbed the snow with what felt like a thousand footprints and the tracks of saucers for sliding down the slight incline of the front yard into the street.

From here, the men's voices were audible. They were talking

about the football game, arguing about which play had lost the game, laughing at something he couldn't catch. He crossed over into their yard. He scooped away snow, making a clearing about five feet from the base of the tree. He placed the cone on the stiff, frozen grass and stood for a moment.

Show time. He took a deep breath, letting it out slowly. Once the sparks began shooting skyward, there would be no time to think, no time for second-guessing. He took another long, slow breath, then lit the cone.

It burned for a few minutes. He stepped back. The cone started to hiss and fizz, shooting sparks in a fountain toward the sky. The sounds grew louder.

The bearded guy stood first.

Hunter backed away toward the neighbor's yard. He pulled the gun out of his pocket and moved toward a tree so he was hidden from view.

Both men stumbled down the porch steps, lumbering through the two-foot deep drifts of snow toward the flaming spectacle in front of them. As they got closer, the sparks shooting upward in an ever brightening display gave off enough light that Hunter could see both of them clearly.

Time was short. In a few more seconds, it would start to fizzle.

He raised the gun and shot the wiry guy first, figuring he was the one more likely to run toward him, and the faster of the two.

He'd expected a cry of outrage, a violent reaction of some kind from the bearded one, but it was entirely different. Instead, the guy stood absolutely still, in shock as his buddy collapsed in the snow, extinguishing the sparks with his body.

Hunter fired again, and the bearded guy was down.

Sprinting across the yard, Hunter stood over them and fired two more bullets into both men. He had to be sure. Lights came on in the house, and as if light could form an echo, lights came on in the neighboring house half a second later.

He ran to the street, crossed over, and climbed into the truck.

297

He started it and put it in gear. He was pulling away as the front door opened and a woman came onto the porch.

The last thing he saw was her face, looking mostly confused. Was she the one who had driven the car, or did she not know who her husband really was?

And that was the other flaw in his plan. The other loose end.

The woman who had driven the car was still out there. Would she put it together that the attack on the bookstore owner and his mother all those months ago had caused this? Would the police connect those dots?

He had to hope not. It had been a long time. He hadn't called in months. He'd disappeared from their radar, hadn't he? They hadn't even looked for the perpetrators. They hadn't been in touch with him to mention suspects or give him any updates. There was no way they would connect these guys to that crime, because they'd never tried.

And that woman driving the car, she wouldn't think about it at all. Would she?

CHAPTER 65

NOW: HUNTER

*N**apa Valley, California*

All Alex had done was go out somewhere with that girl who owned the castle. He'd seen her get out of the car. If this *VIP wine tasting* had been at the castle, what was the big secret? Why was she lying about it?

And he was one hundred percent certain there had not been a VIP wine tasting. She would never dress like that for an event. She hardly dressed that casually for cocktails in Tess's living room. He'd seen a look cross her face that told him she'd considered changing her top and shoes before they'd gone out for Chinese food. She was almost always dressed up in some way. When she was in the Black Mask tasting room, she looked like she was going to dinner in San Francisco.

And when they had gone to dinner in San Francisco, she'd lugged along a pair of high heels in her purse for the occasion, seemingly unable to bear the thought of wearing the comfortable shoes she'd worn to visit Alcatraz.

No, there hadn't been a wine tasting.

So where had they gone? Honestly, he didn't care much about that. He did care about the lie. Or maybe he cared about where she'd gone. What could she possibly be doing with that girl that she felt it necessary to lie about it?

The questions were driving him insane. The lie had succeeded in stirring up everything he'd thought he was finally ready to put to rest.

Was Alex his loose end after all?

Since she'd first lurked outside his office building at sunrise, flirting with him, almost badgering him into asking her to dinner, he'd had nagging, fearful thoughts. Her secretive behavior, her obvious desire for him, yet her refusal to get close enough to do so much as plan a normal trip together made him question everything she did, and often, everything she said.

He could never be sure.

Part of him liked the thrill of always being surprised by her. She was completely different from any woman he'd been with. At the same time, she terrified him. And terrified was not too strong of a word.

Was she the woman who'd been sitting behind the wheel of that black sedan? Had she managed to find him and was this all some elaborate game to punish him for killing those men?

He hadn't gotten a good look at her. He'd hardly looked at all. The brief glimpse had given the impression she was attractive. Maybe. That was it. The darkness hid her features and he couldn't even say what color her hair had been, although Alex was always changing the color of hers, so what did it matter? If he'd been asked by the cops, which he had not been, he would have said her hair was long. But that too wasn't really important. It had been two years now ….

He'd spent a lot of time thinking about what it would take for that woman to make a mental connection between the brother of the man who owned the bookstore and the murders of the two thugs.

Did the woman driving the sedan even know what had happened inside the bookstore that night? The interior wasn't visible from the street. It was possible she wasn't aware of what their feelings were. Maybe she was the wife of one of them. He hadn't seen that car anywhere on either property, but he hadn't seen the garage for the condo.

She might have been a sister or close friend. It wasn't as if the bookstore catered exclusively to the gay community. It was a bookstore. It carried books. Maybe the creeps had told the woman driving the car they were making a quick stop to look for a book on tiling or weight lifting, or a book for a child.

If she did know what they'd done, would their murders, over a year after the attack, make her immediately think of that? Wouldn't she be more likely to think it was random? He supposed the setup of the fireworks removed the likelihood of anyone thinking it was a drive-by. But wouldn't her thoughts go first to an angry customer?

He wasn't sure. He couldn't be sure of anything. It was wishful thinking. He knew that. He wanted it to be impossible.

It was absolutely possible that Alex was the woman who had been driving that black sedan. That she'd figured out he was Zack's brother. That she'd tracked him down at the modeling agency. But then, the favorable outcomes she would have had to orchestrate—getting a job with a company that Pauline ended up hiring for her personal development. She would never be able to engineer that, or go to all that trouble. It was impossibly fantastic.

No, it was his fear taking over. Alex's quirky, secretive behavior. Her commitment phobia. There was no way she was the woman who had been driving that car. His brain was creating patterns where there were none. It's what the brain did. It took his fear, his painful awareness of how far he'd gone in his burning desire to avenge his family, mixed it with the unusual behavior of a woman he was profoundly drawn to, and turned it into a magnificent story that stirred his gut fear.

But still, the thought wouldn't leave him alone—was she, or wasn't she, the woman in the black sedan?

CHAPTER 66

*I*f everyone, or at least Tess and Marcus, as well as Hunter, were to believe that Silas was capable of killing himself over the loss of Amelia, they had to know how serious their relationship was. Tess had to know Silas was lusting after the castle, covering it over with a pretense of absolute devotion to its owner.

It wasn't difficult to maneuver Tess into inviting Silas to dinner. I did it while Hunter was in the room, forcing Tess into a corner where she couldn't politely decline. The daggers coming from her eyes, as if she and I were engaged in a silent film melodrama, were fierce. But as I'd expected, she didn't object because it wasn't how she wanted Hunter to perceive her.

"I've been trying to form a better relationship with Silas," I said as we sipped Chardonnay in the living room.

Damien had noted our choice when Tess offered it, and he continued to punctuate our conversation with amused chortles.

Chardonnay time.

Chardonnay time.

He would pause, as if trying to eavesdrop on what we were

saying, straining to hear from the entryway, and then add his commentary again—*Chardonnay time.*

Hunter laughed every time he said it, which made me smile. I realized Hunter hadn't laughed much the past week or so. Maybe I hadn't laughed much either. It hadn't been the sort of visit I'd envisioned when I invited him. I regretted that I'd become so fixated on Silas that I'd lied to Hunter, and tried to escape his company every chance I got. But it needed to be done.

I moved closer to him on the couch. I put my hand on his leg and leaned into him. He seemed to respond, but it was hard to know. He'd been distant himself. Distracted. He wasn't sure what was going on, and I couldn't do anything to change that because, in some ways, I really had no idea myself.

We were at a standstill, on opposite sides of the country.

"Good to know." Tess took a large swallow of wine.

"Now that Silas and I are forming a good working relationship, I thought it would be really great to cement it with some social engagement. If Marcus is up to it, and I know how he loves to show off his cooking—"

"He's not a show-off," Tess said. "And—"

"I didn't mean that at all. His food is incredible. He could open a restaurant if he wanted to. Don't you agree?" I squeezed Hunter's leg.

"No question," Hunter said.

"Anyway," I gave Tess a winning smile. "It would be *great* to invite Silas and Amelia for dinner."

"Amelia?"

I knew it would knock her off balance.

Now, she was derailed from telling me she didn't want to sit across from her blackmailer and eat dinner. She didn't want him at her table, didn't want him eating her husband's food, didn't want him in her house at all. But if she raised her objections, it would look strange to Hunter. He probably wouldn't notice, wouldn't really care if he did notice, but Tess would think he was noticing, and would care what he was thinking. She wanted Hunter to adore her. She wanted us to be a cozy, friendly four-some. Lifelong friends, starting now. Couples who vacationed together and ate out together and built lives together. I could feel it every time the four of us sat around the dinner table.

"Amelia Monroe. From Windy Hills."

"And *Silas?*"

"They're really taken with each other. I think it's pretty serious."

"She's a kid."

"I told you they were—"

"I know, but I thought … she's not even twenty-one, is she?"

I shrugged.

"He's …" She gave me a confused, slightly concerned look.

"I don't know anything about it. I just know they're really serious about each other and it would be great to have them here as a couple."

"I don't want …" She glanced at Hunter, then turned her attention back to me.

I couldn't see his face without looking. I waited, trying to sense his reaction through any change in the tension of his muscles as I kept my hand loose on his leg. He didn't react, and he didn't speak.

The silence stretched on for half a moment too long. Hunter didn't care, but she didn't recognize that. She wasn't going to allow him to perceive her as ungracious to one of her key employees.

"It would be a great evening and a fun change of pace," I said.

"Are you bored with us?" Tess laughed, almost tittering with hysteria.

"Not at all. But you have that lovely, enormous dining room and that elegant table. We should use it."

She grimaced.

"That pork Marcus served last week was incredible," I said.

"But we just had that. And we don't know if Silas can even—"

"I'm sure he'll make it work." I stood. "Your glass is empty. I'll be right back."

Chardonnay time! Damien shouted.

Later, Tess told me I was cruel. She accused me of betraying her. Of playing games and risking her relationship with Marcus by putting her in a horrible position. I reminded her it was a truism for a reason that you needed to keep your enemies closer than your friends. She glared at me with a look of outraged defeat, but didn't say anything more about it.

Four nights later, the six of us were seated around Marcus and Tess's massive dining table. There were clusters of candles arranged down the center. The overhead lights were dimmed so the flickering candles cast all of our faces in eery, almost threatening shadows.

We were well into another fabulous meal. Everyone had dripped and oozed with compliments over the food. Even Silas had offered what sounded like genuine praise for each dish that was served.

"It's really good to get to know you better, Amelia," I said. "You and Silas make an adorable couple." I raised my wineglass. "To true and lasting love."

Marcus and Hunter said *cheers* in unison.

Tess took a large gulp of wine.

Silas looked smug and in control. Amelia looked uncertain.

"And *cheers* to your new venture at Windy Hills," I said.

"What venture is that?" Tess asked, her tone sharp and extremely wary.

I smiled at Amelia with encouraging warmth. "Amelia's planning to re-establish it as a winery."

"That's ambitious for a girl your age," Tess said.

"Silas is helping." Amelia gave Silas a sideward glance.

I settled back in my chair and took a long, luxurious swallow of wine. It slid down my throat. I felt a smile wanting to make its way across my face—a smile of absolute bliss and satisfaction. Amelia could not have spoken more appropriate words if I'd fed the lines to her myself.

"How is that?" Tess asked.

"Just in an advisory capacity," Silas said.

"I see. Just be careful there's no conflict of interest," Tess said.

"That would never happen," Silas said. "All my loyalty and one hundred and ten percent of my passion belong to Black Mask."

"Good," Marcus said.

I thought the dinner party was a huge success.

CHAPTER 67

I showed up at Silas's office unannounced.

"I hope you aren't planning to make a habit of this," he said. "I'm busy, and I can't drop everything when you're in the mood to stop by."

"This is important."

"You always think you're important. The tasting room is important, you're not. Who's looking after it right now?"

"There's a sign on the door to text me. It takes three minutes to walk over there. Less, probably."

"A sign is unprofessional."

"This will take five minutes. It's nine thirty in the morning. In my experience, there aren't a lot of people going wine tasting at nine thirty on a weekday morning."

"It's still unprofessional."

"Only if someone sees it."

I sat facing his desk.

"What do you want?"

"I have some pictures to show you. Of a document concerning you. Isn't that what you wanted?"

"Is it the contract regarding my ownership of the winery?"

"No, but I'm still looking. I can't go through every single file at once. I can only get into her office for a few minutes at a time. You have to be patient."

"I don't have to be anything. You're not the one running things here. You don't tell me what I *have* to be."

I smiled. "Do you want to see it or not?"

He held out his hand.

I stood and walked around his desk. I unlocked my phone and showed him the image.

The document referenced the sale of the winery to Tess. It was an addendum to the transfer of ownership stating that she was required to pay Silas a bonus of ten thousand dollars, triggered by the sale. It also stated she was required to retain him as an employee for one year after the sale date.

"That's nothing," he said. "I already know all this, obviously."

"It's something."

No wonder he was so aggressive and antsy. The one-year anniversary of when Tess had purchased the winery was approaching quickly. Maybe this was why he'd set up his own backup plan—a dark guarantee of future employment. Although it still wasn't clear to me why he hadn't forced her into anything yet.

It was possible he was deeply uncertain about how she would react. He had the photographs that could destroy her upcoming marriage. But the operative word was *could*. How did he know that Marcus wasn't forgiving and understanding? Maybe Marcus loved Tess so deeply, he would choose to let it go and move past her terrible mistake. Maybe he could see it as simply that, rather than a betrayal that shook their foundation of trust.

Silas shoved the phone back at me. I took it and stepped away, perching on the edge of his desk.

"Don't sit there."

I stood and walked back to the opposite side of the desk. I sat down and slowly, elaborately, crossed my legs. "You asked me to find documents related to your position here."

"That's not the kind of thing I had in mind, and you know it. There has to be more."

"I'm sure there are. But I thought you would want to see this."

"I don't want you running in here with every piece of paper you find. Once you've finished looking through everything, and you have a collection of photographs, then we can talk."

"Aren't you curious?"

"I'm a patient man. I don't have a hair-trigger need to know every minor detail right away. That's not how executives function."

So, he saw himself as an executive. A business-owner. I was fairly sure the document he was hoping to find didn't exist. If it did, Tess would have had her attorneys take care of it. She wouldn't have bought the winery knowing someone else had a legitimate claim to it.

"I guess I misunderstood." I smiled. "You seemed really anxious to know about anything I could find."

"You did misunderstand. And I don't think it's a good idea to be coming in here all the time. If Tess sees you, she'll wonder about it. She might ask questions."

"I can handle Tess."

He smirked. "*Handling* and it being a good idea are not the same. It's better to prevent problems than always doing damage control. But you strike me as someone who's usually in damage-control mode."

"Do I?"

"Is that everything you wanted to talk about?"

"Did you enjoy the dinner?"

"It was great. Marcus is a good cook."

"I mean, did you enjoy socializing, letting everyone know you and Amelia are seriously in love?"

"I didn't think that was necessary."

"Tess should know, don't you think?"

"Why?"

"So she's aware you're in a relationship."

"It's none of her business. And you didn't need to wind her up about my support of Amelia. I don't need her thinking I'm going behind her back." He put his hands behind his head, spreading his elbows out to the side like wings, trying to appear relaxed. He looked tense.

"She didn't think that."

He lowered his hands and sat forward. "I think we're done. When will you have the rest of the files?"

"It's hard to say."

"Not that hard."

"It depends on her schedule, so yes, it is hard."

He stood. "Well, we're running out of time, so figure out how to get in there more often. She has to sleep. You can do it at night."

He was running out of time. I wasn't.

"I'll do my best." I gave him a sweet smile. "But I can't be caught. That wouldn't be good for either of us."

I felt like skipping out of his office. In my mind, I sort of did. Everything was going to work out just fine.

CHAPTER 68

*A*lthough the dinner party had been a pleasant diversion, Hunter had had enough. There was no point in hanging around the winery any longer. He wasn't going to keep Alex in his life by drifting around the Napa Valley. The weather had grown too cold most days for swimming. He could only do so much hiking and walking around vineyards, and Alex was always working or busy with something or another, he couldn't usually say what.

It was time to return to New York. His grasp on his job responsibilities was slipping. If he didn't step up his game, he might find his career on the skids, or sliding into the gutter entirely.

If Alex wasn't who she said she was, and she had some ulterior motive to either fuck with his head, screw up his life, or kill him, she'd already done the first, and she was taking her sweet time with the other two. Logic continued to insist she was not the woman who had been driving the car the night those two assholes almost killed his brother and brutalized his mother.

Only paranoia made him keep returning to that train of thought. Until he discovered something concrete to convince himself otherwise, he was going to force himself to put that concern out of his head.

If Alex wanted a relationship, she needed to figure out what the hell she was doing with her life. Maybe they could make it work—flying back and forth. Maybe they couldn't. But this was unsustainable.

He felt irritable. Part of him wanted to tell her immediately after sex, roll over, and crash into sleep without a discussion. Instead, he decided to do it the right way. He suggested dinner out.

They were seated across the table from each other at a French restaurant. Alex had dressed up as if they were celebrating a milestone birthday or anniversary. She wore a short black dress that was cut open to the center of her back, and almost as low in front, with some complicated arrangements of straps holding it all together around her neck and arms. It mesmerized him. In the center of her breastbone, was the single pearl on a thin gold chain she sometimes wore.

Her lips were dark red, and there was lots of shadowy stuff around her eyes. Her hair flowed around the side of her head and along her neck and over her shoulders in waves of soft silk that made him want to get back in the car, drive home, and carry her upstairs to bed. When he'd seen her descending the sweeping staircase in dangerously high heels before they left the house, he'd wondered what the hell he was doing, telling her he was headed back to New York, almost as if he was dumping her.

Now, she was smiling at him as if he were the most attractive, interesting, sexy man on the planet. As if she couldn't imagine looking at any other guy. As if there weren't any other males in the restaurant. Her gaze held his in a way that made him both excited and a little uncomfortable. He wanted to look away, but he also wanted to grab her right here.

What was it about her? And what was wrong with him? Maybe he was drawing too hard a line, saying he had to leave immediately. But he had a job! He couldn't just stagnate in a mansion for weeks with no end date in sight. Sure, Pauline was fine with the remote work, but he felt disconnected from the organization. He felt as if he was working in a virtual reality world, everyone turning into faces on screens, some reduced to avatars and often, simply words in text boxes.

What did Alex want? She was driving him absolutely insane with her … what was it? Games? Should he call them games? He wasn't even sure that was accurate. Because she didn't seem to be *trying* to manipulate him or mess with his head or control him. She just … was. She lived in her own world and did as she pleased, leaving him spinning wildly out of control.

And she didn't communicate. That was a big part of it. She had all kinds of things scrolling through her mind, a narrative he wasn't privy to, and it left him reeling. At the same time, he was fascinated. He couldn't stop thinking about her, desiring her, needing her, and always … wanting to know more.

Maybe he should tone down what he'd planned to say. Make it less threatening, less final-sounding.

They ordered, and as they slowly ate escargot dripping with butter, he looked at her and felt his heart melt. "I hate saying this, but I really need to get back home. Back to the office." He spoke softly, his voice full of regret, even though he'd hated fifty percent of the hours he'd spent here, feeling like a caged animal inside that enormous, luxurious house.

"The office?" She popped an escargot into her mouth and chewed it with a pleased smile.

He nodded. "Working remotely has been okay, but I've pushed it for too long."

"I understand."

"Do you think … How are we going to make this work?"

"I'm not sure."

"Do you want to?"

She took a sip of wine. "This is amazing." She picked up the escargot fork and held it over the dish, studying the remaining pieces.

He felt as if she'd stabbed the tiny fork in his heart.

Finally, she stabbed one of the snails instead. "I do want to," she said.

He felt as if he'd been holding his breath. "How will we?"

"I'm not sure. I guess we'll have to think about it."

He wasn't sure if he was pleased that she'd said she wanted things to work, or upset that she seemed undisturbed that he was leaving.

"I'll probably take off in a day or so."

She nodded and put the escargot in her mouth.

They didn't discuss it any further. She was warm and lively the rest of the evening. He felt she was thrilled to be having dinner with him. Sex that night was outstanding. He felt as if his head might explode.

He wouldn't walk away from her. He couldn't.

CHAPTER 69

*S*ilas had insisted we meet in the Vineyard at night. I didn't like the arrangement because I didn't want to be standing out in the cold talking to him. And what I had to show him was not going to involve a simple exchange of a few words. It might make him angry, he might tell me I'd found the wrong document, I was wasting his time. Again.

The truth was, I had two documents, but he didn't need to know that. Not yet.

The other reason I wasn't pleased with his insistence that we meet in the dirt mounds running between rows of grapevines while the dark, cold wind blew across the valley was because I would be recording our conversation for Amelia. No matter what he said when he saw the document I had photographed, there was more I needed to entice him into saying for my recording.

I hoped his upset over seeing this document would enable me to lead him into talking about his engagement to Rosé and his lust for Black Mask that had superseded his feelings for his former fiancée. If Amelia could hear who he truly was, if she heard him exposing *himself* and what he wanted, then everything should fall cleanly into place. *If* …

But night and darkness it was.

So I slipped out the pantry door, still a safe exit as the only door to the house without a camera. I wore running shoes, thick black leggings, a black turtleneck sweater, and a thick hooded sweatshirt. Still, I was cold. I shivered, did a few stretches, and started a slow jog through the garden. I paused to open the gate and entered the vineyard. I unlocked my phone, opened the recording app, and set it to start recording. There would be a lot of wasted time since I was still several minutes from our meeting time, but this was my last chance to ensure I wouldn't be observed by Silas. I slid the app to the background and brought my photos to the front, pulling up the one I would be showing Silas.

I ran on the path that circled the vineyard, trying to warm myself, using the flashlight on my phone to see where I was going as I moved farther away from the house and the spray of the outside lights.

Once I left the path, it became increasingly difficult to see. That, and the uneven ground, made even a slow jog impossible.

It wasn't clear exactly where I was meeting Silas. He was supposed to signal me with the light on his phone at twelve thirty in the morning. It was now twelve twenty-eight. I walked slowly, keeping my attention on the lumpy, semi-soft earth.

A few minutes later, a light came on two rows away from me. I maneuvered my way between the grapevines, carefully placing my feet as I went up and down the furrows where they grew.

Finally, I reached the place where he was waiting. "You couldn't have made this more difficult if you'd tried," I said.

"We need to be discreet."

"No one would have noticed us in your office at this hour."

"If someone wakes, they might see the light on."

"They might see the light out here, too," I said.

"It can't be seen from the house."

"If you say so."

"What do you have? And it better be what I'm looking for this

317

time. I don't like how long this is taking. I have a lot of things I'm working on."

"Like getting ownership of Windy Hills?"

"That's none of your business. Show me the document."

I opened my phone and held the photo for him to see. It was risky. If he tried to take the phone, if he tapped it the wrong way, there was a chance the recording app would rear its head. I could imagine his fury if he discovered what I was doing.

Although I didn't want to send any of the images to him, didn't want to give him that power of having something he could show Tess to let her know I'd betrayed her like this, my backup plan was to do exactly that if he tried to take the phone out of my hand. I could probably talk my way out of letting Tess believe I'd betrayed her, convincing her I was trying to help, but she would not like it that I'd been snooping around her office. No one would like that. She would tell me I should have asked. She would have been happy to show me the documents.

But she hadn't been happy to do that. She hadn't told me anything about Silas's situation until I'd forced her into it. She'd acted as if his blackmail were an isolated incident, something that occurred in a vacuum, leaving her utterly without options. In one sense, he did still have a strong hold on her. But she wasn't as helpless as she'd made it appear.

On my phone was a photograph of a loan agreement. Silas had borrowed twenty-five-thousand dollars from the Harpers. As a result, they hadn't given him his copy of the letter of intent, which stated that the winery would transfer to him and his wife when he and Rosé were married. Should their marriage not take place, he would still become the owner, with an absurdly below-market, long-term purchase plan.

"This isn't what I want."

"It explains a lot."

"I need the letter of intent, Alexandra."

"Well, why didn't you tell me that at the beginning? We would have saved a lot of time. Instead, I've been digging around, not knowing what I'm looking for."

"Shh! Lower your voice."

"No one can hear."

"You don't know that. You need to calm down."

"You keep sending me looking for things, and I have no idea what you want."

"You should have figured it out when you read this."

"I wasn't reading. I was taking pictures of things that had your name on them! All I saw when I was in her office was your name and that you owed twenty-five grand. I didn't see that part about a letter of intent until I was looking at the photo later."

"Why didn't you go back?"

"I wanted to show you."

He grabbed my hand, trying to pry the phone out of my fingers. "Give it to me."

I yanked my arm away from him. "You don't need it."

"I need that document."

I laughed. "This isn't the document."

"I need you to get it for me."

"Why? Do you still have to pay Tess? Or was it voided when they sold it?"

"I don't know. No one told me a fucking thing! All I knew was they sold the place right out from under me after that bitch decided she didn't want to be a winemaker, didn't want to be married. And off they went to Italy."

"It sounds like you're the one who needs to calm down." I held my phone in front of me, hoping I was catching his voice clearly. I wanted to put it in my pocket so I could put my hands in my pockets. It was getting colder, and the breeze was getting stronger. I hopped from foot to foot, trying to warm myself.

"I need you to get the document and I need the letter of intent. No more screwing around."

"If you'd told me—"

"Well now, I've told you."

"What will you do when I get it?"

"None of your business."

"I'm taking all these risks for you, but nothing is any of my business?"

"You stepped into it. I didn't ask you to help."

"What's your plan, to own all the wineries in Napa Valley?" I laughed.

"No."

"Just Black Mask and Windy Hills?"

"Just get the documents I asked for."

"I'm not seeing what's in this for me."

"We'll work that out when I have them."

"I want to work it out now. I have no guarantee."

"What do you want?"

"A share."

"How much?"

"I've always wanted a castle."

He laughed so loud, I thought he might wake everyone in the house, maybe half the valley. "You're something else. The castle belongs to Amelia. You know that."

"But you're planning something."

"We'll see. Come up with a reasonable request and we'll discuss it when you have the letter of intent."

"I don't know what you're going to do with it. Tess purchased the winery. The letter of intent isn't valid anymore."

"The sale shouldn't have been executed. Once my attorney gets his hands on that … well, we'll see what's valid."

"You seem more heartbroken over losing Black Mask than you do over losing Rosé."

He grunted.

"Did you even love her, or you just wanted the winery? Maybe that's why she broke off your engagement. Women can sense things like that."

"Don't give me that *women have special senses* BS."

"You don't have to believe it if you don't want to, but you should be careful with Amelia. Women *can* feel things. If your heart isn't in it, if you want something from them. If you're after Windy Hills and she's just—"

"Thanks for the pro tip."

"My pleasure."

"Get the documents."

"I'll do my best."

I turned and tapped on my light. I started making my way along the row of vines.

"And send me the photo of that IOU," he hissed.

I raised my hand to suggest I'd heard. He must have seen my hand, because he didn't say anything more. I had no intention of sending that image. He wouldn't risk sending more than one or two texts about it. If that. All I had to do was avoid him for a few days.

When I slipped into bed beside Hunter, I could feel that he was awake. He didn't ask where I'd been. He didn't even admit he was awake. I stayed well away from him, hoping that if he didn't feel my cold skin, he would assume I'd been in the yoga room or drinking a glass of water.

I really needed this thing with Silas to be over.

CHAPTER 70

THEN: ALEX

*P*ortland, Oregon

Harrison Andrews did not play football during the second quarter of his senior year. The team did not make it to the playoffs. He never knew it was me who sabotaged the last glory days of his career. And no one knew I was the one lacking in school spirit who *stole* our win.

Although that guy had charged way over the line with me, I'd also charged way over the line my brother had recommended before we went to the party. On the way home, Tom had asked me how much I had to drink.

"Not a lot."

"You had more than a few beers."

"I only had two."

"That means you ignored my advice completely and had Jell-O shots. Because you're ripped. I can see it in your eyes."

"How can 'ou see it?"

"I just can. And it's obvious when you talk," he said.

"How much did you have?"

"I'm used to it," he said. "I know how to pace myself. I know my limit."

"The point of going to a party, Tommy, is not having the parents there. So why are you acting like you're my mommy and daddy rolled into one?" He hated being called Tommy. Hated it.

We were almost home before he said anything else. As he turned onto our street, he said, "I hope you didn't do anything stupid."

"Why would you thin' that?"

"Because you sound stupid right now."

I laughed. "Maybe other people did stupid things."

"I told you to only have a few beers. Your body isn't used to alcohol."

"Things changed. They kind of ... spiraled."

"You're sure everything is cool?"

"Yup. Definitely cool."

"Good. How'd you like it?"

"I know what it feels like to get drunk."

He laughed. "That's all you wanted? We could have bought a twelve-pack and gone into the woods."

"You didn't offer. And a party is more fun. It should be. But I don't know ..."

"This one wasn't great," he said. "They vary."

As we climbed the stairs, we heard Mrs. Baxter snoring. I collapsed onto my bed, my head spinning.

* * *

* * *

* * *

After I gave Harrison a tiny portion, although certainly not all of what he deserved, not even close, I decided that drinking was fun. I'd still enjoyed the buzz, to a point. I would have had a better time with different people.

I also decided my brother was right, although I didn't tell him that. He was pretty smart. He'd already been accepted at UC Berkeley. He'd been offered a very nice scholarship. My parents were proud, even though my father was worried because my other brothers were attending colleges in Oregon, where he believed he was keeping an eye on them. In California, all bets were off. My father thought California was a dangerous place, but he couldn't object to a scholarship like that, and a school like that.

Without all those Jell-O shots, I wouldn't have ended up in that bedroom. The whole evening would have gone slightly differently. And slight differences turn into significant differences as things start to unfold, as if they're multiplying as they go.

So I decided to make some rules for myself.

I would modify my rules as I tried more kinds of drinks. But for now, my rule was—one Jell-O shot, one beer. If I had more beer, no Jell-O shots.

No guy who thought he was the star of the show and entitled to all the trophies was going to get the upper hand with me ever again.

CHAPTER 71

NOW: AMELIA

*N*apa Valley, California

Alex had called to say she was coming to the castle at eight the following morning. She hadn't asked if she could come by, she had informed. It was a ridiculously early hour and Amelia had said no, but Alex ignored her.

"I need to see you."

"I won't be dressed," Amelia said. "I won't have had breakfast."

"We can eat together."

"But I—"

"Please make sure someone opens the gate."

The call ended.

When Amelia tried to call her back, it went to voicemail. When she texted, Alex didn't respond. Amelia felt bullied. She thought about getting up before dawn and leaving for the day. Alex could appear at the gates and demand to be let in all she wanted, but Amelia wouldn't be there.

Then, her curiosity, and maybe a little bit of fear, got the best of her.

She was up before the sun, stirred by an increase in that curiosity and fear. She took a long shower. She blew her hair dry, combing the red strands into waves that curled around her shoulders and arms like vines.

Alex was always well-dressed, so Amelia stood in front of her closet for a long time, trying to decide on the perfect outfit for breakfast in the large, cold dining room beside a roaring fire on this rainy morning. She finally chose a white cashmere sweater that made her hair glisten even brighter, taking on the appearance of flames itself. She put on a dark red skirt with black leather insets, and black boots that came up over her knees.

She never wore much makeup. It made her face feel gritty and slightly dirty. She didn't understand why Alex and Tess liked smearing that stuff all over their skin, painting their eyes to look so exotic. Yes, it was fascinating to watch their eyes. It was hard to look away sometimes, but she couldn't imagine doing that to her own eyes, no matter how magnetic it might make them appear.

Downstairs, she made coffee and opened the fridge, wondering at someone who had the gall to invite herself to breakfast the evening before, leaving no time to go to the store. She had eggs and cheese. There was a tomato from the garden and a few mushrooms and onions. She'd make an omelette. Her mother used to make superb omelettes. That, with toast and coffee, was enough for a last-minute self-invite.

Alexandra arrived at two minutes before eight. She didn't apologize for the early hour. She didn't apologize for inviting herself to breakfast, or for refusing to give a reason for her urgent visit.

"Great coffee," Alexandra said after her first sip.

"Thank you. I'm making an omelette."

"Sounds good. I don't have to eat, though, if you have other plans."

"My plans are to eat breakfast." She whisked the eggs and poured them into the pan. "What's the big secret? It feels—"

"I have something you need to listen to."

"What's that?"

"I'll wait until you're finished cooking. So you can hear it without anything interfering."

Alexandra chattered on about the castle, asking what it was like living there alone, asking questions about the wedding staff, about her plans for the winery—a nonstop flow of words that made Amelia wish she'd simply made toast so they could get on with it.

When they were seated at one end of the long table, Alexandra took her phone out of her bag and placed it beside Amelia's plate.

"This is a recording of Silas that you need to hear."

"A recording of what?"

"A conversation I had with him."

Amelia took a sip of coffee, followed by a bite of toast. It needed more butter. She reached for the butter dish and picked up the knife. While she spread butter, Alexandra unlocked her phone and tapped the recording app.

The sound of wind and someone breathing filled the room. "I'll try to skip past this. I should have edited it, but I didn't have time." Alexandra tapped the phone a few times.

Silas's voice came on, the whoosh of the wind enhancing his words with greater drama. Alexandra took her hand away from the phone and picked up her coffee mug.

Amelia listened, feeling her appetite fade as the recording went on. She wasn't sure she understood everything she was hearing, but one thing was clear as the conversation came to an end. She wasn't listening to the same man who had told her she was smart and beautiful. The man who'd believed they were meant to be together from the moment they'd first met. Where was the man who said he cherished her and wanted to hold on to her and take care of her?

He sounded so *angry*.

He didn't even sound like himself.

"Was that ... Silas?"

"Yes."

"It didn't sound like him."

"We were outside. It was night."

"You sounded the same. But he was ..." She didn't want to say what she was thinking. It was too awful. Was he only interested in the castle? Was that the reason for everything? *Everything?!?* Had he kissed her and made love to her and told her they belonged together because he wanted her *property*?

Did he want to help her rebuild the winery like it used to be at Windy Hills and then take it for himself? Because he thought she was young and clueless about everything?

Tears flooded her eyes. She couldn't see Alexandra or the remains of the omelette on her plate. She wanted to drink coffee, if only to have something to do, but her hand felt weak, unable to pick up the mug.

"Why ..." Again, she didn't want to tell Alexandra how she was feeling. She couldn't. She didn't even know herself. Why was Alexandra doing this? Was she trying to hurt her?

"I didn't do it to upset you." Alexandra reached into her bag and pulled out a tissue. She handed it to Amelia. "I wanted you to know what he's doing. You think he's prince charming, but that's not who he is. I'm not telling you what to do. I just want you to know. He's a lot older than you. And when people are that much older, they have more experience. They can manipulate—"

"I get it," Amelia said.

"I just thought—"

"I said, I get it. He's using me. He's no different than my mother. Telling me what to do, deciding how *he* wants things. Treating me like I belong to him. Trying to make me into what he wants me to be."

"You're not a child. You're smart. You understand a lot for someone your age."

"Someone my *age*," Amelia sneered.

"You're smart," Alexandra said. "I'll leave it at that."

Amelia shoved her plate away from her, most of the omelette uneaten. "Was there anything else you wanted?"

"No."

"Thank you for spoiling my morning. My day. Maybe my entire life."

"I'm not the one who spoiled things."

"Why did you tell him you wanted my castle?"

"Because I'd love to own a castle. It's a dream, that's all. A fantasy."

"You can leave now."

When Alexandra was gone, the stone walls felt as if they'd become a prison once again. Amelia felt as if she were inside a tomb. Buried alive.

Silas said he loved her. Hadn't he said that? Or had she been the only one to say those words, and he'd murmured something she couldn't quite decipher? At first, he talked all about what an incredible person she was. But then, he only talked about planting vines and marketing the castle, about the lost potential and the partnership of marriage. He talked constantly about business, explaining how he could advise her. He was always reminding her how young she was—*Since you're not a legal adult, I would probably have to manage all the paperwork and legal stuff*, he'd said. What did that really mean?

Now, she wasn't even sure she wanted a winery. Why? The weddings took care of themselves. The staff knew what to do. She had plenty of money. Besides, the castle was in a trust until she was twenty-one. She'd never told Silas that. She wondered what he would say about that.

Maybe he wouldn't want her after all.

CHAPTER 72

*W*hen Silas came out of his luxury condo at six thirty in the morning, headed toward the carport where his cute red Mini Cooper was parked, he did not look happy to see me.

"How do you know where I live?"

"You told me to go through all the files. I've seen everything."

He glared at me. "This is an invasion of my privacy."

"It's better than constantly meeting where Tess can see us."

"You report to me. Technically. There shouldn't be anything strange about you meeting with me."

"That's not what you said before."

He lowered his eyebrows. "What do you want?" He moved closer to the car, causing it to unlock, but didn't open the door.

"I found another document."

"The letter of intent?"

"No."

"I told you—"

"This is more interesting."

"Let's see."

"I don't have a photo."

"Why not?"

"I thought I heard someone coming, and I had to get out of there."

He folded his arms across his chest. "It sounds like you're bull-shitting me. What game are you playing? If you *heard someone coming ...*" He made air quotes. "... you wouldn't have been able to leave without them seeing you."

"I did. But no photos." I shrugged.

"What did you find?"

"I want to know what our arrangement is before I tell you."

"I said—letter of intent—and then we'll talk."

"That doesn't leave me any negotiating power."

He shrugged.

"That's not fair."

He tried to mimic my voice. "That's not fair." He laughed. "This is business. If you can't handle the business world, and judging by the way you present yourself, flirting and dressing like you do, I'm guessing you don't know shit about business or how things are done. You are not in the power position here."

I knew exactly how things were done, so I gave him a slow, flirty smile. "You like the way I dress?"

He glared at me.

"I think I'm very much in the power position. I have access to her office and you do not."

"I could manage. I could find someone else."

"There's no one else who lives in the house. I'm in a unique position. You need me. And you know it."

He opened the car door.

"I want fifty percent of Black Mask."

He laughed. "I knew the minute you wormed your way into the tasting room you were up to something."

"Did you?"

"You get fifty percent of nothing. Because right now, I have nothing. And until I have something, there's nothing to discuss, negotiate, or take fifty percent of." He smiled as if he were speaking to a small child, telling her kindly she was too young to drive, looking gently at her eager desire to climb behind the wheel and make believe by wildly turning the wheel and pressing all the buttons and switches.

We were both quiet for a few seconds.

"What did you find?" he asked.

"It suggests there's more than the letter of intent."

"More what?"

"That there *was* a contract. Something related to your marriage."

He let out a short laugh. "It does no good. Because if there is, I didn't sign it. What did you find?"

"It's an email print-out."

"Well, what does it say?"

"I don't remember every word. It had a lot of legal jargon, so that makes it harder to remember because I didn't quite understand all of it."

He smirked. "So you went through my employment file that has nothing to do with you, wasting time that could have been spent doing what you were supposed to be doing. And you got sidetracked with email that wasn't what you were supposed to be looking for. And then you thought someone was coming, but you'd wasted so much time, you were interrupted from what you were supposed to be doing. And now you have nothing. And the thing you do have, you can't remember. And that's probably useless because I never saw or signed a contract. An unsigned contract is not a contract."

"If your attorney hasn't seen the email, how can you know what it means? Maybe it's everything."

"You're stringing me along, and I'm not sure why. Because it's not getting you what you say you want. And it's not going to. Maybe you think it gives you some kind of power, but it's only making you look pathetic and incompetent." He climbed into the car. "Don't talk to me again until you have a photograph of the letter of intent." He slammed the door, started the engine, and began backing out.

I thought about standing my ground, forcing him to either brake or back into me. But it would only be a game. The rest wasn't a game, even though he thought it was. The rest was to wind him up. To put him on edge. To make sure he believed he was on top, that he was holding all the cards. Because the next time, that would be it.

CHAPTER 73

*T*ess walked into the conference room in the office building for her weekly meeting with Silas. She was prepared to hear the quarterly update, so she'd allowed two hours. Usually she kept their weekly meetings to an hour, sometimes less. She tried to keep them brief, because every moment was painful. She felt as if she were sitting there naked. Did he look at those images of her every day? Did he salivate over them? Or worse? Was he always remembering that night?

There wasn't a single moment she was in his presence that she wasn't aware of what had happened, of what he knew about her, that Marcus, the one person in the world who was supposed to know everything about her, did not know.

She hated what she'd done, and she hated him. Her flesh writhed when he looked at her. It felt as if a hundred snakes were slithering across her bare skin, winding around her with their silky scales. She felt involuntary shivers convulse across her body, and she wondered if Silas noticed her discomfort.

It was humiliating. Degrading. And she couldn't blame anyone but herself.

She wanted to fire him. But she couldn't.

How had her dream turned into a nightmare in the course of one misspent evening? It was the stupidest thing she'd ever done. She'd been so drunk. She wasn't sure she'd ever been more drunk in her entire life. That wine had hit her like nothing she'd ever experienced. After years in the corporate world, a thousand dinners out with clients, mostly men, she'd thought she knew how to manage her drinking and regulate her alcohol consumption. She knew how to pace herself. She knew what she was doing.

How had she allowed that to happen? Why, in all that was holy and unholy, had she had sex with that creep? She wasn't even attracted to him. She felt as if she'd become an entirely different person that night.

And that was what she'd come to realize after countless, endless nights lying in bed, staring into the darkness, searching for an explanation for her incredibly stupid and shameful behavior.

She was certain Silas had put something in one of the tiny pours of wine. She'd gone back over the evening in her mind, with her tablet in her hand, and listed the wines they'd tasted, calculated the ounces in each glass, up to the time when she recalled starting to lose control. She'd had the equivalent of five large glasses of wine.

It was a lot. There was no doubt about it. But it wasn't enough to make her do what she'd done. She'd overindulged like that other times. She'd gone to company parties and tipped over the edge. She'd heard herself laugh too loudly and listened to herself say things she'd regretted, even as the words flowed without restraint from her lips. She'd shared sloppy kisses with a few work colleagues that never should have happened.

But this? *This?*

He'd put something in one of the glasses. It hadn't been a roofie or GHB or anything like that. She hadn't passed out. She'd stumbled out of there giddy, dazed, and not fully grasping reality.

Finally, she'd decided it must have been Ecstasy. She'd been so happy and filled with such good feelings, so excited about the winery, about the delight that such a glorious thing as wine existed in the world—such a gift and a pleasure. She'd seen Silas through a blurry gaze, a decent-looking guy, fun to hang out with, talking about good wine. And then … her body suddenly ached to be touched.

It was as if she were having sex with a satyr. With a phantom.

And now, she had to sit at a conference table and put on a professional smile while he leered, even if it didn't show on his face. She had to maintain an air of authority and power. She had to act like the owner of this enterprise, his boss. Instead, she felt like a foolish high school girl.

She pulled out a chair and placed her phone and tablet on the table.

Silas was already seated, his closed laptop in front of him. The projector used to display his slides on the screen was dark.

"You can start," she said.

He didn't have the printed report in front of him. Usually, he began by sliding it across the table to her. She'd told him multiple times it wasn't necessary, that he could email her a digital copy for reading on her large desktop display, but he always had a full-color printed copy for her. Today, the table was bare.

"There's something I'd like to discuss before the quarterlies," he said.

"I only have two hours. We'll need all of that for—"

"I would think you'd carve out the time necessary to stay on top of your business."

"Two hours is sufficient. And I'm fully on top of my business."

"You like it on top, right, Tess?"

She felt her face burn. Then, an icy coldness chilled her, so that she felt she couldn't even move her hands from where they rested on her digital devices, as if she were clinging to them for dear life. "What's the issue?"

"How did you find out the Black Mask property was for sale?"

"That's an irrelevant topic."

"I'm in charge of operations now. It's a question I need answered."

"Why?"

"Because, as the head of operations, I want a complete understanding of everything related to the winery, that's why."

"I don't recall."

"This isn't a deposition where you get to fall back on that old crutch," he said.

"That's the answer. I was looking to purchase a winery. Several that were for sale were mentioned to me by various people in the business, and Black Mask was one of them."

"The fact Black Mask was for sale wasn't public knowledge."

She shrugged. "So what?"

"How did you find out? You didn't even live in Napa."

"I don't know, Silas. Someone told me. It was well over a year ago. I was in contact with a lot of people in the Napa Valley and meeting new people every day. It's absurd to think I'm going to remember who told me what about which properties."

"A lot of people were shocked when it sold. And so quickly and quietly."

She shrugged.

"It seems … underhanded."

She laughed.

"Why is that funny? Do you think dodgy business practices are funny?"

"It's time to review the quarterly numbers."

"I don't have an answer to my question."

"You're not going to get one because I have no idea. And there was nothing underhanded or dodgy about my purchase of Black Mask. So you can put that out of your head."

"There was definitely something suspect about it because one day I was overseeing operations and the next day it had been sold, the Harpers were in Italy, and I was running the tasting room."

"I don't know what to tell you. Can we get to the purpose of our meeting now?"

"Since I can't get a straight answer from you, I might have to bring this up with Marcus."

"He'll give you the same answer." She regretted that the moment she said it. This was hers. The winery belonged to her. Marcus was not in charge, or someone to whom this worm could threaten to go over her head. "I'm the owner. I'm the one who purchased the winery. I did the due diligence. I reviewed the books and inventory and brand value, and I signed all the paperwork. Marcus has nothing to do with it."

"You know what I mean."

His smile reminded her of a cartoon snake. But there was nothing cartoonish about it.

Was this it? Was he finally going to make good on the threat that had been hanging over her for months? Was he going to expose her to the love of her life and destroy everything she cared about?

CHAPTER 74

*I*t was pounding, thundering rain. Buckets of water pouring down. The road leading into Black Mask had flooded, so we'd put a sign at the front gate that the tasting room was closed. The storm was only supposed to last for a day and a half.

I was in the workout room using the treadmill. Hunter was still in California, despite the fancy dinner and his announcement he needed to hurry back to New York. He hadn't put a single T-shirt into his suitcase. He seemed suddenly reluctant to go, as if he knew I wouldn't be coming to visit and he wasn't sure when he could make it back to California. He acted as if he thought leaving meant this was the end.

I'd said I wouldn't return to New York, but would I? I wasn't ready for it to be the end of us, so clearly someone had to go somewhere. I just wasn't ready to think about it.

Silas was on my mind. I would have preferred to deal with Silas when Hunter was on the opposite coast. It made me jumpy, thinking about killing him while Hunter was watching every move I made. I found myself mixing two martinis every night.

Rather than giving me the side-eye, Tess joined me. Hunter and Marcus hardly seemed to notice.

I stabbed my finger at the buttons on the treadmill, increasing the speed, increasing the incline, running faster. My muscles burned and still I felt jumpy. I wanted them to burn until they were nothing but ash.

The door opened but I couldn't look away from the machine or I might find myself sprawled across its relentlessly moving belt. I tapped the button to slow it, irritated by the interruption.

"I don't know what to do," Tess said.

I wondered if she should have those words tattooed on the inside of her wrist in a fancy script. Or maybe, in an effort to change her mindset, she should tattoo something to the effect of —*I know exactly what I'm going to do.*

I continued tapping buttons until the machine came to a stop. Without the sound of the treadmill, the rain seemed to slam against the window with more intensity.

"About what?" I asked.

She moved into the room, walking toward me like a zombie, staring through me as if she were watching a horror movie playing out behind me. Her gaze was so sharply focused in the distance behind me, I felt a pressing desire to turn and look, even though I knew I stood only a few yards from the window where the rain gushed down onto a small garden.

"I think Silas is going to tell Marcus."

"Why?"

"Because I tried ... I tried to act like I had control of the situation and I don't think he liked it."

I waited for her to say more.

"Remember? I told you his employment contract had some guarantees? There was a clause that he would remain employed here for one year if the winery was sold. The anniversary of when I purchased the winery is next month. I think he's decided he's almost out of time to force me into giving him something."

"What did he ask for?"

"I … I'm not really sure."

I laughed. "That makes no sense."

Most women might have started crying at this point, but Tess just looked stunned. She stared at me as if the wind had been knocked out of her. As if her brain couldn't put the words together, allowing her to speak coherently.

"I think he just wants to … I guess he thinks he …" She started laughing. "Maybe he wasn't thinking. I don't know why he would tell Marcus what I did at this point. Because what he wants from me is such a small thing. And I don't have what he wants!" Her last words came out with a note of high-pitched hysteria. "I honestly don't know what he wants from me. Ultimately, I think he wants the winery." She started laughing, harder this time, uncontrollably.

She stopped suddenly. "I don't know what Silas is doing. All I know is he seems to think the winery should belong to him and he's going to use this horrible, stupid thing I did to torment and humiliate me until I lose my mind and … I don't know. Maybe until he drives Marcus and I apart? I'm done trying to figure out what he's up to." She laughed again, with more bitterness this time. "Just speaking it out loud helped. So thank you. I'm going to tell Marcus. That's the thing that's making me insane. Once Marcus knows, Silas can't do a damn thing. I'll be free and I can put all this nonsense behind me. And if Silas does have some legal claim I'm not aware of, that wasn't disclosed, my attorney can handle it properly." She gave me a confident, triumphant smile.

"You're going to tell Marcus what you did?"

"Yes. We've told each other everything about our lives. That's what makes our relationship so amazing. Total honesty and transparency. Keeping this secret will destroy us, no matter what's going on with Silas and the winery. I have to tell him. He'll get it. We all make idiotic mistakes. He'll see that. He adores me."

"Sometimes when people tell their partner they cheated they—"

"I didn't cheat. I didn't decide I wanted someone other than Marcus. This is different. It's not cheating at all."

I gave her a neutral smile. "Are you sure you're not just making yourself feel better, clearing the air and feeling as if you're completely transparent in your own head, but filling Marcus's head with something awful?"

"No. That's not it. We need to be a unified team."

"But he'll have to live with it. How is that love? You're dumping something you don't like dealing with onto him, so you'll feel better and he feels worse."

"That's not what I'm doing. Besides, you said I should tell him. It was the only way to be free of Silas."

"If Silas was really going to show those pictures to Marcus, he would have done it by now. Maybe he's just trying to pressure you. And once he realizes you can't be pressured, he'll give up. Maybe he's realized that telling Marcus won't make you cave. It's only the threat that will make you cave. Right? Once he tells him, that's it. So he'll just keep threatening. If you can stand up to that, you're fine."

She was quiet for a moment. "That's an interesting point."

"Telling Marcus will hurt him. What happened is over. You can't undo it, and why put that in Marcus's head? That's not true love, is it? Making the other person suffer?"

I'd read this in an Instagram reel and I thought it fit the situation perfectly.

Tess threw her arms around me. She pressed her face into my slightly damp neck. "I was worried you didn't give any thought to what it meant to be in love with someone. I was wrong."

I patted her back.

Finally, she let go of me. She looked sublimely happy.

I would look equally happy when I'd polished off Silas. Hopefully, that would be soon.

CHAPTER 75

*H*unter's suitcase remained in the closet. He hadn't said anything about what day he actually planned to leave. I hadn't seen him book a flight, not that I'd been tracking him twenty-four-seven, but he hadn't mentioned a flight.

If I hadn't sat across from him in one of the two cute black dresses I'd brought to California, eating escargot, listening to him try to capture our relationship in words, and explain why he needed to return to New York *soon*, I would have thought I'd dreamt the whole thing.

I was eager for him to leave. I needed to start moving on my plan to be rid of Silas. I wasn't one hundred percent sure I'd persuaded Tess not to tell Marcus that Silas was blackmailing her. She'd seemed content and enlightened with my suggestion that Silas would lose all his power once he did tell Marcus. Therefore, there was no motivation to ever do so, but Tess changed her mind often and without cause. I couldn't rely on her not deciding to tell Marcus after consuming two fabulous bottles of wine over a dinner meant to melt her into his arms, if that's what his dinners were designed to do. It sometimes appeared that way.

If Amelia was still as angry as she'd looked when I left her in the massive dining room, standing by the fire, she might end their relationship any day. And what I'd planned for Silas needed to take place soon after that.

He would appear to die by his own hand, bereft over the loss of his sweet, young intended. Another love ripped from his arms. I needed to have everything in place when she told him she was finished with him.

I was counting on her to do that. I hadn't been flattering her when I told her she was smart. She was. Deeply and profoundly naïve, but she was learning fast.

One thing she didn't want was to be owned by anyone. Once she fully realized that was exactly what Silas intended, she would be finished with him. I really didn't have to do anything at all to make her see what *she* needed to do.

I suggested to Hunter it would be nice to spend an afternoon and evening in San Francisco. There were some things I needed to buy anonymously. I didn't tell him that part, obviously. Just the part about being together in San Francisco.

The MOMA was first on our list. We spent two hours there, which wasn't nearly enough, according to Hunter, but plenty for me because my blood was pumping furiously, my mind racing around the details of what I needed and how I would manage to ditch him for at least an hour, probably two.

I'd decided Silas was going to die of a drug overdose. It wasn't the ideal choice, but it was the only one I could manage cleanly. Anything else risked leaving DNA of my own, or making a mistake that raised questions about whether he'd really done it himself. I'd gone over it a hundred, possibly three hundred times, in my mind.

No one knew Silas as a person who used drugs. It would seem strange and out of character, but there was no way, once he was gone, to question it. And as long as I wiped out all evidence of my presence with him, it seemed relatively safe. And clean. I liked clean.

A note, tapped out on his phone in a text to Amelia, was an unusual way to send one's last words to the world, but it seemed to fit his quirky, self-conscious and dramatic character. I wasn't aware of any close family in the area. The winery and his dream of ownership had made him a loner.

After the MOMA, I suggested we visit the Japanese tea garden in Golden Gate Park. The torrential rain of the past two days had disappeared as suddenly as it had gushed out of the sky. All that remained was a vast expanse of blue with huge fluffy white clouds and a cold, mild breeze. We wandered around the gardens, not talking, just enjoying being outside in a place that was different from what we were used to.

It's something that's underrated—changing the scenery. Everyone thinks they have to travel to an exotic location, spend thousands of dollars and book complex travel arrangements and luxury hotel rooms. But really, all you have to do is walk out the front door and turn left instead of right. Take a different exit off the freeway and park your car at some place you've never seen. Take a different subway or train line. Simply get off at an unfamiliar stop.

I took lots of photos of Hunter, using it as an excuse to check the time. We would be going to dinner at a tapas place he'd read about and I wanted to finish my errand before that.

As we finished wandering, he glanced at his own phone. "What do you want to do now? It's four."

"Let's go to Union Square. We can check out the stores. Maybe get a coffee or something."

He nodded. He didn't look excited, but it was close enough to Market Street, and Market Street led to some grungy areas where I would be able to find someone selling what I needed to buy.

As we wandered in and out of stores, I stopped to look at purses and shoes, sweaters and jewelry, slowing my pace with each counter and display we passed. Finally, I managed to drift far enough away from Hunter that I was well out of his sight. I turned and walked quickly in the opposite direction.

He was going to be upset with me, but if I explained I needed to pick something up, even if I told him it was a surprise, he would pester me with all kinds of questions. As soon as I reached the entrance doors to the department store, I shoved through and started running. I was wearing boots, but they had the flattest heel that could still be called a heel, so I easily managed a light jog, although I certainly couldn't sprint.

I walked and jogged as fast as I could to the decrepit section of Market Street. I found a bar and ducked inside. I bought enough fentanyl to knock two men into their graves.

With the fentanyl tucked into the zippered pocket inside my bag, I jogged all the way back to Union Square. My phone was buzzing with text messages from Hunter. He'd called three times, leaving voice mails with each call. If I didn't hurry, I would probably be greeting the police when I found him again.

I dipped into an art gallery, purchased a blown glass vase, and waited with burning impatience while it was carefully wrapped.

As I stepped out the door, I texted Hunter my location.

A few minutes later, he was walking toward me, his expression a mixture of irritation, upset, and a healthy amount of worry. "What *happened* to you?"

"I had to …" I held up the glossy white bag with silver lettering.

"I was worried. Why didn't you answer my texts?"

"I was busy and—"

"You were gone for almost an hour and a half."

"I know. I—"

"Why didn't you text me? Or pick up?" He ran his hand through his hair and left his fingers buried in the strands, gripping his scalp. He turned away, shoving his other hand into his pocket. He stared at the traffic, which moved in an achingly slow stream up Post Street.

After a few seconds, he started walking in the direction of the traffic. I took a few long strides to catch up.

Without looking at me, he asked, "Aren't you going to apologize?"

"I wanted to surprise you."

"It's not a surprise to ignore someone's messages. You just disappeared. It's rude. And insulting. And disrespectful. And scary. And a whole bunch of other things."

"Like what other things?"

He snapped his head toward me, glaring, then turned forward, increasing his pace.

"Are we still going to dinner?" I asked.

"What's wrong with you?"

"I wanted to get a host and hostess gift for you to give Tess and Marcus before you left. I wasn't sure you would—"

"So you think I'm a loser houseguest?"

"No. I wanted to help. I know you're thinking about work."

"The question remains—what's wrong with you?"

"Because I didn't answer?"

"That. And you just walked away. Do you even realize how disrespectful that is?"

"I won't do it again."

"Why did you do it this time? I don't understand you."

"Sometimes when I'm focused on one thing, that's all I can think about." It was the best I could do. It was the truth, for the most part. It would have to do.

We did go to dinner, but he was upset with me all the way there, all through the ordering and the appetizer and our salads. He didn't relax until we'd finished our first glass of wine. And even after that, he wasn't himself.

But I'd done what needed doing. This was why I'd wanted him gone. I needed to focus on Silas. I hoped there wouldn't be any more trouble with Hunter.

CHAPTER 76

The things Silas had said had been echoing inside Amelia's skull on continuous replay since she'd heard Alexandra's recording. His voice had sounded strange, she'd realized, because her first thought had been the truth—He was a different person. An entirely different person. It wasn't the wind, sounding louder than it did when you were standing outdoors, picked up by the microphone and amplified until it distorted the voices.

He was a man who desperately wanted something. But it wasn't her. She was sure of it.

She'd been stupid to believe he was falling in love with her. And stupid to believe she was feeling the same. She wasn't even sure she knew what falling in love really meant. And he was old. She was still a teenager, at least for a little while.

He was an adult who had lived an entire life while she was locked up in her tower. He knew things she'd never even heard about. It was impossible to know how many women he'd been with, how many girls he'd loved. Maybe he still loved the one he'd been engaged to, and that's why he was so upset about the Black Mask Winery.

She wasn't ready to be in love, to get married, to have a man telling her what to do. Expecting things from her. What if he wanted children? They hadn't even talked about that. She was almost a child herself.

She shivered.

The recording had saved her from something horrible. It was almost as if Alexandra was sent by the fairy godmother who had rescued Amelia from the tower by helping her set it on fire, killing her parents, releasing her from captivity.

That thought also made her shiver. Fairy godmothers didn't exist. They belonged in fairytales. Princes didn't exist either. Not really. There might be some countries where people still held those titles, but what did it mean? The people who were called by royal titles were nothing like the men in fairytales, appearing out of nowhere to rescue princesses. Why did she need rescuing, anyway? She'd already been rescued.

She owned a castle and land and a wedding business that gave her a good income. She needed to learn about *life*. She should travel and see the world, not lock herself up in this castle all over again, this time by her own free will! What had she been thinking?

It was almost as if she'd handed Silas the key to the tower herself, giving him permission to lock her inside.

Later, when she walked into Silas's office, he welcomed her with a smile. He stood and came around his desk. He took one of her hands, pinning it to his thigh as he pulled her close. He kissed her. A long, deep kiss that made her feel squeamish and eager to be finished with her unpleasant task.

As he released her lips, still keeping her hand pinned to his thigh, she was overcome with a desire to wipe the moisture from her mouth. Finally, he let go of her hand.

"What a brilliant surprise," he said. "If you have time to wait for about half an hour, I'll take you to lunch."

"I don't have time."

"Oh." He gave her a mock pout. "Why not? What could be more important than lunch with your lover?"

"I'm planning a trip. I'm meeting with a travel agent in an hour."

"A trip? Where? I ... that's sudden."

She smiled. "I'm going to London and visiting some other parts of England. I thought it would be interesting to see some real castles."

"I can help you organize that. You don't need a travel agent. We can—"

"I've never done it before, so I'd prefer an expert's help."

"I said I can help. But I'll need to check when I can get away. It might be a while." He drummed his fingers on the desk.

"I'm going by myself. I'm really sorry, but I don't want to be with you anymore."

"You ... you're breaking up with me? No."

"Yes. It's ... I don't think I'm in love with you. And you're a lot older than I am, and—"

"No. You're not thinking ..." He laughed. "Love takes time. You can't break up with me. We have a great thing going." He stood. "Why are you doing this?!"

"I just told you."

"No!"

She began backing toward the door.

He laughed softly, then smiled gently, although to Amelia it looked more as if he wanted to lick her face or something equally disgusting. She shivered, moving closer to the door. Why had she closed it? She hadn't wanted anyone to hear what she was planning to say, but now she felt trapped with the solid wood door behind her and Silas striding toward her.

What was he going to do? The first time he kissed her, she'd felt ... what had she felt? She couldn't even remember. She'd thought it was magical. Was that because it had been strange and different? New? So many feelings she'd never experienced before?

She didn't want to think about any of this right now. She wanted to get out of here. She turned and grabbed the doorknob.

Silas's hand was on her wrist. "Don't go."

"I need to."

"You can't just walk out. We're in love. What about our plans? What happened?"

"Nothing happened. I'm only nineteen."

"Then we'll slow things down a little." He laughed. "I get that. I adore you, Amelia. I can't lose you."

She wanted to ask whether he didn't want to lose *her*, or her castle, but something kept her tongue locked behind her teeth. She'd already given him too much. She didn't owe him any more of her thoughts, or any explanation. She wanted to leave, and he needed to let her.

"I don't want to get married or be engaged. I don't want anything. It's too much. Please let go of me."

"You're acting crazy. A few days ago, you were in love with me. Something happened. Why would you change your mind? Tell me what happened? You're not making sense."

"I'm not crazy. I decided I'm too young."

"You're not too young. You're so smart and you seem so much older. I don't even think about your age."

"Well, *I* do. Let go of me. I don't want to talk about it anymore."

He squeezed her wrist, twisting slightly. "You can't do this to me. After everything I've done, everything I'm going to do for you."

"Let go of me."

He released her wrist. "We'll talk after you have time to think about it. You'll be so lonely without me." He touched her face.

She shook her head, as if twitching a fly off her skin.

He looked hurt, but she wasn't sure if it was hurt, or fear.

"I'll call you. I'll come over tomorrow."

"Please don't," she said.

"You can't—"

"Don't bother me."

"*Bother* you?!" His voice was a sudden roar.

She slapped her hands over her ears, pressing her back against the door. "Stop." She jerked around and grabbed the doorknob. She turned it sharply and opened the door. She stepped out of his office, backing away slowly as he loomed in the doorway. Because he was slender, he wasn't a physically intimidating man, but she still felt he might come after her. She still thought about the stairs to the first floor, fearing they were too close, scared to break his gaze because he might take that moment to lunge at her and shove her down the stairs.

"I'm leaving." It didn't need to be said, but she felt compelled to say something, some words to mark that things were over. There was no going back. But she wasn't sure he saw it that way.

"I'll call you."

She ran down the stairs, wondering how hard it was to get a new phone with a different number. Wondering why she thought that was easier than simply not answering his calls.

CHAPTER 77

I didn't need to see Amelia or receive a text from her to know that she'd removed Silas's groping hands from her life, and his hooks from her property.

Silas came into the tasting room while I was reorganizing the gift shop, the only thing I could think of to keep myself busy on a cloudy afternoon when we hadn't had visitors since one o'clock. All the sweatshirts were stacked where the hats had previously been displayed. I was trying to think of a way to arrange them so the various messages on the front were visible without customers having to pick up every shirt, leaving them in disarray.

His face, the set of his shoulders, his stride, and the force with which the door had opened all announced he was an unhappy man. Not hurt and feeling rejected from losing the woman, rather the girl, he said he loved, but furious at losing the girl he wanted. The girl he needed. The girl who he believed would help him double his future holdings.

"When are you going to finish photographing the files?" he asked.

I laughed. "Is that what I'm doing? Photographing every single file?"

He crossed the room in less than four strides and was standing right beside the counter where the sweatshirts were piled. "You know what I'm talking about."

"I already told you, I have to be careful. I have to wait until the timing is right."

"You're taking too fucking long. I think you're stalling."

"Why would I do that?"

"Because you're trying to force me to give you what you want before you've done your part."

"I'm not trying to force you to do anything. I thought this was a business arrangement."

"It doesn't feel like that," he said. "It feels like … It just shouldn't be this much work."

"Feelings have nothing to do with it. I can't rush it. Do you want the document or not? If she catches me in her office, I won't be living here anymore. I won't be working here. And you'll never get your document."

"Well, figure it out. Fast. I'm tired of waiting."

"What's the rush? And why are you so angry?"

"I'm not angry." He grabbed a sweatshirt, unfolded it, and held it up. "Why are you moving everything around?"

"Things could be better displayed, so they catch more attention."

"You think you know better than everyone about everything, don't you?"

"No. I just have some ideas."

"Watch it."

"What does that mean?"

"Don't get so full of yourself."

I moved away from the counter. "You need to calm down. We're partners and we—"

"We are not partners. Not by any stretch."

"Why are you so agitated? Trouble in your love life?"

He grabbed the edge of the table and shook it. "Why do you

think that? Did you do something? Did you tell her something bad about me?"

"What?"

He gave the table a quick shove. "Did you say something?"

"Something about what?" I hoped I looked confused and slightly nervous.

He moved closer. "It's strange that ..." He backed up suddenly. "Never mind. Just get me that fucking document. By tomorrow."

I smiled. "I'll do my best. But I've already explained the constraints."

He left with as much bluster as he'd arrived.

I did plan to *get the document* that night, but there wasn't any document. If there ever had been such a document, the Harpers hadn't turned it over to Tess. It wasn't clear why they'd left the record of his debt with her, or why they'd walked away from that debt. Maybe, like Tess, they simply wanted to be rid of him.

Now that Amelia had broken up with Silas, and would verify that fact when his body was found, I was free to move forward with engineering his death to have the appearance of a suicide.

This was one of the riskiest things I'd ever done. I'd given it a lot of thought, and I'd decided I needed some additional security in order to leave Tess's house for several hours without any chance of being discovered.

Although Tess and Marcus and Hunter never suffered from insomnia, at least as far as I knew, almost everyone wakes in the middle of the night once in a while. Sometimes it's simply a barking dog, even in the widely spaced properties of Napa Valley. Sometimes it's an unwelcome dream that startles us awake. At other times, rich food or too much alcohol or a hundred other physical anomalies interrupt sleep, even for a moment or two.

Especially Hunter, sleeping a few inches from my pillow, needed to be out for the night in a way that allowed me to roam freely. My work with Silas required a long leash. No leash at all, really. And the only way to get that was to give all three of them what I typically gave my murder victims.

They would sleep well. They would sleep deeply, undisturbed, and without dreams. In the morning, they would feel disoriented and confused. They would entertain suspicions that something wasn't right, but their thoughts were unlikely to consider the truth. It was too far outside their realm of typical experience.

The following morning, I suggested an evening spent shooting pool on their walnut pool table covered in luscious pink felt in their third-floor game room. Pool and a few cocktails, enhanced by me, would allow Marcus and Tess to stumble safely down the hall to bed once the GHB began making its way through their bloodstream. I would delay the timing of when I added the drug to Hunter's drink. When he became disoriented, I would help him safely down the stairs to our room and into bed.

The pool room had a full bar in one corner, so mixing cocktails and adding another substance to each one without being seen was a somewhat straightforward task.

After the others agreed to a competition around the pool table, I went looking for Silas. We'd arranged most of our meetings verbally, but now it was more critical than ever that his message history didn't include anything from me. If all went smoothly, as I knew it would, his phone records would be checked by the police —presumed suicide or not.

I entered the office building and slipped inside the small conference room on the first floor. I closed the door partially. Anyone entering the building wouldn't notice me, listening for Silas's distinctive footsteps rapping across the floor like gunshots as the heels of his pompous, pointy-toed boots hit the ceramic tiles.

He was late. His lateness was going to make me late opening the tasting room.

He didn't show up until twenty past ten. The tasting room opened at ten.

When I finally heard him come in, I bolted out of the conference room as if I were charging into his arms after a lengthy separation from my lover. Maybe that was exactly what I wanted to project at this point. Not that he would believe it for a minute. But if he believed it for half a second, that was all I needed.

"Silas. I was worried about you."

He stopped. "Why?"

"You're late. Which you never are! And because of what happened with Amelia, I ..." I twisted my face into one of fear and heartbreak, as close to what I imagined threatening tears should look like.

I thought he might laugh, but he didn't. He looked unsettled, as if he wasn't sure what I was up to. Which he wasn't. Ever.

"What do you want?" He continued walking toward the stairs.

I hurried after him, reaching out to touch the back of his arm. He stopped and turned. "What do you *want?*"

"I have it."

He narrowed his eyes.

"Remember? You told me to get the photograph by today. I did."

"Let's see."

I shook my head. "Someone could walk in any minute. I thought we could meet at your place tonight." I touched his arm again, letting my fingers trail down to his hand. Not a lot, not aggressively, not in a way that would make him think I was mocking him. Just a friendly, soothing, and oh-so-softly suggestive touch.

He was a man with a larger-than-average ego. And it worked as it's nearly guaranteed to work on a man of his mindset and hubris. A man who had been dumped by a girl whom he thought he controlled to the point of ownership.

How dare a teenager, a more than typically naïve teenager, dump a guy like *him?* He was smart and savvy, sexy and sophisticated. He was a dream come true. Every girl should want a man like him. Every girl *did* want a man like him, he was absolutely certain of it.

But somewhere, buried beneath all that absolute certainty, he was desperate to know that he was *the man*. And I was there, ready to assure him that was the truth. He had all the power, didn't he? He was poised to bring Tess to her knees, claw back the winery he thought he'd been promised. And he now believed I was desperate for a piece of it.

He had a new woman he might be able to own. Maybe he could own me in more ways than one! Of course, he could own me in more ways than one. He was *The Man*.

"Sure," he said. "Tonight. What time?"

"One thirty."

"Why so fucking late?"

I gave him a slow, teasing smile.

He didn't say anything more.

CHAPTER 78

I needed to be in top form for the night that lay ahead of me. The minute the clock ticked to five p.m., I locked the tasting room door, hurried up to our room, and changed into running clothes.

"You're going running in the dark?" Hunter asked.

"I do it all the time," I said.

"Should I go—"

"No. I'm fine."

I nearly started my run as I left the room, needing to put distance between us before he could shove his feet into shoes and trail along after me. I ran for three miles, my mind working through the timeline and every detail of the evening four or five times as my feet pounded over the familiar route.

After a shower and Tess's barley soup, complemented by salad and sourdough bread, we headed upstairs to play pool.

We teamed up boys against girls, which was a pretty fair match because Marcus had only played pool about ten times in his entire life, and Tess was a pro at it. Early in her career, when she worked for several startups, two of them had rec rooms featuring pool tables where the employees brainstormed the future of their companies over late night games.

I kept my eye on my phone. I planned to add the GHB to the second round of drinks. The most challenging part would be ensuring that the second round of drinks started when I expected them to.

I'd calculated that my time with Silas would take about four hours, including travel time. I needed all of them to sleep soundly until well past seven in the morning. Because I'd chosen a Friday night, habit was on my side. Saturday was the only day Marcus slept late—the only time it was the weekend around the globe and he was less likely to have urgent emails from Asia or Australia waiting for him. Not that security issues only happened on weekdays, but since I'd arrived, he'd consistently taken Saturdays to sleep until seven or so.

Marcus and Hunter won the first two games. I didn't care. All I cared about was that second round of drinks.

But Tess cared. "Stop looking at your phone. You're not paying attention."

I wasn't aware I'd been doing it that much. I needed to relax. Arousing their suspicion was worse than a few minutes of delay. What mattered was my attention to the contents of their glasses, and that I was the one to mix the second round.

After that, she and I began to do better.

We won the third game. She was smiling again when I offered to mix the drinks.

"I'll have a beer," Hunter said.

A beer was okay. In fact, it might be better. He would drink it more quickly and I could add his dose to the next beer. Once he switched to beer, he would stay there.

I pulled a beer out and handed it to Hunter with a kiss on his lips. Tess and Marcus had been drinking corpse revivers, which had given me an unpleasant image when she suggested it before we started playing. I mixed a second round for her and Marcus, marveling again over their well-stocked bar that had ingredients like absinthe on hand. Although if you're fond of corpse revivers, I suppose you always do have absinthe on hand. I splashed some Black Mask Pinot Noir into a glass for myself.

"No martini?" Tess asked.

"One is enough for today."

"What happened to you?" She handed the pool cue to me. "I've never heard you say that."

"Are you sure?"

"Not ever."

"I don't think you've been listening."

"I'm always listening," she said.

I broke the balls, and we continued playing. I handed Hunter his beer each time I saw it sitting for more than a few minutes. He finished it quickly, as I'd hoped. I went behind the bar, opened another bottle, and added the GHB. It was so much easier than having to crush and dissolve roofies as I had in the past. Just a few drops of the colorless liquid and I was done. I took the beer to him, offering a longer kiss this time.

As he took his first sip, I watched closely, but just like Tess and Marcus before him, he was unaware of the addition to his drink.

First, they were feeling great, a little giddy and high, but before they had time to wonder at the strange effects of just two drinks, Tess and Marcus said they'd never felt so tired. They were going to bed. They apologized profusely for spoiling the evening. Hunter said he was feeling more tired than usual and didn't mind an early night himself.

Forty minutes later, with everyone tucked in and sleeping like babies, I changed into my usual black leggings. I put on a low-cut black top. I stuffed a black long-sleeved T-shirt and a few necessary supplies into my messenger bag. When I heard a snore come from Hunter's lips, I took the keys to the rental car. I slipped out of the house through the pantry door into the fenced area with its trash can and recycling container, and its camera-free route to freedom.

CHAPTER 79

*W*hen I was close to Silas's condo, I pulled onto a side street and parked. There was a chance I might be seen walking, but I hoped that with my ponytail and running shoes, I looked like a woman returning from a late workout at a twenty-four-hour gym. It was better than leaving the rental car where it might be noted as an unfamiliar vehicle near an upscale condominium complex, the carports filled with luxury cars. A white, four-year-old Toyota might embed itself in someone's memory.

Silas opened the door wearing an eager expression on his face that suggested he was definitely expecting more than a photograph of the document I claimed to have found in Tess's file.

"Let's see it," he said.

I laughed. "Calm down." I pulled a bottle of very expensive wine, not from Black Mask, out of my messenger bag. "Why don't we relax first?"

"Because I want to see it."

"Don't you trust me?"

"No."

"I'm super tense from all this sneaking around. I'd like a glass of wine. We can relax for a minute and talk about what happens next."

"After I see it."

"No, Silas. We're going to have a glass of wine like the classy people we are." I walked into his kitchen and took two glasses off the open shelf. I pulled a wine opener out of my bag. I'd expected him to object. I didn't want a discussion about finding an opener to slow my progress in getting wine, and the drugs, into his system. "Go sit down."

"You're not the one running things here. I already told you—"

"And I told you, we're partners. Tess is my friend. I'm the one who took the risk here. You won't be seeing the letter unless we have a conversation first. So sit down while I pour the wine." I gave him a charming smile. "We can enjoy each other's company and get to know each other a bit better. Won't that be nice?"

He seemed to like the sound of that. He settled on the white sofa facing a massive TV. He stretched out his legs and propped his feet on the glass coffee table.

I had to move quickly. Silas was not a man with a lot of patience. The faster I ushered him into unconsciousness and out of this life, the better. Otherwise, I faced a long night of arguing, and possibly a lot of physical conflict as he tried to make good on what I'd led him to believe he was getting along with his document.

I poured the fentanyl into his wineglass and carried both glasses into the living room. I handed the glass to him and took a sip from mine.

"No toast?" he said.

"I want to get right to business."

"Which business? Showing me what you found, or something more fun?" He raised his eyebrows in a way that could only be described as corny.

"Discussing what my share is."

"That's not what you implied." He took a sip of wine.

I drank more, giving him a seductive smile, hoping he would mirror my drinking while he waited for me to settle beside him on the couch.

He swirled the wine in the glass, but didn't drink.

"Sure, then. Let's have a toast." I moved closer and put my leg between his, pressing it against his right leg. "To getting along after all. In more ways than one."

He grinned. "I'll drink to that." He took a sip.

I felt a physical ache for him to drink it faster. I took a long, slow breath. I needed to calm down, but I wasn't entirely sure he was going to drink all the wine I'd poured. He was obviously much more focused on getting me to sit beside him, running his hand along the cushion.

Sipping more wine, I rubbed his leg with my knee, pressing it into his thigh. "Isn't this wine amazing?"

"Mmm."

"You don't sound impressed."

"I'm more impressed with you."

"Do you want to know what it cost?"

"Why don't you sit down and tell me?"

"Have another taste and guess."

"I don't want to guess."

"Please." I moved my knee higher up his leg.

He leaned his head back.

I moved my leg. I was pushing him away from drinking more wine. If I wasn't careful, he would either put the glass on the table and forget all about it, or spill it.

"Sit down." He grabbed my wrist and pulled me toward him.

"Don't be in such a hurry. Getting there is half the fun."

"Is it?"

"You should know that. Aren't you a connoisseur of fine things? Food and wine and women?"

He laughed. "Is that what you think? You sure didn't act that way until recently."

"I misjudged you."

"Your loss."

"Besides, you were with Amelia. I don't step on other women's toes."

"I wasn't with her when you first met me."

"Fair enough." I took a long swallow of wine. "Aren't you going to guess what it cost?"

We continued this dance for nearly forty-five minutes, but I finally got him to drink the entire glass. He never did guess the price. I only had to give up three long, nauseating kisses, as well as the feel of his steamy hands sliding under my bra, moving it around in a such an awkward way I worried it wasn't going to recover.

The fentanyl came over him quite suddenly.

He yanked his hands out from under my shirt. "I don' feel good."

"Let me get you some water." I stood and picked up his phone off the table. "Open your phone and I'll air drop the photos of the document."

"Now?"

"We don't want to forget. Since … you know. I have to get back soon."

He nodded vaguely, looking like he might be sick or pass out any minute. His skin was so white, he looked dead already. I placed the phone in his hand. "Here."

He stared at the screen, looking unsure about what he was supposed to do, but that was enough. It unlocked. I took it from him just as his head lolled onto the back of the couch, then to the side. He started to vomit, and I turned away.

I hurried into the bathroom, tapping his phone to keep it awake.

In the bathroom, I pulled out my phone. I opened a blank email on Silas's phone. I copied the email I'd written earlier when

I had time to think about how to word it in a way that sounded believable and echoed, as best I could, his way of speaking.

I tapped in Amelia's email address, then set the message to send in ninety minutes. It didn't give me a lot of flexibility, but I had to make sure it went out in a timeframe that would line up with whatever they determined his time of death was. It might be slightly off, but hopefully not so far that a detective would dig in and start asking detailed questions. I didn't think they could pinpoint his death to the minute. It would be more of a window—like waiting for an appliance to be delivered, or for the cable guy to show up.

With all the evidence of a suicide, there wouldn't be a lot of reason to go looking for too much scientific detail. There was no motive for murder as far as the police would be able to determine. Tess certainly would not say anything.

Next, I found the app for his security camera and deleted the evidence of my arrival. I would leave through the sliding glass door onto his back deck, where there was no camera because it was a four-foot drop to the ground. I guess he figured no one would show up with a stepladder to make that climb, so he hadn't installed a camera there. I also poked around until I found the blackmail photos of him and Tess all those months ago. I deleted them from the app and from the trash.

I remained in the bathroom for another half hour. I wasn't sure exactly how long it would take. The fentanyl was dangerous to his respiratory system—it would essentially make him forget to breathe—and I'd given him far more than was recreationally sane.

That was the other risk. When they saw how much he'd taken, they'd wonder at the extreme nature of it. But at the same time, they probably wouldn't think he'd overdosed accidentally. There wouldn't be questions about why a man who never used drugs had started getting high with the worst drug imaginable. The emailed note would push them to believe he'd done it with a purpose in mind. A one time trip to end his life because he couldn't live without Amelia Monroe.

There hadn't been any sounds from the living room for over twenty minutes.

I walked quietly down the hallway and stopped, peering around the corner. One glance at the horrifying state of his body told me he was dead.

I was not looking forward to working around him to clean up the evidence of my presence.

For that reason, I worked with more speed than usual. I put on a face mask to reduce the smell. I pulled on surgical gloves and started my cleanup by using duct tape to remove all the hair that had fallen out of my head on the couch and carpet. I wiped the coffee table with a microfiber cloth, rubbing hard to remove my prints and skin cells.

I took my wineglass into the kitchen, washed and dried it, and put it back on the shelf. I found his wine opener and placed it beside the bottle, then wiped down the bottle with a second cloth, as well as the counters and everything else I'd touched in the kitchen.

I cleaned the bathroom and his phone, then placed his phone beside him on the couch. I took a deep breath, picked up his hand and touched his fingers to the screen in a few places to leave his prints. After I let go of his hand, I rushed to the kitchen and scrubbed my hands with soap and hot water, then wiped down the sink.

After a complete survey of every surface I'd touched and place I'd stepped, I packed my bag, pulled up the hood on my sweat-shirt, put on a pair of distinctive black-rimmed eyeglasses, and went out the back door. I dropped my bag over the railing, climbed up, and jumped to the ground.

I walked to the car and drove home at a casual pace that belied the adrenaline racing through every nerve in my body.

CHAPTER 80

*I*t took fifty-six hours. I know because it felt as if I counted every single one, as well as all two thousand-eight hundred-twenty minutes in between those fifty-six hours.

Obviously, I didn't. But I did count quite a lot of them. I was constantly looking at my phone, checking the time. When I wasn't looking at it, I was telling myself I didn't need to look. I had *just looked*. I was scanning the local news for information about a man found on his living room couch, dead of a drug overdose.

All of this because, as it turned out, Amelia didn't check her email for nearly three days.

Inquiries to the Windy Hills Castle went to the Windy Hills email account. Since Amelia had grown up without knowing email or any kind of electronic messaging even existed, she didn't have the compulsive habit wired into her DNA like the rest of us do. She did carry a phone, but when it vibrated with a text message, she often didn't look at those if the phone was in her purse. She didn't feel the need to keep it in her pocket so she could respond to its every pulse and desire, like the rest of us do.

Silas was usually at the winery on Saturdays. When he hadn't shown up by noon, Tess sent him several texts. She called him, but she was more annoyed than worried. It didn't cross her mind to call the police. I'm not sure they would have done anything because an adult man hadn't shown up for work on a Saturday.

On Sunday afternoon, Tess mentioned it was strange he'd never responded to her messages, but then wrote it off to Silas and his games and his lack of respect. It wasn't as if she relished hearing from the guy.

During those long hours of waiting, wondering if the scenario I'd carefully constructed would be believed by the police, wondering how thoroughly each detail would be checked, if I'd added enough of a second layer to make it look plausible, I wondered how, and when, he would be found.

Did the neighbors speak to him often enough that someone would report him missing? From that perspective, the time had been short.

When Amelia finally got to her email, what would she do? Contact Tess? Me? Would she immediately call the police? Would she go to his condo to see if it was true, checking on her own to see whether he was trying to manipulate her into going back to him? She might not believe it. The horror of it might be too much. With her mind steeped in dramatic stories more than actual life experience, she might think he was trying to frighten her into his arms.

In the end, her naïveté drove her actions.

She called me, her voice wavering with uncertainty and disbelief.

"I don't know what to do," she whispered.

"About what?"

"I got this really strange email from Silas. I think he's trying to make me feel badly. I just want him to leave me alone."

"What strange email?"

"It says ... I don't even want to say."

"Can you forward it to me?"

"It's too awful."

"You can't forward it or tell me what it says?"

"It's so personal. But it's scary. And I feel like he wants to upset me. And I'm really upset." Her voice trembled. When she spoke again, it had grown so soft I could barely hear. "I don't know why he would write this to me."

"What does it say?"

"I'll come over and show it to you."

I wondered if she truly believed in her gut that he'd written it simply to upset her. Didn't she realize, on some level, it might be real? I'd thought the words I'd chosen were straightforward, free from melodrama. But maybe, at nineteen, it was impossible to believe. Still, she'd witnessed horrible deaths. It wasn't as if she didn't know the terrible realities of unexpected, gruesome death.

When she arrived, she handed her phone to me without speaking.

I read my own words.

Amelia ~

I thought we were meant for each other. You destroyed me, and I can't be in the world without you, so I'm leaving for good. Take flight, my little sparrow. I hope all your dreams come true in your castle on the hill. Goodbye my only love. Forever.

* * *

I handed the phone back to her.

"Do you think he …." She whimpered. "It sounds like … I don't think he would *kill* himself. Do you?"

"No. Absolutely not. He's not the type," I said. "I mean, he sounds different. He sounds … not like himself. Sad? Maybe hopeless?"

"Yes." Tears flooded her eyes. "I feel so awful. I didn't know I would make him feel so terrible. But I—"

"His feelings aren't your responsibility," I said.

"But I made him feel that way."

"You aren't obligated to do what other people want just because it might make them feel badly. You didn't want to be with him. You're allowed to decide who you want to be with. Even if it's no one."

"Do you think he's ... do you think he killed himself?"

"I don't know. I'm not ..." I paused.

"Should I go over there?"

"No. You ended it."

"But someone needs to see if he's okay."

"You broke up with him. That's your responsibility. Let's show this to Tess. He didn't show up for work Saturday. So maybe ..."

Amelia started crying.

"If something happened, it's not your fault."

"Something didn't just *happen*. He killed himself. What if he killed himself because he loved me and I told him I didn't and—"

"You get to choose who you love. You can't love every man who claims he loves you. Silas is almost fifteen years older than you. And even if he was only twenty, it doesn't matter. You get to decide, not him. And he gets to decide what to do with his life. If that's what he actually did, if that's what he decided ... but we don't even know."

I started walking toward the house.

We went through the entryway. Damien must have sensed Amelia's despair because he was respectfully quiet, making a low murmuring sound that was almost like a cluck.

Amelia followed me up the stairs to Tess's office. The door was open, and we went in.

Tess read the email message and returned the phone to Amelia. She picked up her own phone and placed a call. A moment later, she was talking to the police, asking for a welfare check on Silas Birch, tapping her computer to look up his address while she spoke.

For another two hours, I waited for the others to learn what I already knew.

For two days after that, I waited to find out how the police would interpret the condition of Silas's body, the half empty bottle of wine, the single glass with a residue of fentanyl, the packet of fentanyl I'd left in the kitchen, the email they asked Amelia to forward to them, and the history of calls and messages and emails on his phone.

In the end, there was no evidence to suggest his death was anything but self-inflicted. Because of the email, it appeared to be suicide, although the circumstances of overdosing on fentanyl were noted as highly unusual for a person who had no history of drug use. The ingestion via a glass of wine was noted as inexplicable.

But there was nothing to indicate anyone else had been inside his condo that day, or for several days before. No source for the fentanyl was found. No receipt for the wine was found, which was noted as another oddity without explanation. It might have been a gift he'd kept for weeks, if not years.

Two weeks later, there was a memorial service for Silas at the Black Mask Winery. It turned out he had a brother who lived in Southern California. The brother made all the arrangements for the disposal of his ashes and his property.

No one cried at his memorial, but as we stood among the grapevines and searched for complimentary words to speak about him, we all wore dark glasses to hide our lack of tears.

CHAPTER 81

*H*unter had extended his departure long past the point of reason. The discovery of Silas Birch's body and the planning and execution of the memorial service had gripped him with morbid fascination. He wasn't sure why. If he had a typical relationship, he would have said his girlfriend needed him there for emotional support. But that mythical girlfriend who needed emotional support in the face of her colleague's suicide was not Alexandra Mallory.

Alex handled it all as if it were a minor disruption. She seemed to feel almost nothing about the horror of the circumstances. Aside from the fact that she hadn't been a huge fan of the guy, most people would still feel shock and sadness, and an almost guilty sense of loss when a person with whom they'd had a complicated relationship died in that way.

But Alex was more focused on ensuring that Amelia was freed from her guilt. It was almost as if Alex saw herself as some kind of priestess, needing to make sure the girl didn't carry a burden that Alex insisted did not belong to her. Alex talked about it incessantly, discussing the unfortunate wording of the suicide note, wondering why it had seemed to place blame on Amelia. The way

Alex went on about it, you'd think she'd written the damn suicide note herself!

Hunter grew tired of hearing her speculate about how she might get Amelia to recognize the fact that the suicide had absolutely nothing to do with her. That any choice that man had made was his alone.

Finally, by the time the memorial service took place, Alex seemed to have convinced Amelia to see things her way. But Hunter almost wondered if she'd gone too far. Wasn't Amelia's reaction normal? Not that Amelia owed Silas anything whatsoever, or that she should have stayed with him. She was clearly too young. It was disturbing that a man his age was so taken with a nineteen-year-old girl. It was healthy that Amelia had found the wherewithal to end things.

Still. Some regret and sadness were normal.

Now Alex was finally putting it behind her. She seemed to be able to give her attention to Hunter. Too little, too late, in some ways. After all the weeks he'd been here, feeling shoved into a corner, her eyes always looking at some point beyond or behind him. Her thoughts were always somewhere else, so much that she often didn't respond to what he'd said. Now she looked into his eyes as if she wanted to sink into his soul.

Or did she?

What *did* she want? He did not have a clue.

He continued to experience moments when he thought she had to be the woman who had driven those two assholes to beat up his brother. What else explained her inexplicable behavior?

And now, here they were, lying in bed, staring into the darkness.

He felt deeply satisfied after consuming every part of her body, and she his. Satisfied physically, that is. His mind continued to twist itself into a knotted cord of unanswered questions.

"Have you figured out what we're going to do?" He slid his arm under her shoulders and pulled her toward him.

"No. Have you?"

"It seems unsolvable."

"Nothing is unsolvable," she said.

"Are you sure?"

"Yes."

"Do you want to be with me?" he asked.

"You already asked me that."

"I'm asking again."

"Yes."

"But you refuse to come to New York."

"And you seem to have zero interest in coming to California."

He buried his face in her hair, feeling the soft silk across his cheeks and forehead. "I have a career and a home in New York city."

"I have a job too."

"But it's not—"

"For now, it's what I have," she said.

"You're essentially homeless. Couch surfing."

She laughed.

"What do you want? Are you even trying to make plans?"

"I will."

"When?"

"I'm not like other women."

"I'm aware." He squeezed her upper arm gently.

"Can you handle that?" she asked.

"I'm not sure what's all involved."

"I don't always make plans, for one thing. Except when I do. And I ... well, I'm just different. I need space."

That was a good way to describe it. He hadn't put it into words, but it made him relax, hearing her say it, describing the pull he felt, as if she were trying to move away from him. As if she were a magnet and often, she flipped without warning to the opposing pole, a repellent force that no matter how he moved, he couldn't make a connection.

She seemed to like him. But what guy, this far into a relationship, was grasping for evidence that a woman *liked* him? He shouldn't have to do that. At the same time, he had secrets of his own. So perhaps he was asking more of her than he was willing to give. "Maybe I'm not like other men. Can you handle that?"

She ran her hand across his chest, leaving it there as if searching for his heartbeat, feeling it beneath the muscle and bone, as if that might tell her the answer.

The way she ran her hands across his body, he thought he was a fool for wondering if she was the woman who had driven that black sedan. The nagging question remained, but maybe it was there because he'd thought about it so much it had burrowed its way into his brain until it felt rational simply because he'd considered it so frequently.

She wasn't that woman. She *couldn't* be.

But just as she wasn't like other women, he wasn't like other men. And not in any way that Alex might imagine he was different. The difference in him was serious. Deal-breaking.

He was a killer. He had all the justification in the world, but in the end, he was still a killer.

He didn't regret it. He hadn't regretted it for a single moment. No one was going to punish those two fuckers, and they didn't deserve to walk around, laughing and enjoying life after what they'd stolen from Zack and his mother. His mother would never be the same. There was a tiny flicker of fear in her eyes whenever he looked at her now, even when she smiled.

No, there wasn't a single heartbeat of regret for what he'd done. But he'd stepped over a line that would separate him from other men for the rest of his life. There was no going back. He'd done the worst thing imaginable.

The question was—would he ever tell Alex? *Would* she be able to handle that?

CHAPTER 82

The evening after Hunter left, Marcus flew to Singapore for a week of customer meetings.

It was raining endlessly. Tess and I sat in her living room with blankets over our legs, and the gas fire creating a mesmerizing glow in the darkened room. Rain pounded against the bifold doors. The palm trees swayed like unearthly creatures waving their arms, trying to get our attention.

I took a sip of my martini.

Bad storm! Damien shouted from the entryway. *Bad storm!*

The storm had been a topic of conversation for two days, and every time Marcus came into the kitchen, he and Tess had discussed it, their voices carrying to the entryway. Now, Damien mentioned it almost once an hour, as if he were providing the weather forecast on the nightly news. He hadn't asked for mango or commented on Chardonnay all afternoon and evening.

The house felt large and slightly empty without Hunter and Marcus, although I liked watching the fire and not talking much. I liked stretching out in the king-sized bed without crashing into another pair of legs. I was sure in another few days, I would find myself wishing Hunter was beside me again.

I couldn't stop thinking about what he'd said—that he wasn't like other men. The way he'd said it, I didn't think he was trying to compete with me or mirror my words. I wondered what he meant. I knew he was different, because who he was hadn't been laid on the table in the first thirty minutes I'd known him. He was fun and interesting and kept a lot of things to himself. I suspected it would take me a long time to figure him out, if I ever did.

But what did that mean—*not like other men?*

I had no idea when I would see him again or how we were going to figure that out either. I was probably going to have to return to New York for my things. I'd texted Eileen, and she hadn't offered to even move my furniture out for donation, not to mention packing up my clothes. She certainly wasn't going to go to the trouble of selling anything. And she'd used about twenty exclamation points on her message after telling me that fact.

It was absurd to walk away from everything I owned. I could probably manage a short visit without running into Ned. And even if I did, so what? He didn't know anything. Not really.

I took another sip of my drink and ate an olive.

"What are you thinking about?" Tess asked.

"Plans."

"With Hunter?"

I ate another olive.

She laughed.

Dangerous woman! Damien shouted.

She raised her glass. "This is really … not a nice thing to say, but here goes." She smiled. "To freedom!"

We clicked our glasses and drank.

She didn't know I'd set her free, but she absolutely knew I was the only person in the world who would allow her to celebrate a man's death because it had set her free. And that I would celebrate with her.

A NOTE FROM CATHRYN

When I first started writing about Alexandra Mallory, I thought she would be a character threatened by a strange roommate in a standalone psychological thriller—The Woman In the Mirror. Within a few chapters of starting that novel, Alex took on a life of her own. Her voice came into my head in a way I had never experienced with other characters. By the time I finished writing that book, I knew she would have a few more stories … and here we are, with the fourteenth book and no end in sight. Yet.

The response to this woman with clear sociopathic tendencies and deeply held opinions on everything from olives to the place of religion in the world has overwhelmed me at times. Readers have told me she scares them, they see a small piece of themselves in her, and they've felt empowered by her. The greatest thrill for me is that I've experienced all of those reactions myself.

There are no words to express the gratitude I feel in knowing people enjoy reading my books and find a few hours of escape through the stories I tell. Knowing that you've enjoyed this character through so many books is humbling and an honor that I don't take lightly.

Thank you so much for reading. It means the world to me.

ABOUT THE AUTHOR

Cathryn is the author of over thirty psychological suspense novels, including the ALEXANDRA MALLORY series featuring a sociopath you can't help but love. Readers have called the series "addictive".

The things that torment us in real life—obsession and revenge, guilt and envy and longing—are endlessly fascinating in fiction and she never grows tired of writing stories about characters struggling to overcome the worst.

Cathryn also writes ghost stories because who knows what lies beyond our senses—The Haunted Ship Trilogy and the Madison Keith series of novellas.

When she's not writing, she's usually reading, walking on the beach, or playing golf, going way out of her way to avoid hitting her ball in the sand or the water. She lives on the Central California Coast with her husband and her cat, Cleopatra.

You can get in touch with her by email, find her social media links, or sign up for her monthly newsletter at

cathryngrant.com/contact.

As a thank you for signing up, you'll receive a free short story about Alexandra Mallory.